CW00420805

HUGO WILCKEN was born i
educated there and in Lond<
His first novel, *The Execι
critical acclai

Visit www.AuthorTracker.co.uk for exclusive
information on your favourite HarperCollins authors.

Also by Hugo Wilcken

The Execution

HUGO WILCKEN

COLONY

A Novel

HARPER PERENNIAL

London, New York, Toronto and Sydney

Harper Perennial
An imprint of HarperCollins*Publishers*
77–85 Fulham Palace Road
Hammersmith
London W6 8JB

www.harperperennial.co.uk

First published in Great Britain by Harper Perennial 2007

A catalogue record for this book is
available from the British Library

ISBN-13 978-0-00-710648-6

Set in Minion

For Julie and Léon

COLONY ONE

I did not die – yet nothing of life remained

Dante, *Inferno*, Canto XXXIV

I

Lurid rumours abound about life in the penal colony. There are the labour camps where they make you work naked under the sun; the jungle parasites that bore through your feet and crawl up to your brain; the island where they intern leper convicts; the silent punishment blocks where the guards wear felt-soled shoes; the botched escapes that end in cannibalism. As the stories move through the prison ship, they mutate at such a rate that it becomes impossible to gauge their truth.

In Sabir's cage, there's only one man who's already been out there and actually knows what it's like. He's a grizzled assassin called Bonifacio. Although not tall, he's bulkily built, with the bulging, tattooed biceps of a Paris hoodlum. His cool menace unnerves most prisoners but doesn't stop a few from pestering him for information. The questions obviously irritate him and he only bothers to reply when bribed with cigarettes, which are in short supply on board. Sabir asks nothing himself, but listens as he lies on his hammock, gazing through the tiny porthole into the punishing intensity of the blue outside. It's from these overheard fragments that he gradually builds up a picture of what awaits him across the ocean. He now knows that they'll disembark at Saint-Laurent, a small frontier town on the banks of a river called the Maroni, somewhere north of the Amazon, somewhere south of Venezuela. A splinter of France lost in the jungle.

'That's where the main penitentiary is. Where they do the selection,' he hears Bonifacio explain one day in his thick Corsican accent, shot through with Montmartre. 'If they think you're dangerous, you go straight to the islands. There are three of them. Diable is for political prisoners. The main barracks are on Royale and the punishment cells on Saint-Joseph. If you end up on the islands, there's no chance of escape. But you won't have to do hard labour.

'If you don't have a trade, they'll send you to one of the forest camps. Some are near Saint-Laurent, some are on the coast. Do anything to avoid them. They're the worst. You're out in the sun all day chopping trees. If you don't fill your quota, you don't get your rations. You end up with fever, dysentery. If you're down for the camps, bribe the bookkeeper to get you a job at Saint-Laurent. If that doesn't work, pay one of the Blacks or Arabs to chop your wood for you. Then buy your way out as quick as you can.

'If you've got a trade they can use, you get to stay at Saint-Laurent. Or they send you up to the capital, Cayenne. You work for the Administration. There are cooks, butchers, bakers, mechanics, bookkeepers, porters . . . If you get a job, make sure it's outside the penitentiary. That way, you're out during the day, you're unguarded. Best thing is to work for an official, as houseboy or cook. You get to sleep at their house. But you won't score a job like that first off.

'To survive, you need dough. To escape, you need dough. To get it, you need a scam. Everyone's got a scam. The guys who work at the hospital steal quinine and sell it on. The iron-mongers make knives and *plans* and sell them on. In the camps they catch butterflies and sell them to the guards, who sell them to collectors in America. Everyone's got a scam.'

So much to take in. During the long sleepless nights, Sabir turns it all over in his mind. In the solitude of the darkness, problems seem insurmountable. How to avoid these forest camps, for instance? As far as he knows, Sabir hasn't been classed dangerous, but he has no particular skill other than basic soldiery. He has no money. He knows that most of the other prisoners do, banknotes tightly fitted into the little screw-top cylinder they call a *plan*, hidden in the rectum. Money given to them by their families. Sabir's father has disowned him; his mother is dead. No trade, no money; no brawn either: Sabir is a smallish man with a slight build. There are nights when a paralysing nervousness invades him, worse even than the anxiety attacks of the Belgian trenches. It's such a long time since he's had to consider a future. He's got too used to being a judicial object, shunted from prison to prison, prison to court, court to prison. He's got used to lawyers talking for him, being his voice, just as all the others talk about him and around him. Almost as if he weren't there at all.

The new life that awaits him seems very different. Not at all like a mainland prison. Deeply strange and yet somehow familiar: it's the world of the *romans à quatre sous*, the pulp novels that Sabir used to devour when on leave from the front. In Sabir's mind, the *bagne* – as the penal colony is called – is a savage fantasy land, peopled with shaven-headed convicts in striped pyjamas, boldly tattooed from head to foot, guarded by men in pith helmets and dress whites. The coastline is an impenetrable wall of green jungle; gaudy parrots scream from the trees; crocodiles lurk just below the water's surface; natives glide to and fro in dugout canoes; bare-breasted women tend to children in palm-roofed huts; wide-mouthed rivers disgorge into an infinite ocean. It's a netherworld of no definable location, surging up out of the tropics like an anti-Atlantis. When he was a child, Sabir's mother would tell him that unless he behaved, '*tu finiras bien au bagne.*' This oft-repeated threat was every bit as real, and yet every bit as fantastic as his long-dead grandmother's warning that Robespierre stole naughty boys away in their sleep. And every day on the streets of Paris you could hear people grumbling: '*Quel bagne! Quelle galère! C'est le bagne!*'

What strikes Sabir about most of the other prisoners on board is their extreme youth and vulnerability. Very few of them actually seem like Bonifacio, like the tough *hommes du milieu* that populate the Paris or Marseilles underworld of Sabir's imagination: the pimps, the drug dealers, safe crackers, hit men, gangsters. Gaspard, for example – the nervy, cowering country lad to Sabir's left who cries himself to sleep – looks barely sixteen. One evening, without any prompting, Gaspard sobs out his story, banal and tragic in equal parts. He and another farmhand friend broke into the village café one night for a dare, and forced the till. The café owner came down to see what the disturbance was. Panicked, Gaspard grabbed a bottle of spirits, hurled it at the owner and fled. The man slipped on the stone floor, cracked his head open and bled to death overnight. The gendarmes picked Gaspard up the next day and he confessed that same morning. This boy seems typical of so many of the *transportés* on board: juvenile, illiterate, from peasant stock, lost, bewildered, completely out of his depth. Only thirty himself, Sabir feels ancient and worldly among these petrified adolescents. As though he's lived and died an entire life in comparison.

Discipline on board is lax, not at all like in a mainland prison. Most of the men have stripped off and wear nothing but towels around their waists. They sit in small groups, chatting quietly, smoking, fretting, occasionally fighting. The hard men from the military jails in the African colonies – the *forts-à-bras* – even run a poker game with a makeshift pack of cards cut from cardboard. A stained blanket on the steel floor serves as the card table. These men are generally much older than the others, and everyone's scared of them. Little cliques have already formed in each of the eight prison cages: the Parisians band together, as do the Corsicans, the Bretons, the Marseillais, the Arabs, the Indo-Chinese. There are a couple of Germans too in Sabir's cage, deserters from the Foreign Legion who speak hardly any French and sit whispering together. A tall, thin man huddles in the corner and pores obsessively over a tattered map torn from an atlas. Over and over he mouths a string of unfamiliar words, like a magic incantation: Paramaribo, Albina, Maroni, Orinoco, Oyapock, Sinnamary...

As the boat reaches the tropics, the heat and lack of air inside the cages become almost unbearable. Walking, standing, sitting or lying, it's impossible to get comfortable and just as impossible to sleep. Twice a day the prisoners are given a collective shower: sailors come down into the hold with hoses and drench the men with fresh salt water. It's a delicious relief, but five minutes later Sabir is dry again and horribly itchy from the salt. Thirst is now an overriding problem; the drinking water has become contaminated and the guards pour rum into the barrels to make it more palatable. On this final leg of the voyage, Sabir feels constantly dizzy, but he can't tell whether it's because of the heat, the bad water, the rum, the seasickness or just the stench of six hundred bodies. The men lie listlessly now in their hammocks and conversations have died down to a low mutter, barely audible over the groan of the engine room.

One day the birds finally reappear, at first trailing in the boat's wake then wheeling around the funnels, filling the air with their sad cries. It's dawn. Sabir's hammock is hooked up by a porthole and he can just make out a dark blade cutting across the horizon. Over the next hour the blade thickens and resolves into a vivid green. Not long after, the sea turns yellow. It happens literally from one moment to the next, as if the boat has just crossed a border. A gargantuan river mouth comes into view, several kilometres across. Everyone flocks to the portholes as the river swallows the boat up. An air of nervous expectation hangs over the cages; only Bonifacio remains impassive, unshakeable, as he lies in his hammock smoking cigarette after cigarette.

To avoid mudbanks the boat has to zigzag its way upstream, sometimes steaming down the middle, sometimes straying perilously close to the French bank – almost close enough for a man to reach out and touch the green foliage that bursts out over the water. On one occasion they pass what they take to be an Indian village: a rudimentary collection of five or six huts, a few inhabitants by the shore. It's hard to make out what the Indians are actually doing as they gaze out across the river and beyond, apparently quite uninterested in the faces pressed to the portholes. Occasionally the boat gives a piercing hoot, although there's no sign of other traffic on the river. And each time it does, great clouds of birds rise gracefully from the trees before dispersing into the sky.

At around noon, their destination finally comes into view: a couple of boulevards hewn out of the jungle, heading into nowhere; a large complex of buildings to the left of a long pier; then beyond that a neatly laid-out residential quarter. Saint-Laurent has the air of an unremarkable French village, miraculously transplanted to the South American jungle. Its little pink bungalows and spruce gardens look faintly ridiculous, cowed by this river and rainforest of unearthly proportions. With so many prisoners now jostling for a glimpse, Sabir manages only brief moments at the porthole. The trees that imprison the town are the tallest Sabir has ever seen. Some of them even sprout out of the river itself, blurring the boundary between land and water. It is indeed the green wall of Sabir's imagination, sliding slowly along the bank as the boat steams towards Saint-Laurent. The immensity of the forest frightens him, because he knows that from now on he'll have to live surrounded by it, and that one day soon he'll have to escape through it.

When the engine cuts out, the silence is extraordinary. Sabir can hear the river lapping at the side of the boat. His blue cloth uniform, which had offered so little protection against the European winter, now suffocates him and he has to resist the temptation to rip it off. Sabir sets his cloth cap carefully on his head. Strange how you feel some vanity even in such circumstances. The town lies ahead, quite still in the dead of the noonday sun. They have been twenty-four days at sea. The air shimmers in the dripping heat. The date is 29 February 1928. It's Ash Wednesday.

II

The march to the penitentiary takes only minutes. Sabir is struck by the colourful headdresses of the Creole women among the crowd lining the boulevard, curious to see the new convoy. Some of these women are laughing, calling out to the convicts: '*Allez, les gars . . . bonne chance . . . t'es beau, toi!*' The banter sounds too spontaneous, too unnatural; it's a peculiar counterpart to the scenes on the other side of the Atlantic, just a few weeks before, as the men boarded the ship. Then, the women were weeping, not laughing. Then, Sabir vainly searched the crowd of female faces for a glimpse of his fiancée. Was she there? Most likely not. Sabir had asked her to stay away. Nonetheless a violent feeling, almost hate, grips him now as he thinks of her probable absence that day. It's practically the first time he's thought of her since boarding the ship.

To the right, colonial buildings with wide, inviting verandas. To the left, a statue of a man staring imperiously into the river, two black men crouching down beside him. As he marches, Sabir follows the statue's gaze, beyond the river to the other side. The Dutch bank, according to Bonifacio. There, too, is a smart, whitewashed colonial village: the mirror image of Saint-Laurent. It, too, is completely surrounded by jungle, perched uncertainly by the water as if cornered by an invading army. Although it looks exactly the same, this other side of the river is in fact like a photographic negative, Sabir realises. Because it's not French. Not a penal colony. Its jungle looks seductive, alive with possibility. A man might disappear into it and emerge on the other side completely changed, a different person.

Little knots of convicts stand idly by the penitentiary gates; they appear to be totally unsupervised. In their red and white striped uniforms and wide straw hats, they remind Sabir of the vaudeville clowns in the shows his mother used to take him to as a boy. As the new convoy are marched through the gates, one of the convicts shouts out: 'Anyone from Lyons in your cage?' No one dares answer. Another convict sidles up to the tall man marching beside Sabir – the one who spent the whole trip staring at his tattered map. Apparently they know each other. 'I'll send you a note tonight,' Sabir overhears the convict whisper. 'I'm working in the botanical gardens. It's a good job. We're a man short. When they ask what you do, say you're a gardener.'

Even once the convoy are inside, the gates of the penitentiary stay open. Convicts seem to wander in and out as they please. This laxness perplexes Sabir because it makes escape look easy, when he's heard that it isn't at all. They're herded into a vast hall with an array of equipment: height gauges, scales, a camera mounted on a tripod, a table with ink-pads for fingerprinting. While Sabir strips, a clerk makes an inventory of the various marks on his body, every wart and mole. Sabir has a small flower tattooed on his left shoulder blade, dating from his army days. The clerk – who Sabir only now realises is actually another convict – examines it very carefully, devotes a short paragraph to it in the *registre matricule*. 'What sort of flower is it? What's its name?' Flummoxed, Sabir has no response. But later, when he's asked what his profession is, Bonifacio's warning about what happens to unskilled prisoners comes back to him. He remembers the convict at the gates and says: 'Gardener.'

Before lock-up, an officer issues everyone with a sheet of writing paper and a stamped envelope. He tells them that there's no postal service out in the forest camps, and that, in any case, in future they'll have to buy their own stamps and paper. Sabir spends the rest of the afternoon earning a couple of francs writing letters for the illiterate convicts. Pleas to wives to stay faithful; to come to Guiana; to on no account come to Guiana. Letters begging lovers not to forget them; to brothers commending the care of their wives and children to them; to parents asking for money, assuring them that everything's all right, that they're doing well. Appeals to the Ministry of Justice for pardons; instructions to lawyers in the hope of last-minute miracles; threats of vengeance; last wills and testaments . . .

Those with money have already bought coffee and cigarettes from one of the turnkeys. One prisoner has bought a fresh supply of cigarettes for Bonifacio as well. He has crouched down, wetted his finger and traced a rough map of the river and coastline on the dirt floor. He's explaining the three routes out of Saint-Laurent: west, across the river; east, through the jungle; and north, down the river and into the sea.

'Across the river gets you out of French territory and into Dutch Guiana. Opposite you've got the town of Albina. From there, there's a road to the capital, Paramaribo, on the coast. But your uniform'll give you away. The Dutch will send you back across the river. So you need false papers and workman's clothes. That way you can pretend you're working in one of the mines down the river. Even then, they'll check back with Saint-Laurent if they think you're French.

'Or you can try the jungle. It looks the easiest way, but it's the hardest. I don't know anyone who's made it through to Brazil. Jungle's so thick you can only do a couple of kilometres in a day. There are huge rivers to cross. Without a gun there's nothing you can catch. You'll poison yourself eating the fruit. Or the Indians will find you. They're paid ten francs for each convict they bring back. Or you'll go crazy with hunger and come back after a few days. If you can find your way back.

'Then there's the sea. It's the riskiest way. The hardest to organise. But it's your best bet. You need a lot of dough. You need a boat with a sail, food and water for at least ten days. You paddle down the river at night, to catch the dawn tide. Then you're in open sea. Because of the winds you can't go south. So you have to head north-west till you get to Trinidad. The English won't let you stay. But they won't hand you back to the French either. They give you a few days to sort yourself out and find fresh supplies. Then you have to sail on. You can't put to shore in Venezuela, because they'll send you back to Saint-Laurent. But if you make it to Colombia, you're free.'

In the tropics, night approaches with almost visible speed, sweeping across the forest like a black tide. Within the barracks a feeble night-light casts spindly shadows: everything is obscure, humid. The night brings no particular relief from the heat and the smallest movement seems to take an enormous effort. Unfamiliar noises reach Sabir through the bars, but in the barracks itself there's silence. It's as if the strain and shame of their arrival has exhausted everyone to the point where there's no room for any further emotion. It's not just the silence that's different, but the stillness too. Sabir had got used to the gentle rocking of the boat, and the knot in his gut is like a reverse seasickness. For Sabir, this absolute stillness feels as though something that had once been faintly alive has now finally died.

The barracks holds sixty men – roughly the same ones as in Sabir's cage on the prison boat, minus those already admitted to hospital. Unconsciously, they've reconstructed the cage in the barracks, as if afraid of what novelty might bring. To Sabir's right lies Bonifacio; to his left Gaspard the country lad – who has tearfully dictated a wrenching letter to his parents begging forgiveness. Despite the heat and humidity, he's shivering and curled up in foetal position: already Sabir has noticed the intense pressure the boy is under from the *forts-à-bras* to give in to their advances. Soon he might have to choose one of them, if only to protect himself from the others. 'Don't worry, I'll keep an eye out for you,' Sabir told him as he wrote the boy's letter. 'I'll try to help you if I can.' And somehow this promise felt like an act of rebellion, not against the life of the *bagne* as imposed by the authorities, but against a convict-created world.

Bonifacio, on the other hand, is dozing peacefully. He's stripped to the waist; a huge tattoo of a Christian cross covers his back. Sabir remembers how, early on in the trip, someone made a mocking remark about this tattoo. Bonifacio simply got out of his hammock and delivered a single, perfectly executed blow to the man's stomach, then lay back down. The man was so badly winded that everyone thought he was going to die. Even as he snores now, Bonifacio's muscleman biceps remain taut, threatening.

Like a proper professional, Bonifacio has never bragged, never once talked about his past. But Sabir has already heard his story, from another prisoner on the ship. Years before, Bonifacio got twenty years' transportation with hard labour for a run of jewel heists. He was sent out to French Guiana but escaped eighteen months later, making his way to Argentina.

There, he was helped out by friends in the prostitution racket. Eventually, he set himself up in the business, running a network of French girls in Buenos Aires. It was a comfortable, prosperous existence, but there was one thing that still rankled. During his trial, Bonifacio had arranged for a fence to send him his cut from the jewel heists. He never got the money. It was quite a fortune – easily enough to have financed an escape from the penal colony as soon as he got there.

One day, years after his escape to Argentina, he risked a return to France. Back in the Paris underworld, there was stupefaction at his sudden reappearance. But thanks to his reputation as an *homme régulier*, friends helped him trace the man he was after. Bonifacio soon found his former fence living in a bourgeois apartment building not far from the Bois de Boulogne. The man begged for mercy, but Bonifacio showed him none. He gunned him down in front of his wife and children. A few days later, Bonifacio was picked up again, as he strolled down the boulevard Clichy with his Argentinian mistress. Someone had betrayed him to the police. Scared off by Bonifacio's underworld friends, the fence's wife refused to testify against him. Unable to pin the murder on him, the authorities simply put Bonifacio on the next prison ship out to Saint-Laurent to finish his original sentence.

Throughout the afternoon, various convicts from other barracks have come up to the bars to talk with Bonifacio in low voices. Sabir also notices that Bonifacio hasn't bothered to write his letter: he's sold his paper and envelope to one of the German prisoners for a few *sous*. Sabir hasn't had time for his own letter yet. There's only one he wishes to write, and after that there'll be no further need. On the boat he dreamt up all sorts of fantasies about escaping back to France, maybe reuniting with his fiancée, somehow returning to his former life. He was going to write to her to tell her he'd arrived safely. But now he changes his mind. Already, something has moved inside him since his arrival in the *bagne*. During the long, humid afternoon spent transcribing the impossible wishes of others, the realisation has grown in him that his old life is dead. That he can now never expect to resurrect it. That his survival – should he want it – depends on sloughing off this dead skin. That his only real hope is to become someone else entirely.

Thoughts. They become so clear in the darkness. Wondering now what to write to his fiancée, Sabir is inevitably reminded of all the things he's lost. He recalls his arrival at the holding prison in France before embarkation: the bundle of prison clothes and clumsy wooden-soled shoes he was handed; the humiliating body inspection; the inventory of his personal effects the guard had made. It was only then that he was told that he could send on his things to his family if he wished, otherwise they'd be destroyed. There was a moment of anguish before relinquishing these few mementoes of a different life. He hadn't realised he'd have to part with them. The letters and photo of his fiancée; a faded picture of his mother as a young girl; his military citation, along with the medal his unit had been awarded. He hadn't realised these things were important to him. Particularly the photos. How would he be able to remember what his fiancée looked like? Already the face is blurred. It's the feel of her breasts and body that remains with him most viscerally. Or perhaps it's just the ghost of any young woman's body – here in this world of men.

'I'm never coming back,' he now scribbles under the gloom of the night-light. 'Consider me dead, and think of me no longer.'

III

A week later, at dawn parade, an officer singles out a dozen men, including Sabir. They're to leave immediately for Renée, a new forest camp twenty kilometres down the river. 'You've got until nightfall to report to the chief guard. Otherwise, you'll be counted as missing.'

An Arab turnkey doles out their day's rations and walks them out of the penitentiary. It's the first time since his arrival that Sabir's been outside, and as he's watched the crowds of convicts herded in and out of the gates every day, as he's listened to the incessant chatter about goings-on in town, Saint-Laurent has expanded in his mind. It is, after all, a capital city of sorts. The capital of the *bagne*. But now as they leave, he's reminded again of how small it is, how insignificant it seems, compared with what surrounds it. After only a few minutes' walk, the almost elegant boulevard crumbles into little more than a dirt track through a dusty shanty town.

The turnkey stops as they approach a little shop; a Chinaman lounges by its entrance, puffing on an ivory pipe of a type Sabir hasn't seen before. 'If you want to buy anything before you leave, you can get it here,' says the turnkey. No doubt he gets his cut for bringing them here, that's his scam. Inside there's a counter with tobacco, rum, bananas, coconuts, loaves of bread, some kind of boiled meat and rice. Sabir has a few francs he's earned as an *écrivain*: he'll need plenty more to finance his escape, but the temptation to buy something is overwhelming. Such a thing hasn't been allowed in so long! It's these half-tastes of freedom that are so dizzying. Sabir parts with some of his cash for a glass of rum – a ridiculous extravagance – and also some tobacco, since he's heard that in the forest camps smoking is the best way to keep off the mosquitoes.

The turnkey leads them to a place where the dirt road disappears into the trees. 'You have to follow that path. Camp Renée's less than a day's walk from here. You should get there by late afternoon.' He turns away and is gone without a word: here, no one bothers with hellos or goodbyes. The men wait at the spot for a few minutes, too astonished to do anything. Sabir gazes over to Dutch Guiana across the river. Surely there must be a guard hidden somewhere, watching them, checking up on them, ready to shout, ready to fire on them if they try to get away... Eventually they hurry off down the trail the turnkey had pointed to. Sabir rounds each bend expecting to find a guard there, waiting to pick them up and take them to the camp. But there's no one. They're alone in the jungle. At times a darkness envelopes them: trees bow over the trail like two sides of a steeple, a violent blue only occasionally piercing the thick canopy.

Sabir doesn't know the other men; they aren't from his barracks. But no one introduces himself. They're wraiths, walking in silence, each sunk in his own thoughts. It's the shock of suddenly being alone, unsupervised, for the first time in months. The forest has no bars or walls – and yet the old hands back at the penitentiary have impressed on everyone that, in itself, it offers no salvation. To wander off unprepared, with no plan or rations, is to condemn yourself to failure. Sabir lets the other men get ahead until he really is by himself. The weird forest silence is punctuated by squawks and rustling sounds that might be the wind, a small animal or a snake or bird. Sometimes these noises make him start involuntarily. What would it be like to be here in the forest at night? It's good to be alone, though, in daylight hours at least. The forced company of other prisoners merely accentuates the loneliness. Only when Sabir's alone does a sense of himself as a man among others come back to him.

The forest camps, hard labour. He hasn't been able to avoid that fate after all. Foolishly, he'd assumed he'd get a job at Saint-Laurent as a gardener. Such stupid faith in your hopes and dreams is one of the dangers of prison life. The past is dead, the future stolen away, the present an endless desert – so you retreat into a fantasy world, where finally you're in control. Among the lifers he's known, Sabir has seen the syndrome time and time again. You lose yourself in grandiose plans, unrealisable dreams, until life becomes a mirage. And escape can be the worst dream of all. It's the fantasy paradise of the *bagnards*, just as the *bagne* is the fantasy hell for everyone else. Sabir must be on his guard against such daydreaming, because it's never innocent. If he really is to escape, his plans must be firmly grounded in the real world.

At around noon, judging by the sun's position, Sabir stops at a clearing. It's on a small hill, in an otherwise flat terrain. It looks as though someone thought it a good idea to build here, cleared the high land, and then gave up. Before he sits down to eat his bread and dried sausage, Sabir hoists himself a few metres up a tree. For the first time he's able to look right across the forest he's in. A horizonless sea of green merges seamlessly into the primary blue of the tropical sky. Whatever direction you look in, it's the same: blue, green, blue, green. If you stare long enough, the colours start to coalesce until it feels as if there's no up or down, no left or right. Nothing to grab on to, except the filament of river and its random twists. Feeling giddy, Sabir climbs back down. His rations spill out of his tattered cloth sack.

As he eats his lunch, Sabir thinks of his fiancée, for the first time since writing that letter to her under the barracks night-light. It's the stale, lumpy bread he's chewing on that reminds him of her: when they'd been together, she'd been working in a bakery. Now, before him, he sees the room he briefly shared with her in Belleville, just around the corner from that bakery. The shabby chair, the table and the water jug: the vision is suddenly vivid and desperately alive. On the sagging single bed, his fiancée, naked and smiling. He stretches out his hand. But as soon as he's able to discern her features, to focus on the curves of her body, she's gone – the room, too. He finds himself staring at a line of ants on a tree as the picture fades. Ants, ants everywhere. This is the real life of the dead forest. It takes him a minute to pull out of the dazed sensation his vision has left him with, and finish his bread and sausage.

Now on the move again, through the forest. At times the narrow path feels horribly claustrophobic, barely making its way through the thick vegetation. Looking up can bring on vertigo: the trees stretch up twenty metres and more. There are moments of peculiar beauty – two trees of different species growing towards each other, their different-coloured leaves intermingling to form a dappled, stained-glass effect. Vines stringing from one trunk to another, like wild-growing lace. On one of those vines, Sabir sees a bunch of little white flowers miraculously high up among the dense green.

An hour more until Sabir passes near the first camp, Saigon. A dozen gaunt convicts are bent over, apparently hoeing at some cleared ground. Their movements are jerky, puppet-like. Hard to imagine what crop they might be trying to grow out here: most of the ground is hard caked mud and a tangle of tree roots. To one side, a turnkey stands chatting and smoking with a guard. All the convicts look up at Sabir and one asks where he's going. The guard, however, just points to a new trail on the other side of the cleared ground and tells him to keep moving.

Sabir picks up his pace as he dives back into the darkness of the forest. In a way, he's eager to get to his camp. However dire the situation, imagining one's fate tends to be worse than living it – even in Belgium, the shelling and the attacks were not as bad as the nauseous dread that preceded them. Not long after his encounter with the labouring convicts, Sabir sees a group of practically naked men with axes, half-jogging along the path back to Camp Saigon. One of them stops and calls out Sabir's name. He turns around to see a man with a hooked nose and a face that is lined and hollow, burnt black by the sun. The man stares at Sabir, shakes his head, murmurs: 'Got pretty thin, haven't I? You don't recognise me.'

'I do. But I thought you were dead.'

'Likewise. And yet, here we are. Safe and sound.'

Edouard laughs mirthlessly at his own joke. That faintly aristocratic voice and laugh are his, and yet the ghostly face and bony body belong to someone else entirely. He's not the first acquaintance Sabir's bumped into in this colony, although he's certainly the closest. In Belgium, Edouard and Sabir were stationed on the same trench section for months on end – an eternity of waiting and tedium. And during that time, they shared everything. Food, drink, tobacco, jokes, news, rumours, philosophical musings, card games, clothes, boots, lice – such pairings-off were both practical and more or less the norm in the trenches. Over winter they even slept together to conserve heat, a single blanket wrapped around them both. In short, they lived the life of a couple with more intensity than many husbands and wives. No doubt they saved each other's lives on occasion, too. Sabir has a distinct memory of Edouard bringing him down with a tackle one morning while he was shaving in the rear 'bathroom' trench section. A rifle had been pointing out from a bomb crater not twenty metres away behind the lines. All day they played cat and mouse with the sniper, but Edouard got him in the end. Much later came the attack in 1917 that definitively broke up the unit. When the straggles of survivors finally assembled in one place, Edouard wasn't there.

'You know, I've often thought of you,' Sabir finds himself saying now. 'When you didn't come back that morning, I was sure you'd been killed. We all did. What happened?'

'Shrapnel in the eye. Knocked out in a foxhole. They didn't pick me up for another three days. I was raving; thirst, I suppose. Month in hospital, then invalided out.'

'It's amazing, I . . .' Sabir is on the verge of telling him how he tried to find Edouard's family after the war, but stops himself. He stares. When Edouard looks his way, his eyes aren't completely aligned. One appears to be glass. It's difficult to tell with his tanned skin, but there doesn't seem to be any scarring at all around the eye or anywhere else on his face. Unusual to be hit by shrapnel so precisely in the eye and nowhere else.

'I haven't thought of that time for so long,' says Edouard. He chuckles to himself. 'D'you remember that chap Durand? That madman who always wore a spiked helmet he'd looted from some dead German?'

'Yes. I remember.'

'Did you hear what happened to him?'

'Don't think so.'

'Someone bet him fifty francs he wouldn't walk into that bar in Lille with the spiked helmet on and order a beer in German.'

'What happened?'

'Some drunk English officer drinking there got up and shot him dead!'

They laugh. A flood of faces from the war return to Sabir. Julien Pardieu; le Petit Clouzot; that man with the purple birthmark on his face . . . most dead, but what has happened to the survivors? Married, with children and jobs? Or more like Sabir and Edouard? For a moment, Sabir's back in the trenches. Once again, the days of shelling, the nights with prostitutes. His months there seem like the best of times, the camaraderie so different from the suspicion and isolation that reign here.

'You're going back to that camp over there?' asks Sabir.

Edouard nods. 'We're supposed to be wood chopping. But if you're quick, you can get your quota done earlier. Then you can go out butterfly hunting. There are a lot of Morphos round here; you get a franc a piece for them. So you came in on the last convoy?'

'Yeah. I'm heading for Camp Renée. Know anything about it?'

'I know it. Got a good friend there. It's not so bad. Not exactly lax, but the *chef de camp* is new. The place has only been open a few months. All the clearing's been done. There's just construction work, no wood chopping. And that's what kills you. The chopping.'

They stand chatting uncertainly for a few more minutes, about the camps and the Colony, but not any more about the past. Edouard's conversation is punctuated by various expressions and convict jargon that Sabir only half-grasps. Still so much to learn: a whole new language, a whole new mythology. When Edouard smiles, which he does only once, his face is rigid like a mask. At one point, he abruptly asks: 'What about money? Got any money?'

'Few francs, that's all.'

Edouard quickly changes the subject. He doesn't elaborate on the purpose of his question. Eventually, he says: 'Well, I'll be off now. You've got another couple of hours before you reach Renée. When you get there, go and see Carpette. He's the keeper of one of the barracks. Tell him you're a friend of mine. Tell him I asked him to do whatever he can for you.'

'I'll do that. Thanks.'

'Camp Renée . . . you struck lucky . . . there are worse places . . . well, be seeing you.'

Edouard disappears back down the trail towards Camp Saigon. And Sabir continues his journey through the forest, at first thinking about Edouard, about his glass eye, and then about Edouard's friend in Camp Renée who might be able to help him. Such recommendations don't mean a lot out here, though. Sabir thinks back to his own foolish promise to help the country boy Gaspard. It weighs on him, although no doubt he'll never see the boy again. Not unless he, too, is sent to this Camp Renée. A camp with a woman's name, odd that. He wonders at Edouard's last words: 'Be seeing you.' What was the likelihood of that?

At some point in the afternoon the rain comes crashing out of the sky, but Sabir barely notices, lost in self-absorption. In any case, it means that it's four o'clock and he has only a couple of hours till nightfall. The path winds by the river: the other shore seems to be melting under the lashing rain, collapsing like a flimsy stage set. It hits you hard, this rain, and yet brings no great relief from the heat. That's what makes it feel so foreign.

The path ends abruptly. Coming out of the forest is like coming out of a dream. Ahead, lined with palm trees, an avenue – vertiginously wide after the confines of the forest. Swathes of jungle have been cleared, perhaps a couple of hundred hectares in all. A number of small buildings have been erected there. At the bottom, six whitewashed barracks with thatched roofs, three on either side of the avenue. The effect is almost pretty. A few convicts wander about, but otherwise the place is almost deserted.

Sabir reports to the bookkeeper as he's been told to do; after his name and number have been registered, he's taken to his barracks. It's set out in the same way as the one in Saint-Laurent, with long planks of wood by the walls that serve as communal beds. Unlike in Saint-Laurent, though, this barracks has a wretched lived-in feel. Threadbare rags and battered tin bowls lie at the base of the bed plank, along with little statuettes and other objects half-carved out of the heavy tropical wood. They're to be sold to the guards, probably, who'll then sell them on as souvenirs in Saint-Laurent or Cayenne. On the walls, pictures of glamorous women torn from ancient copies of *La Vie Parisienne*. And family photos, warped in the heat and damp, of wives, mothers, daughters, sisters, mistresses.

Sabir is told to dump his cloth sack in the far corner and report immediately to the camp commandant. The book-keeper points out the path he's to take, to the left of the grand avenue. After a ten-minute walk through the jungle, he comes to a clearing by the river. Here, there are convicts at work, levelling the ground, erecting a wall, building a large house. Sabir can hear a gramophone. Classical music – crisp piano notes and a male voice singing in German. In itself, it's jolting, since German will always remind Sabir of the front, and those odd fragments of conversation that used to drift across the Flemish mud when the wind was right. Sabir knows nothing about classical music, but the frozen, precise tones seem starkly out of place as they echo across the trees and water, here in the suffocating humidity of the equatorial forest.

Inside, the ground floor of the house appears to be more or less complete and habitable; beyond a short corridor there's a sitting room. The gramophone in one corner. A table in the middle, and a man sitting by it, his head in his hands – as if in pain or in prayer. He looks up. 'Ah, the gardener!' He gets to his feet and extends his hand. Sabir takes a moment to extend his own: it's a long time since anyone offered to shake hands with him. It feels like reaching into another world.

'I don't know where to start. I've got some rough plans drawn up here. Or we could go and see the terrain now; perhaps that would be best. If you'll follow me out here, the back way...'

Sabir keeps right behind the commandant. They're looking out over land that's been cleared, some of it levelled as well. 'There'll be a series of steps here once I get the stone,' the commandant continues, 'and then to the right there'll be a fountain. That has nothing to do with you, of course; I've got a stonemason working on that. Over here, in front, I want a lawn, if I can get the turf, with the flower beds to the side away from the river, and beyond a *jardin anglais*. You're going to have to write up some specifications for plant species. I've got seeds from France and I have a shipment of seedlings coming from Florida.'

Bewildered, Sabir says nothing throughout, but the commandant, carried away by his own enthusiasm, doesn't notice. They stroll about the terrain, while the commandant continues to spill out a jumble of horticultural plans that Sabir can barely take in: a hedge to cut the river from the lawn; a fishpond in the *jardin anglais*, in front of the folly he's having built. But the fish are a problem since none of the river species would survive. Sabir nods, watches the commandant. He towers over Sabir and is noticeably thin – like a convict rather than an Administration official, most of whom run to fat. He has a carefully trimmed black moustache. His hair is dark, what's left of it: at the front most of it has gone and he's cut the rest extremely short. This too, coupled with his tanned face, reinforces the convict look. It's difficult to say how old he might be. Thirty-five? Forty-five? There's a certain Teutonic stiffness about him – Sabir wonders whether he's from one of the 'German' *départements*, Alsace or Lorraine.

Now they're back in the sitting room, poring over plans. 'A lot of this I want done within the next four weeks, before my wife arrives. All the basic landscaping at the very least must be done by then. I can give you half a dozen men; it should be sufficient if you're well organised.' The commandant has lit a cigarette, a proper French one, not the sawdust-cut rubbish the convicts smoke. Ignored, the cigarette consumes itself in the ashtray: it's torture to watch. Out of the blue, the commandant shoots Sabir a question: 'So what's your experience? Who did you work for?'

'I was head gardener for the Comtesse d'Entremeuse, sir. I looked after the gardens at the Château Ben Ali.'

'Really? How interesting . . .'

Within seconds, Sabir has a whole story worked out in his head, with all sorts of baroque details. But already the commandant has lost interest and has started talking about his garden again.

Nightfall, after the evening meal. Stretched out on the hard board bunk, hands behind his head, Sabir watches the to and fro of the barracks. There's a night-light between the two bed boards but many of the men have their own little lamps as well, fashioned out of empty tins. There's not much conversation. A few of the convicts have quizzed Sabir about Saint-Laurent, but once they realise that he's got no interesting news and no money, they drift off to their own corners. One man is mending his butterfly net, another is carving something out of a wood block, yet another is squeezing parasites from the soles of his feet. In the middle, a card game is in progress.

A bell rings. A guard and a turnkey appear. The keeper of the barracks shouts out: 'All present and accounted for, *chef.*' The turnkey bolts the doors before moving on to the next barracks; one by one, the little makeshift lamps are winked out and after a while only the central night-light is left burning, silhouetting the men as they lie slumped on the boards, most of them still in their sweaty work clothes.

Although he's exhausted, Sabir can't sleep. He hasn't had a proper night's rest since the holding prison in France. Sleep was impossible on the ship and it's turning out to be just as difficult in the barracks. He can't get used to the hard boards, can't get used to sharing the barracks – and the bed board – with so many men. In France, he sometimes had a cell to himself, and never shared with more than four or five other prisoners. In the half-gloom, his mind wanders back to his meeting with the commandant. Sabir knows nothing whatsoever about horticulture or landscape gardening. His story about working for the Comtesse d'Entremeuse surprised even himself, and it takes him a moment to work out where he got the name from. On the prison ship, there was a prisoner called Lacroix, who was always bragging about how he was the valet for this Comtesse d'Entremeuse – apparently he'd been caught stealing jewellery from her dressing table. All the other prisoners thought him a pompous idiot. Throughout the voyage, he bored everybody stupid with his stories of the Comtesse, the château and the high life they led there. As if he thought her nobility had somehow rubbed off on him. Then, just a few days before reaching the South American coast, he fell ill. He turned yellow and started shaking. Within hours he was dead.

Sabir is thinking about his new job as a landscape gardener. As a working-class Parisian, he's never even been into a private garden before. His friend Edouard, on the other hand, would know about such things. Sabir remembers now that in civilian life Edouard ran a nursery. He recalls Edouard telling him how he'd import exotic varieties and sell them to rich families at absurdly inflated prices. And how the bottom had fallen out of it all, once the war came. Sabir wonders whether there'll be any way he can communicate with Edouard, ask his advice.

There's one incident about Edouard that sticks in his mind. At one time, behind the trenches, soldiers used to maintain little *jardins potagers*, which they planted with potatoes and other root vegetables to supplement their diet. Edouard some-how managed to grow a rosebush on his patch. He tended it with great care and, in the summer of 1917, it finally blossomed into an explosion of red. Set against the fields of mud and the trees stripped of leaves, the effect was bizarre. For a brief moment, the rosebush became one of the sights of the sector; men used to stop by it on their way to the bombed-out village just behind the lines, where the mobile brothel had been set up.

A month later came the major assault, after all those months of immobility. And it was then that Edouard disappeared.

For whatever reason, this incident comes to mind as Sabir thinks about his job. And although he knows nothing about gardens, he's certainly met people like the commandant before: men fizzing with ideas, carried away by their own enthusiasm. They're eternally planning and constructing, but more often than not their plans come to nothing. There were officers like that in the army, and he knew how to handle them.

As Sabir lies there, lost in speculation, he sees a man get up and go over to the night-light. The man leans over as if to light a cigarette from it, but Sabir sees him deliberately blow the lamp out. Everything's black – there's no noise save the occasional snore and a mysterious shuffling sound. A tingling fear invades Sabir. All those stories he's heard about what happens in the barracks at night . . . He draws his feet up, ready to kick out should anyone attack him. Why didn't he get himself a knife in Saint-Laurent when he had the chance? As his eyes get accustomed to the dark, he can make out a grotesque ballet of shadows. He can hear whisperings too, but it's impossible to work out what's happening. He holds his position, nerves on a hair trigger, muscles tensing at every click or rustle, until he can feel an ache crawling up his legs, towards his gut and arms. An hour or more passes like that. Eventually he hears a mutter: it's the keeper of the barracks. In the dark, Sabir sees him rise from the bed board and move towards the lamp. The flash of a match illuminates the barracks with a terrible violence.

The lamp is lit again and all the shadowy forms Sabir thought he could see melt away to nothing. But there'll be no sleep now.

IV

It's this lack of sleep that lends everything its air of unreality. As though he were on the other side of a glass wall, observing a diorama. When he's working, and often at night too, the vision of his fiancée returns to him, catching him unawares, just as it did during the journey in the forest. Back in France, when she was still near, when she was still a possibility, he thought of other things. Other women even. Now, as he's trying his best to forget her, this is when she decides to haunt him. To wait for him. Dream back to the summer before last, and the dark hair that framed her face. Once again, she trembles beneath him. Her nakedness troubles him, but he resists the urge to masturbate; he recognises the mental danger of associating sexual relief with her image.

After an uneasy first few days, work on the garden proceeds smoothly. The six men under Sabir's orders are all country lads: they know about the land, how to prepare a field, how to build drystone walls, the rudiments of landscaping. Thanks to them, he can get by on bluff, delegation and wile. Sabir is careful always to have one of his men along with him whenever the commandant takes him on a tour of the site to explain what he wants done. Already, the lawn area has been levelled and some of the land by the river drained. Once this heavy work is completed, once the seedlings arrive and it's a question of digging and planting flower beds or rock gardens and preparing hedges, Sabir realises that his job will prove more difficult.

Every day he sees the commandant, and an unlikely relationship develops between the two. The commandant is not such an easy man to fathom after all. While the guards live in bungalows with airy verandas up by the wide avenue at the main camp, he prefers his half-built house down by the river. And he stays there completely by himself, when other officials of his rank keep whole armies of convict servants.

Sometimes, at the end of the afternoon, he asks Sabir into his sitting room, where they look over plans for the garden. During these sessions, in the last hour before the sun goes down, conversation sometimes veers away from the garden and construction work. The commandant never asks about Sabir's past, but on occasion talks about his own. An idyllic childhood beneath the French Alps; student escapades at the Saint-Cyr military school; the Paris life of a young man about town – a life that could never have conceivably intersected with Sabir's.

Despite his military career, the one thing the commandant never talks about is the war. One afternoon, though, he does mention a tour of duty in the French colony of Algeria. From one instant to the next, he becomes heated and angry. Algeria, where 'we build roads, railways, we plant vineyards, create industries, open schools, we allow the colony to prosper ... and yet what have we ever managed to do here in Guiana? What has this colony ever done for the Republic? Why do we still have to import all our food, when the Dutch and British farm their land? Why are there bauxite mines in Dutch Guiana, sugar plantations in British Guiana, and nothing here? It's a damned disgrace! But what can you expect of a colony that has only butterfly wings and stuffed monkeys to send to the *Exposition Coloniale*?'

The rant takes Sabir by surprise. Later, he finds out that it's by no means unusual: one of the commandant's pet obsessions is reform. 'This absurd colony – corrupt from top to bottom!' he explodes on another occasion. 'I go to Saint-Laurent, I order a new batch of trousers for the men here. What do I find? The Administration has none to issue. The storehouse is empty. Why? No one in the Administration will tell me. But I find out from a convict. The keeper of the stores has sold the lot to Brazilian contrabandists! He's robbed the government of five hundred pairs of trousers! Will he be arrested? Of course not! He's paid off everyone with the proceeds of the sale. At best, he'll be sent back to France. It's outrageous!' The commandant slams his fist down on the table with a rage that hints at something else, some deeper frustration or violence.

One afternoon a new batch of convicts arrives at the camp. Only one of them is assigned to Sabir's barracks – a Basque boy nicknamed Say-Say. Lying back on the bed board, gazing up at the rafters, Sabir listens as Say-Say reports the news from Saint-Laurent. Bonifacio has pulled off a sensational escape.

'They'd taken all the dangerous guys from the barracks and put them in cells. They were going to be shipped out to the islands next morning. During the night, Bonifacio got out somehow. Knocked out the turnkey, then stabbed that guard, Muratti. In the stomach. I was on cleaning detail the next day – what a mess. Like an abattoir. The guy didn't die immediately, though. They took him to the hospital, unconscious. One of the porters told me that, just before he died, he woke up and started screaming.'

Muratti: Sabir remembers this guard. A Corsican, like Bonifacio. A lot of the guards are Corsican, as are a lot of the convicts. They all seem to know each other and they're all connected in some way, through complex family alliances or ancient, obscure feuds. This guard, Muratti, had something against Bonifacio. Maybe it was personal, maybe it was to do with Bonifacio's previous escape, maybe it was Corsican business. In any case, Muratti came to the barracks the very day the new convoy arrived, to crow over Bonifacio's recapture – or perhaps goad him into doing something stupid. Although Sabir could see that it'd taken enormous self-restraint, Bonifacio managed to hold his tongue and ignore the guard's gibes. Muratti soon got bored with Bonifacio's silence and went away.

'Anyway,' continues Say-Say, 'the afternoon before the escape, we're all being exercised in the yard. Bonifacio's just standing about smoking. Muratti comes up to him, starts talking: "Still here, then?" he says. "Thought you'd be long gone by now." Bonifacio doesn't say anything, completely ignores the guy. Muratti keeps baiting him: "When's the big escape, then? Today? Tomorrow? The next day?" Finally, Bonifacio says: "Tonight. I'm out of this shithole tonight." "Too fucking late," says Muratti, "because I'm moving you to the cells after exercise. The boat gets in tomorrow morning." And he was right, Bonifacio was moved straight after. But then, in the middle of the night, he gets out anyway. How the hell he did it I don't know, but Jesus . . .'

He's interrupted by one of the camp guards. There's silence during the headcount, but straight after lock-up an argument over Bonifacio's escape flares up. In the camps, news is a scarce resource, and every morsel must be carefully chewed.

Say-Say continues: 'He must have paid off the turnkey to open the cell door for him. Then knocked the guy out afterwards, to make him look innocent.'

'Bullshit,' says one of the *forts-à-bras*. 'I've been here since 1921 and I can't remember a single escape that relied on a turnkey. Can't trust 'em. They got too much to lose.'

'He must have paid *someone* off. What about the walls? How could he have got over the walls? With all those sentries at night.'

'Maybe he didn't. Maybe he hid out in the stores and sneaked out during the day.'

And so on. The only question in Sabir's mind is why Bonifacio took the stupid risk of knifing Muratti. Because if he's ever caught, there's no doubt now as to what his sentence will be. Either way, he'll have escaped the *bagne* for ever.

Another long, restless night stretches out before Sabir. It's under cover of darkness that men settle their differences, go thieving, go to their lovers. The shuffle of bodies, the muffled cries – the sound of pain or pleasure? Not always easy to know. Sleep comes rarely, but when it does, it brings uneasy dreams. Only in Sabir's waking moments does his fiancée appear to him, beckon him. When he sleeps, his dreams are different. He's in a wasteland of green. Like the Flemish battlefields in every respect except colour. Back then it was grey skies and kilometre upon kilometre of grey mud; now, it's an endless expanse of tangled undergrowth that doesn't seem to be growing so much as dying.

A fresh dispute has broken out, cranking up the tension in the barracks. Antillais is a black convict who's quite a bit older than the others, maybe even as old as sixty. Until recently, he's always kept himself to himself, spending all his spare time doting on his pet cat. Every night after lock-up, the cat would get in through a hole in the roof, then laboriously make its way down the wall onto the dirt floor, where Antillais would feed it meat scraps he saved from dinner. He's even built the cat a little wooden manger where it slept, by the bed board. But one day, one of the *forts-à-bras,* known as Masque because of his tattooed face, complained about the way the cat pissed and shat all over the barracks. The two men practically came to blows over it, and Masque threatened to strangle the cat if he ever saw it again. Not long after that, the cat disappeared. For a few days, Antillais was broken with grief. A rumour started to do the rounds that Masque had killed the cat and, what's worse, had cooked and eaten it with friends in the jungle one afternoon after work. Now, Antillais is given to talking to himself and mumbling terrible threats.

Masque fears Antillais, because Antillais is mad enough to risk his own life for revenge. But since Antillais is an old man, it'd be an act of cowardice to have him killed, so Masque can't do that. He can't even take normal precautions in the barracks without losing face among the other *forts-à-bras.* And the strain is beginning to show. Masque is one of the worst of the bullies, and there are plenty of men who wouldn't mind if something happened to him. The other day, Sabir even noticed one of Masque's enemies, a convict named Pierrot, pulling Antillais aside and talking to him in a low whisper. Not long ago, Pierrot had been sitting on the bed board counting some gambling winnings when Masque had stridden up, snatched half of the notes from him, pulled a knife and shouted: 'Take it off me, if you think you fucking can!' No one's saying anything, but everyone's mentally prepared for a bloodletting.

Sabir stares at the scratch marks on the wall opposite, where the cat used to shimmy down. He's still thinking about

Bonifacio's escape – and about his own. There've already been a few failed attempts since his arrival, two from his barracks alone. Men who've just taken off, unprepared. They get across the river easily enough, only to be picked up by Dutch soldiers on the other side and sent back to Saint-Laurent. No, the only way is the properly planned, properly financed escape with like-minded individuals. It takes Sabir right back to the money problem. You can earn a few francs hunting butterflies, but even then you need a net. A decent one costs fifteen francs, and it's weeks before you're any good with it. He was hoping to make money as an *écrivain*, but it wasn't long before he realised that wouldn't work either. Not that most here aren't illiterate, because they are. Rather, it's that so few men have any desire to write letters any more. There's the scarcity of paper in the camps, the problem of getting the letters back to Saint-Laurent – but that's not the real reason. It takes four or five months to get a reply, and the longer you're in the Colony, the wider the gulf grows. Pretty quickly, you've got nothing left to say to that other world; relentlessly, the Colony absorbs you until there *is* no other world. As for the rest – the faded photograph, the tattered letter with its protestation of love – all that becomes a hopeless fiction.

As Sabir closes his eyes, images of Bonifacio's escape come to him. A fantasy unfolds: instead of Bonifacio escaping, it's Sabir in that cell, waiting. The cell door is open. The turnkey calls for Muratti the guard, then bows his head, readying himself for the blow from Sabir that will knock him out. It's done in the blur of a moment. Then Muratti appears. Sabir can feel the blade of a knife against his palm as he hides behind the door. That knife, ready to slip between a man's ribs. And the thrust . . . but then everything blanks out, and Sabir finds that he can follow that particular fantasy no further.

Bonifacio's escape is the violent miracle that can't be ignored. Sabir realises that, if anything, news of it has made him feel anxious and despondent. Because soon enough, money or no money, he'll have to emulate Bonifacio. And run those same risks that this other man took so nonchalantly. For Sabir, the thought of escape involuntarily brings up jumbled images of his first school fight; of that night he tried to lose his virginity; of being shelled for the first time in Belgium; of the first corpse he came across in the fields behind the trenches. Bonifacio is gone, like a magic trick, and in an obscure way Sabir feels orphaned.

The next day passes in a dream. Sabir's work isn't onerous; in fact, he's even started to enjoy it. Having never before given even a passing thought to gardening, he's now beginning to see how there might be something in it. The commandant has brought a small library with him to the camp, and it includes several old books on botany and horticulture. He's encouraged Sabir to look through these books and take anything that catches his eye. They're fairly useless from a practical perspective – a history of the château gardens of the Loire Valley; a tome on flowers and orchids native to France – and at first Sabir borrowed merely to show willing. But now it's become his habit to sit down with a book during the half-hour the convicts have for their lunch. They make for difficult reading and are often boring; on the other hand, they're the only books he has access to at the camp.

Today, Sabir has taken a nineteenth-century treatise on horticulture from the library. After breaking his bread, he opens the book and reads the first lines of the first page: 'From the intimate union of art and nature is born the perfect composition of a garden, which Time, purifying public taste, now promises to bring us. In such a garden, the majesty of nature is ever present, but it is nature reduced to human proportions and thus transformed into a haven against the rude shocks of our mortal existence.'

Not easy to get the hang of sentences like these. During the war, Sabir was a voracious reader, devouring the adventure stories, novels of intrigue and penny dreadfuls that were specially printed for soldiers at the front. At times, he was gripped by a terrible hunger. He'd crunch through novel after novel, day and night, barely aware of what was happening in and around the trenches. But those books were different. The words and phrases flew effortlessly by, their meaning self-evident. With the commandant's books, on the other hand, you have to concentrate on every line. And yet, as he rereads the passage from the treatise, Sabir has his tiny flash of revelation. Since the war, Sabir has been in and out of factory work. But this business of gardening is clearly something more than the pastoral equivalent of that. There's plenty to learn, if one ever cared to learn it. It's what it might be like to have a craft, or a special skill. Again he recalls Edouard's rosebush behind the trenches, and the care he lavished on it. Indeed, it's a measure of the unreason of this colony that Edouard is out chopping wood while Sabir is in charge of creating a garden. For a brief moment, Sabir catches a glimpse of a different kind of life.

But when the end of the day approaches, when it's time to go back to the barracks, he's filled with fear and anxiety again. There are any number of reasons for escaping – one of them, he's beginning to realise, is to get away from the other convicts. Those endless nights with their whispers and pressing tensions; the bullying *forts-à-bras*, self-esteem set on a hair trigger; the night noises that shred your nerves and leave you exhausted in the morning. As he walks back along the path to the main camp, he thinks of Edouard and their meeting in the jungle. He remembers how Edouard told him to go and see a friend of his named Carpette, one of the keepers of the barracks. And that Edouard would ask this Carpette to do what he could to help Sabir.

He didn't know what a keeper was before he came here; he's since learnt that it's a prized position. While the others are out at work, the keeper has to clean the barracks, fill the water urn from the river, and make sure nothing's stolen. But it's also the keeper who sells the convicts the oil he siphons off from the barrack supplies, the coffee he skims from breakfast rations, as well as tobacco, matches, onions, bread and all sorts of other wares. Some of this stuff is pilfered from the kitchen; the rest he gets the turnkeys to bring in from Saint-Laurent when they go into town. The keeper buys wholesale and makes his money selling piecemeal to the convicts at night. It's a lucrative business.

Sabir collects his dinner rations and walks down the avenue towards the end barracks, of which Carpette is the keeper. By the time he finds the man he's looking for, there are only a few minutes left until lock-up. Carpette turns out to be a smallish, fastidious-looking man. He grabs Sabir's arm and leads him to the privy, where they can talk away from the others. Eyeing Sabir suspiciously, he subjects him to a sort of interrogation.

'How do you know Edouard?'

'We were together during the war.'

'Really? How did you know he's here?'

'Bumped into him, on my way to camp.'

'When was the last time you'd seen him before that?'

'Haven't seen him since the war. I thought he was dead.'

'Did you notice his false eye?'

'Yes. I noticed it.'

'Did he tell you how he lost his eye?'

'In the war, I think he said.'

Carpette gives a short laugh, as if to dismiss the story. 'Yes, well, Edouard's told me all about you. Says you're broke, though.'

'That's true,' Sabir replies, mystified by the interrogation and the question about the false eye. He hurries to the point: 'Look, I need to get out of here. I'll do whatever I have to. Edouard said you could help me.'

'Get out of here?' Carpette continues to stare, as if sizing up a rival. Unlike other convicts, his hair has grown out a little, enough for a side parting. It's the privilege of a keeper to wear one's hair like that, and it sets him apart from the others, giving him an air of purpose and authority. Finally he says: 'You work down by the river, don't you? You sometimes go into his house, don't you?'

'Yes.'

'Can you get in there alone?'

'Sometimes.'

'There must be plenty to steal there. Booze, food, tobacco, oil, clothes, cutlery, pens, ink, paper . . . Look around, for Christ's sake.'

'All right. I will.'

'Don't be greedy. Don't steal too much. Couple of bottles of rum, not the whole case.'

'I understand.'

'Problem is, whatever you take, you won't be able to sell it here. Because it'll be spotted by the guards. They'll find out who's doing it, then they'll bleed you dry. But I can fence it for you. I can get someone to take the stuff down to Saint-Laurent.'

The evening bell rings; Sabir hurries back to his own barracks. That night, although sleep seems just as impossible,

Sabir is less anxious than usual. The meeting with Carpette was ambiguous; he must now earn the man's trust. Carpette has merely offered to fence stolen goods for him, no doubt in order to take his own cut. But he's noticed that while most other convicts go about in dirty rags or half-naked, Carpette looks after himself: his striped convict shirt had been clean and in good condition. In other words, he's a survivor, he hasn't let the Colony entirely degrade him. That's a good sign, and he's glad to have made contact with someone like that.

He wonders why it hasn't occurred to him before to steal from the commandant. Now he thinks about it, he's noticed how things are always going missing down by the river. The bricks and timber arrive by boat, but by the time they're unloaded, there's always less than on the order form. At times, the pilfering has seriously impeded his own work. Three spades disappeared and he had to wait for new ones to come up from Saint-Laurent before he could continue with the digging. He now realises it was probably his own men who took them.

It's this question of money and how to get it that creates so much of the anxiety, that makes the Colony so different from Sabir's prison experiences in France. In a mainland prison, there were times when it felt like going back to childhood – you were fed and housed and all the important decisions of your life were taken by someone else. Here in the Colony, that's all stripped away. Inaction is no kind of option: the pursuit of money is the pursuit of life over death.

V

Five forty-five, the morning bell, not quite light. Men lined up in the dull green of the tropical dawn, queuing for breakfast rations: a crust of bread and a splash of coffee. The coolness of the air on Sabir's body feels good – this hour before daybreak offers the only real respite from the heat. Standing in line next to Sabir is Antillais, the man whose cat has vanished. The night before, Antillais calmly announced to the barracks that his tormentor Masque would be dead within the week. Masque attempted to laugh it off. Surely he'll kill Antillais now. The tension in the barracks is palpable.

It's difficult to tell how old Antillais really is. Not just because of his colour, but because people age more quickly in the Colony. Someone told Sabir, though, that Antillais has been here over thirty years. In other words, since before the twentieth century. What would that be like? But thirty years is perhaps no different from five. When everything else stops, time accelerates towards the horizon. One moment you're a young man; seconds later you're old, ready to die. It's all over. Perhaps, in Antillais's position, Sabir would also risk his life to avenge the death of a pet. Why not? In some way, the *bagne* actually lessens your sense of mortality. It's like during the war, at the front, when you'd find yourself taking incredible risks for the smallest things. An image of Edouard comes to mind, calmly climbing out of the trench to recover a packet of cigarettes.

This morning, some of the commandant's wife's luggage is arriving by boat. It'll be Sabir's job to oversee its delivery to the house, make sure nothing's stolen. Not easy, since he'll have to watch not only the convicts bringing the crates up to the house, but also the Bonis who'll ferry them to the riverbank in their canoes. The Bonis live in tribes up and down the river, but they're not Indians, they're the descendants of runaway slaves. They're incorrigible thieves (a convict told Sabir he'd once come across a whole village of them dressed in striped convict shirts), but expert boatsmen as well. They make their living ferrying goods and people across the river. And sometimes they supply convicts with the boats they need for their escapes. But they're ruthless businessmen and the boats never come cheap.

The commandant is generally up at the main camp during the day, but this morning he's stayed down by the river to await the arrival of the ship. He seems excited about it and his eyes have a glow to them. Perhaps he's already started on the rum; Sabir has noticed that he's a bit of a drinker. Not that it's anything unusual here. The commandant might even pass as fairly abstemious, compared with the guards.

It's impossible to know exactly when the boat will get in, since there's no direct communication with Saint-Laurent. No telegraph or phone lines. There used to be, and there probably will be again, but something always happens to the cables. They're too easy to cut and it's always in somebody's interests to cut them. So now the camp is as isolated as a medieval village. The commandant has invited Sabir into his house while they wait, ostensibly to talk about progress on the garden, but his mind is elsewhere. He drifts back to his favourite subject, the reform of the Colony: 'I'm not interested in setting up just another logging camp, where we slowly work the men to death. What's the point of that? How will it benefit the Colony? How will it benefit France? Logging would be a good idea, if we had professional loggers with proper equipment exporting the wood to Europe. That doesn't happen here. We have convicts with rusty, clapped-out axes. The timber ends up being used for fuel in Saint-Laurent. The *bagne* feeds the *bagne*. It's slowly consuming itself.

'Once the building work's finished, I'm going to open up that flat land to the north, by the river. We've got no livestock here to feed the *bagne*, let alone the rest of the Colony. All that meat has to be imported. It's costing us a fortune! We have fresh water in abundance and all we need to do is open up suitable grazing land.'

But Sabir has switched off. He's heard this about the live-stock before. According to Bébert, one of the country lads Sabir works with on the garden, this plan to carve grasslands out of the forest is doomed to failure. Once the trees are cleared, the topsoil's quickly washed away and it's impossible to maintain any kind of pasture. You just end up with huge expanses of mud. Bébert's been here six years, has tried to escape twice. Now, he appears to be resigned to his fate and spends his money gambling. 'He hasn't been here long enough,' he said about the commandant, 'but he'll learn. He'll learn.'

Nonetheless, through sheer enthusiasm and willpower, the commandant has achieved an awful lot in a short space of time. There's the land cleared up by the main camp, the buildings there and the avenue; and then there's this grand house by the river, already nearing completion, and the garden Sabir is in charge of creating. Rumour has it that the commandant is a very wealthy man, that his house and garden are being built at his own cost – albeit with free convict labour. Perhaps it's true. The things Sabir has managed to sneak out of the house over the past week and hide in the undergrowth – bottles of burgundy, silver spoons, a *jambon de Bayonne* – suggest someone who's made no concession to colonial life, regardless of cost. Despite this, the commandant appears to be a man of ascetic habits. It's a paradox. Sabir's even seen him lunching off dry bread and broth – convict rations, in other words.

The commandant's still talking; Sabir slowly tunes back in. 'You're a good man,' he's saying, 'you're doing a fine job with this garden. My wife will be so pleased. I know she'll like you.'

Past eleven now and the boat still hasn't arrived. The commandant can wait no longer; he has business up at the main camp. Sabir is left on his own. There's a guard and a dozen men working down by the river, but they're too far away to see what he's up to. For once, there's no one in the vicinity, and he has the perfect right to be in the house – he can take a good look around without fear of being caught out.

Upstairs, two rooms are finished; the rest of the floor is in a skeletal state. Sabir pushes the door to one of the rooms. The first thing he notices is the full-length looking glass. It's a shock to catch sight of himself like that. While he sees his fiancée's face everywhere, his own has been a blank all these weeks and months. There are no mirrors out here, none that a convict can use, in any case. You can stare into your dinner tin, and it gives you a blurred, distorted image. Other than that, there's imagination and memory. Which are always wrong. Always telling you what you want to hear, that you're the same as when you were arrested, that the months of imprisonment have had no effect, nor will the years to come in this scorched colony. The person that now stares out at Sabir seems to be someone else. The shaved head, the leathery, sun-hardened skin and the gaunt features give his face the skull appearance that he's noticed in others. He's been here such a brief time, and yet the transformation has already happened.

In the room there's a bed, a chest of drawers, a chair and table, a few other pieces of furniture. Sabir jerks open one of the drawers; there's nothing in it. This is to be the wife's bedroom, evidently. The curtains are frilly, feminine. The sole other decoration is a framed photograph sitting on the bedside table. It's of a house by a river. Sabir does a double take: the house looks just like the one he's in right now, built at the same angle to the river, with the same garden layout. He takes a closer look at the photograph. No, actually it's a different river, with European trees and vegetation. A different house. Nonetheless, the similarity is striking.

The other bedroom's clearly occupied. The bed's unmade, there are clothes on the chair and piles of books on the floor. Downstairs is a similar mess of books, paper, food, clothes, cutlery. It's what makes it so easy to steal from here: what Sabir takes, the commandant will assume is lost somewhere. Or he simply won't care. He shows little interest in possessions. It's occasionally the way with the rich, Sabir has noticed. Those who've never had to struggle to own anything.

He picks up one of the books: *The Principles of Hydro-Engineering: An Introduction.* He flicks through it – it's full of notes. Most of the other books have some practical slant as well. The man's a self-starter, a Robinson Crusoe. On top of one of these piles of books, there's an album crammed with photographs. Some have been stuck in, others just jammed between the pages, so they spill out when Sabir opens the album. He bends down to collect the ones he's dropped, shuffles through them. There's one of the commandant as a boy, in a sailor suit. Another of a frowning man in a top hat, beside a matronly woman in a voluminous dress. Several photos of the house – that same house from the picture in the wife's bedroom. And several more of an attractive, dark-haired woman in her mid- to late twenties. The commandant's wife, Sabir supposes. There's something odd about her, although Sabir can't immediately put his finger on it. Her face is completely expressionless in each image – like that of a saint, or of a dead body. There's just one image of her smiling, at the beach. She's wearing a swimming costume, revealing the curve of her hips and breasts. Sabir slips this photo into his pocket.

Before lock-up he has another rendezvous with Carpette, down by the edge of the forest. Sabir has some more stolen goods for him. This time, Carpette has specifically asked for paper and ink. Very easy to spirit away from the commandant's desk: he's one of those men who's always firing off a mess of ideas, and that's what his desk looks like. In general, it's not the thieving that's so difficult, it's hiding the stuff and then getting it up to the main camp. The endless trips he has to make down an indistinct path running parallel to the main one, to avoid the guards . . .

It seems, though, that he's managed to allay Carpette's suspicions of him. And so far, Carpette's been as good as his word: he's fenced the things Sabir's brought him and paid up promptly. No doubt Carpette's swindling him – the silver spoons he'd stolen are probably worth ten times what Carpette gave him. And yet Sabir couldn't care less – he's at least getting some proper money, for the first time since his arrival. That immediately makes him feel better, less vulnerable. The first payment went to buying a *plan* and a knife. Since then he's been saving. And buying food to supplement his rations: above all, it's important to stay in decent health.

The dealings between the two have until now been furtive, brief. But this afternoon there's more time, and as they exchange goods and money, Carpette asks Sabir if he has any plans.

'I'm getting out, of course,' Sabir says, 'as soon as I've got the dough.'

Carpette shakes his head. 'You'll need a lot more than that.'

'I know.'

He offers Carpette one of the cigarettes he's just stolen from the commandant; together, they smoke in silence. A bloated sun hovers over the green horizon. Never before has it looked so huge, so near. Back in France, Sabir didn't know what the sun was really like. Out here, it's the true fire. It penetrates your body like a knife. And burns with an intensity that reduces a whole life to a mere moment.

'Edouard says I can trust you. So I'll tell you that we're getting out, too.' Carpette says nothing further, and neither does Sabir. It's such a pleasure to smoke a real cigarette. Carpette exhales languidly; he doesn't gulp down the smoke like most convicts. The sun nudges the horizon now; it's sinking into the forest. It'll be dark very soon. Here, night falls like a stone.

As they walk back to the barracks, Sabir can see the men queuing for their dinner ration. Theoretically, it's the keeper's job to collect the rations from the kitchen and dole them out – but no doubt Carpette's paid someone else to do it. There's nothing you absolutely have to do in this colony, if you have the money to avoid it.

'Edouard used to work in the botanical gardens,' Carpette now continues as they walk. 'But he has his enemies in Saint-Laurent. That's why he was sent to the camp. That's why they won't transfer him back. And that's why I bribed my way into this job, out here. It cost me all my savings. Back in Saint-Laurent, I used to run the postal service. It was a damn good job. We were *happy* in Saint-Laurent!' He spits out the word *happy* with a bizarre violence. 'So now we'll escape. We'll need a boat and sail; that's not a problem. I don't know why, but Edouard trusts you. If you want in, though, you'll need two hundred francs up front. A hundred for the boat, fifty for the sails, fifty for the food and water. Then another few hundred for when we get to Colombia, if you want to make a go of it. The problem is finding someone to sail the boat. If there's anyone in your barracks who's likely, sound him out. Tell him his expenses'll be covered.'

Night again. The knife in his hand makes him feel no safer. It just emphasises the fact that in here everyone has knives. They're locked in behind heavy iron doors, the guards are nowhere near, and there's no way out in case of trouble. Certainly, everyone's extremely wary tonight and practically nobody's asleep. Antillais is stretched out on the bed board, hands behind his head. He's spent the past half-hour at work on a toy boat he's building, using the wood from his cat's manger. Masque is in the corner near the privy, arguing with another *fort-à-bras*. He looks drawn, tired. The atmosphere is weirdly calm. Sabir forces his mind onto other things.

He thinks back to his conversation with Carpette. Something new has happened. For the first time since he's been here, escape is not just an abstract project, but a real, concrete prospect. Visions of a different world come to mind. Dark-haired men with large moustaches and sombreros. Is that Colombia? Or maybe it's Mexico he's thinking of. Sabir knows nothing of any of these countries, except that they all speak

Spanish there – a language of which he has no knowledge. He knows nothing of boats either. And yet Carpette's proposing an epic ocean voyage of, what, hundreds of kilometres? Or thousands? In a way, it's all the same. His dreams are a blank canvas that he can colour with whatever images he chooses.

What of Carpette and Edouard? He didn't see it at first, but Sabir now recognises Carpette as one of two 'types' who generally manage the best here. The first are the *forts-à-bras*, who use brute force, intimidation and protection rackets to get what they want. And then there are the hustler types like Carpette, the small-time capitalists who keep a low profile but build up networks of accomplices to create mini-trading empires. The *forts-à-bras* are to be avoided, but it's useful to know the hustlers.

Carpette is also a somewhat effeminate man. In a mainland prison, he'd have to hide it, or get regularly beaten up. Not here. The hyper-virility of the *bagne* craves its opposite. It's the men in the middle – men like Sabir – who are the invisible ones, who play no part in the sexual economy. Without even really thinking about it, Sabir assumes that Carpette and Edouard are lovers. It's the only form of solidarity that exists out here, after all. Otherwise, you're utterly on your own. There's no such thing as friendship or camaraderie, as there was at the front.

Sabir tries to remember what Edouard was like in those days, when they shared a trench section and much else besides. It's not easy. In a relationship like theirs, the other person is the mirror you gaze into, and his real nature remains obscure. Edouard now strikes Sabir as something of a mysterious character, although he didn't feel that at the time. Taciturn, given to acid remarks and black humour. There was that day he let slip that he was a widower: 'She was thrown from a horse and died the next day. We were married just long enough for us to realise we couldn't stand each other!' No, he certainly wasn't like other enlisted men. For a start, he wasn't even working class. He was educated, he read educated books. He had a business, he'd been an importer of exotic plants. Why did he join the infantry, when he was clearly officer class? He had the reputation of being a brave soldier, in any case. Scrambling up the dirt walls to take potshots at the German wire-cutters with his old hunting rifle, in full view of the enemy lines. Reckless, death-wish behaviour. Sabir also recalls that Edouard used to be a keen sketcher. He always carried a little sketchbook with him. Sabir once flicked through one of them and found it full of desolate landscapes. A single tree stump in a field, a dark farmhouse against the sky...

Darkness smothers the barracks. Over by the night-light, a card game is getting under way. The game they play here is called the *marseillaise*, a version of baccarat. Often it goes on until dawn. Not that Sabir has ever joined in. It's too easy to get addicted to gambling, and once that happens, it's the end. You'll never get out. You'll start winning, maybe huge amounts; you'll find yourself living for the game, thinking about it incessantly all day and playing it all night. Then, after a while, you'll start losing. When you've exhausted your funds, you'll borrow money you can't hope to pay back. Soon you'll owe half the barracks. You'll become an outcast, no one will play with you. You start receiving threats. Your nerves are gone, you're pulling your knife at the slightest provocation. You're in a hopeless spiral that can only end one way.

Masque is the banker. He rattles the money box and a few convicts get off the bed board to join in. It's the banker's job to deal the cards, manage the game, settle any disputes. He gets a ten per cent cut of all the winnings, so it's a lucrative position. You've got to be ruthless to do it, though, ready to defend yourself and draw your knife the moment there's any trouble. Consequently, it's always the toughest *fort-à-bras* who takes the job. Masque has been banker for the past month, but lately he's let his second take over the role almost every night. Maybe he thinks it makes him too vulnerable to an attack from Antillais. If so, he seems to have changed his mind tonight. The tension in the barracks visibly eases: if Masque doesn't think he's going to be attacked, he must have good reason.

Sabir watches the game from his corner. Behind the players, several people wait in attendance. There's the man who earns a few *sous* spreading the blanket they play on. Another convict puts the cigarettes in front of each player; yet another pours the coffee: an entire mini-economy revolves around the game. Masque says nothing as he deals. His tattoos are a carnival joke. He's bald on top but has tattooed in his hair. Around his eyes, tattooed glasses. On one cheek, an ace of spades; on the other, an ace of clubs. On his upper lip, a purple moustache. In civil society, he'd be a freak. But men like Masque rarely try to escape; the *bagne* is their life and it's impossible for them to live outside it.

One by one, the makeshift lamps go out. But the game goes on. One of the players, Sabir notices, is the Basque boy Say-Say, the one who'd come up from Saint-Laurent with the story of Bonifacio's escape. He looks about seventeen, has freckles, big jug-handle ears and bad teeth. Too ugly to appeal to the *forts-à-bras*, but they've found another way to misuse him anyway. He had a full *plan* on arrival in the camp, and was too young and inexperienced to shut up about it. So the *forts-à-bras* coerced him into the card game and are in the process of picking him clean. Once they've done that, there'll no longer be any future for him in this camp. Being from the Basque country, though, Say-Say probably knows his way around a sailing boat. As he watches the boy lose again, Sabir recalls the lad who'd bunked beside him on the journey out. Gaspard, with the country accent you could hardly understand. What happened to him, he wonders. Is he still alive? He remembers the promise he made to the boy to look out for him and feels a stab of shame. Perhaps he can redeem himself by transferring the promise to this other hopeless case.

Hard rain starts to pound the roof. That means it's about midnight. Before coming here, Sabir would never have believed how clockwork the weather could be. Life's uncertainties have become certain, and vice versa. He listens to the dead sound of cards being shuffled, fingered, slapped down onto the blanket. There's an occasional muttered curse. Everyone not involved in the game is lying down now, except a toothless old convict who's darning a pair of trousers. Out of the corner of his eye, Sabir notices Antillais silently rising from the bed board. He moves like a ghost towards the card game. Masque has his back to him. A flash of something in Antillais's hand. Sabir can feel a hundred eyes flaming up in the night. But Antillais sails straight past the card game. Nothing happens. Masque doesn't even turn round. And Antillais continues down the short corridor, into the privy.

For a minute, Masque continues with the card game. Then suddenly he tosses the pack to his assistant and leaps noise-lessly to his feet, like a cat. Again, a flash of something in the reflection of the night-light. The assistant starts dealing. In a second, Masque has disappeared down the corridor to the privy.

Now another man jumps up. Impossible to see who it is; he's too quick. He's been lying on the bed board right by the privy. The corridor swallows up his shadow as well. Nobody moves. The players freeze mid-game. In the vacuum, the sound of an uneven drip fills the air like a tolling bell. Suddenly, a scuffling. The noise of a garment being ripped, a muffled grunt. Then a pig's squeal of a scream that splits open the night. It's followed by a gurgling, guttural noise, like someone trying to clear his throat. Then nothing. The barracks is engulfed in a chaotic silence.

A tiny, eternal moment of stillness before everyone snaps into action, in a storm of energy. The remaining little lamps are snuffed out. Players grab their money from the floor and race to the bed board. Men scramble to hide their knives. The *marseillaise* blanket and money box disappear and once again silence invades the barracks. Outside, the rain thunders on. And from the privy, groans, growing ever fainter.

A man walks back out through the corridor. It's Pierrot. The convict whose winnings Masque had brazenly made off with a few weeks back. He strolls over to the water barrel, starts washing his hands. He takes off his shirt, plunges it into the water barrel as well, wrings it out and casually tosses it over a piece of string to dry. Then he lies back down on the bed board by the privy. Another man walks out of the privy. Antillais. He's muttering to himself. He too finds his spot on the bed board and lies down. Even he stops mumbling now, as an expectant hush shrouds the barracks.

Minutes later, the bars of the door are rattled. 'On your feet, all of you! Up! Up!' The captain-at-arms is surrounded by guards, their revolvers unholstered. They pour into the barracks, dashing about like nervous dogs. Turnkeys with lamps follow them in; no doubt it's the night-duty turnkey who signalled the alarm. The convicts get up from the bed board clumsily, as if drowsy from sleep. A couple of the guards go straight to the privy: it's where the premeditated murders almost always take place. A minute later, they're out again, dragging the body between them, trying hard not to get any blood on their uniforms. Masque is obviously dead, although no one's actually bothering to formally verify it. He's already nothing, an ugly lump of meat. Soon it'll be as if he never lived at all. Or he'll be incarnated in one of those amusing stories convicts like to tell. The man who was killed for cooking a cat.

'Everyone out! Everyone out!'

As the convicts file out of the door, the captain-at-arms examines their hands and clothes for signs of blood. Pierrot passes through, so does Antillais. No doubt the turnkeys know all about Masque, Antillais and the cat. The convicts march out into a sheet of tropical rain.

Now the guards do a quick inspection of the barracks. They find half a dozen knives and a few other illicit items. But most of the men have hidden their knives well enough to pass such a cursory search. The rain stops from one moment to the next – here, everything happens abruptly, even the weather: the *longueurs* may be disorientating, but they're always punctuated by sudden dramas. The men are marched back into the barracks, dripping wet. A smeary crimson trail leads from the privy to where Masque's body is now laid out.

'Stand to attention!' shouts the captain-at-arms. He's pacing about the barracks, taking a good look at each man. 'Well, then. Who did it? Who's the guilty man?' Silence from the convicts as he walks by, inspecting each one. They're all staring into the middle distance. Two minutes pass. 'So no one saw anything, is that it? No one killed him. He stabbed himself in the back. Is that it?' Still no one says anything. The captain paces the length of the barracks once more, then suddenly yawns, as if he finds the whole affair not only distasteful but boring as well. 'We'll see about all this in the morning. You two, get this thing out of here. Go and get a stretcher.'

One of the men designated for stretcher duty is Pierrot. He plays it coolly, not hesitating for a second. Once they come back from the guardhouse with the stretcher, they lift the lifeless body onto it with some difficulty: Masque was a big man. Sabir notices how Pierrot manages to get a fair amount of blood on his trousers. Clever. It makes for a pretty good excuse, should his shirt still have any of Masque's blood on it the next day.

VI

The commandant sits across from Sabir, behind his heavy brazil-wood desk. It's littered with a confusion of reports, journals, papers covered in a tiny spider scrawl, piles of books. He picks one up, theatrically lets it drop back onto the desk. 'If I'd known the climate was as bad as this, I'd never have brought all these books with me. Within a year, they'll be eaten away by mould. Within three, there'll be nothing left at all.'

Sabir remains silent. He stares through the glassless window to the punishment cells opposite. Outside one of them, a prisoner and guard sit handcuffed together. The guard is smoking a cigarette. Every time he lifts the cigarette to his mouth, the prisoner has to lift his hand as well. Why doesn't the guard change hands?

'Anyway, I've had news from Saint-Laurent. My shipment of orchids has arrived there from Florida. There's a Dutch ship due up from the bauxite mines. The captain will pick up my shipment and deliver it here on the way up to the coast. I imagine it'll arrive in a couple of days. You're to stop work on the hedging and start preparing the orchid nursery.'

'Yes, sir.'

'The captain-at-arms has already interviewed you?'

'Yes, sir.'

'And you've nothing further to add about last night's . . . unpleasantness?' The commandant briefly looks away, as though out of embarrassment.

'No, sir.'

'Very well. You can get started immediately. No need to return to barracks. I'll send your men down to you.'

Sabir collects his lunch rations and walks slowly back down through the jungle to the house and garden by the river, buried in thought. He's ragged from the night's events, the captain-at-arms's morning interrogations, and yet almost as agitated by the interview he's just had with the commandant. He's to build an orchid nursery now? Sabir has vague images in his head of the flamboyant, strikingly coloured flowers he's occasionally seen in the *fleuristes* of Paris. His job as a gardener seems to be moving onto a higher plane. The heavy, brute work is mostly finished with; soon, it'll be difficult to keep up the pretence. For Sabir, the feeling of being an impostor has always been there. Maybe even for years. Only now it's as sharp as ever. And yet what a tragedy if he were moved from his position before this escape that Edouard and Carpette are planning.

When the commandant's up at the camp, Sabir now has free run of the house. This new status has developed imperceptibly, without anyone commenting on it. The guards who spend the day down here are suspicious of him and suspicious of his relationship with the commandant; but they leave him be, since they don't know what the commandant has sanctioned and don't wish to ask him. And when he's here by himself, Sabir can fall into a sort of fantasy. That it's *his* house, his garden, and the guards are under his authority.

He's noticed one change since he was here in the commandant's reception room yesterday. The commandant has chosen a photograph from his photo album upstairs, framed it and placed it on a sideboard. A studio shot of his wife. It reminds Sabir of something. Lately, the visions he has of his fiancée have subtly changed. Her face seems to be replaced with that of a young woman at the beach. She has a curious smile, dark hair and a striped swimming costume.

Sabir scans the commandant's library. There actually is a book about orchids here somewhere; he noticed it before. A crinkly paged volume, entitled *On the Various Contrivances by Which Orchids are Fertilised by Insects*. Sabir pulls it out and turns to the introduction: 'The Orchidaceae is a broad family of perennial plants, characterised by one fertile stamen and a three-petalled flower.' There's a lot more in that vein. But no practical advice on how to care for them. The rest of the book is hopelessly scientific, meaningless. Damn the commandant for not having anything more relevant, less highbrow. Damn his nineteenth-century learning!

What to do for this nursery he's to build? The commandant has said nothing specific about it, save where it's to be located. The only image that comes to mind is that of a greenhouse. Clearly, you don't build greenhouses in tropical climates. At the back of the house, his men are lounging about near where the hedge is to be planted, smoking, doing nothing. He sets them to work on a low walled enclosure by the pond. He has a notion that the flowers will at least need protection from the harsh sun and beating tropical rain, so he envisages thick poles at each corner, and some sort of palm thatch. Rush matting for the inner walls, to let in the air. Beyond that, he has no particular idea. Then again, is the commandant going to know any better than him?

Once he's got the men working, he returns to the house – to think, to sit down, to smoke one of the commandant's cigarettes. He should be looking for things to steal. And yet he feels emptied by the strain of last night. In a way, it's been good having to organise the nursery; it's occupied his mind. Masque's murder now seems unreal. It's the dream that lingers after you wake, then follows you around all day. At the same time, it's impossible to focus on it directly. Instead, Sabir finds himself recalling other deaths. Distant ones. He thinks of his mother. Of his grandmother. Of all sorts of men he knew at the front. Their young faces surprisingly fresh in his mind.

The commandant doesn't arrive at his house until a little before dusk. In the early days of the garden, he'd carry out daily inspections of the work; now, he generally invites Sabir into the house to report on the day's progress. And the first thing he usually does in these meetings is pour himself a rum. Today, for the first time, he offers Sabir a glass as well. This simple act raises their relationship to a different level, if only for the time it takes to drink the rum. There's something fundamentally social about sharing a drink which makes it impossible to maintain roles of jailer and prisoner, punisher and punished. There's something perverse about it as well.

'You've got them started on the nursery?'

'The men are building the outer wall, sir. I'm using the bricks we ordered for the retaining wall by the jetty. We'll need around eight dozen more bricks, though, sir. Shall I place an order with the kiln? Or will we have to go to Saint-Laurent?'

'Whatever you think necessary. Write it down and I'll sign the order tomorrow morning.'

Sabir has the impression that the commandant knows even less than he does about what's needed, and that's a comfort. He can feel the rum moving through his body: a prickling sensation crawling down his arms and legs. He hasn't had any alcohol since that glass of rum at the store on the way out of Saint-Laurent. It's easy enough to get here, and there are plenty of convicts who drink. But they all end up alcoholics. They're old at thirty. They rack up huge debts. And they never, ever leave.

'It's for my wife, you see,' says the commandant. 'She loves orchids. When she was a child, I used to take her out on mountain rambles sometimes. There was one Alpine orchid flower we used to find all over the place ... with its two yellow petals ...' The commandant quickly downs his rum and pours himself another. For a minute or two he's silent, seemingly lost in memories. He snaps out of his reverie. 'And that's why I ordered the shipment. Something of an extravagance, of course.'

Outside, it's growing dim. The commandant tends to get carried away with his conversation, and often at these meetings Sabir has to remind him that he needs to go, if he's to make the barracks for dinner and lock-up. Today, he pretends to forget. It's partly the rum. But mostly it's the murder. Masque's blue body and his blue face. Would there be reprisals against Pierrot and Antillais tonight? When Sabir left the barracks this morning to be interrogated, the two seemed supremely calm. Antillais was still building his little boat, Pierrot was cleaning his nails with his knife – the same one that had killed a man. Perhaps they're safe. Perhaps Masque had too many enemies and his empire has crumbled at first touch. All Sabir knows is that he can't spend another night in the barracks. Not with his knife clenched to his side, in a delirious haze of insomnia.

The commandant is pouring the rum again. 'She's been ill, you see. Not physically ill. A nervous complaint. She's spent some time in Switzerland. Now she's much better. I took this wretched job for her, do you see? She said she wanted to be as far away from Europe as possible. One of the African colonies, or Indochina. But when this post came up, she told me to take it. She couldn't wait any longer. She said she wouldn't marry me unless I took an overseas post. So I took it. Now I want everything to be just right for her arrival. I want her to regret nothing.'

It's not clear whether the commandant is talking to Sabir or himself. The man's hands are shaking. Maybe from drinking, but Sabir thinks not. He gets the impression that the commandant is like a ravenous animal, physically hungry perhaps, emotionally starving certainly. This unceasing tide of words and plans – Sabir is a mere shadow to him, an object in a room, solid to touch but nothing more than a receptacle for this outpouring.

Across the trees, a bell tolls, and echoes back across the river to ghostly effect.

'The evening bell. You've missed lock-up.'

'Yes, sir. I wasn't thinking of the time. I'm sorry, sir.'

'No. It's my fault. I've been talking too much.'

'They'll probably send a guard down, once they do the headcount.'

'Yes. They probably will.' The commandant strokes his chin. 'But they won't open up the barracks for you. You'll have to sleep out tonight. If a guard comes down, I'll tell him what's happened. I'll make sure there's no trouble for you.'

'Thank you, sir.'

'In the meantime . . .'

Sabir can see what's going through the commandant's mind. His natural instinct is to offer Sabir a bed for the night, but that would hardly be appropriate, given their different circumstances. He could let Sabir sleep on the floor downstairs, but even that would be regarded as peculiar, should a guard come down.

'Sir, if I might take a lamp, could I suggest that you allow me to sleep in the folly? We put the palm thatch on two days ago, so that way I could at least get some protection from the rain.'

The commandant looks relieved. 'Why, yes, I think that would be a good solution.'

A few hundred metres from the house, at the back of the garden, there's a narrow path that leads to a perfectly circular clearing, in the centre of which is the folly. It, too, is circular, with a diameter that's just big enough for a man to lie down, fully stretched out. The floor decking is no more or less comfortable than the bed board in the barracks. But what a relief to be able to lie down on your own, with only your thoughts and dreams to accompany you. It's as if the world has expanded and breathes again.

The commandant has given Sabir a blanket. They waited in the house for a guard to come, but none did. In the meantime, the two dined on cold meat. For all the guards know back at the camp, Sabir could have murdered the commandant – and yet no one has bothered to come down to investigate. Tomorrow, he'll ask permission to move out of the barracks and stay down here, in the folly. He knows the commandant will agree. Nonetheless, anger wells up in Sabir. The commandant, letting Sabir in on his plans and secrets like that – as if they're the centre of this world, and Sabir's own life and aspirations are of no consequence. He sits up, takes the photograph of the commandant's wife from his pocket, holds it to the lamp and stares at it for a long time. Outside the folly, everything is obscure, lugubrious. A world of solid night. There's nothing else here except Sabir, the lamp and the photograph.

Staring at the photograph, Sabir thinks back to what the commandant said about his wife: the 'nervous complaint' she suffers from; the recuperation in Switzerland; the desire to be 'as far away from Europe as possible'. To Sabir, it sounds like the bare bones of some impossibly mysterious story. Perhaps she's still pining for a lost lover killed in the war. Or she's committed a *crime passionnel* and has had to leave the country. Or she's succumbed to some dark thread of family madness that runs back through generations.

There is nothing tragic or dramatic about Sabir's fiancée. No story to tell. She's the hard-nosed type. No doubt she's already found herself another man. There was just one occasion, Sabir now remembers. One moment of true drama in his relationship with her. Sabir had been flirting – innocently enough – with a girl at a friend's wedding. His fiancée was furious with him over it. She went off to stay with her mother, and her parting words were: 'If I ever find out you've slept with another woman, I'll kill you.' She said it in such a matter-of-fact voice that he knew she meant it quite literally. That night, he spent his wages at a local brothel. It was the first time he'd visited one since the war.

The commandant's wife now stands before him. She's slipped out of her dress. Her underwear resembles the swimming costume she wears in the photo. From the house, Sabir can hear the gramophone playing its German songs, resonating through the forest. Sabir's vision is more intense than anything he's seen in the jungle camp. Out here, it can be days or even weeks before you catch sight of a woman: the feminine is a country of the imagination. 'I knew you'd find me,' she whispers to him. She smiles, puts her arms around him. This is their secret hideaway. This is where they retreat to when she can get away from the commandant. She's the bored wife of a chilly colonial administrator, cast into a tropical wilderness. She's hungry for connection, for company, emotion, sex. And he's the skilful gardener, tending her beloved grove of orchids. Together they talk, exchange histories. Sabir's banal existence suddenly seems heroic. As a soldier, he fought for his country. As a convict, his country repaid him with exile.

He lights a cigarette from the lamp, puts the photo back into his pocket. The gramophone music has stopped. It's given way to an aria of frog croaks, insect clicks, monkey howls and other random noises of the night. Sabir stretches out, finishes his cigarette and closes his eyes. Moments later, the dawn light streams in through the shutter lattices. It's the first proper night's sleep he's had in weeks.

VII

Edouard has health problems. He doesn't see as well with his good eye as he used to. It's this terrible sun he's exposed to, out chopping wood every day. All in all, says Carpette as he and Sabir meet one afternoon, it's best they get out as soon as possible, while Edouard's still healthy enough to undertake the journey. Carpette's arranging the purchase of a boat from one of the Boni ferrymen. He needs the money for it very soon. Does Sabir have his share of the money? They want to leave within two weeks. They still need someone to sail the boat. Has Sabir talked to that Basque boy he mentioned the other day? Is Sabir in, or is he out? I'm in, he replies, with sudden desperation. I'm in.

That day, Sabir has hauled up a whole case of rum for Carpette to dispose of. He's sure the commandant has no idea how much he drinks, wouldn't necessarily miss the case, wouldn't investigate if he did. And yet the commandant must have realised by now that all sorts of things have gone missing from the house. He could hardly be that stupid or absent-minded. If so, then he must also realise that Sabir is the culprit. Because no one else has the kind of access to the house that he has. And the fact that the commandant's done nothing about it has merely emboldened Sabir even further.

Now that he's moved to the folly, Sabir's meetings with the commandant sometimes extend into the night. Sabir accepts the commandant's rum and wine as well, but is careful to remain sober. The commandant, on the other hand, drinks too much. And when he does, his talk grows ever more grandiose.

'The trouble is administrators don't stay here long enough,' he says one night. 'They see this as a cursed post to escape from as fast as possible, with as much loot as possible. Well, I'm different. I plan on staying. And damn the rest of the Colony. I have my own little kingdom here. I'll organise it as I see fit. I'll continue building on the avenue. I'll get the convicts out of the barracks. I'll give them concessions. I'll let them farm the land, earn an honest living, open up the Colony. Forge a new country. The English managed it in Australia, why can't we do it here? I'll build a settlement to rival Saint-Laurent. A new city. Built on republican virtues, of justice and equality before the law.'

Justice? Equality? Back now in the darkness of his folly, Sabir muses briefly on the commandant's words before sleep overcomes him. Sabir, for one, has never expected or asked for life to be just or equal. These ideas are a luxury that only certain people can afford. People like the commandant. For Sabir and those like him, life is a perpetual struggle, one which leaves little room for such abstraction. And when not engaged in this struggle for survival, Sabir would be consumed with the usual desires, for companionship, intoxication, sex; his free moments would be spent assuaging these desires as best he could. That's how things had been, until his arrest at least.

In his time, he's come across those agitators for change – the communists, fascists, anarchists. The pamphleteers. On the factory floor, in the bars he'd drink at. He's never paid them much heed. The only long stretches of time he ever had for proper thinking was at the front. Even then, the goal of thinking was to achieve the peace of not having to think any more. And the commandant's books are almost the first he's read since that time.

Sabir's mind now wanders back hypnotically to the years of freedom, between demob and the prison gates. In those days, Paris felt dark and oppressive. The city's monolithic buildings, immense avenues, gold domes and sumptuous façades could lock you into a state of powerless awe. Not that it struck him like that at the time. It's only once you've lost something that you can make sense of it. But no, he now realises, he has no great nostalgia for his native city. No desire to find himself back there, even if it were possible. Now is the moment to escape into a different dream.

The commandant's shipment of orchids is due. Standing on the riverbank the following day, Sabir glimpses funnels poking out over the trees as the ship twists its way through the forest. While he waits, fretting over what to do with the orchids when they arrive, one of the Boni ferrymen sidles up to him, taking him by surprise. 'Friend of Carpette? Friend of Carpette?' Sabir glances about: a couple of guards are lounging by the river drinking, but they're some distance away.

With a mixture of gesticulation, broken Dutch and French, the ferryman makes Sabir understand that he's the one who's selling the boat to Carpette, Edouard and himself. That they'll have it late next week. That he'll sink it and secure it with stones in one of the creeks downstream, but he won't tell them which one and where until he gets the money, all of it. Throughout, he punctuates his disjointed speech with a staccato laugh.

Sabir nods. 'I understand.'

At that, the man wanders off to his canoe. Sabir notices the ritual scarring he has on his back – horizontal and vertical lines which look almost like a Christian cross. He climbs into his canoe and paddles his way across the river to the Dutch side – shrinking until he's nothing but a black spot against the brutal green of the trees on the far bank. Finally he melts into the backdrop.

The escape. That's what's important. That morning, Sabir went up to the main camp at dawn – ostensibly to commandeer some convicts to help with the orchid shipment, but actually to see Say-Say, the young Basque from his old barracks. His real name is unpronounceable, and his nickname comes from the terrible stutter he gets when nervous. The Colony is a hive of speech difficulties: Say-Say is hardly the only stutterer, and there are also plenty of lispers, mutes, those with all manner of speech tics. Not to mention the convicts who talk to themselves. Sabir has even caught himself at it, on occasion.

Say-Say wasn't in the barracks; Sabir tracked him down to the camp's hospital – a grand word for the row of dirty mattresses in a converted barracks, looked after by a convict orderly. He seemed in a bad state. His jug ears bright red, his eyes shining with a fever that shook his body.

'Here, roll me a smoke, will you? I can't do it.'

It was true; his hands were trembling too much. Was there any chance he'd be well enough by the time of the escape? Then again, the thing about fevers is that you never know how they'll play out. A bad one can carry a man off within hours. But some pass in a day or two, with no real consequences.

As he rolled Say-Say a cigarette, Sabir went through the escape plan he and Carpette had worked out, dropping to a low whisper when he thought one of the other convicts was taking too close an interest. Here in the Colony, Sabir has by now realised, it's not the guards who are your main enemy, it's the other convicts. He kept talking as they smoked together – explaining about the boat, the sail, the provisions, the paddle down the river before dawn, the ocean crossing to Trinidad, then along the coast to Colombia. The plan had been formed in bits and pieces over several meetings and, spoken out loud like that in its entirety, it sounded too fantastic. As if Sabir were recounting one of those escape yarns you'd hear from someone who'd heard it from someone else. Like so many of the tales that do the rounds here, you can't quite bring yourself to believe it.

'We're not going to hang about until you're better, though. Either you're well enough by next week, or we'll have to find someone else.'

Say-Say leant towards him, gripped Sabir's arm. 'Listen, I'm not as bad as I look. I've been smoking quinine.'

Quinine: one of the tricks for shamming sickness. You add it to your tobacco and it puts your temperature up, makes you look as if you've got a fever.

'Why?'

'Had to get out of barracks. I owe Pierrot. Not that much! But he started threatening me. Now he's sent word here. I've got to get out of camp, too. It's that or...'

Sabir looked around the hall. Men lying flat, their bodies glistening, staring up into nothing. Only one of them was sitting up: a man counting endlessly on his fingers: '27, 28, 29 – 27, 28, 29 – 27, 28, 29...' A few mattresses down from him, Sabir noticed Antillais, Masque's co-murderer. He, too, was shivering away a fever. With him was a kitten, attached to his wrist with a length of twine. So he'd wasted no time in getting another pet. The kitten jumped onto his chest, mistaking his shaking as a desire to play.

Say-Say grabbed at him again. 'Did I ever tell you what I got done for?'

'No.'

'Smuggling. We used to run a fishing boat from Bayonne to San Sebastian.'

'Really. What did you smuggle?'

'Oh, all sorts of things. People. And arms. To the fighters.'

'What fighters?'

Another shaking fit took hold of Say-Say. He was trying to convince Sabir he knew about boats – except that the story was so fanciful as to be unbelievable. Sabir wasn't even sure that Say-Say was shamming his fever: if he already had gambling debts, then where would he get the money to buy the quinine? He was one of those nervy convicts who was always making up stories to impress the others. Nonetheless, Sabir remembered the promise he'd made to the country boy Gaspard, that he'd now silently transferred to Say-Say. He'd been swindled out of his money by the *forts-à-bras*; it wasn't his fault. He couldn't survive here. He'd have to get transferred, or escape. And Sabir would help him escape. In some way, it was liberating to help someone else. It was even liberating to feel pity for someone other than himself.

'I'll be back up on Monday. If you're clear of fever, then it's on. Otherwise . . . '

'I'll be all right. Don't worry. I can't go back to barracks, though. Either they let me stay on here, or I'll have to hide out in the forest.'

'If it comes to that, make your way down to the river. There's a trail that runs thirty metres to the right of the main path. Use that. As you approach the house, you'll see the garden to your right. Track round to the other side of it. You'll find a path that leads to a small circular building. Go inside, stay put. I'll come by in the evening. I'll bring food.'

The Boni ferrymen are unloading crates onto the riverbank. Sabir thought there'd be pots, not crates, and he has no clear idea of what to expect inside them. In the book on orchids he's borrowed from the commandant's library, there are careful line drawings of intricate, bizarre flowers, of a sort he's never seen before. One of them has wavy, drooped petals like hair extending all the way down the stem; another is like a cat with its jaws open; another like a dragon; yet another like a wizened head. Some are repulsive, some lushly sensual, some crudely sexual. Most look like anything but flowers. In fact they are curiously animal-like, and what they remind Sabir of are the thin, fantastical creatures in a picture book his mother gave him as a child. Although the creatures were supposed to be comical, Sabir was frightened of them; in his dreams, they'd emerge from under his bed like grotesque insects. When he finally confided his fear to his mother, she laughed at him. 'Don't worry,' she said, 'there's nothing to be afraid of. There's nothing living under your bed.'

Foliage peeks out through the slats of the crates. Once they've been transported to the nursery, Sabir prises off a lid. What he finds inside is a chaotic jumble of bulbous, gnarled roots, stems, browning leaves, earth . . . but no flowers. It looks like a box of weeds removed from a flower bed. The plants are all sodden, as well – no doubt the crates were doused with water on board. Perplexed, Sabir stands there staring. What would Edouard do under these circumstances? He's the real gardener, the real expert. Not for the first time, Sabir feels guilty that it's he who's in this relatively exalted position, who's lied his way to privilege, while his old comrade Edouard's out there some-where chopping wood.

One of the convicts on his team says: 'Well, what's all this muck, then?'

Another remarks: 'Whatever they were, they're all dead now.'

Not quite. Here and there a plant seems to be alive – and then on closer inspection, maybe a good quarter of them are.

'You're right,' answers Sabir, after a minute's sun-struck silence. 'Looks like they're good for nothing.' They remove the lids from the rest of crates. It occurs to Sabir to put two of the deadest-looking crates aside, to show the commandant when he comes down. 'We'll get rid of the rest of them, though. You can dump the lot in the jungle, behind the folly.'

Once his men have gone with the crates, Sabir turns back to the house. Halfway across the garden he has second thoughts. It's a relief that most of the plants are dead. It's even more convenient to say that they all are. The commandant won't be down from the main camp for another hour. Sabir goes back to the two crates the convicts have left behind and carefully sifts through them, pulling out any plants that look as if they're still alive and tossing them into the river.

Working under the noon sun can produce a kind of delirium. Afterwards, Sabir sits down under a tree with his back to the river, at the point at which the garden reaches the water. Sometimes there's a breeze here, but not today. This wet heat that permeates everything, that even has its own colour, its own smell. Men in the distance seem hazy, uncertain against the background, like wraiths on the shoreline.

Sabir can hear a low buzz, which at first he takes to be an insect. Then, out of the corner of his eye, he spots something high up in the sky, glistening in the brilliant light. It's vividly red, like a tiny drop of blood against the blue infinity. A biplane, following the river into the interior. But there's no airfield at Saint-Laurent. Beyond Saint-Laurent there's another camp and then nothing – just Boni and Indian villages carved out of the forest, plus various mining camps. Certainly nowhere to land a plane. Sabir watches the red splotch as it continues deeper and deeper into the jungle until it disappears altogether.

Now he's thinking about the orchids again. With or without them, he realises, the garden is nonetheless taking shape. Gazing out at the shimmering expanse of newly laid lawn, Sabir is seized with a certain proprietorial pleasure. The layout is the same as the one in the photo of the house and garden he'd seen upstairs, in the wife's bedroom. Ever since that evening when the commandant mentioned his wife, Sabir has been eager to learn more about her. One thing that he's found out is that her name is Renée. Whether the commandant has named Camp Renée after her or it's simply a coincidence, he doesn't know. If the former, then it's a strange sort of homage to pay, to say the least. Although on several occasions it's seemed as if the commandant's on the verge of talking about her again, only once has he actually done so. It was an evening of strangulated monkey howls – no doubt some sort of mating ritual. The commandant had had several rums. 'You know,' he said, 'she was never like any other women. To me, the others are dead. Quite dead! Only *she* is truly alive.'

Now Sabir's back in the house. The commandant will return soon, but there's time enough to look out for any titbits to steal. The office is its usual mess of books, blueprints, papers, empty glasses, full ashtrays. In the corner, under the drinks cabinet, there's a cupboard. It's always locked. In fact, it's the only thing in the house that always is. Sabir has contemplated forcing the lock before, but has so far drawn back from doing so. If the commandant discovered it had been tampered with, he'd have to know it was Sabir. And then what would happen? He might lose all his privileges. And get sent to another camp, where he'd end up chopping trees in the sun, like Edouard. Yet there's another, more obscure reason for not doing it. To Sabir, locking the cupboard seems to be a message to him from the commandant: take what you want here, anything, except what's in this cupboard. Spare this and the rest is yours.

It's the first time he's seen the key in the cupboard. Sabir pauses, pricked with a sense of guilt that's gone within the second. Through the window he can see the commandant emerging from the forest, ant-like against the immensity of the trees. He'll be here in five or six minutes. Sabir turns the key and yanks the cupboard door open. Inside, a few neat piles of papers and letters. He pulls a few out of their envelopes, expecting them to be from the commandant's wife. Disappointment: they're not. Some are to do with business affairs, others appear to be from a family member. One envelope has a Swiss stamp. The typed letter inside is on headed paper: Dr Martineau, Eves-les-Bains, near Geneva. *Monsieur*, I am replying to your letter of 22nd January, 1927, concerning your wife. Sabir pushes the letter back into its envelope and shoves it into his pocket. Beside the piles of letters and papers, a small metal box; inside, a tidy wad of fifty-franc notes. Sabir takes a few of them – best not be too greedy – then shuts the box, locks the cupboard door and slips out of the study.

Minutes later, Sabir watches as the commandant's face colours with surprise and frustration. 'What, none of them survived? Not a single one?'

'No, sir.'

'Well, I'll be . . . damned!' The commandant's on the verge of some explosive rage. He starts to pace about impotently, his struggle to keep calm filling the room. 'Of course, they did tell me most of them wouldn't survive. I'll give them that. But then they promised a good quarter would be all right.'

'I'm sorry, sir. I've left two crates out for you to inspect.'

An unpleasant feeling invades Sabir as they walk out under a terrible sun to where the orchid nursery was to be. It takes him a moment to identify this feeling as remorse; it's gone almost as soon as it had come. The commandant bends down to inspect the crates and sift through the steaming, sodden plants. Most of them are just a sludgy mess now: decomposition sets in so quickly here. One he holds up to the sun, like a farmer inspecting a stillborn animal. This climate – which doesn't so much nurture the living, as liquefy it . . . The commandant sighs, his anger now changed to resignation. 'I suppose that's it, then. No point in keeping this stuff.'

The fate of the orchids hangs over the rest of the day. Sabir spends the afternoon digging holes for a boundary fence. The commandant has been most particular about this fence, but whether it's to keep the jungle out or the garden in, Sabir has no idea. Not long before the end of the workday, the commandant wanders over. He seems muted, deflated. At first he says nothing, looking on as Sabir self-consciously goes about his work.

'Such a pity about the orchids,' he murmurs finally. 'I so much wanted my wife to have them, when she arrived.'

Sabir doesn't know what to say but momentarily stops what he's doing, and the commandant places his hand on Sabir's shoulder as if in commiseration with a son – or even a lover.

'When will she be arriving, sir?'

'She's taken a berth on the *Queen Wilhelmina*. The boat's due in at Saint-Laurent early on Thursday morning.'

'You must be looking forward to it, sir.'

'Indeed I am.'

Thursday. And the proposed date for the escape is Friday. She might well stay in Saint-Laurent a day or two. Or she might come straight here. In which case, Sabir may just get to see her before the escape. He imagines her on a boat down the river, sitting upright in the canoe like a haughty princess, to be ferried ashore by the Bonis like so much cargo ... The trouble is that when he thinks of the commandant's wife, she is so very real. And yet when he dreams of escape, it feels like fantasy.

This is the first time in his life that he's felt a small measure of fulfilment. Since leaving the barracks, things have been very different. He's decently fed now, and he has work to do that doesn't grind him down, not in the way factory work did. He's a gardener. He's developing a skill. The garden offers possibilities. A sort of liberty, even. Because life before his arrest – when he never had the luxury to think past the next meal, the next few francs – was anything but free.

'What about you?' the commandant says. 'Did you have a girl back home? Do you have a girl here?'

A girl here? He wonders how the camp commandant could understand so little of convict life.

'No girl here, sir. A girl back home, though. My fiancée.'

'Really? What's her name?'

'Renée.'

It isn't; the name just came out like that. He'd been hoping for the commandant to say how strange, that's my wife's name, too. But he doesn't. He doesn't even pick up on the coincidence.

'She's waiting for me, sir,' Sabir continues. 'She's what makes it all bearable. She writes to me every week. When I get a stable position here, when I get a land concession, I'm going to send for her.'

'I see, I see. Very good.'

It's the first time the commandant has ever asked him

anything personal, but already he's lost interest. The questions were nothing more than an expression of boredom, politeness, or simply a desire to bridge the silence. Sabir intuits that although the commandant's attitude towards the convicts is different from other functionaries, the men are no more real to him.

The sun is low in the sky now. It'll be dark in half an hour. Together they walk back to the house. Sabir's long shadow paints the door, and as he moves towards it, it's as if he's falling into his own negative.

Later that night, in the folly, Sabir pulls the stolen money from his pocket and counts it: three hundred francs. Enough for the escape and plenty more besides. Now he has this money, he feels changed. In the holding prison, on the boat, in Saint-Laurent, in the camp barracks, during all this time, everything in his mind has been organised around the idea of escape. Now that it's possible, even probable that it'll happen, the idea is starting to lose some of its mystic power. He's wondering whether he shouldn't sit it out here for a while. After all, he could hardly have hoped for things to have turned out as well as they have. He's avoided hard labour, avoided barracks life, he has an occupation he likes, he has money, and it seems he has a protector in the shape of the commandant. What's more, he knows that, in an emergency, he'll always be able to force the cupboard door and make off with the rest of the money. And then there's the commandant's wife.

He tries to decipher the letter from the Swiss doctor that he's stolen, only half-understanding: '... symptoms reflecting an excessively morbid disposition ... they are, to my mind, of a largely psychosomatic nature, provoked by profound guilt at the death of her cousin ... this morbidity manifests itself, at the deepest level, in a transference of fortunes ... when she speaks of her own body as "dead meat", she is merely expressing a desire for the converse to be true of her cousin's body ... it is this hysterical notion of sacrifice that must be confronted in the most vigorous manner possible.' The letter is studded with psychiatric jargon unknown to Sabir, throwing the meaning of whole sentences into doubt. Even so, even if he understood all the terms, it's clear that what he has here is not the story itself, but a commentary on the story.

Under one of the floorboards, Sabir has hidden a glass jar where he keeps his 'treasure'. Although the jar is sealed against humidity, the photos inside are already fraying at the edges. He gets them out, spreads them by the lamp, stares at them. That picture of her at the beach. Several others he's stolen since. Her, with a man in uniform, not the commandant. Her, sitting thoughtfully, reading a book. The book cover is visible, but the photo isn't clear enough to read the title.

My cousin was a military man, she now tells Sabir. A captain of the tenth regiment. We were in love. Marriage, for the moment, was impossible, he had no money. I urged him not to worry about that, but, no, wait until after the war, that was what he kept telling me. I have an army friend who'll put up the money for a business, he'd say. After family dinners, we'd sneak off, we'd meet up in a folly at the bottom of the garden ... a folly just like this one. And we'd lose ourselves, among the orchids. On the last night, the night before he had to go up to the front, we embraced. I was ready – but no, he said again, I respect you too much for that; we'll wait until after the war. I was angry at his refusal. Naked for the first time in front of a man, I was changed. I didn't want his respect. I wanted him to be driven by the same lust for me as I felt for him.

She's naked in front of Sabir. Mosquitoes fizzle and hiss in the lamp flame. She steps forward and he embraces her, buries his head in her breasts. Sabir, back from the front to reclaim his lover. The cousin is dead, and she'd thought she was lost. Well, now here he is again. With a different face. Toughened by war. And hardly now the type to reject a beautiful woman's advances. 'I've found you again,' she says. The curve of a shoulder; a beauty spot beneath the breast. They fuck. No more of this pretension of respecting or disrespecting anyone or anything. It's beyond that, Sabir now knows. It's beyond anything. Once you step off into that cool vacuum, what else could possibly matter?

VIII

Sabir half-expects something to happen after breaking into the cupboard – but nothing does. It gives him the feeling that the commandant will never move against him. Some of the money's gone to paying off the escape, the rest is safely in his *plan*. And the doctor's letter is with the rest of his 'treasure' in the glass jar. He thought of putting it back in the cupboard, should he ever find it open again, and he thought of burning it over the lamp. In the end, he kept it. Somewhere in the back of his mind is the memory of that day in the holding prison, when they took his letters and photos from him.

As he wanders back to his folly one evening after rum with the commandant, he wonders why he's been given such leeway. No doubt the commandant has checked his record – and there he'll have found that Sabir served in Belgium; that he was even decorated. It might be part of the reason. The commandant himself has never mentioned the war, and Sabir guesses it's because he didn't fight in it. Perhaps he was posted to Algeria for the duration. A man like the commandant would take that hard. And overcompensate in his other endeavours. Such abstract guilt is another of those luxuries of his class. As for Sabir, he didn't join up out of any sense of duty. The patriotism was certainly there, but only skin-deep. It affected him no more than the cheap sentiment of a music-hall melody. Going to war was simply what young, working-class men of his generation did.

And yet he'd never seriously considered deserting, either. He recalls now one particular night in 1917. All through the afternoon, word had been spreading along the lines that the offensive would begin at four o'clock the next morning. Sabir remembers nothing of this offensive, nothing at all of going over the top. All he can recall is that evening when the nervous young officer finally told them, after the weeks of waiting. Some men were in shock and babbling in the trenches that night, but in general the news had a tranquillising effect. Men who normally jumped at the sound of every mortar now went about their business quite calmly. To Sabir it felt like relief – the relief one might experience on learning one had a terminal illness, after months of suspecting it. As usual, after dinner they played cards – Sabir, Edouard and a couple of other fellows in the trench section. It was simply an evening like any other, only more so – to a pitch of intensity that drove away consideration of anything else but the game. As it got dark they continued to play, until they could barely see the cards, until it became impossible to go on. Even then, they stayed sitting at the 'card table' for another half-hour. And while they played, they remained almost silent, with an absorption that had been absolute. Nothing else – not the occasional shell or desultory gunfire, not the officers shouting orders, not the sordid hustle of trench life, nor the lice nor the rats – nothing could penetrate their world.

Later, probably an hour or two before the offensive, Sabir stared up at the stars. In his state of heightened awareness, they seemed like tiny cysts covering the night's black skin. A lot of the men were sucking on the morphine-soaked pieces of cardboard that chemists sold to wives and mothers, who sent them on to the soldiers. When the signal came, they'd climb up in a drugged haze, not properly understanding what was happening. Perhaps, like a drunk in an accident, they'd actually fare better than the other soldiers.

Even now, there was the chance of getting out, of deserting, if you really wanted to. There was a conduit from a disused trench section that led to a field just behind the lines, and from there you could make it under cover of night to the nearest village, which was surprisingly close by, or to the town, some twenty kilometres distant. It was a well-known escape route, occasionally used by the men for sorties to local bars and brothels. As long as you were back by morning, as long as you didn't abuse the privilege, no one said anything. Even the officers knew about it, and judged it a useful pressure outlet. And it would have been conceivable to use it now. You'd have had to get civilian clothes from somewhere, you'd have had to cover an awful lot of ground in a short space of time, but it could have been done. It was a comforting thought in a way, because it made Sabir realise he actually had no desire to desert. And it certainly wasn't anything to do with duty, honour, bravery, pride or even fear of the firing squad. Here in the Colony, as he walks towards his folly, as he thinks about that night for the first time in years, it remains unfathomable to him.

The last embers of sunlight have died away, although a full moon casts a silver sheen over the forest. The folly stands there in its clearing, like a miniature lighthouse. Something's not right about it, although for a moment Sabir can't see what. The door's open. A shadow stains the back wall against the moonlight. Someone is slumped on the floor. The shadow somehow seems more substantial than the body itself. Sabir freezes by the door – it's not Say-Say, as he thought it would be at first. Sabir can feel fear moving down his legs, his arms and to his fingertips, the way the nicotine does after the first morning drag on a cigarette. He could turn around now, go back to the house, or sleep out in the garden, or in the aborted orchid nursery, which he's already marked out as his next home once the commandant's wife gets here and reclaims the folly.

Bonifacio's not asleep. Just lying down, watching Sabir carefully, without a word, without a trace of panic. He's like a wounded animal. His bare feet are ripped and raw – a mess of blood and bruises. What agony it must have been to walk on them.

'Who the fuck are you?'

'I'm . . . I'm . . . the gardener.' Sabir waves feebly in the direction of the house. It's all he can do to get the words out of his mouth.

Bonifacio lets out a low chuckle. 'The gardener, eh? The gardener . . .' The chuckle turns into a racking cough, which continues for a minute or so. It gradually subsides. His breathing is shallow, like an animal panting. It seems he doesn't recognise Sabir, despite the fact that their hammocks were hooked up side by side on the boat out. Sabir wonders how much he's changed since. Then again, perhaps Bonifacio never noticed him in the first place.

'What are you doing out here at this hour?'

'I . . . I sleep down here. While the work on the house . . .' Sabir's words trail off.

'You know who I am?'

'No. I mean, yes. I think so.'

'You think so . . . Well, listen, Mr Gardener. I need to eat. Understand me? Food.'

'I'll see what I can do.'

Bonifacio stares at Sabir. Moonlight reflects off his eyes, making them look otherworldly, cat-like.

'Yes. You see what you can do.'

The house is dark. Sabir makes his way across the garden by moonlight. He toys with the idea of waking the commandant, denouncing Bonifacio, but decides against it. No doubt Bonifacio has his friends and colleagues among the convict population. He remembers the story he was told about Bonifacio, how he'd risked travelling thousands of kilometres back to France just to kill a man. And he remembers that punch he gave a man on the boat, immediately winding him into silence, irrelevance.

Sabir tries the French windows at the back, which look out over the river. There'll be a patio here, once the building is finished, and a path down to a jetty. He can already picture the commandant's wife wandering out through the windows, strolling down this path in her swimming costume to read her book by the water. He's thinking of forcing the windows open, but in fact finds they're unlocked. Careless of the commandant. Too easy for someone to slip in and kill him. Perhaps that's exactly what'll happen one day. The *bagnards* are locked up at night, but dozens of *évadés*, like Bonifacio, wander up and down the river.

As he silently creeps his way through the house, Sabir notices that he's shaking; he hasn't done that since the war. The sound of drunken snoring from upstairs; moonlight flooding in through the window, creating a world of shadow: lines criss-cross the walls, like giant cracks. They remind Sabir of the orchid drawings in the commandant's book. In the larder, he finds some meat slices and a loaf of bread.

Bonifacio's sitting up. He's bandaged his feet with what

Sabir recognises as one of his own shirts. Blood has soaked right through, and with his stubby legs it looks as though all he has is two bloody stumps. In front of him is Sabir's glass jar. It was well hidden under a floorboard, and yet he's found it anyway. Thank God Sabir has his money in his *plan*. Bonifacio's smoking one of Sabir's cigarettes too, and flicking through his photos.

'Fancy-looking girl you got there. Who is she?'

'My fiancée.'

'She French?'

'Yes.'

'Doesn't look it.'

Sabir shoves the food in Bonifacio's direction to forestall any more questions. Bonifacio drops the photos and rips into the loaf like a zoo animal. The tendons on his neck jut out, hard as wire. In a few minutes, the food is gone. The click and whirr of insects fill the air. Bonifacio says nothing for a long time, as if the effort to digest is taking up all his concentration. He's breathing heavily. Eventually he looks up at Sabir. 'This where you sleep?'

'Yes.'

'I'm sleeping here tonight. You sleep by the door.'

'Yes.'

'We'll talk in the morning.'

'Yes.'

Bonifacio picks up the photos, hands them back to Sabir. 'Don't forget your sweetheart. Hope she hasn't forgotten you.'

He has a shirt on; it's filthy and torn. He pulls it off to use as a pillow and lies down, stretches himself out from wall to wall, the same way Sabir usually does, lying on his stomach. He's snoring within the minute. The gigantic cross he has tattooed on his back rises up and down, glistening with sweat. Sabir sits hunched up by the door, watching Bonifacio sleeping in the lamplight. Sabir's shake hasn't gone; he crosses his arms, as if against the cold, although it's still steaming hot.

It wouldn't be so difficult to kill Bonifacio now if he wanted to. He pictures himself plunging his knife into the back of Bonifacio's neck. The death convulsions. Then dragging the body out into the forest. The humidity and the wildlife would do the rest. He shakes the idea from his head. Quite apart from whether he's capable of it, he might as well see what Bonifacio's planning first. Surely he's not going to risk sticking around here for long. He'll push off in a couple of days, once he's recovered. Sabir stays awake deep into the night, smoking, until the folly is thick with the fumes and even the insects are driven away. It's his habit to drift off to sleep thinking about the commandant's wife, thinking about undressing her, swimming with her in the river. Tonight that's impossible. Bonifacio has chased her away, and for that Sabir feels angry with him.

He wonders what Bonifacio's been up to all this time. Probably hiding out by the river on his own, for weeks on end, stealing food where he can. Must have been difficult, though. Escaped prisoners are a commonplace; guard killers are not. They're the one category of prisoner the Administration makes every effort to recapture – all the more so with a celebrity like Bonifacio. There's a price on his head. He'd have to steer clear of the Indians and Bonis. Even other escaped *bagnards* camping out in the forest would be wary of him, since the penalty for aiding a guard killer is permanent removal to the islands.

Sleep comes a few hours before dawn. In Sabir's dreams, he's back in the trenches, playing cards with Edouard, Masque and Bonifacio. It's hard to focus on his cards, though – every time he looks, they seem to have reconfigured themselves and it's impossible to tell whether his hand is a winner or not. Too late, the stakes are too high, there's nothing to do now but play on. Occasionally he looks up to see Edouard opposite him, penetrating him with his gaze, his glass eye fixing Sabir to the spot.

Day breaks through the slats of the shutters. Sabir opens his eyes, tries to focus. His head is dull with the ache of too little sleep, his throat dry. Bonifacio is already sitting up, staring at him, smoking. The bandages on his feet are stiff with dried blood.

'Gimme your shoes.'

'But I only have this pair!'

Bonifacio pushes his hand into his trousers, pulls out an oily wad of money. He thumbs off a few notes and hands them over to Sabir. 'Get yourself a new pair. A new shirt as well.'

Sabir struggles up, takes the money. Apart from the state of his feet, Bonifacio seems better than he was last night. The food and sleep must have done him some good.

'Second, my friend, you're going to do some business for me. You're going to hire yourself a canoe and go down to the nearest Boni village. Find someone to sell you a boat and sail. I'll give you the dough for the down payment. Then you go up to the main camp. Buy supplies from one of the barracks keepers. Then find someone who knows all about sailing boats. Tell him you have a boat ready. Tell him the good news: it won't cost him a *sou*. And whether he likes it or not, he's the damn skipper. You're going to do all this today, my friend. I have no more time to waste in this shithole.'

This last sentence he spits out with venom. Still befuddled by sleep, Sabir says nothing. All this time, Bonifacio hasn't stopped staring at him. It's a gaze that's like a drawn knife. Sabir looks away, and in that instant realises that he's played it all wrong, he's lost. If he'd immediately said yes, I'll do all that, or if he'd immediately said no, it's impossible, he might have got away with it.

'You're hiding something from me,' says Bonifacio. 'Aren't you?'

Still Sabir doesn't reply, tries to keep his face as blank as possible.

'Know what I think, my friend? I think you already know about buying boats and finding sailor boys.'

Sabir tries one last time to meet Bonifacio's gaze. 'I've got to get up to the camp for the roll call.'

'Sure,' says Bonifacio. He's barring the way, though. They're both smallish men, but Bonifacio's bigger and bulkier, his body flexed and taut like a single muscle. 'First, why don't you tell me about this sailing trip? When are you skipping out?'

'I...' Sabir's thinking furiously. Can he lie and get away with it? Put on the spot like that, he goes for the safer option. 'Friday, dawn.'

'How many men?'

'Me and three others.'

'Where's the boat?'

'Don't know. One of the other men has the details.'

'How big is it?'

'Big enough for four men, that's all I know.'

'If it's big enough for four, it's big enough for five.'

'I'll have to ask the others.'

'You won't ask the others. You won't say anything to them. This'll be our secret. But you'll find out where the boat's hidden.'

Sabir's walking up the path to the main camp as the sun flickers over the horizon. It's a terrible relief to be away from

Bonifacio: he can breathe again. Everything becomes blazingly clear. He's been edging towards it for the past few days, but it's taken the trauma of Bonifacio for him to realise. All those things, the good things that might have happened if he stayed here, employed as a gardener, under the benevolent patronage of the commandant. Who knows, he might even have got a pardon: such things are rare but not unknown. He could have set up business as a gardener to functionaries in Saint-Laurent or Cayenne. He could have learnt all about the exotic plants here and exported them back to Europe. He might even have made his fortune that way. The door of another future opens, just enough for him to peer inside, before it slams firmly in his face.

He should have told Carpette that he's changed his mind. That he no longer wants to escape. That he's happy to write off the money he's already supplied for it. Because why exchange this present for the uncertainties of the high seas and, if he's lucky, a country about which he knows nothing? His position here is the best he can hope for, for the moment at least. And there's the commandant's wife. He thinks of the photographs of her. The frozen face. The vacant expression caught in the lens, forever attached with an importance that it was never meant to bear. The ache is almost physical. Too late, too late.

And yet who knows, he tries to persuade himself. After all, he's a convict, dependent on the goodwill of one man, the commandant. Sabir can't help feeling that sooner or later, the Colony will consume the commandant too, just as it's consumed so many of his charges. He has a vision of how things will collapse here. No matter how much money the commandant has, nothing will work if everyone, guard and convict alike, is stealing all the time, as is the case. The commandant's projects are condemned to failure; he'll become disillusioned. Paris and France may have ceased to exist for Sabir, but they're still very much alive for the commandant. No doubt he still has his apartment in the 16th *arrondissement*, his family home in the Savoie, that he can return to at a moment of his choosing. The commandant's escape, at least, is a certainty.

No, Sabir's fantasy of a new life as a gardener is surely no more or less a flimsy construct than the boat awaiting him in a nearby creek. This colony is not his home. Paris wasn't his home. But perhaps it's still there to be found, in Colombia. Or Panama. Or Brazil, or the wastes of Patagonia. For a second, he pictures a life of endless roaming.

Without even realising it, he's come to the end of the trail, has made his way up the main avenue and arrived at his old barracks. He tries to snap out of this torment of thought and fantasy that's leading nowhere. Barracks roll call. The names are rapped out. He almost forgets to answer to his own. Say-Say is there, looking ragged and ill. He's evidently been kicked out of the hospital. And yet he told Sabir that he couldn't come back to barracks, that Pierrot had threatened him. He could have hidden in the folly, as Sabir had offered.

Out of the corner of his eye he spots Carpette. He seems to be in a state of uncharacteristic anxiety, hopping nervously from one foot to the other. And as the roll call continues, Sabir notices Carpette furtively glancing towards him. Now it's over. The men wander off to work or back into the barracks.

Carpette approaches. 'It's off, it's all off.'

'For Christ's sake!' hisses Sabir. 'There are people around!' He guides Carpette through the barracks and into the privy. 'What the hell's the matter?'

'Edouard's disappeared.'

'How do you mean, disappeared?'

'He wasn't at roll call yesterday. Not the morning one or the evening one. He's gone.'

'Maybe he's just hiding out in the forest. Waiting for Friday.'

'No. We've got this hiding spot where we meet up. A shack I built for us. He hasn't been there. Anyway, if he was going to do that, he'd have told me.' Carpette gives an involuntary shrug and a strained giggle. His hair is unparted, his shirt stained. 'We don't have any secrets, Edouard and me. He'd have told me, that's all. Just like he told me about you.'

'Let's wait and see what happens,' replies Sabir, baffled by Carpette's last remark. 'It's only Wednesday. Let's wait and see if he turns up. We can always put everything off to next week.'

'We can't do anything. Not until I know what's happened to him.'

Sabir spends the rest of the day working in a state of coiled tension. His mind involuntarily grinding its way through thought after thought, consuming them, discarding them, one after the other. It's the first time he's seen Carpette lose his composure; it's disturbing. He's never exactly trusted Carpette, but has nevertheless relied on him as the one who has the answers. Now there's the question of what to tell Bonifacio. Carpette knows where the boat's hidden, but he's not about to tell Sabir, not until he finds Edouard.

Edouard and his glass eye. Sabir recalls how, straight after the war, he caught the train to the town in the Ardennes where Edouard had told him his family was from. He did it partly out of a genuine desire to know whether his friend was alive or dead, partly because Edouard was from a wealthy family who might help him get a job. And yet after three days in Charleville, sleeping out in fields at night, he found no trace of Edouard's family. As if it didn't exist at all, and never had. He remembers

Carpette telling him that Edouard had worked in the botanical gardens in Saint-Laurent. And he remembers the whisper he overheard on his first day in the Colony, only now making the connection: 'I'm working in the botanical gardens. It's a good job. We're one man short. When they ask what you do, say you're a gardener.'

All day, the idea of killing Bonifacio plays at the corner of his thoughts. At lunch, he went back to the folly with food for Bonifacio, but he wasn't there. Nonetheless, Sabir knows he'll be back in the evening. He remembers what Bonifacio said just before Sabir had left for camp: 'Don't do anything stupid. I've been keeping an eye on you for the past few days. I know your habits.' Bonifacio's around somewhere nearby, in the forest no doubt, keeping tabs on Sabir, forever watching him. There's no escape.

IX

Night is falling. The commandant is sharing the last of a bottle of rum. Usually Sabir restricts himself to a single glass; this evening he's had three. A clump of bread and some salted beef lie in his bag, for Bonifacio. The gramophone scratches out the sound of a German song that refuses to resolve into any easy melody. As the commandant speaks, Sabir can feel the rum rising to his head, like noonday heat.

'These gramophone records are warping with the humidity. Soon they'll be unplayable. How stupid I was to bring them out here. But I thought my wife would like some music.'

'Sounds all right to me, sir.'

'The speed varies horribly; can't you hear it? Curiously, I quite like it this way, though. I don't know why.'

Sabir's only half-listening; the other half of his mind has already crossed the lawn, is already in the folly, wondering what he'll find there. And hoping unreasonably that there'll be no Bonifacio.

'Do you know this music? Do you like it?'

'I've heard you play it before, sir. Very nice, sir.'

'Well, I don't think it's very nice. I think it's rather bleak. It's from *Winterreise*. One of my wife's favourites.'

As he says this, the commandant seems overcome by some obscure emotion. He puts his hand to his eye, as if to wipe away a tear, although there's nothing there. The moment passes.

'As you know, I'll be going to Saint-Laurent tomorrow, to collect my wife, of course, and also for some administrative duties. But I have something I wish to talk to you about before I go.'

He gets up, fishes about in his pocket for a set of keys, then crouches down beside the cupboard. He's unlocking it, Sabir realises with horror. Sabir remains clamped to his seat. The commandant's fumbling about in the cupboard – he's taking an eternity about it. He gets back up, turns towards Sabir. There's a fifty-franc note in his hand. He's smiling.

'I'd like you to have this.'

'I ... I'm not sure what to say, sir.'

'I wanted to give you some token of appreciation for the hard work you've done, for me, for my wife, on the garden. Of course, I'm counting on you to keep this strictly between ourselves. I know prisoners aren't allowed money. I also know you can't easily survive without it. In any case, that's all going to change. Soon enough, I'll put the men here to doing useful work – growing crops, raising livestock – and I'll make sure they're properly paid for their work.'

'Well, thank you very much, sir,' Sabir replies as he pushes the note to the bottom of his pocket.

'You know, with a few more men of your calibre, we can make a go of things out here. I'm convinced there's real potential. We could make a good team. I just want you to know I appreciate what you've done here and ... well, you've good reason to hope that your position will improve. That's all I'll say for now.' The commandant drains the last of the rum. 'I'll be leaving in the morning at five, so I probably won't see you until my return. I imagine we'll be back by Thursday evening.'

Sabir darts across the lawn, through the *jardin anglais* to the folly as fast as he can, not giving himself any more time to contemplate what's awaiting him there. The folly is dark, but Sabir can already feel there's someone in it. In some indefinable way it's not the same as it was when he left it at lunchtime.

'Took your fucking time.'

Bonifacio's standing, smoking. He's looking so much better than twenty-four hours ago; it's remarkable how quickly he's recovered. He's shirtless – biceps oiled with sweat like a boxer's. Sabir notices the shoes Bonifacio's wearing, Sabir's own, while he himself goes barefoot. He didn't have the time to buy new ones. On Bonifacio, his old shoes seem to be a good fit. He opens his bag, hands over the food.

Bonifacio eats in silence, more slowly and deliberately than last night, when he tore at the meat ravenously. Sabir sits down on the floor. As he watches Bonifacio eating, the image of the commandant briefly comes to mind. Whatever happens, Sabir's not likely ever to see the man again. You've good reason to hope that your position will improve, he said. Recalling these words, Sabir feels an emptiness in the pit of his stomach. He puts his hand to his pocket where the fifty-franc note is. The commandant hadn't even noticed the missing money. All that cleverness and learning of his, combined with this monumental lack of nous, that Sabir has found so often typifies the officer class.

'That girl of yours,' says Bonifacio now, wiping his mouth with the back of his hand, 'the one in all those photos of yours. What's she like?'

'How do you mean?'

'You know. What's she like in bed? Is she a good *fuck*?'

Bonifacio utters this last word with studied violence. Sabir says nothing, refuses to meet Bonifacio's gaze.

'Well? Does she take it like a whore? Or do you have to slap it out of her?'

'I don't want to talk about it.'

'Frigid, is she? Stuck-up type? Looks it. Or did you never bed her? Is that it? Never had the balls for it? She wore the trousers, is that it?'

'I said, I don't want to talk about it.'

Bonifacio chuckles to himself. 'Have it your own way, then.' He's lying down on his back now, hands behind his head. 'See your friend up at the camp?'

'Yes.'

'He tell you where the boat is?'

'No.'

'You even ask him?'

'No.'

'Thought I told you to ask him. Thought I asked you to find out where the fucking thing is.'

Sabir says nothing. He's trembling again, and it feels weird not to be able to control one's own body. As though his quivering hands are in fact someone else's.

Bonifacio has sat up. His face is dark and taut; for a moment it seems as if he's going to explode into violence. Suddenly he relaxes. His face creases into an ugly smile, he chuckles again. 'Take it easy, my friend. But next time, do what I tell you ... Here, get me another smoke.' Sabir tosses the packet to him and Bonifacio lies down again. 'What's the plan, then?'

'Meeting at dusk the day after tomorrow, then we'll go down to the creek.'

'You don't even know which creek?'

'No.'

'How much dough did you give this friend of yours?'

'Two hundred.'

'Shouldn't have cost that much. You're one trusting guy. How do you know he hasn't pocketed the dough? How do you know he's not skipping out without you? Find out which creek tomorrow. Don't mess it up this time.'

Once again, Bonifacio is snoring within minutes – the sound sleep of a man with no doubts. It's this very cocksureness that makes it so difficult to contemplate murdering him. Sabir imagines himself raising the dagger over the prone Bonifacio, ready to plunge it into the back of his neck, and yet at the same time Bonifacio whips round to disarm him and pin him to the floor...The longer he thinks about doing it, the more impossible it becomes. He pictures Pierrot after he and Antillais killed Masque: the casual way in which Pierrot strolled up to the water urn afterwards, to wash the murder away.

The commandant's wife is now beside him, for the first time in days. Her appearance is unexpected, fatally diminished by Bonifacio's presence. Bonifacio, who's lying there exactly where she and Sabir have so often lain down together, naked and trembling. Her hair brushes the back of his neck. She's whispering in his ear: 'You have to. Go on, do it now. It's the only hope, our only way out.' She's behind him now, clasping her arms around his waist. 'I've found you again.'

Sabir turns away from Bonifacio to face her. Impossible to speak, though, impotent as he is in the face of her expectations. 'Don't worry,' she says, sadly. 'I understand. Don't worry.' She kisses him on the lips, not as a prelude to sex but more as a farewell. Does he detect a *moue* of distaste on her face? She's moved away from him now. She's walking out of the door, back across the garden to the house. He should be running after her, and yet Bonifacio's magnetic control draws him back, keeps him here in his folly.

Sabir blinks himself awake. He has the feeling that he's been asleep for minutes only, but that can't be true – the grimy shadow cast by the half-open shutter means that dawn isn't far off. Bonifacio has already disappeared; he can feel his absence even before he sees it.

The sense of being trapped at the centre, and therefore unable to see the whole clearly... On his way back up to camp, Sabir turns his thoughts to Carpette, and whether Carpette might be taking him for a ride. What, after all, is this business about Edouard disappearing, just before the escape? The instant he starts musing on any one possibility, he can't help believing in it completely, even if only for a moment. He's filled with a terror that Carpette's vanished in the night, leaving him at the mercy of Bonifacio.

At roll call, Sabir spots Say-Say. He looks in a pitiful state; he's been roughed up. Pierrot is there, too, lounging about over on the other side of the barracks, chatting and laughing with one of the other convicts. Say-Say claims that Pierrot has threatened to kill him. Pierrot's certainly a killer, but would he go that far, Sabir now wonders. The Masque murder was quite a different affair.

Say-Say's name is at the top of the roll call list, and he bolts like a terrified cat as soon as he answers to it. Pierrot is called soon after, while Sabir's name is right at the bottom. Pierrot hasn't wandered off like the rest of the men, though; he lies back down on the bed board and slips one of the younger convicts a couple of *sous* to bring him some coffee. He's rich enough to pay someone else to do his work quota. There are a few others like him, all *forts-à-bras* who know how to work the system. They generally sleep through the morning, then go about their business – whatever their particular scam is – in the afternoon.

Say-Say's nowhere to be seen now. No matter, Sabir will send him a note later, once he's seen Carpette and finally understood what's going on. On the spur of the moment, he signals for Pierrot to follow him into the privy. It's the first time he's ever had anything to do with the man – as a rule he steers clear of the tough nuts.

'It's about Say-Say.'

Pierrot raises his eyebrows. 'What about him?'

'What did you do to him?'

'Kid got what was coming to him,' Pierrot replies with a shrug of the shoulders. 'Some cheek, coming back here without the dough he owes me. What the hell's it to you, anyway?'

For a moment, Pierrot was coiled and ready for action. But he's quickly sized Sabir up and realised he's no *fort-à-bras*.

'How much does he owe you?'

'Fifty. Damn well better have it today.'

Sabir reaches into his pocket, pulls out the banknote the commandant has given him. 'Take it.'

It's gone in an instant – even in the privy, there's no point in a note that large being visible any longer than it has to be. As they leave, Pierrot says: 'It was nothing bad. No blood. Just to let him know what he was in for if he didn't square the debt.'

'No hard feelings.'

'But if I was you, I'd get him out of barracks.'

'I'll do that.'

No doubt Pierrot imagines that Sabir and Say-Say are lovers. Well, let him think that. Sabir hurries down the avenue, through a mêlée of men making their way to work. As he walks, he wonders idly how much money Pierrot would want to kill

Bonifacio. A lot: more wads of cash from the commandant's cupboard. But would he accept such a job? It'd be risky. And ultimately just as risky for the contractor. He's arrived at the end barracks now, where Carpette is keeper. He's half-expecting to be told that Carpette has disappeared, but no, there he is, sweeping out his barracks, one of the keeper's morning tasks. He looks different from yesterday; no longer dishevelled, not quite himself, either.

'Any news of Edouard?'

'I was going to send you a note. He's back.'

'Back? From where? Where'd he go?'

Carpette stops sweeping, leans on his broom, stares into the middle distance. 'Yesterday afternoon, I went down to the shack. The one I told you about. About an hour's walk from here, in the forest. I wasn't expecting anything. But I had to go just to make sure. He was there. At first, he wouldn't tell me where he'd been. I guessed Saint-Laurent, of course. Finally he admitted it. Bloody stupid, dangerous thing to do. Anyway, he's been reported missing now.'

The consequences flash through Sabir's mind: if you're absent from roll call, you have twenty-four hours to show up, before the official missing report goes out. Once that happens, even if you turn up voluntarily, you'll be sent to the *blockhaus* in Saint-Laurent, to appear before the tribunal. If Edouard has a clean record and no enemies, the punishment might be light: a short stint in a punishment camp. But there's always the chance he'll be sent to the Islands.

'He wouldn't tell me why he'd been to Saint-Laurent. Came back with a big sack, though. Won't tell me what's in that, either. It smells strange. He keeps hold of it the whole time, like he's afraid I'm going to nick it off him or something.'

Carpette's looking at Sabir with some sort of expectation.

What exactly does he want Sabir to say, though? He's often had this feeling that Carpette thinks he knows some secret about Edouard. At this moment, he's acutely aware that he knows nothing about Carpette, and that Edouard is a different kind of mystery. And yet he feels a sudden urge to 'confess', to tell Carpette all about Bonifacio. Finally he mutters: 'So it's on again?'

'You know Serpent's Creek? The one beyond the Boni village. That's where the boat is. The supplies are down by the river. In the jungle, behind the pier at the commandant's house. There's an old ruin there, at the edge of the trees; know where I mean?'

'Yeah.'

'I hid the supplies behind the wall there. I was going to get a Boni to ship them down to the creek, but the only one I trust won't do it, the coward. Says there are a couple of guards in the house now, with rifles.'

'The commandant put them in there while he's away. Or maybe they're there for good, now the wife's moving in. I don't know.'

'Why the hell didn't you tell me before?' says Carpette irritably. 'Anyway, we're going to have to carry the supplies down to the creek ourselves now. We'll have to do it late afternoon tomorrow, and hope for the best. At four, I think. No later, 'cause we won't be able to find the boat in the dark. Better tell your Basque boy.'

Sabir grabs a young convict who's willing to go and find Say-Say in exchange for a few *sous*, and scribbles out a note for him with the details. Four o'clock tomorrow, by the ruin in the jungle behind the pier. On his way back down to the river for a last day's work, Sabir briefly wonders whether Say-Say can read, decides he probably can't. He'll get someone to read the note out to him, no doubt, which inevitably means divulging the escape plan to a third party. The messenger will probably read it too, if he's able. Sabir should have been more careful with what he wrote.

A tranquilising feeling of fatalism invades Sabir. The escape, Bonifacio, the commandant's wife, Edouard, the penal colony – none of it matters, under this annihilating sun. He dimly perceives his life as if it were an object in front of him. A warm breeze is coming off the river, shaking the branches of a dead tree that's leaning over the path. Leaves flutter free from their branches and are borne off on the wind back towards the camp.

X

Mid-afternoon, the following day. The commandant's still away in Saint-Laurent collecting his wife. As a consequence, nobody – guard or convict – is bothering to work much. The two guards stationed at the commandant's house have already found the rum supply and made a start on it; that's a good sign. Sabir has given his men on gardening detail leave to remain in barracks, and although he doesn't actually have the authority to do that, no one questions him – without the commandant, the power structure becomes strangely fluid.

Bonifacio. Yes, he returned to the folly yesterday at noon, and Sabir brought him some food. As he gnawed at it, he quizzed Sabir about the boat; Sabir told him immediately where it is. No point in holding out; no point in lying. No strength or guile for it. After that, Bonifacio smoked two of Sabir's cigarettes, and then disappeared without saying anything of his plans. He didn't return in the evening, either – Sabir slept alone – and wasn't there this morning. It's half past three now, and Sabir has returned to the folly for the last time. Still no one there. Sabir has the feeling that Bonifacio's cleared out for good – although it's impossible to tell, since he had no possessions to return for. But a certain oppressiveness that has lately haunted the place seems to have dissipated. As the afternoon light filters in through the shutters, it's as if Bonifacio had never really existed at all.

Alone again in the folly, but for a few minutes only. A smell wafts in through the door – half sweet, half rank. The orchids he dumped behind the folly, rotting away under the sun and rain. He thinks back to that afternoon when the commandant put his hand on Sabir's shoulders, as if Sabir shared in his disappointment at the dead orchids. In a way, he pities the commandant's failure to please his wife in this respect. He lifts the floorboard where he's hidden the photos of the commandant's wife, and a few other things besides. He lights up the lamp for the last time, pulls out the letter from the Swiss doctor he stole from the cupboard, holds it over the flame. The paper is slightly damp and it takes a while for it to burn properly. Not like the moths he used to watch at night, as they crashed ceaselessly into the lamp, sometimes even knocking it over in their violence. Often he absorbed himself in that drama: the shadows on the wall, surrounding him, magnified many times, wings flapping as if the creature were trying to smother the flames, its podgy body twisting and squirming in the heat.

The letter's in cinders now. A few cryptic phrases will remain in Sabir's brain for a few more weeks or months, and then they too will be gone for ever. The photos of the commandant's wife are in his hand. He can't bear to burn them, can't bear to take them with him, either. In the end, he stuffs them back in the jar, screws the lid on tightly and puts it back in its hiding place. The money in his *plan*, a change of clothes, the new shoes that hurt his feet – it's all he need take with him. Once again, the man without a past. He sits on the floor for a few minutes, not even smoking a cigarette, just thinking about the folly and the commandant's wife, trying to get a feel of what he's leaving behind. She's here somewhere, head bowed, naked, turned away from him. It's something like hate she feels for him now, for in the end he proved not to be the hard surface she needed to grind against. Sabir is filled with a yearning for a future that will never be. It washes through him, finally leaving him empty, and he realises it's time to leave.

'Did you see where the guards are?'

'In the house. Downstairs, in the study. Getting plastered on rum.'

'Good.'

Sabir, Carpette, Edouard and Say-Say are all crouched behind a crumbling wall, just back from the edge of the jungle, not far from the pier – a leftover from some earlier, failed colonial occupation. At one point, Sabir remembers, the commandant had toyed with the idea of incorporating this ruin into the garden as another picturesque folly, but in the end decided against it. This is where, in a hole covered with branches, Carpette has hidden the provisions. Three lidded barrels to carry down to the creek, plus an empty urn for the drinking water.

Seeing Edouard again is bizarre. Over the weeks, Sabir has thought quite a bit about him. He's gone over many times in his mind that one meeting of theirs in the forest, and how shocked he was at Edouard's appearance. And then there was Carpette's constant talk of Edouard's poor health, how they had to get out now before it deteriorated any further. He's been expecting to see a wreck of a man. And yet Edouard looks in remarkably good shape, by convict standards at least. He doesn't seem to have any problems seeing out of his one eye; his upper arms are relatively muscly, the sign of a decent diet. Can this be the same person he hardly even recognised six weeks ago? Sabir thinks of his own body, and it occurs to him that it's not Edouard who's changed, but himself. Not only has he got used to the convict 'look' – the thin, skull-like face, the watery eyes, the concave chest, the hooked nose – but he has been transformed into it.

Say-Say, in sharp contrast to Edouard, is in a terrible state: cowed, shivering, sweating. Nothing to do with any roughing-up Pierrot might have given him: it's a bad case of fever. He's shirtless, hugging himself. Sabir notices for the first time the few words he has poorly tattooed in black ink across his hairless chest: *J'ai vu, j'ai cru, j'ai pleuré.*

'Another hour till dusk,' says Carpette. 'There's nothing for it, we'll have to shift these now. Wait any longer and we won't be able to find the boat in the dark.'

'I know that path,' says Sabir. 'There won't be any guards down there – not unless we're unlucky. They'll all have gone back up to camp by now. They won't want to be stuck out here in the afternoon rain.'

'Yeah, that's what I was thinking. There's just those damn guards at the house.'

'They're at the back. They won't see a thing. They won't come out.'

'Let's go, then. Edouard, you take this,' says Carpette, handing him the empty water urn.

'Give it to the boy. Can't you see he can't handle a full barrel?'

It's true, Say-Say looks as if he'll have a hard time walking, let alone carrying anything. Carpette and Edouard exchange looks that are difficult to translate. Immediately, though, it's clear to Sabir that there's tension between them, over and above any generated by the escape.

Say-Say has nothing with him; Carpette and Sabir have their small cloth sacks. Edouard, on the other hand, has a large, unwieldy bag slung over his back, making it difficult to carry his barrel. They make their way along the side of the garden, down to the path that starts at the pier. It's the last time Sabir will see this garden into which he's put so much effort. The grass has taken on a greyish hue – perhaps the turf hasn't taken properly and it's dying. Or it might be a reflection of the bruise-blue rain clouds that now swirl and roll about in the sky like ocean waves.

Past the pier, along the riverbank path. Sabir takes up the rear, behind Say-Say, who's lagging. For the first time in weeks, he allows himself a fleeting fantasy about a life after the escape. He won't stay in Colombia – he's heard the climate there is as hellish as it is here. No, what he'll do is head down south, to Argentina. There are plenty of Frenchmen in Buenos Aires, he's been told, and the city itself is supposedly a bit like Paris, with long, graceful avenues. Then again, a make-believe Paris is not what he's after. He'll head even further south. What's south of Buenos Aires? He has no notion, just the word Patagonia, and a vision of prairie land or perhaps a white wilderness.

Ahead of him, he sees Say-Say flop down like a broken puppet. Edouard and Carpette are out of sight, round a bend. Sabir catches up with the boy; his face is pale, his breathing laboured.

'Too sick. I can't make it.'

'Don't be stupid. We can't stop now.'

'No,' the boy croaks, 'I mean it. Don't wanna go on. I'll stay here. And get back up to camp in the morning.'

'You can't do that. What about Pierrot?'

'Pierrot . . . Saw him this afternoon. Told me we're quits. Told me to forget about it.'

'So you think it's all right to go back to barracks now?'

'They won't report me. So long as I show up in the morning.'

A rage boils up in Sabir. He grabs the boy by the shoulders, hisses furiously: 'Listen, you wouldn't last another month in the barracks; hasn't anyone told you that? Haven't you figured that out? You've got no dough. This is your only chance! Who the hell do you think paid off Pierrot, eh? Who do you think did that?'

Say-Say's staring at him, stunned and incapable of speech, while Sabir continues shaking the boy's shoulders in a frenzy of anger. '*I* paid him off! *My* money! Understand? You'll *never* get another chance like this. Even if you wanted to back down now, we wouldn't let you. You're the navigator. You don't want to continue, we've all had it. You don't want to continue, I'll slit your throat right here!'

He hears a voice from ahead: 'What the hell's going on?' It's Carpette, he must have backtracked to see what the matter was.

Sabir's face is flushed and his hands are shaking; he realises he's been shouting. He lets go of Say-Say's shoulders, tries to compose himself. 'Kid's sick.'

'Too bad. Look over there!' Carpette points in the direction of the river. In the distance, maybe five hundred metres away, Sabir can make out a small boat chugging along the bank. 'Looks like . . . I'd say the patrol boat from Saint-Laurent. What the hell's it doing this far up? Better take cover.'

Sabir picks Say-Say up, drags him off the path. They're all lying down in the scrub now, waiting for the boat to pass. Sabir can feel his heart thumping hard against the ground, not because of the patrol boat, but as a residue of his sudden rage against Say-Say. It took him quite by surprise and has left him perplexed. He has his knife in his pocket; he was moments away from brandishing it when Carpette appeared. And yet now he feels almost teary-eyed; why can't he control himself? Nerves, nerves. The loss of control disturbs him anyway. Say-Say's there beside him, shocked and wide-eyed, uncomprehending of what's happened, what's still happening. The boat's zigzagging about to avoid sandbanks.

'Stopping off at camp, I'll bet,' whispers Carpette. 'Can't see how the pilot's going to get back in the dark, though.'

The others are lying well away from the path now, but Sabir's on his stomach, peering at the boat through the scrub, squinting to see better. There's the familiar heaviness in the air, the clouds overhead pregnant with storm. The boat, which was about fifty metres out from the shore, now veers slowly back to the bank, and at one point it seems as if it's heading directly at Sabir. As it moves nearer he can make out three people on board. A pilot and another man in the front section of the boat, and then a woman sitting by herself at the back, in the open air.

Closer, closer . . . Sabir could practically hit it with a stone. Someone on the boat might even catch sight of his head through the scrub. Too late, he can't move now. Snatches of conversation float off the river, filtered through the jerky moan of the engine. Impossible to make out what they're saying, though; just a jumble of half-words. The commandant is in front, chatting to a uniformed man at the wheel. An occasional laugh breaks through.

Sabir wonders why he has left his wife unattended at the back of the boat. Fresh off the ship from Europe, she must be feeling overwhelmed, disorientated, frightened even. She's wearing a sleeveless dress – fashionable in Paris perhaps but utterly bizarre here, out on this kilometres-wide expanse of muddy water. Her hair's cut into a dark helmet of a bob. Rarely has Sabir seen someone who looks quite so singular, so alone, as she fans herself listlessly in the pre-storm humidity. She's staring out into the forest, and for a second or two, as the boat goes by, Sabir has the feeling that their eyes lock, that she's staring right through his eye sockets to the back of his skull, his mind naked and transparent to her gaze. The moment stretches out to an infinity. How amazingly pale she looks. She's more world-weary, older than he'd imagined her, but not by much. She's quietly weeping – at least he thinks so, it's hard to tell from where he's hidden. It's exactly how Sabir dreamt the scene, days or weeks before. He finds himself thinking: 'You don't weep like that unless you've known happiness first.' He recalls that first day in the forest on his way to camp, when he stopped in a clearing to eat his lunch, and the vision he had of his fiancée in their bedsit in Belleville.

The boat slips by, barely rippling the water, as if hovering just above the surface. And now it recedes into the distance, an apparition shimmering uncertainly under the bulge of the sun hanging low in the sky, until finally it melts away into the river.

'C'mon. It'll be dark soon enough.'

Carpette's words snap Sabir out of his dazed state. The world comes back into focus: Edouard has already moved on, Carpette's now following him. Carpette's the one who speaks, who relays orders, and yet it's Edouard who leads. Say-Say's still there beside him. Sabir hoists the boy up by the armpits. 'You can rest up once we get to the creek. Anyway, you won't have anything to do till we get into open sea.'

They pass by the Boni village. There seem to be no men about. Naked children play in the dirt; semi-naked women sit cross-legged on the ground, breastfeeding babies or working at something intricate, although Sabir can't make out what. There's always the possibility they'll report the *évadés*, but it's unlikely at this hour. Most of the women don't even bother to look up from their work as the convicts pass. One seems slightly startled but then stares up into the distance beyond

Sabir, as if she's heard the noise but the men themselves are somehow invisible.

Just after the village, the clouds open up like bags slit with a knife. Visibility shrinks and the going is tougher under the rage of wind and rain. Edouard and Carpette have disappeared ahead; Sabir's practically carrying Say-Say along with him – hard, slow work, what with his barrel plus the water urn. As the rain tumbles down, Sabir is assaulted by a welter of thoughts. He wonders what Edouard is hiding in his bag, about his apparent well-being in the face of Carpette's stories of his ill health. He thinks back to those few days he spent in Charleville, fruitlessly trying to track down Edouard's family.

They trudge along for another quarter of an hour. There's a break in the rain and now Sabir can see Edouard and Carpette stopped at a curve in the path. They're arguing about something; Carpette's wagging his finger at Edouard. He can't hear what they're saying, but from their expressions, their body language, from the enigmatic remarks Carpette's made in the past, Sabir intuitively grasps the underlying situation. For Carpette, Edouard is everything, an obsession. But for Edouard, Carpette is temporary, a means to an end. Perhaps he needed Carpette for the money, for his wheeler-dealing instincts. Or for sex. Or for company and friendship. Or simply because in order to survive in this colony, two is always better than one. They stop arguing as Sabir approaches.

'The creek's down there,' says Carpette. 'We've got to go and find the boat. The spot should be marked with a pile of stones. Leave the stuff here with the kid.'

Sabir sets the boy down under a tree for protection against the rain – quite pointless since they're all drenched through now. Sick and terrified, Say-Say doesn't say a word. No doubt if he wasn't so sick, he'd skip off back to camp once he was on his own, thinks Sabir. He consoles himself with the thought that no matter what Say-Say wants right now, this escape attempt is his best chance of staying alive. He, Sabir, knows what's best for the boy, even if the boy can't understand that.

The three of them scramble down the bank and wade along the shallow creek. The rain's slowly clearing and the sun's occasionally visible again, casting long evening shadows along the disturbed water. They continue in silence, with nothing but the sound of the creek washing about their feet and the crunch of pebbles. Far away across the river, a lone bird shrieks as it wheels in the sky. They're less than an hour from the commandant's house, only twenty minutes from the Boni village, and yet this closeness merely seems to emphasise the isolation. Never has the human world felt quite so far away, so fragile.

Edouard's voice breaks through Sabir's thoughts: 'I see it. Over there.'

The pile of rocks, on the other side of the creek. Edouard and Sabir plunge forward across the water. The creek gets deeper and deeper, and once it reaches his chest, Sabir starts up a clumsy breaststroke. Carpette has held back; now he shouts: 'You two should manage it. I'll stay here on the other bank.' In a few strokes, Edouard and Sabir have made it over to the other bank. The water's muddy, impossible to see anything, but under the water by the rock pile, Sabir's knee hits against something solid. He feels about in the water. It's the boat, weighted down with stones; it takes a few minutes to clear it of the stones, then they try to haul it out.

'Too heavy,' Sabir calls to Carpette. 'Come over and give us a hand!'

His own voice echoes back to him from across the water. No reply from Carpette, though.

'He won't come over,' Edouard says. 'He's scared to get out of his depth.'

'He can't swim?'

'No!'

They're the first words they've exchanged since their meeting in the forest all those weeks ago. Edouard flashes him a sour grin that perfectly conveys the absurdity of a non-swimmer escaping across the ocean. It reminds Sabir of old times, the camaraderie and the black jokes that used to punctuate the days and months in the trenches.

'We'll just have to get this done ourselves.'

They set to it in a sudden fire of enthusiasm. A few failed attempts later, they finally manage to beach the boat and then roll it over to get the water out. It's a back-breaking job, but it feels good to be working with Edouard again. When they're through, the two slump down next to the boat, exhausted by the effort. Carpette shouts out: 'The sails! They're under the rocks!' Sabir wearily climbs back up the bank to the rocks. They're a patchwork affair, these sails, sewn together from old flour sacks – who knows if they'll survive the winds of the open sea. He puts them down by the boat, takes off his dripping shirt, sits down again to get his breath back.

'I'd forgotten that,' says Edouard.

'What?'

'Your back. The tattoo. Remember?' Edouard takes off his shirt as well to reveal a tattooed flower that's the mirror image of Sabir's – his is on his right shoulder blade, while Sabir's is on the left.

'God, yes. That's right.'

'*Sobralia fragrans.* They probably grow somewhere not far from here. I used to ship them to France before the war.'

Sabir had forgotten, too. It was the dog days of summer,

1917, and there hadn't been much action on their trench section for weeks, other than the morning shellings. Together they got a couple of days' leave, and spent it in the bars and *maisons closes* of Lille. There was a tattooist who worked out of one of the brothels they frequented, and Edouard had become friendly with him. One evening, all three were sharing a drink and the man offered to tattoo them for free. Edouard immediately agreed. This surprised Sabir, since Edouard, unlike almost all of the other enlisted men, had bourgeois manners and an accent to match. Even among the respectable working class, a tattoo marked you out as a thief, ruffian or sailor. Edouard opened his satchel, pulled out his notebook and quickly sketched out a flower in strong, clear lines. 'Here, let's see what you can do with that,' he said to the tattooist.

'Anyway, let's get this thing back over to the other side.'

They push the boat out into the water, paddle it to where Carpette's standing, with his arms crossed. 'Shit!' he mutters as he climbs clumsily into the boat. 'Little bastard told me it was five metres long. Lying little bastard!'

'I've seen worse,' Edouard replies.

The sun has dipped below the horizon and it's getting difficult to see as they paddle their way back towards the mouth of the creek. Yes, the boat's small enough, not too much bigger than a dinghy. Sabir didn't really notice that in the effort to get it up out of the water, when it had seemed so huge and unmanageable. It's a river boat, certainly not built for high winds and ocean waves. Sabir is pricked by a terrible doubt about the conventional wisdom of the old lags. Surely taking your chances through the jungle would be better than this.

'Looks sound enough, at least,' says Carpette after a long silence, more to persuade himself than anyone else, it seems. 'If the weather holds, we'll be all right.'

'And if it doesn't?' Sabir asks.

Edouard jumps in. 'If it doesn't, it'll all be over so quick you won't have time to think about it.'

Silence again. They paddle on for a minute or so before Carpette suddenly starts. 'Who's that with the boy? There's a man there!'

'Where?'

Say-Say's propped up where Sabir left him. Impossible to tell whether he's dead or alive. Crouched down beside him, against the luminescent horizon, is the shadow of a man.

'Turn around! Let's turn around!'

'No,' says Edouard. 'He'll have seen us anyway.'

They paddle closer. As they approach, Bonifacio moves away from the boy and climbs down towards the bank. Edouard has his hand to his pocket; Sabir too has his knife at the ready, but his hand is shaking and he knows he wouldn't be able to get it out in time.

'Ahoy there!' Bonifacio's tone is *faux*-jovial. The boat nudges at the bank and Bonifacio pulls at it as if to help them beach it. 'Fine-looking vessel you got there.'

'Leave it alone!' Edouard shouts. He jumps into the water, up to his knees.

'Easy, boys, easy, boys.'

'I said leave the boat alone!'

'Easy now.'

Bonifacio takes his hands off the boat with an exaggerated gesture. He and Edouard are facing each other in the shallow water, a couple of metres apart.

'Who are you? What're you doing here?'

'No need to get all aggressive about it.' Bonifacio points towards Sabir, who's still sitting in the boat with Carpette. 'Didn't your friend tell you who I am? He knows.'

It's too sombre to make out much of Bonifacio's face now, although Sabir can still see Carpette's, which is twisted into an astonished scowl. But he can feel Bonifacio's gaze penetrating and confusing him once again.

'Well?' says Edouard.

'He's . . . he's . . .' Sabir stutters to a halt.

'We been helping each other out, right?'

'Yeah . . . that's right.'

'Kipping down together, eating together . . . just like a married couple, isn't that so?'

'I know who you are,' says Carpette. 'You're the guy who killed a guard.'

Bonifacio ignores Carpette. 'And we became friends. Such damn good friends that he told me all about this little escapade. Asked me along, too. Wasn't too sure at first. Then I figured what the hell. So here I am!'

Sabir and Carpette climb out of the boat. Bonifacio has a big fake grin on his face. All four of them are standing in the water, but Carpette immediately moves to Edouard's side, leaving Sabir next to Bonifacio, as if two camps had formed.

'What makes you think you can just hitch a ride?' says Edouard. 'We all paid good money for this.'

'Fair point. Let's cut a deal right now, then.' Bonifacio pushes his hand into his pocket. Sabir tenses up, but all Bonifacio brings out is a wad of money. 'Lad here told me he paid two hundred. Sounds over the odds to me, but I'll play along. In fact, I'll throw in another hundred for you.'

'You're a guard killer. If we get caught . . .'

Bonifacio laughs. 'Oh, we won't get caught!'

The two-edged reply hangs in the air. Bonifacio makes a move over to Edouard and Carpette. Despite the fact that it's

Edouard who's done most of the talking, Bonifacio proffers the money to Carpette. 'Here, you divvy up.'

'Wait,' says Edouard. 'Leave us alone for a second. Go over there while we talk this over.'

Bonifacio freezes for a few seconds, as if affronted, then finally says: 'Sure. Anything you say. You're the boss.'

Edouard and Carpette get out of the water and huddle together. They don't invite Sabir over. Sabir moves to the bank as well and sits down on the ground, not far from Bonifacio, who says nothing to him, acts as if Sabir isn't even there. Furious whisperings from Edouard and Carpette. Sabir can imagine it easily enough: Carpette's tempted by the money; Edouard doesn't care about that and doesn't like the look of Bonifacio. Still, does he have any choice? Sabir inwardly shivers. If they don't accept Bonifacio, he doesn't quite know what'll happen, but there'll be some kind of bloodletting. Bonifacio will take Edouard by surprise – kill him quickly and impose his will on the rest of them. And kill Carpette, too. Or perhaps not: some kind of crew is necessary, Sabir supposes. For a moment, he thinks back to the killing of Masque in the barracks, and how petrified he was then. Now, it's quite different. He considers the various possibilities in a detached frame of mind, as if watching a performance or looking at a picture. The image of the woman on the boat comes back to him. He sees her tearful face again, and he realises that, in some way, he envies her tears.

'All right. We'll take the money.'

'Thought you'd see sense, boys.'

'Let's pack the supplies in the boat before it gets too dark.'

The storm has completely dissipated – almost as if it never happened at all. A still night now, not a breath of wind in the air;

stars creeping across the sky. The water, smooth as mercury, is dark silver under a glittering loop of moon. It's too perfect, this moon; it belongs to the world of fairy tales.

The boat's been made ready for the pre-dawn tidal run. It's too dangerous to light a fire, and the men sitting by Sabir have dissolved into dim half-presences under the moonlight. Bonifacio has a couple of bottles of rum with him. They're from the commandant's cellar, Sabir's pretty sure of it – where else would he have got hold of them? The nerve, risking the guillotine just to pinch rum from the commandant's house. It reinforces this feeling of Bonifacio being everything, every-where. He uncorks a bottle, shouts out: 'To the whores of Pigalle!' The forest replies with a ferocious silence. It's a minute before the usual assortment of insect hums, animal rustlings and monkey howls slowly fade back in.

'Here, have a swig.'

'No,' says Edouard, but Carpette grabs the bottle from Bonifacio and takes a long draught. Sabir too has his turn, the alcohol ripping through his empty stomach.

'Hey, stutterer, y-y-you want some t-t-t-oo?'

Say-Say shakes his head. He's looking better, the fever seems to have died down for the moment. He's no longer trembling, but seems just as wiped out and terrified.

'Well, I say you have some!'

Bonifacio seizes the back of the boy's head, tips the bottle down his throat until Say-Say's practically choking on it. He's trying to get us all dead drunk, thinks Sabir, so there's less chance of any of us attacking him in the night.

'That boat's no ocean liner,' says Bonifacio a little later on, once most of the first bottle has gone. 'I say we feed ourselves up now, so there's less to carry. We dump everything we don't need for the trip. Everything. We've all got plenty of dough now, boys, eh? We buy anything else once we get there . . . What do you need all that for?' He points to Edouard and the unwieldy bag he has slung over his shoulder. 'We're not moving house, for fuck's sake.'

'Bag stays with me.'

'What've you got in there?'

'That's my business.'

'And I say the bag goes!' Bonifacio thumps the bottle of rum down on the ground. 'No room for it. Look at the size of the boat. It's a damn thimble!'

'The bag stays with me. You don't like it, then *fuck* you!'

Edouard's uncharacteristic outburst slices through the febrile atmosphere. Carpette and Sabir are sitting between Edouard and Bonifacio – impossible to read anyone's face in the dim moonlight. Sabir watches the other men's hands, dares not make any movement with his own.

'Okay,' says Bonifacio finally. 'If that's the way you want it. It's your plan. Your escape. You're the boss.'

Carpette breaks open one of the barrels, hands out some biscuits and salted meat. The immediate tension has been defused, but a sullen silence reigns. As he chews at the meat, Sabir reflects on Bonifacio. He's struck once again by his sense of assurance in keeping his money in his pocket rather than in a *plan*. Bonifacio's no simpleton *fort-à-bras*; he uses anger coldly for a purpose. He's violent when he needs to be, conciliatory when it's to his advantage. He knows how to back off without losing face. Perhaps he was testing how far he could push Edouard – or he'd calculated his chances of leaping at Edouard's throat and decided against it. Edouard's wise not to get drunk like the rest of them. He knows well enough that they've exchanged one form of imprisonment for another.

As for Sabir, he's cushioned from the worst of the fear by

this feeling that it's all happening to someone else. As if he's looking down at himself from above. The confused thought strikes him as he drifts off into drink-induced stupor that, in any case, the various futures have already been lived out, played out, and all one can do is wearily continue along these set paths. Only the past remains obscure. It hasn't happened and perhaps it never will.

XI

The sky is still a wall of night, although the horizon's now tinged with the faintest of pre-dawn glimmers. Sabir's arms and face are sticky with blood – a cloud of mosquitoes descended upon them in the middle of the night, so thick it was even difficult to breathe. He sat up with the others, furiously smoking, in the hope it'd drive the insects away. His face is swollen and itching terribly.

Edouard climbs up from the bank. 'Tide's definitely running out. Should've left an hour ago.'

Slowly they nose the boat out into the grey river; then with a lurch it swings into the current. At this time of year, the river runs very fast with the tide and there's no need for paddling, just a little rudimentary steering. Edouard's at the helm, Say-Say lies curled up at the bottom of the boat. At one point Sabir and Bonifacio have to get out to push the boat off a mudbank, but it's the sole incident as they make their way easily down the river. Saint-Laurent and the other river camps are all upstream; there's nothing but Boni and Indian villages until the river mouth. The one disconcerting thing is how low the boat sits in the water; but for all Sabir knows about sailing, this might be quite normal. His mouth is dry, he's hungover and exhausted from lack of sleep and the mosquito attack. The others seem to be faring little better.

The long night felt not unlike the wait in the trench before an assault, when time slowed to an agonising crawl. In contrast, the run down the river feels as if it's over in a moment. The river widens, widens, quickens, until the current breaks into exhilarating waves as the tide speeds out. Then the flash of lights at the heads. The Galibi light to the left, on the Dutch side, the Hattes light on the French side. There's a camp at Les Hattes, probably a patrol boat too. But the *évadés* are relatively safe once they reach the heads. Even if they're spotted now, no patrol boat would chase them, because it'd get stranded in the open sea until the tide comes in again.

The boat skips over the tidal waves towards the black sky. It's not clear at which point they cross from river to open sea, but gradually, over a period of twenty minutes, the boat slows until finally there's just a steady lap of water against the bows – no more waves, no strong current. The lights are well behind them now, indistinguishable from the stars.

'All right, let's hoist the sail.'

Edouard keeps the helm while Carpette and Sabir try to raise the mast. It proves surprisingly difficult. It's still dark, and there must be a technique to standing up in a boat, but neither of the men have it and both nearly fall overboard over the next half-hour. Eventually they manage to get the mast upright, steadying it with planks of wood and the thick twisted vine the Bonis use for rigging. It doesn't look too secure, but Sabir gives it a few good knocks and it refuses to budge. The sail goes up, billowing in the gentle wind.

'It's a southeasterly; that's good,' says Edouard. 'The star on the horizon. It's the North Star. We have to steer to the left of that.'

Bonifacio gives Say-Say a kick. 'Hey, time to earn your passage.'

Say-Say writhes at the bottom of the hold and moans: 'C-c-c-can't. Too sick.'

'I'll stay at the tiller,' says Edouard. 'It's easy going for now. The boy can take it when it gets rougher.'

Dawn breaks slowly. A monstrous sun rises up from under the ocean, and the switch from night to day feels like exchanging one world for another. It's perfectly clear weather, the sea preternaturally calm. Behind them, the faint green line of jungle; ahead, a vast canvas of blue.

'We've got to clear the coast,' says Bonifacio. 'I say take it straight out, then steer north-west.'

'No. It'll be faster with the wind directly behind us. We'll be out of sight of the coast in an hour.'

Everyone except Edouard lies back in the boat for a while, worn out by the night, by the flight up the river, the hoisting of the mast, the grinding tension of it all. Somehow, Sabir has managed to get soaking wet and he's enjoying simply lying there in the dawn sun, drying off, recovering from his hangover. The sea salt seems to have soothed the mosquito bites, and brought down the swelling as well. For once, there's nothing to do, nothing he *can* do. It's the first time he's actually taken pleasure from the sun since arriving in the Colony, and the sensation brings forth a confused matrix of memories. A beach holiday with relatives in Normandy, just after his mother died, and the faint recollection of building walls of sand against the tide. Then another holiday, many years later, with his fiancée – the taste of salt on his lips now evokes an acutely physical memory of sex and the smell of sea on his fiancée's body. All this in turn bleeds into the photo of the commandant's wife at the seaside – he watches the seductive sway of her hips as she saunters along the sand towards him, smiling. And now he sees her again, this time in the patrol boat on the river. Older, sadder, bowed by the mystery of tragedy. He realises he prefers her that way and once again feels the blue of her eyes piercing him. The memory of the experience is even more intense than the experience itself, and he has to force himself back to the reality of the ocean, the boat, the four people he's sharing it with.

Out of the corner of his eye, he sees Carpette grappling with one of the supply barrels. He extracts a small stove from it, which he lights with some difficulty. The seawater will soon get into everything, Sabir reflects, and how then will they keep the matches dry? Carpette's brewing some tea – its fresh bitter-sweetness fills the air, mingling with the ocean's salt smell.

'Tea up!'

The others prop themselves upright as Carpette pours the tea into stolen tin cups. It's strong, revitalising, thirst-quenching. Under the tension of the first hour of the escape, Sabir didn't realise how dehydrated he was. How stupid to have got drunk the night before, when water supplies will be so strictly rationed. And why didn't he think to drink a litre or two before leaving the freshwater creek?

The tea has visibly lifted everyone's spirits, though, and a manic euphoria invades the boat. 'We're on our way!' Bonifacio crows. 'We've left that shithole for good!' He breaks into song – a pre-war music-hall melody. Soon everyone's singing along except Edouard, who's still at the tiller, quietly sipping at his tea and staring into the blankness of the ocean. Even Say-Say looks on the way to recovery, and that makes Sabir feel relieved. The euphoria is infectious – mad images jump into Sabir's mind. What was that thought about all futures having already been played out? It's exactly the opposite he's feeling now.

What before was a narrow tunnel with its single exit into the dark now seems more like a sunlit field, with different prospects on every horizon.

At one point, Bonifacio notices that Edouard isn't singing. 'What's up with you, then?' he asks. 'Lost your voice?'

There's viciousness in Bonifacio's tone, as if he's deliberately trying to pick a fight. At first Edouard appears not to hear, and continues staring out at the horizon. Then he replies: 'There's a long way to go yet.'

'What? On an ocean like this, perfect breeze behind us, perfect weather, provisions for a couple of weeks? Couldn't have had it better if the governor himself had planned it!'

'We've got at least another ten days. Plenty of time to get becalmed, sunk in a storm, get lost, picked up . . . it's a bit early for celebrations.'

'Killjoy,' Bonifacio mutters. He now turns to Say-Say, gives him another kick. 'You're an ugly p-p-p-prick, aren't you? Bet you never had a woman in your life. Get us across the ocean in one piece, and I'll buy you the most expensive girl in the best brothel in Colombia. How's that sound?'

Say-Say mumbles something inaudible, crawls back to the bottom of the boat. The singing's over, the elation of a few moments ago dissipates into silence as the hangovers take hold again. The sun's risen well up over the horizon now. Edouard's got his spare shirt wrapped around his head, turban-style. Sabir does the same, and unrolls his shirtsleeves as well. His arms are already burnt – it's the sun's reflection on the water, which seems to double its strength and deadliness. Now he lies back down again. High in the sky, a bird circles about directly above them. Probably a bird of prey: the wingspan's too big for a gull. Sabir tries to imagine what the boat looks like from so high up – a speck of human society afloat in the blue.

Minutes, hours pass in silence and immobility, each man occasionally shifting around to get more comfortable or find some shade from the sail. No one offers to take the tiller from Edouard, nor does he ask anyone to do so. For a long time, Sabir can't stop himself staring intently at some tiny detail of the boat, and completely losing himself in it – a notch on the mast, or the letter 'A' printed upside down on one of the flour sacks-cum-sails. If you stare long and hard enough at any particular spot, he learnt long ago in a prison cell, then it starts to move. It's as if the power of concentration can bring anything to life, even a splotch of dirt on the hull. Sabir's mind wanders disjointedly from one thought or image to the next. Memories ... Stay still for long enough, deprive your brain of stimulation for long enough, and they'll always assault you. Faces from the past, people you haven't thought of in months or years, some still alive, but most dead. Men from the prisons, men from the trenches, they all crowd together in the theatre of Sabir's mind. Strange how you can forget names, forget almost everything about a person, but somehow the face remains.

'So you were the commandant's gardener, then?'

Edouard's question crashes through Sabir's reflections, and it takes him a moment to collect himself and reply: 'Yeah. I was.'

'What in God's name was he growing down there?'

'We hadn't planted the beds yet. He's brought seed over from France. Seedlings, too. He was getting them from Martinique.'

Edouard makes an indistinct, disapproving noise, then lapses into silence. The commandant and his garden already seem like another world – further away, more alien than the war comrades and prison acquaintances who invaded Sabir's mind moments before.

Ten minutes later, Edouard abruptly continues, as though

he's been ruminating on the subject all this time: 'Doubt if he'll have any luck with seed from France, though. Why didn't he go to the botanical gardens? Why bother with Martinique when we cross-breed quite a few European varieties for this climate, right in Saint-Laurent?'

'I just did what he told me. I don't know anything about plants. He's got the money to do what he wants, I suppose. He even shipped crates of orchids in from Florida.'

Edouard snorts. 'The idiot wants to import orchids from America when the forest is awash with them!'

Another long silence, then another question: 'So what did you do with the orchids?'

'Most of them were dead.'

'Most of them would be, though. Buyers are warned of that.'

'Well, I didn't know that. I threw the lot away in the end.'

Edouard chuckles, says: 'You did the right thing, though! The rest would have died anyway. Even in the botanical gardens, even with the indigenous species, I had the devil of a time keeping the buggers alive.'

Carpette's been listening in with barely disguised jealousy; he now moves over to where Edouard's sitting and whispers something in his ear. But Bonifacio shouts out: 'Hey! We're all in this together. No secrets, no whispering.'

After that, silence sets in, as everyone muses on Bonifacio's warning. No whispering – yes, it's easy enough to see why. Whispering means conspiracy. Once two or more people have taken against someone, it's not hard to push that person overboard. So, from now on, all relations will have to be public. It's a new constraint that not even the penal colony could have enforced. Life on board is not life in the Colony, Sabir muses, nor is it the life of free men. Rather, it's a limbo, a closed world with its own rules and strategies.

Sabir mentally reviews what he knows of each man, tries to get a feel for their motivations. There's Bonifacio. It's difficult to know what to think of Bonifacio. He's tactically ceded some authority to Edouard, but Sabir can see well enough that Edouard has rubbed him up the wrong way, and that ultimately he'll react. If Sabir could take Edouard aside, he'd tell him that it'd be far safer to let Bonifacio take the lead now. After all, once they get to Colombia, or maybe even Trinidad, they'll be free to go their separate ways.

In Belgium too, Sabir recalls, Edouard always provoked this kind of reaction among those in authority, or those who aspired to it. Officers invariably disliked him; he was as reckless with their commands as he was with his own life. Often enough he disobeyed orders, but in a way which showed them up as absurd, making the insubordination difficult to punish. Sabir remembers an incident in which an officer received a bullet wound to the wrist. At first he claimed that Edouard had shot him in a heated argument, and Edouard was briefly detained. The following day, however, the officer withdrew the claim and reported the wound as a self-inflicted accident. Edouard never told Sabir what had really happened. In fact, it was rare for him ever to say too much about himself. And what he did say usually came out in enigmatic dribs and drabs. Edouard was something of a cold fish – yet Sabir can't help feeling that the black jokes, the ironies, the insouciance in the face of death, they were all a front. For what, he's at a loss to say. Some sort of passion. In certain ways, it strikes him now, Edouard is like the commandant.

Then there's Carpette. He's followed on from his position as barracks keeper to take charge of food and drink on the boat, that's his role. Sabir's wary of him now. Judging from the occasional hostile glance, it seems that Carpette has taken against him. Because of his conversations with Edouard, but also because it was his fault that Bonifacio's on board. In turn, Sabir feels a certain anger towards Carpette, which at first he finds difficult to explain to himself. But as the day wears on, it occurs to him that the boat is not unlike a trench, with its confined space and its tedium. Because of this, his wartime relationship with Edouard feels resuscitated, as if they're still the paired-off comrades-in-arms – or *époux*, to use the trench argot of the time. It's jealousy he's feeling.

Which leaves Say-Say, lying sick at the bottom of the boat, although no longer shaking with fever. The navigator. Who is this frightened boy? Arriving in the barracks, and eager to impress, he boasted about his full *plan*. There's his stutter that comes and goes. Sabir, too, once had a mild stutter. It largely disappeared at puberty, materialising only occasionally at moments of high stress. But then in Belgium, in the trenches, it vanished altogether, never to return.

Carpette, Edouard, Say-Say, Paris, Belgium . . . thoughts follow ever-meandering paths, bifurcating, dwindling away until there's nothing left but a mental daze. By the afternoon, it's searingly hot, and difficult to think clearly about anything. Sabir opens his eyes occasionally and is struck by the over-whelming blueness. Never has the world seemed so simple, so bare. Boat, sea, sky, sun, horizon. A few other men, like fractured reflections of oneself. A light so strong it's almost disintegrating. World without adjectives – except hot, hot, hot.

At some point, Carpette hands out some dried meat and stale bread, together with a ration of water – refreshing, but it doesn't kill off Sabir's thirst, which he realises will remain with him until they reach Trinidad. Say-Say gets up briefly to relieve himself over the side of the boat and very nearly falls in. The laughter on board has a sun-struck, hysterical edge to it. Every time someone gets up, there's a fear that he'll fall overboard, or even capsize the boat.

Soon after, the sky opens up. For a while they sit there enjoying the rainwater washing away the salt that's dried out their skin and worsened the effect of the sunburn. Carpette takes off the top of the urn to catch as much of the water as possible; Sabir gulps down whatever he can cup in his hands. The heavy lash of tropical rains mingles with the monotonous sounds of the sea to mesmerising effect. At the same time, the ferocity of the deluge is disturbing. The bottom of the boat starts to fill with water, and they spend the next hour bailing out as best they can.

Abruptly the rain stops and, a quarter of an hour later, the clouds clear. The giant sun has sunk low in the sky – night's not far off. Where did the day disappear to? The escape down the river feels like either a moment ago, or a lifetime ago. Sabir looks over to Edouard. He's been at the tiller from the very beginning, for more than twelve hours. Sabir can see the tension running down Edouard's arm, the muscles and tendons prominent. His hand is raw and cracked from the salt and sun, his face set like a mask.

'Here, let me take it for a while,' says Sabir. But Carpette heads him off and grabs the tiller from Edouard.

'On the horizon,' directs Edouard, 'the North Star. Steer to the left of it.'

There's not enough time to dry off properly before the sun goes down, and Sabir's sodden clothes stick to his body uncomfortably. Day and night overlap each other briefly as stars prick against the orange sky, but the dark soon smothers all colour. It's a relief to be able to relax one's eyes: only now does Sabir realise that he's been squinting against the sunlight all day and that's why his face muscles hurt. The men settle in for the night; Sabir lies down, too. Again, the confusion of thoughts, from which he wishes more than ever that there could be some escape. But he finds it impossible to doze for more than a few minutes at a time, despite his exhaustion from the sun.

Edouard's still sitting up, unable to unwind after the gruelling day at the tiller. His and Sabir's eyes meet briefly under the starlight. Edouard's expression is surprisingly probing, and yet he says nothing. The image of the rosebush Edouard grew behind the lines in Belgium returns to Sabir. In his mind's eye, he sees the red violence of the rosebuds as they burst open like exit wounds. Later, when the time's right, he'll ask Edouard about that rosebush.

Bonifacio's making a snuffling sound that might be a snore. Now would be the moment to dispose of him. He and Edouard could manage it, although there'd always be the risk of capsizing. Then again, why kill him now? Better to let things ride and see if they can get to Trinidad in one piece. Nevertheless, Sabir can't help wondering about it, fantasising about it, picking over his own impotence in the matter. Stare up at the sky instead, with its billion peepholes. For a second or two, a shooting star flits across his field of vision. With its silver filament against the night, it looks like ordnance sailing over the trenches. Shooting stars – good luck or bad luck? Sabir can't remember. The moon's rising at a near-visible pace and is now almost directly above him. A gaping white hole punched through the blackness. The moonlight feels almost dazzling and Sabir makes an involuntary move with his hand as if to shade his eyes from it.

At one point Sabir finds himself mentally humming something that's both familiar and unfamiliar. It takes him a moment to work out what it is: one of those German songs the commandant used to play. Sabir resists the difficulty of the melody – so different from the music-hall tunes he's used to – but is drawn into it at the same time. Impossible to tell if it's a happy piece of music or a sad one, since it sounds so alien to him. He remembers now how the commandant said that it was one of his wife's favourites.

He imagines the commandant's wife as she disembarks at the pier near the house for the first time. Puzzlement: something not quite right but she can't think what it is. As the commandant takes her on a tour of the gardens, it slowly dawns on her. The house is an exact copy of her family estate, back home in France. There's the lawn where they used to have English-style tea parties in the summer. The tree by the river that she used to sit under, reading her book. And the folly. Where she and her cousin used to meet, where once she tried to seduce him and he refused her. It's all the same, and yet not the same. Decay has set in. It's like an old memory that becomes distorted in a nightmare. The lawn is brown, looks as if it's dying. The windows lack panes of glass. The orchid nursery has no plants in it. And the folly . . .

The commandant leads her upstairs to the bedroom, the one with the photo of her old house on the bedside table. He wants to have sex immediately; she submits. She undresses without ceremony; it's a relief to be naked in this heat. She can see that the commandant's a little afraid of her nudity. The sex is desperate, mechanical. It's their first time – she refused after the wedding, refused until they were safely out of France. Everything is over quickly enough. No trace of blood on the damp, starched sheets; the commandant has noticed it, but says nothing.

Sabir's eyes are full of the stars, and it's almost as if the boat and the ocean aren't there at all. He hears some noise behind him and turns his head; it takes him a few seconds to focus. It's the tiller, knocking against the side of the boat. Carpette has his head in his arms; he's fallen asleep. The boat's slowly turning around on itself.

'The tiller, the tiller!'

Carpette rouses himself, grabs at the tiller. Edouard and Bonifacio are awake now.

'Here, why don't you let me take it for a while?' says Sabir.

'I'm all right. I'm all right,' replies Carpette angrily, as though Sabir has been deliberately trying to humiliate him. The men settle back down. Sabir wonders how long they have been drifting like that. One hour? Eight hours? Impossible to tell in this timeless night. Impossible to do anything except let one's mind stray from thought to memory to dream and back again.

Bonifacio's voice emerging from the dark, sometime later: 'What's that? Can you hear it?'

Sabir rouses himself from a light doze. Yes, he can hear it, too. A muffled rumbling sound, coming from far away.

'Thunder,' says Edouard.

'Don't think so; sounds too regular,' replies Bonifacio. 'Boat engine maybe. A steamer.'

'No, it's thunder.'

'How could it be? There are stars up there.'

Edouard gives a derisory snort. 'Shows how much *you* know about the sea. We could be minutes from a storm.'

Edouard sounds so certain that Bonifacio doesn't bother to reply. They sit there motionless in the boat, straining to hear the sound again. A cold, heavy dew has settled, and everything in the boat is wet and slimy to the touch. After a while, the rumbling loses its faraway tone and the sea starts to swell. There's a minute or two when one might still pretend it's nothing, just one of those random stirrings you can get on the calmest of seas. But soon enough it's clear that they're on the edge of a storm. And all the time, the rumbling's gaining in intensity, louder, louder.

'That's it – we're in the rollers!'

Bonifacio barks to Say-Say: 'Hey, sailor boy! Take the helm!'

'I'm . . . I'm too sick.'

Bonifacio gives him a violent kick and shouts: 'You got a free ride 'cause you're the navigator. So get up and fucking navigate! Take the helm, I tell you!'

'I . . . I . . . c-c-c-can't,' the boy whimpers. He's cowering in a foetal position, his hands over his head.

Edouard intervenes. 'No time for this. I'll take it; I've been sailing in my time.'

There's a stiff breeze now and a light rain has settled in. The boat skips over the waves at a fair pace but Edouard seems to be in control. The trouble is that at this speed quite a lot of water's sloshing in over the side and Carpette, Bonifacio and Sabir bail furiously. The situation remains constant for quite some time – although Sabir can already feel nerves slowly shredding, beginning to go. Just when it seems that it can get no worse, the swell rises vertiginously. And then the big waves come.

'Sail down, sail down!'

A gust has ripped through the sails; Sabir struggles against the wind to try and get what's left down. As he's balancing himself on the rigging, the boat knifes its way across another incoming wave. The bows spank down hard in the trough with a violence that sends Sabir crashing against the mast. Dazed, he sits down again, tries to regain his equilibrium. He puts his hand to his head: a little blood, he's gashed his forehead. But without the mast he might easily have been swept overboard.

Between the waves everyone's desperately bailing. The mast's still standing but the sails are lifeless rags, flapping in the gale. At one point Sabir hears someone mutter 'This is it,' and he turns round: from the starboard side, a mountain of water surges forward. Amazingly high up, its crest is trimmed with a lace-like froth. The wave takes an interminable time coming, then seems to pause above the boat. Sabir has the time to think 'Has it hit yet?' at least a couple of times before it finally crashes over them with a force that knocks the wind out of him. An otherworldly moment of underwater silence: Sabir wonders whether he's still on board or not. Then he surfaces to shouts, a confusion of bodies, barrels, rain and the ocean still washing over the boat. He's gasping for breath, floundering like a landed fish. And he sees Edouard, coldly handsome, still clinging to the tiller, yelling: 'Bail, bail, bail, bail!'

One of the barrels is open – Sabir grabs it, empties it to use as a bucket. Frantic bailing: every few minutes a new wave breaks over the boat, although none as big as the giant that somehow didn't sink them. As each wave washes over, Sabir puts his head down and hunches his shoulders to protect himself. He's struck by a sense of *déjà vu*: he realises it's the same posture he used to take as a soldier when walking into gunfire. Head down, shoulders hunched. Always walk *slowly* towards enemy lines once you've gone over the top, the officers would insist, never run. If you ran ahead, you were likely to be shot by your own side. How difficult it was to walk *slowly* through no-man's-land, though.

He hears Edouard's voice: 'I think we've passed the last line of them . . .'

They're back into the normal swell – still large, but not threatening if they bail fast enough. It's getting light by the time they've got most of the water out. There's another five or six centimetres in the bottom, but that's it, they're out of danger for the moment. Sabir collapses, exhausted. Silence for a good half an hour, save the slap of water against the bows. Barrels, tins, other bits and pieces from the supplies bob about in the bottom of the boat. Bonifacio, Carpette, Edouard, Say-Say, they all now lie about haphazardly, like the morning after a debauched party. All there, no one overboard.

The new day brings a desolate calm – the ocean has returned to the glassy flatness of the morning before. Someone stirs. It's Carpette, salvaging what he can of the supplies. A little later, Bonifacio raises himself as well. 'Made it by a miracle,' he says. 'And no help from this *cunt*!' Bonifacio gives a massive kick to Say-Say's prostrate form. Say-Say's body quivers with the shock. Bonifacio lies back down again; the effort's exhausted him.

The sun, the sun: a new punishment after the events of the night. No cover from it, no sail. Sabir looks about for his cloth bag, but it doesn't seem to be anywhere, it must have been washed overboard. Miraculously, Edouard still has his big bag hoisted over his shoulder.

'Only one thing to do now,' Edouard says. 'We tack south till we hit land. We're probably only a day away.'

That means Dutch or British Guiana. Neither is safe. No one replies. An air of despondent lethargy hangs over the boat. Only Carpette is active, fussing about with what's left of the supplies. At some point he remarks: 'Water urn survived. But I think some seawater's got in.'

'Is it drinkable?' asks Edouard.

Carpette takes a sip, grimaces. 'Maybe if I stick some condensed milk in.'

'That settles it. We've got to make for land.'

'How are we going to do that?' says Bonifacio, with a gesture of the hand that takes in all the devastation of the boat.

Amazingly, the mast is still upright, but the sails are gone. The tiller hangs limply in the stern: the rudder's been shorn off.

'There's a little wind,' replies Edouard as he takes off his shirt. 'We'll have to use our shirts for sails. I'll see what I can do about the rudder.'

Sabir takes charge of securing the shirts to the mast. Not very effective, but enough to inch the boat forward. In the meantime, Edouard's fiddling with the tiller, trying to attach a paddle to act as a rudder.

'It'll only work if it stays this calm,' says Bonifacio.

Edouard shrugs. 'At least let's bail out the rest of the water. To lighten the load.'

But no one moves to do it. Under the sun, it requires just too much energy.

Bonifacio says: 'I know one way to lighten the load. We toss this lump of shit to the sharks.' He delivers another powerful kick to Say-Say's body. Say-Say squeals in pain. 'Why didn't you get up and navigate? What the fuck did you think you were getting a free ride for?'

'I'm sorry... I'm sorry...'

'Could've killed us all.' Bonifacio leans down, starts shaking Say-Say by the shoulders. 'Answer me, answer me!'

'D-d-d-don't know anything about boats. I lied. I'm sorry... I'm sorry...'

'*Fuck!*' Bonifacio spits out the word as if it were a physical obstruction. Then he sits back. 'You've just signed your death warrant.'

'Had-had to get out of camp. He-he was going to kill me. I'm sorry... I'm sorry...'

Say-Say's seized with some sort of convulsion, whether from terror or fever, it's hard to tell. Out of nowhere a knife has appeared in Bonifacio's hand. Sabir somehow finds his voice and speaks up. 'Leave the boy alone. Can't you see he's sick?'

Say-Say looks to Sabir, points to him with his shaking hand, starts shouting in a disturbed, high-pitched scream: 'You did it! Your fault! I'd changed my mind. I wanted to go back to camp. You wouldn't let me. You bastard!'

He continues in this vein for a while, his words increasingly incoherent, then he launches himself at Sabir, punching him uselessly in the chest. Taken by surprise, Sabir's slow to respond – the two wrestle for a while before collapsing to the bottom of the boat, entwined like exhausted lovers. The boat rocks dangerously.

Edouard steps in. 'What's done is done. The main thing is to get this boat to shore.'

'I want him off the boat,' replies Bonifacio.

'No one's kicking anyone off the boat.'

Sabir has managed to pull himself away from Say-Say, who's dissolved into tears. He catches a split-second glance from Edouard that's hard to interpret – there's something about his glass eye which makes his face unreadable, volatile.

'Listen, we've all got knives here,' says Edouard to Bonifacio; 'there's no point in knifeplay. We'll all end in the water.'

Bonifacio stares at him for a moment, then suddenly sits down in the bows, overwhelmed by the sun.

'Just get us to shore.'

XII

Not long after, they sight the low green line on the horizon. The storm must have pushed them much closer to the land than Edouard had realised. There's no time to feel relief, though, since the boat has sprung a leak and everyone except Edouard at the tiller is bailing like crazy. Carpette's cursing the Boni who sold him the boat: 'Never would have got us to Trinidad anyway. Never would have got us to Trinidad anyway.' He repeats the phrase over and over again, with exactly the same intonation, until Bonifacio finally shouts: 'Shut it, for God's sake!'

Closer to land a wind begins to blow; minutes later, they're riding the offshore swells. Ahead, a beach, but no easy way to guide the boat in. Edouard heads it blindly into the surf and it shoots up through the breaking rollers. A final wave dumps them on the sand with a loud crack. Hauling the boat out of the water takes the last of Sabir's strength and he flops down on the beach.

Bonifacio has grabbed hold of Say-Say by the shoulders. 'I don't know why I don't kill you. Maybe it's 'cause I don't like to kill young boys.' He fixes Say-Say with his stare that's so hard to pull away from, then points towards the palm trees which border the beach. 'Get going before I change my mind.'

Bonifacio has his knife in his hand again. Say-Say moves slowly away, up the beach, head hanging low like a punished schoolboy, feet dragging against the sand. Edouard's clearly too tired to remonstrate – for the first time since the riverbank, Bonifacio has managed to impose his will without challenge. Sabir watches as Say-Say disappears into the coastal jungle. No one says a word, and for the moment Sabir has no energy to think about anything, either.

It's sometime in the early afternoon. The men sit and lie about in a daze at the water's edge. Sabir's skin has started to blister; he should look for shade but he's too tired for it. At some point Edouard gets up and starts tinkering with the boat. He's gone awhile but eventually returns to sit with the other three. 'The bows are split. The boat's had it, that's for sure.'

'Where do you think we are?'

'Dutch Guiana. At a pinch, British Guiana.'

Bonifacio shakes his head. 'Christ's sake. We'd have done better just crossing over the river.'

'Well, we can't set sail in that boat again. No way of repairing it. We'll have to continue on foot.'

'We'd better head north,' says Bonifacio. 'If we're in British Guiana and we can make it to Georgetown, I know someone there. Maybe we can get a boat. If we've landed too low, we'll have to try Paramaribo.'

'You're right. North's our best bet. Do we all agree?'

Sabir mumbles something, Carpette just sits there without saying a word.

'What about supplies?'

Now Carpette rouses himself and replies in a flat tone: 'Sack of condensed milk tins. Another sack of tapioca, but it's wet through. If we spread it out to dry, it might be all right.'

'That's it?'

'Few onions. We lost the meat and rice. Stove, water urn, cups survived. Everything else went overboard.'

The bad news sinks in. They sit listening to the crashing waves and the cry of the gulls. 'I say we stay the night on the beach,' Edouard says. 'We're in no state to move on now.'

No replies, but no desire to move. At some point in the afternoon, Sabir manages to raise himself and get his shirt off the mast. It's ripped but still wearable, painful to slip over his blistered, sunburnt skin. He moves up from the water's edge to lie under the palms. He's feeling weak and finds himself shaking a little – he wonders whether it's fever. That could be a death sentence in present circumstances. But maybe it's just a delayed reaction to the events of the night. He finds himself thinking about Edouard again, and how he turned out to be so proficient at the tiller. Sabir can't remember his ever mentioning sailing to him. His family's from the Ardennes, nowhere near the coast.

On top of the blisters, Sabir notices a dark purple bruise on his chest. From when Say-Say assaulted him on the boat. A shiver of guilt runs through him. He sees now that he'd already sensed Say-Say's secret. Already at the hospital he'd realised Say-Say knew nothing about boats. Somehow Sabir managed to put this realisation aside and not act on it. He's at a loss to explain it to himself. But perhaps Say-Say will be lucky, and find his way to a settlement where someone will take pity on him. It's out of Sabir's hands now.

At some stage he falls into a deep, dreamless sleep, awaking only when the four o'clock rain crashes out of the sky. Sabir waits it out huddled under a palm tree, cupping his hands for rainwater. The deluge stops after twenty minutes; in another twenty minutes he's dry again. Sabir gets up gingerly, both refreshed from the sleep and weak from thirst and hunger. The sun hovers low at the edge of the forest. On the beach, someone's breaking up the boat for firewood – Carpette, judging by his silhouette. Bonifacio and Edouard are over by some rocks in the distance. It's hard to see what they're up to. Sabir stays put, not wanting to talk to Carpette, and only moves down when he sees the other men walking back.

Edouard has a barrel with him. 'Crabs. Size of your hand. We can toss them on the fire.'

Carpette's pouring water from the battered water urn. He hands a cup to Bonifacio, who takes a swig then spits half of it out. 'Disgusting.'

'It's that or nothing.'

'Should have tried for some run-off from the rain.'

'What could I catch it in?'

'There'll be creeks along the coast,' says Edouard, 'once we get started.' He's busy trying to get the fire going, using a method Sabir's not seen before: rubbing a pointed stick into a piece of thick bark, surrounded by dry weeds. Smoke soon rises from the bark and Edouard starts to blow hard on it. The whole process is astonishingly quick, as if Edouard's been doing this all his life. Where on earth did he learn that?

The dinner of fresh crabs and condensed milk revitalises everyone. 'Better than that shit they served up in Saint-Laurent,' remarks Bonifacio. It's not really enough to eat, though, and there's the nagging thirst that'll be unbearable under the sun. Already, Sabir's finding it difficult to swallow. At least back in camp the river provided an endless water supply. He thinks back to the days he spent gazing into the Maroni, fascinated at the way every cloud and patch of light was perfectly mirrored in the river, so that it no longer looked like a reflection, but the thing itself.

The sun over the ocean wakes Sabir. The sand's littered with crab shells, empty tins, the remains of last night's dinner. In the ruins of the fire he can still distinguish the burnt-out shape of the boat's bows. Bonifacio is sitting up, facing the jungle, staring up along the beach. Edouard and Carpette are nowhere to be seen. Sabir follows Bonifacio's gaze: in the distance, some-one's hobbling towards them. As the person draws closer, Sabir's shocked to see it's Say-Say. When he's about thirty paces away, he stops, then shouts out: 'Everywhere back there is flood-ed. I can't get through. There's no way through.'

Bonifacio gets up and walks slowly towards him. Say-Say just stands there, frozen. He's shirtless, his shoulders red raw, ribcage visible. His feet and calves covered in scabs and scratches. He's so weak, thinks Sabir, it probably took his last strength to get back here. And he knows there's no point in running. Bonifacio stops a metre or so in front of Say-Say. The two face each other, motionless, wordless. It's as if they're about to shake hands. Sabir can't see Bonifacio's face, but Say-Say's is animated by a hopeless resignation. The scene seems almost intimate.

It's over in a second. Bonifacio leaps forward, Say-Say falls noiselessly to the sand. His body shudders, quivers for an instant and then is still. It takes Sabir a few moments to under-stand what's happened. Only when he sees the blood leaking out from the neck onto the sand does he realise that Say-Say hasn't simply fallen or been pushed over. Bonifacio gives the body a short kick to check for life, then rolls it over onto its side.

Sabir spots Edouard and Carpette, up by the palm trees where he'd slept the day before. Looks as if they've witnessed the whole thing. By now Bonifacio's dragged Say-Say's body by the feet down to the edge of the water. The tide and the sharks will take it later. He strolls calmly back to the fireplace, sits down and busies himself cleaning his knife with a bit of old rag he's found somewhere. All done with the practised ease of a local butcher. What's just happened seems so matter-of-fact, so banal, that it leaves Sabir numb, unable to think, feel or imagine.

A little later, Edouard and Carpette come back down. There's a shocked, dismal silence as Carpette divides up what's left of the supplies: a few tins of condensed milk and a couple of onions each, plus some tapioca that's been drying out on the beach. Sabir's waiting for Edouard to say something about Say-Say, or even for a fight to break out. But nothing happens, nothing's said. Edouard's very subdued, his mind elsewhere.

It's Bonifacio who finally breaks the weird silence. 'Better get going.' The men set off up the beach, stopping briefly at the rocks where Edouard and Bonifacio had caught the crabs. They poke about in the rock pools, but there's nothing there – must be the wrong time of day. Beyond the rocks there's an expanse of sand that takes an hour or two to trudge along. The men spread out along the beach, no one keeping anyone company. The blank numbness hasn't left Sabir.

Half-thoughts flicker on and off in his mind, rarely finding their focus. There's his raging sore throat, brought on by thirst. There's Say-Say's death. He can form no real feeling about it. So different from the murder of Masque, who was killed away from view, in the privy. How easy it is to conjure up the horror of the unseen.

And yet few convicts would complain about Bonifacio's sense of justice. By saying he knew how to sail a boat, Say-Say endangered all their lives. Without Edouard's skill at the helm they'd be dead now. But it was Sabir who insisted that Say-Say come along. He wouldn't have survived long in camp anyway, Sabir reasons now. The boy would've died, one way or the other. There was a terrible inevitability about it. He knew boys like that at the front, saw it in their faces. Sabir feels a moistness in his puffed-up eyes. A childhood image returns to him: his mother waiting for him one day after school, with a bag of sweets from the *boulangerie*. He'll find out Say-Say's real name, he thinks to himself, he'll write to his mother, tell her that her son hadn't suffered. Tell her beautiful lies.

The beach dissolves into messy mangrove swamps, and they're forced to move inland to avoid them. It's just as Say-Say said: there are flooded savannahs everywhere, and it's almost impossible to plot a course through them. For a while you plod along with the mud and water at your ankles, then suddenly you find you're up to your waist in it. And the only way out is the way you came in. They tramp all day without stopping, hoping to cross the swamps before nightfall. But by late afternoon there's no sign of an end to them. Edouard spots a triangle of dry ground and they decide to stop there for the night. There's just enough time to build a little lean-to before the afternoon rains come down: they stand with their hands cupped and open mouths pointed to the sky. After the deluge, they take off their clothes and wring them over the tin cups for drinking water.

They're on a little island in the swamps, with nothing to use for firewood. Edouard has tried to get a fire going with mangrove roots, but with no success. And without the smoke, there's no avoiding the thick clouds of swamp mosquitoes. Dinner is a few sips of condensed milk, half an onion, some salty tapioca that simply aggravates the thirst.

At dusk, the swamp suddenly comes alive with all sorts of

birdlife. Hundreds, maybe even thousands of them, blackening the skies and paddling among the mangroves, raucously calling to each other like boys in a playground. Edouard tries half-heartedly to hit an ibis with a rock: it looks their way briefly, not in the least scared or interested in them. If only they had a gun . . . As the sun sinks below the horizon, the birds disappear as suddenly as they came.

'How far do you think we got today?' Bonifacio asks Edouard.

'Don't know. With all the going backwards and forwards. Four kilometres along the beach maybe, one or two through the swamps.'

A terrible day, and just a paltry few kilometres on. Everyone's too depressed to talk, which is probably just as well, since the resentment in the air is palpable. They sit there picking the leeches off their bodies. The mosquitoes are intolerable. Sabir takes handfuls of mud to smear over his face, arms, legs, but it does little good, and the stink is so great that he finds it hard to sleep.

At dawn they break camp. They're in a horribly exhausted state, and yet no one wants to stay a moment longer in this pest-infested swamp. The going is slightly better than the day before, and after an hour they catch a glimpse of the ocean. How abstract and pure it looks, after this interminable mess of mud, sludge, roots, insects. They swing sharply to the left, away from the ocean. The idea is that if they head directly inland, they'll eventually clear the coastal swamps and get to dry land.

The slog is mesmerising; Sabir's mind drifts off. He's back in Belgium. Wading through the mud of no-man's-land. There was that one dreadful autumn of lashing rain and sleet, when it felt as if the whole of Flanders was an oozing mire. When it wasn't so uncommon to come across men drowned in their foxholes. And the constant flooding of the trenches – they even had to bring over engineers from England to build new drainage systems. Until now, crossing no-man's-land to get to the enemy lines was something he'd never been able to recall. In the trenches before the assault, yes. In the trenches after the assault, yes. But the actual crossing . . . Only now, on the boat and here in this swamp, has that feeling returned to him with the force of a dream.

Ahead, Edouard has stopped and turned around. 'I can see the sea ahead of us.'

'Can't be right,' says Bonifacio.

'It is, though, look.'

Beyond Edouard is a treeless swathe of swamp, which in turn disappears into the sea.

'Can we have somehow turned a full circle?'

'No, the sun's still behind us.'

Of the four men, Sabir has the slightest build, and he's hoisted up a mangrove tree to get a better look. Once he's climbed to the top and got his bearings, it quickly becomes clear what the problem is. They've been wandering up a broad, flat peninsula which stretches into the sea from the south. In other words, there's no way to reach the mainland to the north; it's a dead end. The news is met with a sour silence.

'Don't have a lot of choice, do we?' says Edouard. 'All we can do is retrace our steps.'

They start back in a daze of exhaustion, hunger, depression. Another slog through kilometres of swamp and savannah. No question of stopping to rest: they must get to the beach by nightfall. It takes a terrible concentration to will their feet forward with every step.

The endless mud; the self-recrimination. How did I end up

here? What am I being punished for? Could it have been different? It could have been different. Wrong decisions; missed opportunities. Sabir recalls a fellow soldier who offered to go halves with him in a business venture after the war. He declined. And his comrade-in-arms went on to make his fortune. Years later, Sabir bumped into him, on one of those grand avenues that bisect the *beaux quartiers* of Paris. Suit and tie, married with a child, apartment in Neuilly. A short conversation, but Sabir didn't know what to say, was too ashamed to ask for his help.

He's passed through some physical barrier – the legs start to move by themselves, and he's no longer quite there. The present recedes again, against the relentless pressure of the past. The monsters he dreamt of as a child. The creatures who lived under his bed. His mother laughed, assured him that none of that existed. It's clear now that she was wrong.

He's in the Bois de Vincennes with his mother, by the lake. Nearby, a family is picnicking. There's a little boy who's caught something and is now proceeding to kill it with a rock. A lizard. Its desperate wriggling is testimony enough of the will to live. As Sabir pushes his toy boat out onto the lake, the thought strikes him that in many years' time, that boy too would be dead. And that many years on from then, his children, should he ever have any, would also be dead. Instinctively he realises that, with this knowledge, he's not quite the same boy as he'd been that morning, before the trip to the woods.

He's in the cemetery in Paris – it must be his mother's funeral. Père Lachaise, with the tombs that are like houses. A real city of the dead. With its wealthy suburbs – monstrously huge monuments decorated with statues – as well as its shanty towns, its jumble of broken tombstones displaced by tree roots. Standing by a grave, Sabir puts his hand to his face, and he feels something wet. Tears? No, it's blood, from the bites of the swarms of sandflies that infest the swamp.

Hours later, he stumbles onto the beach without even realising it. The others have collapsed on the sand, motionless. Edouard lying beside Carpette, his bag still slung over his neck. All the way through the swamp and back, with that big bag of his. Sabir too lies down on the beach, the feeling of his legs and the pain gradually coming back to him. There's the roar of the surf and the enveloping darkness. He closes his eyes and, as sleep overpowers him, his mind still spinning, he has the sensation of falling through the night.

XIII

'Can't see what we can do but continue south,' Edouard says next morning.

'Agreed,' replies Bonifacio. 'But what happens if we hit swamps there, too?'

Edouard shrugs. 'Somewhere south, this peninsula must connect up with the mainland. That's what we've got to aim for.'

They carry on down the beach. An hour or two later, they pass the place where they landed. The fireplace, the remains of the boat are still there. But no sign of Say-Say's body. It's been washed away. As they trudge past, Sabir reflects on Say-Say's last few days alive. Yes, he'd have realised he couldn't stay in the barracks. Not with a debt to a known killer. Luckily, he comes down with fever and is sent to hospital. Even more luckily, he's offered a chance to escape, on condition that he sail the boat. So he lies. Who'd have acted differently? Then, at the last moment, his tormentor Pierrot tells him he's free of the debt. He goes down to meet the other *évadés* in a state of turmoil. Halfway to the creek, he takes fright. Decides that with the debt out of the way, he'd rather risk camp than the high seas. But Sabir, he thinks he knows better. Sabir, the judge; Bonifacio was merely the executioner.

At midday they come across a trickle of water spilling over the sands, making its way to the ocean. They follow it back up the beach. The sand turns to rocks, the trickle becomes a shallow creek. The men stop to scoop up the water. What an ecstatic feeling to be able to drink until the thirst is gone – for a moment, it's impossible to concentrate on anything but this extraordinary physical pleasure.

When they've all had their fill, Edouard says: 'There's an incline here. What with this creek, we must be on the mainland. I think we must have passed the swamplands.'

'What do you think we should do?' asks Bonifacio.

'We can't go north. We'll just hit the swamps on the other side of the peninsula. Or we'll have to cut through kilometres of jungle to get around them. But we can't do that, because we've only got a couple of days' provisions. Then, even if we manage that, we're still somewhere in Dutch Guiana, probably nowhere near Paramaribo. And even if we get to Paramaribo, we'll get picked up immediately in these clothes without papers. Unless anyone's got friends there. Has anyone?'

A long, dead silence as it sinks in. They've been struggling with short-term survival and have lost sight of the long-term hopelessness of the situation.

'What do you suggest, then?'

'We're probably only fifty kilometres from the Maroni.'

'You're saying go back to French Guiana?'

'Got a better idea? We can probably get to the Maroni in a few days. We've all got money. We probably all know people who'll help us out. We'll lie low by the river until we get hold of another boat.'

'That's crazy.'

Edouard shrugs. 'As I said, if you've got a better idea, let's hear it.'

The two men talk for a little longer, while Carpette and Sabir sit in silence. Edouard's plan is counter-intuitive, but Sabir has grasped that it's the only real solution. It's dawning on Bonifacio as well: quickly enough, he comes round to it. Above all, it's the idea of an end to this wandering, however temporary, that's psychologically appealing. There are plenty of escaped convicts up and down the river. Most never get out; they subsist on catching and selling butterflies, or banditry. Eventually they die, or return to camp, or are recaptured. But with money and resolution, Sabir and the others should manage better than most.

They decide to follow the creek up the incline. Half an hour in, Edouard spots and catches a small turtle, no bigger than a man's hand. They desperately scour the creek for more turtles as they wade up, but none are to be found. A couple of hundred metres upstream, the creek mysteriously disappears underground. They're in a broken, uneven terrain and, to continue, they have to scramble over stretches of slippery, moss-covered rock. Huge clumps of bamboo impede their progress – they're impossible to cut into and you have to either walk right round them or duck and weave your way through. The further in they get, the thicker the snarled jungle becomes. They work out a system: two men up front, slashing a way through the undergrowth with their knives, and two men behind, carrying what's left of the supplies. Every hour or two, the teams change duties.

At nightfall, they come across another creek and decide to stay there for the night. Edouard lights the fire while the others fruitlessly search the stream for more food. Divided between four men, Edouard's turtle comes to nothing much, a mere taste washed down with a few sips of condensed milk.

A handful of tapioca and that's dinner. The men lie down. Hunger and exhaustion have subdued everyone – although Sabir has the impression he's doing a bit better than the others, thanks to his slight build.

Bonifacio kicks at Carpette. 'Hey, sing us a song or something. Tell us a story. Anything to get my mind off my stomach.' Carpette remains silent. 'C'mon. Give us the tragic story of your life.' Still nothing from Carpette, and Bonifacio bellows: 'Hey, I'm talking to you!'

'What do you want to know?' replies Carpette nervously.

'Well, what did you get done for?'

'Forgery. Banknotes.'

'Really. And you?' he says to Edouard.

'Me? I was seeing a girl from one of the shows in Montmartre,' Edouard replies tonelessly. 'We were crossing the Pont Henri IV. We had an argument. I pushed her off the bridge.'

'That's more like it.' He turns to Sabir. 'What about you, lover boy? Same story? That pretty girl of yours. Bumped her off, did you?' Sabir says nothing, and Bonifacio cackles. 'He's got these photos of some fancy lass. She's not really yours, though, is she? Too posh by half. They're just some old photos you found, aren't they?'

'Shut up!'

Sabir wonders whether Bonifacio will do something to him. He feels quite fatalistic about the possibility – it might even be what he wants. But nothing happens. Bonifacio simply laughs his mirthless laugh.

'Some company you lot are,' he mumbles, then rolls over.

The crackle of the fire, the odd rustle in the forest, the monkey howls, the weirdly mechanical insect clicks. But Sabir's no longer scared of the night, its sudden noises and grotesque shadows. He's lying on his back, hands behind his head, staring up beyond the canopy to the stars. So Edouard killed a showgirl on a bridge over the Seine, he's thinking. Funny, all that time he was in Paris, so was Edouard. They might well have bumped into each other. In fact, it's strange that they didn't. But then he has a doubt. It's not like Edouard to come out with anything so direct about his past. Surely he was just fobbing Bonifacio off with a silly story. It sounds too pat. Like the melodramatic tales convicts tell to cover up their ignominious past as muggers or house robbers. Edouard often said how much he disliked Paris, how he'd never live there.

Through the next morning, they gradually work their way up to higher ground. Here, the trees soar to stupendous heights, cutting off most of the light. Mosses, vines and ferns string their way overhead, forming a low roof as if they're in a vast green cave. And everywhere the constant drip, drip of rainwater running off the leaves, echoing dully through the forest. The undergrowth has thinned out and the going's easier: for long stretches they can walk without having to cut a way through. It lifts their spirits, since it makes it more likely that they'll get to the Maroni within a day or two.

If that's the case, what happens next? Sabir wonders what's on Edouard's mind. Because, on reflection, it's not so simple as getting back to the river and negotiating the purchase of a new boat. Bonifacio's a guard killer. It's too dangerous to stay any length of time in French Guiana with him. Besides, there's his murder of Say-Say. They'd still have to 'lose' Bonifacio somehow. It brings Sabir straight back to the old question.

'Stop!' he hears Edouard hiss. The men freeze. A couple of metres up a tree, an iguana, the size of an arm. Edouard noiselessly picks up a rock, aims, throws hard. The iguana drops to the ground with a heavy thump. 'Good shot!' says Bonifacio. The men gingerly approach. Edouard pokes it with a stick and it scuttles off under some ferns. They all pummel the ferns with rocks – but when they search them, the iguana's nowhere to be found.

At noon, they eat the last of the tapioca in gloomy silence. All that remains now is a few cans of condensed milk. The thought of the iguana they almost caught simply sharpens the hunger, adds to the horrible nervy frustration. Back in camp, Sabir heard convicts say you could last up to a month in the jungle without food, as long as you had water. Perhaps, if you're not walking and cutting your way through the forest.

Another long march all afternoon, making a fair distance in the absence of thick undergrowth. What bothers the men most now is some kind of low-growing plant with tough, thorn-bordered leaves that scratch and tear at their legs. In the late afternoon they reach a stream. In theory they could walk on for another hour or two before nightfall, but they're too exhausted. Edouard gets a fire going for the mosquitoes, but there's nothing to cook on it. There are some small fish in the stream, but no way of catching them. Even if there were, they'd be barely a mouthful. The best the men can manage is to collect the grass that's growing along the side of the stream, put it in a tin with water, boil it up and drink it as a soup. But it has little effect. The hunger and exhaustion have brought on a heightened, febrile atmosphere, with the pre-storm heaviness in the air only adding to the tension. Bonifacio in particular seems to be in a state of some excitement.

'How far d'you think we've got?' he asks Edouard.

'I'd say we've covered almost half the distance.'

'Almost half? Is that all?'

'If we were closer to the river, we'd have come across something by now. Jungle paths, Indians, some sign of life. I think we've got another thirty kilometres to go.'

'Jesus.' Bonifacio's hands are shaking slightly. Bad time to get the fever, if that's what it is. 'Got to eat something, or I'll go mad.' He wades back into the stream, stares into it, plunges his hand down as if to grab at something. After a few attempts he tires of that game and clambers back up the bank. Now he approaches Edouard again. 'You and that fucking bag of yours. Dragging it all this way. What the hell have you got in there?'

'That's my business.'

'We're all in this together. It's all of our business.'

'No. It's my business.'

'You're hoarding food, is that it?'

'No.'

'What else would it be? I've seen you. Sneaking off by yourself.'

Bonifacio is standing over Edouard now, as he's fixing a palm cover for the fire to protect it from the rain. The bag's sitting by his feet. It's clear that Bonifacio is working himself up into a rage.

'Give me the bag.'

'No.'

'And I say give me the bag!'

Bonifacio makes a move for it; Edouard kicks his hand away. Bonifacio explodes in a frenzy of anger, all the simmering tensions between them finally spilling over. Edouard has his knife out, but Bonifacio simply picks him up and throws him into the stream. There's a gash along Bonifacio's arm where Edouard must have caught him before being thrown in.

'Fuck you!' Bonifacio screams. 'You've fucked us all! You sailed us straight into that fucking storm . . . fuck you . . .' He's in such a state as he tears at Edouard's bag that he's practically bawling. 'What's this…what's this…?' He's pulling out sheaves of paper, throwing them in the air. There seem to be hundreds of sheets, and on each is one of Edouard's precise, careful little drawings of a plant or a flower – they scatter and billow about in the wind like confetti. Sabir recognises the creamy texture of the paper as the expensive type the commandant used – not the normal, crumbly stuff you got from the Administration. He remembers how Carpette asked him to steal it, how he delivered bundles of it to him.

'Fuck you…' Now Bonifacio is pulling something else from the bag – there are half a dozen of them, they're about a metre long, and they look like dark, gnarled tree roots. Bonifacio sinks his teeth into one of them, spits it out, then throws the lot at Edouard in the river. 'What the fuck are these?'

It starts pouring down. Before long, the campsite and nearby vegetation are plastered with soggy paper, the rain-smudged ink running down the sheets like mascara on a tearful face. The rain seems to have brought Bonifacio back to his senses. He sits down by the fire and pulls his rag of a shirt off. A gash along the biceps of his left arm is dripping blood. It doesn't look like a deep wound, but he tears a strip off his shirt to tie round his arm. On the other side of the stream, Carpette is helping Edouard out of the water. Edouard looks blank, shocked. At one point he says to Carpette: 'No, no,' and gets back into the water, feeling about on the bed of the stream. Perhaps he's dropped his knife.

If Edouard and Carpette were to launch an attack on Bonifacio now, Sabir would join in. Or if they made a run for it through the jungle, Sabir would follow. But nothing happens. When the rain eases off, Edouard crosses back over the stream to collect the sheets of paper from the ground and bushes. Most come apart in his hand, although that doesn't stop him. He's like a zombie. He lays the sodden remains carefully on the ground, then wades back into the stream and fishes out a couple of those knobbly, root-like objects that had been in his bag. He places them next to the pile of paper. Nearby, Bonifacio's watching wordlessly, still as a reptile.

Edouard joins Carpette on the other bank. The two of them are speaking lowly, urgently. Sabir expects Bonifacio to say something, to stop them as he'd done on the boat. But he remains silent. More furious whispering, then Carpette shouts angrily: 'I've seen the tattoo!' At that, the whispering abruptly stops, leaving Sabir mystified as to the meaning of Carpette's remark.

As darkness descends over the campsite, the two men get up to cross the stream and move over to the fire. Bonifacio finally speaks up: 'No. You two stay over there on the other side.'

'We'll get eaten alive by the mosquitoes.'

'That's your problem. You're not sleeping by the fire tonight.'

Edouard stands there undecided for a moment, then starts to scout about for more firewood. Within twenty minutes, he has a new fire burning on the other side of the stream. It leaves Sabir stranded with Bonifacio: crossing over now would surely be some sort of provocation. Edouard has lain down on the ground, while Carpette sits by the fire. They must have some agreement to take turns to keep watch.

'Give me your knife.' Bonifacio's standing over Sabir. He doesn't have his own knife out, but his right hand's resting by his pocket. 'I'll give it back to you in the morning.'

It's not done to ask another convict for his knife; and it's seen as a humiliation to hand it over to anyone else. It hardly matters, though. They're far from convict society now, with its perverse niceties. Sabir takes his knife out, hands it to Bonifacio, handle first. He feels relieved to be rid of it. Bonifacio lies down on his stomach; he's shirtless, and the gigantic cross on his back rises up and down with his slow breathing.

Somehow, Sabir has managed to sleep. He's not sure if any of the others have: Bonifacio looks drawn, bleary-eyed. The bandage around his biceps has stained a vivid red, although he doesn't seem to have any trouble using the arm. Sabir remembers that Bonifacio has been living out in the jungle much longer than the others – probably since the night he murdered the Corsican guard, all those weeks ago. It can only be down to his bull-like strength that he's alive at all.

Sabir's vaguely surprised to see Edouard and Carpette still there, on the other side of the stream. Edouard has boiled up some more grass, but Sabir doesn't have any: he's got mild diarrhoea from last night's soup. The weird atmosphere again. No one knows any more how to respond to the other – it's as if the men are in some play and have forgotten how it goes. Bonifacio and Edouard stare at each other across the stream. Edouard has managed to patch up his bag and has slung it back over his shoulder. Sabir's knife is on the ground by the fire; he picks it up, thinks about pocketing it and then puts it down again.

They move off through the trees, into the dark of the forest. Bonifacio first, then Sabir, then Edouard and Carpette. Well spaced out, to prevent anyone being able to sneak up on anyone else. Relatively little undergrowth now. They're following some kind of narrow path, or an animal run – tapirs, or the wild pigs that they've caught frustrating glimpses of in the distance.

They walk all day without a break, keeping the sun to their right shoulder. Although the going is fairly easy, compared with most of the terrain they've crossed, Sabir has the impression they're not covering as much ground as they should. On top of the exhaustion and hunger, they're cut and bleeding, limping, their wounds are festering. On occasions, Sabir's overcome with a light-headedness, and an overpowering desire to sit down, lie down. It passes after a minute or two. But the attacks seem to be getting ever more frequent.

The mind spools back. He remembers that evening Bonifacio was waiting for him for the first time in the folly. And how just before then, he'd been crossing the garden, lost in a memory about the trenches. He'd been thinking about that time before the assault, when he'd considered deserting, and had decided against it. He'd been wondering why he'd taken that decision. There's an easy answer to that, he now realises. Deserting would have condemned him to a life of wandering. A life of exile. He'd have had to change his name, become someone else. And yet all these things have come to pass anyway. The forest stretches out before him like an ocean.

Hours of walking in a stupor of memories and vague sensations. Now Bonifacio has stopped dead ahead. The afternoon light, filtered through the branches and vines, streaks his body and makes him look like some wild animal. As Sabir gets closer, he sees that Bonifacio's holding the half-rotting carcass of a large bird.

'If we give it a damn good roasting, it should be edible.'

They sit down and wait for the others. After ten minutes or so, Carpette appears.

'Where's your friend?' asks Bonifacio.

'Lagging behind. He was feeling sick. Should be along soon.'

They wait in silence. A good half-hour passes. Bonifacio's getting increasingly nervy and irritated, since Edouard's the only one who can get a fire going easily. Sabir spends minutes at a time staring at the dead bird. Hours before, he'd have been virtually hysterical at the thought of roast meat. Now he almost couldn't care. He knows he's hallucinating from fatigue and hunger, but the carcass looks as if it's decomposing in front of him. Living or dead, the forest absorbs everything – ingests it, digests it, excretes it, in an eternal cycle of decay.

Still no Edouard. After a while, they start to call out through the vast silence of the forest. There's no answer.

'We won't find him if he doesn't want to be found,' says Bonifacio presently. 'He's fucked off in some other direction. Good riddance.'

They spend a few minutes collecting firewood, then Bonifacio busies about trying to get a fire going. Carpette's just sitting there staring into the ground, his face completely vacant. Sabir's thinking about Edouard. On the one hand, he's wondering why Carpette's not making more of an effort to find him. On the other hand, he's thinking back to the trenches, when he and Edouard formed a 'couple'. He remembers that time when Edouard climbed out of the trench to recover a packet of cigarettes, under sporadic enemy fire. When Sabir remonstrated with him later for taking a stupid risk, he laughed bitterly. 'I'd rather die for a cigarette than for my country.'

Sabir gets up. 'I'm going back to look for Edouard. Something might have happened to him.'

Bonifacio shrugs. 'Suit yourself. Don't expect me to save any meat for you.'

Carpette looks up briefly. Impossible to read his quizzical expression. Sabir disappears down the trail they've just come from. Judging from the sun, he's got enough time to backtrack a good kilometre, and still return before dark. At intervals, he lets out a shout: 'Edouard! Edouard!' There's no echo – the trees deaden the sound. The high fronds of the ferns sway menacingly in the breeze. After a while his own voice starts to frighten him, and he continues on silently down the trail. Impossible to see the sun through the trees now, and in the fading light he has the impression of being swallowed up by the forest.

It's just as he decides to turn back that he sees it. A pile of cut branches by the edge of the trail. He moves closer to get a better look. Underneath, a pair of bare feet are just visible. Sabir tosses the branches aside.

He's a mess. One side of his face is smashed in. It's like one of those long-dead frozen corpses you'd stumble over in no-man's-land in a February snowstorm. Only Edouard isn't quite dead. Carpette must have thought he was, though. Sometimes it can be so hard to kill someone. There are men, even mortally sick ones, who don't want to die, who hang on through sheer willpower. And yet there's no way that Edouard will survive. Even if he were anywhere near a hospital. Sabir has seen enough men in this state to know. The breathing is shallow, hesitant. Through the mask of blood, Sabir detects a tightening of face muscles. Edouard's attempting a smile. Or a grimace. The mouth moves, ever so slightly. It's a whispering croak: 'Jules Cotard.'

'Yes.'

That was the name Sabir used in the army. Nothing more for a while, and Sabir wonders if Edouard has died. But he hasn't, not yet. Sabir stares into his face, into the eye on the side that hasn't been smashed in. And the eye stares back, holds Sabir in its gaze.

Edouard feebly gestures towards Sabir. Sabir leans forward, until his ear is almost touching Edouard's bloody mouth. It whispers again, slowly, trying hard to enunciate each word through the slurring: 'Do you remember that dream?'

'What dream, Edouard?'

'Remember it? Do you?'

'Yes. I remember that dream.'

'We talked about it so many times.'

Edouard smiles again, then sighs. He moves his head, almost imperceptibly, as though to shake it. He's trying to form more words in his mouth, but nothing's coming out except little bubbles of bloody spittle. A few more moments of mouthing into the void, then a final straining to be heard. 'Finish me off.'

'I can't do that.'

He mouths again and then is still. Edouard's hand, by his side, is frozen mid-grasp like a statue's. The moment was indistinct, but he's gone now, there's no doubt about it. No need to kill him; there never was. It almost sounded as if he were asking for something else, an embrace.

Sabir moves away from Edouard's body and sits down on some sort of rotting log. He feels so tired. Edouard with his bloody face lies before him, in that unnatural pose of a dead body. It's obscene. Sabir thinks about burying Edouard. He really wants to bury him, but has no digging implement, nor the strength to do it. Possibly he does have the strength, but he doesn't want to waste it. Nevertheless, it doesn't seem right to leave Edouard here like this. Men should be buried. An unburied body is no longer alive, not properly dead, either.

The things they went through together. The bodies they saw. Tears come to Sabir's eyes. Confused, he puts his head in his hands. For a moment, it seems he can't continue. The moment passes, though. He gets up, gathers the branches up again and places them over Edouard's body. Nearby, he spots the pole Carpette had been using as a walking stick – stained dark red at the heavy end. And Edouard's bag, split open, rifled through. The dried-out sheets of paper with their little drawings of flowers. What was Carpette looking for? Money? Sabir puts a couple of the drawings in his pocket, as proof that he's found Edouard's body, if proof he needs. Then he starts along the trail back to where Bonifacio and Carpette are camped.

As he walks, he's reminded of that first walk through the forest to Camp Renée. Although it feels like a lifetime ago, the memory of it is still very clear. Climbing up that tree. The vision of his fiancée. Meeting Edouard. Not recognising him at first. Noticing his glass eye . . . It occurs to him now that the eye he's just been staring into, which held him so fixedly in its gaze, that eye was not actually Edouard's real one. So how did he know that it was Sabir?

He wonders what Edouard could have meant with his last words. Remember that dream. What was he supposed to remember? What did they talk about so many times? But there's no point in trying to attach any sense to the ramblings of a dying man. The meaning of his final plea is clearer. During the war, it was very common for comrades-in-arms to enter into pacts by which one would kill the other if either was wounded grievously in the groin or face. It was certainly something he and Edouard would have discussed in the trenches.

It's dark by the time Sabir gets back to where Bonifacio and Carpette have camped. One of them's managed to get a fire going. To one side are the remains of the bird, half-eaten. Sabir picks at it: even cooked, even burnt through, it still tastes rancid, and he can only manage a few mouthfuls, washed down with condensed milk. He wonders whether he'll be able to hold it all down.

'Did you find anything?'

He and Carpette stare at each other across the fire. Why didn't he notice how suspiciously Carpette was acting before, how surprised he seemed when Sabir said he'd go and look for Edouard? He shakes his head.

Bonifacio's stretched out on the ground. Carpette's sitting

by the fire snivelling. Occasionally he mutters: 'He was my friend . . . he was my friend . . .' The act is understated, convincing. Carpette might even believe it himself. Out here in the forest, cut off from human society, it might be possible to believe anything. Sabir stares at Carpette for some time, then switches his gaze to the hypnotic flames of the fire. He doesn't want to give anything away. But he half-suspects that Carpette knows well enough what he's found.

XIV

The morning sun and its dappled light. The trail has widened out and has crossed over a couple of other tracks. This part of the jungle seems to be populated – by Indians, at least. The question is how far they are from the nearest Dutch settlement. If they're reasonably close, then the danger is being betrayed by the Indians. Bonifacio moves on ahead, followed by Sabir, then Carpette. They're not so far from the river now, Sabir suspects. In any case, it's coming to an end very soon. Sabir can feel it; feel something closing in.

The forest is an insomniac blur – the fear of Carpette attacking him kept Sabir awake most of the night. Staring into the jungle, there's the temptation to simply disappear into it. At other times, the trees on either side of the trail are like the walls of solitary confinement. Sabir thinks of the commandant for the first time since the boat. Perhaps it's because they're heading back to French Guiana. He'll hide out near the house, he decides. After all, it's the only corner of the Colony he's familiar with. He'll know what to steal, who to contact. The camp, the garden. He gets a dim sense of why the commandant wanted to build that house, that garden, to put the convicts to work.

Bonifacio sidles up to Sabir. 'Tell me now, then. What did you find?'

'What d'you mean?'

'You know what I mean. I trust you well enough. I want to know if I can trust *him*.'

Sabir says nothing for a moment. After so long in the jungle, so long without proper food, he knows he's not thinking properly. Nor, probably, is Bonifacio. Sabir the judge, Bonifacio the executioner. Only this time it's merited, by any law of any civilised land. Thinking about Edouard, Sabir is seized with a befuddled anger. What was it the commandant once said about justice? There are times when the punishment must go beyond anything one can know. There must be something terrible, something greater than us . . . He feels himself shaking again.

He pulls out Edouard's drawings from his pocket, shows them to Bonifacio. 'Murdered.'

Bonifacio nods. 'You go on. I'll catch you up.'

Sabir walks on in a daze. He might be wrong, it might all be his imagination. Edouard might have been killed by someone else, an Indian. The truth is that he doesn't care any more. He trudges on, waiting for Bonifacio to catch him up again. Ten minutes pass, twenty minutes, half an hour. He doesn't even bother to consider what may have happened to Bonifacio or Carpette. He passes by another one of the criss-crossing tracks. Quite apart from the danger of being caught with a guard killer, the thought of being alone with Bonifacio again is intolerable.

He turns right off the trail. Away from the river, in all probability. Even better, because Bonifacio's less likely to follow him up a track going the wrong way. Over the first hundred metres, he's careful not to leave any visible tracks. The idea of Bonifacio haunts him for a while; but after twenty minutes of walking, he begins to feel easier in his mind and he slows his pace. The conviction that Bonifacio isn't following him flows through him like a gulp of rum. He's on his own again, truly on his own.

He's tempted to stop and lie low for a day, before continuing on down to the river. But he wonders whether he'll be able to get up again if he sits down. Best continue for the moment, even if it *is* the wrong direction. Best continue until he's clearer in his head. His torn shirt is in the final stages of disintegration, falling from his body. The shirt with its unique number that sits above his heart, that tells him he's been examined, quantified, qualified, found to be a negative asset, found to be worth ten years of hard labour in a foreign land. He gives it a final rip and tosses it into the jungle.

Now he has the image of Edouard in his head again. On one level, he knows very little about Edouard, and nothing at all about his life after the war. On another level, he knows everything that's important. It seems as if he held on until Sabir found him, before allowing himself to die. The tears come as he thinks about how he wasn't able to bury him. He pulls out from his pocket the two drawings he took from Edouard's bag. He hasn't properly looked at them before. They remind him of the orchid drawings in that book of the commandant's he once looked through – flowers that don't look like flowers, that look like the fanciful creations of an artist. One has its petals complicatedly intersecting to form a good likeness of a crucifix, complete with black markings that might be the man hanging from it. The flower – or the drawing of it – is neither beautiful nor ugly. It's bizarre. But it commands attention: once Sabir looks at it, it takes an effort to pull away.

He's climbing a gentle incline, a sure enough sign that he's moving away from the river. At one point, the vines that form the low canopy thin out. A brilliant tropical sun paints the vegetation in vivid colours. The very air feels luminous. Looking up, Sabir notices bunches of wild-growing bananas, sheltering in the shade of the higher trees. He jumps up to catch a low-lying branch, swings his way onto a tree, and starts climbing. Halfway up, he has another of those attacks of dizziness. It's very strong and for a moment he thinks he's going to lose his balance. But the moment passes. Just before he reaches the bananas, he gets a clear view down the slope. There's the silver thread of the river – closer than any of them had realised. They'd been following a trail that runs parallel to it, a kilometre or two into Dutch Guiana. All Sabir has to do is go back the way he came, cross over the trail and continue straight on.

With some difficulty he manages to knock a few banana bunches to the ground, then he climbs back down. The fruit tastes sour and sweet at the same time. Not unpleasant to eat, not particularly nice, either, but it fills his belly. He gorges on it. Halfway through eating, he realises that the bananas are going to make him sick, but it doesn't stop him.

Sabir continues a little way up the incline, not really knowing what he's doing. His trousers are almost as ragged as his shirt was, shredded by the rapier weeds he's had to walk through. There's no good way to hold them up any more, and he decides that it'd be easier to discard them as well and simply walk on naked, like an Indian.

Up here, in any case, the going is easier. Not long after the bananas, he glimpses something through the trees that looks like a stone wall. Sabir clambers his way across the forest to investigate. It's some sort of ruin. The jungle has reclaimed most of it. What's left is a crumbling wall, a rusty saw, an old wheel – a world that merely alludes to the whole. There's also what must have been an enclosure once, a large kitchen garden, now overgrown with ferns and forest undergrowth. What it all reminds him of is the ruin where they gathered, just before the escape.

Sabir lies down by the wall, convulsed by horrible stomach pains. Moments later he's violently sick. It goes on for ages. Even when there's nothing left to throw up, it continues: there are brief moments of respite before the retching begins again, and then again. In among the green-yellow of the half-digested fruit he sees bits of pink and red, as if he's vomiting up his stomach lining as well.

When it's all over, maybe an hour later, he's shivering and bathed in a rank-smelling sweat. The stomach pains are largely gone, but his chest and throat muscles ache from the retching. He's far too weak to move. The wall gives him shelter from the afternoon rains, and the water eventually washes away the vomit that surrounds him. The light fades, then seems to cut out as if it has been switched off.

It's night. Stars glisten through the rain. He manages to prop himself up against the wall at one point, but that's the best he can manage. He's very ill. He wonders whether he'll be any better in the morning. But it seems unimportant.

A memory comes back to him: months ago he shared a cell with a man nicknamed Lazare. He was quite famous, newspaper articles had been written about him. He'd been condemned to death for the murder of his wife's lover. His execution was scheduled for dawn one day – he'd been given his last meal, the guillotine had been set up and the guards had even marched him to the place of execution, when a presidential reprieve was announced. He'd been a minute or two from losing his head. Sabir questioned Lazare about the incident and he didn't seem to mind talking about it. 'You're marched out of your cell, aware of every second, every part of every second. The smallest sensations are amazingly intense and somehow more real than usual. And yet at the same time it's almost as if it's not happening to you at all. As if you're watching a scene from afar . . .' All night Sabir drifts in and out of sleep, his mind shifting between memories, dreams, fantasies. He remembers how when he first arrived in the Colony, he wrote that letter to his fiancée. How it struck him then that the only way out, the only solution, was to change, become someone else.

Light again. Sabir opens his eyes. The wall is gone. Now he's lying by the edge of the river. He has no idea how he got there; in fact, it seems impossible. But he accepts that it is so. He wants to move, tries to hoist himself up, fails, collapses back on the ground. Then again, no doubt he's as good here as he is anywhere. The wandering is over. And this mysterious journey to the river was the end of it. He props his head up with his arm and gazes across the water. He even fancies he can make out the commandant's house, on the other side. He'd planned on making his way there. Back to the garden he created. Back to the folly, unsullied by Bonifacio. To the commandant's wife. To her naked body, and the annihilating desire.

He remembers lying low by the river, opposite where he is now, watching the boat go by. The look she gave him as their eyes locked was one of absolute recognition. Let her find him here, then. On the other side. He thinks of the wall and the ruined garden enclosure he found, back up the hill, away from the river. One day, he'll take her there. And the garden will be more alive than any the commandant could have envisaged. He imagines it filled with all manner of bizarre flowers, like the ones Edouard had sketched in his little drawings. It was

Edouard who took the decision to return, after all. Edouard and his glass eye.

Twilight: an entire day has passed in a moment. From now on, every day will be like this. It's getting difficult to focus on anything, to feel anything, to draw the line where he might end and the world begins. Sabir shifts position, puts his head down on the soft, moist ground and stares up at the sky. Only now does he realise that he's lying half on the bank, half in the river. Water laps over him.

After a while, he closes his eyes. The river and forest have vanished, the Colony, too. It's 1917 again. It always will be. He's nineteen years old, by now battle-hardened. Night falling, the stink of the trenches. Officers patrolling behind the lines. Some in armoured vehicles, some on horses. Messages relayed, field telephones cranked up, German voices drifting across the wasteland.

Those bodies. The men who are about to perish. Many of them fathers, all of them sons. All children. The sky explodes into a beautiful fireworks of artillery barrage. There really is nothing more going on than the card game they're playing, he and Edouard and a couple of other soldiers in his trench section. It's the only reality. Nothing since has ever been so real.

He sees his fiancée, Marie. He remembers the beginning, meeting her for the first time at a baptism. The happy moments of an unhappy life – could anything be more perfect than that? They fucked only hours later. He remembers the end, too: that night before his arrest, when finally he realised it was hopeless. On opposite sides of the bedroom, the screaming distance between them: 'We can save it! We can change it!'

* * *

Pulling him down, headlong into a bottomless pit – then gazing back up at the boundless sky. All the voices in his head dying down, reduced to a garbled murmur.

A mother's farewell, as you dash away to war. The still-ticking watch on a dead soldier's wrist. The sound of cards, shuffled, fingered, slapped down on the makeshift table. The artillery rumble. Distant but insistent, like the muffled cries of a baby. Do you remember that dream? We talked about it so many times. The flat, desolate landscape in the twilight. The silhouette of a single tree stump. And the dark farmhouse against the sky.

COLONY TWO

I

'After so many years of travelling, I feel as if I've killed every last certainty within me.'

The line stared out at Manne from an otherwise blank page in his journal. It was in his neat script, but he couldn't remember writing it. For a minute, he let his pen hover over the words before putting it down again. So early in the morning, and yet the air already shimmered with the heat. He sat back deep in his deckchair, his mind empty as he stared out into the hypnotic blue.

By the rails, he could see one of the merchant sailors standing with a female passenger, very young but not especially attractive. The sailor was openly flirting with her, and she was doing nothing to discourage him. He'd put a bronzed arm around her waist, and was now edging it ever lower. Manne couldn't hear what they were saying, but as in any exchange it was always the bodies that expressed the essential, never the words. He watched them for a while, idly wondering whether they'd sleep together before the end of the voyage, or even the day. The girl, Manne had learnt at the captain's table, had come out from France, changing boats in Guadeloupe.

She was engaged to marry a prison guard at Cayenne. They hadn't met before, only exchanged letters and photographs. Apparently it was quite a common arrangement: the girl was probably an orphan or prostitute, or both, and getting married would extricate her from a difficult situation. As for the guard, it was his only means of meeting and marrying a white woman.

Manne's mind strayed back to dinner the night before, where he'd heard about the girl. The conversation had mostly been colonial chitchat – and yet there'd been this sexual tension among the passengers, split roughly evenly between men and women. Ribald jokes, flushed faces, hands drifting over hands, *décolletés* tugged down. It felt like the desperation of the war years, and Manne couldn't help tying it in some way with the boat's ultimate destination – the penal colony. Mere whimsy, no doubt. It was not so different from the bohemian *soirées* he remembered from Paris before the war, with the endless café-hopping, the occasional bed-hopping. The dynamics of the captain's table were simply those of a late supper in Montparnasse after a show.

Talk on board generally veered away from the *bagne*. In fact, mention of the girl and the prison guard had been the first whisper of it at the captain's table. It made the Colony seem both stranger and more banal than the mental picture Manne had drawn from books he'd read – memoirs with titles such as *My Green Hell, Ten Years Among the Dead* or *Dry Guillotine*. In the years Manne had spent criss-crossing the Americas, the *bagne*, if it came up at all, was usually spoken of with irritation, even anger. The brothels of Buenos Aires were all run by escaped *bagnards*, it was said, and in northern Brazil they terrorised the local population. That France would send its undesirables to this continent clearly injured some native sense of pride.

The sailor and the girl wandered off, arm in arm, leaving Manne alone on deck. For a while he sat reading his book – Baudelaire's translation of *Arthur Gordon Pym* – before dozing and broiling in the morning sun. An hour later he woke with a start, his skin prickly with sweat and heat. He'd been dreaming of Edouard again. It had been very fragmentary, and all he could recall now was Edouard's face, and his glass eye as it stared back lifelessly at him. It took him a moment to shake himself free of this image and notice the other people now leaning over railings, looking out towards the green line on the horizon. The boat was approaching Georgetown, its first stop on the mainland. Manne watched as the line thickened and clarified. He'd been to British Guiana once before, years ago. He'd worked his passage across on a boat from Liverpool, when he'd started to feel unsafe in England. A brief stop in Georgetown, of which he remembered almost nothing, before sailing on to Belém and along the Brazilian coast.

He stayed up on deck as the boat docked. A few passengers left the boat at Georgetown; a few more disembarked to lunch in town. Manne wasn't hungry; he contented himself with a stroll up and down the quay, watching the dockers as they loaded up goods for Cayenne. A kaleidoscopic crowd bustled about by the boat: British sailors in their crisp whites; black policemen in bobby's helmets; Chinese men peddling food; Indians shifting implausibly huge sacks; Creole women in their vivid headdresses.

As he was about to reboard, Manne noticed a tall British officer striding towards the boat from one of the dockside buildings, trailing a couple of armed customs officials and a dozen pitifully dressed white men. The captain rushed down the gangplank to remonstrate. 'No no no,' Manne could hear him bellowing, 'I don't have handcuffs, don't have bars, I've nowhere to put them, I can't take them!'

The captain was barring the way. Eventually the British officer conferred with one of the customs men, who was sent off on an errand. Another of the customs officials gave an order and the men in rags sat down on the ground by the boat. No one else on the quay seemed to pay any attention to them. Manne dawdled by, watching them sprawled over the paving stones as if squashed to the ground by the force of the sun. Every now and then, one of them would throw an impotent glance in the direction of the boat. But most seemed as uninterested in their fate as the people who hurried along the docks. One man held his head between his knees; the others gazed about vacantly, like zoo animals.

What struck Manne most forcibly was how stunted they were – almost as short as the pygmies he'd encountered once, years before, on an expedition to the Congo. Half were without shoes and their feet were a mess of bites, wounds, bruises the colour of bad meat. All were bearded, except a couple who were too young for it. And they all shared the same starved stare, the bowed shoulders, the cow-like docility.

Manne sidled up to one of them. 'Where did you come from?'

'Saint-Laurent.'

'What happened?'

The man shrugged his shoulders. 'Stole a boat. But it washed ashore.'

'What'll happen to you?'

Silence, another shrug of indifference. The customs officer was back now with a podgy little man in a cravat, obviously French. The consul, Manne supposed. He and the captain clearly knew each other, but they didn't shake hands.

'Georgetown prison doesn't want them,' the podgy man was saying. 'What d'you expect me to do? Adopt them?'

The captain shook his head. 'I don't have anywhere to put them.'

'Put 'em in the hold with the cargo! Listen, if you won't take 'em, I'll wire Cayenne. They'll wire back the order before you leave. Then you'll have to take them. Don't force me to waste my time.'

'All right,' said the captain with an angry wave of the hand. 'You'd better get me some handcuffs or leg irons. I'm not having them free to roam about the ship.'

A short while later the men were marched on board. Just behind them, Manne noticed the sailor and the girl walking together up the gangplank, hand in hand, the same ones he'd seen earlier on deck. They were relaxed and easy with each other, as though something had been resolved. Pointing ahead to the men in rags with her other hand, the girl seemed momentarily anguished. 'What if they seize the ship or something?'

The sailor laughed. 'Look at the buggers. Couldn't kick a dog, let alone seize a ship. Better get used to 'em anyway, where you're heading.'

Another day and night at sea, shadowing the coast. Then Paramaribo, Dutch Guiana, under a ferocious morning sun – it was where Manne was disembarking. No point in going on to Cayenne with the other passengers, since there was no road from Cayenne to Saint-Laurent. Easier to get off here, and make his way down to the border town of Albina, a boat ride away from the penitentiary.

A black porter rushed up to him as he stepped off the gangplank, but Manne waved him away. His two smallish suitcases were easy enough to carry – all they contained were a few changes of clothes, some books, cash, bank orders, letters, papers. Any other possessions had long ago been sold off, or abandoned in Europe. And over the last few years, he'd continued to pare down his belongings, at first unconsciously but later deliberately. Because in the end, it was surprising what little one needed to keep going. Manne cleared customs and made his way to the ticketing office. A boat would be leaving in two hours down the Commewijne River for Moengo, the ticket man said. From there, he could get a lift to Albina.

Barely past breakfast time, but Manne was already slick and sticky from the heat, in need of a wash. No point in checking into a hotel, though, with just a couple of hours to spare. Instead he strolled along the streets near the docks. The feeling was of a town that had yet to gel into any particular style. Its wooden buildings looked vaguely Scandinavian. The rice-laden barges paddled by rows of Malay men made one think of the Far East. Whatever it was, it felt foreign, after the Gallic claustrophobia of the boat. Manne ducked into a barber shop, hidden among a bazaar of little storefronts. The barber quickly lathered him up and started to shave.

'Just got in?'

'That's right.'

'From Guadeloupe?'

'On that boat, yes. I got on at Port-of-Spain.'

'So what's your business here?'

'Passing through.'

'Where are you heading?'

'Moengo. Then down to the Maroni.'

'You don't want to go down there. Terrible country.'

'Why?'

'Full of fever. If the fever doesn't get you, the bandits will. Crawling with escaped convicts. Bad country.'

They were talking in French, but then the barber broke off to jabber something in Creole to a young boy loitering outside. Tattered Dutch and English magazines lay on a table by Manne's chair. The barber was one of those types Manne had come across so often in the colonies – of European origin, fluent in four or five languages, and yet impossible to tell where he was really from, if anywhere.

'No, what you want to do is head up to the highlands,' the barber continued. 'It's healthier. More gold up there. And it's a damn sight easier to get at than on the Maroni.'

'Really?'

The barber stopped shaving for a moment. 'Look, if you're interested, I know someone you should talk to. He's got a mining concession on a river up in the highlands. You never know, he might sell it to you. I hear there are giant nuggets up that way. Men shipping gold by the kilo.'

'If that's true, why aren't you up there?'

'I'm a barber,' the man mumbled. 'Not a prospector.'

He carried on shaving in silence. Always the same in prospecting country, with even the barbers trying to sell you worthless concessions.

'Ever see any of those escaped convicts you were talking about?' asked Manne after a pause.

'Seen plenty of them,' the barber replied, without much interest. 'Bloody thieves and murderers, the lot of them.'

'Ever been down that way?'

The barber shook his head. 'I told you. It's no good down there. A graveyard.'

Enough time for coffee, then a stroll back to the docks to board the next boat. A very different affair from the one he'd arrived on, where most of the passengers had been French or

French Creole, and a Gallic decorum had prevailed. On this boat, people were herded on like cattle, and no single nationality dominated. There were American engineers, Dutch soldiers, Javanese labourers, Chinese traders, miners and prospectors, chancers of every sort.

Minutes out of Paramaribo, and they were in thick jungle. A sluggish breeze made the heat bearable, and for a while Manne paced the upper deck to get some air. Gradually, the ever-twisting river narrowed until there was hardly room for the boat to get through. Nonetheless, it steamed on at a reckless pace. The water was deep right to the banks, and bushes reached metres out over the river, acting like fenders to stop the boat from running aground. Native dugouts scurried out of the way as the boat approached. Kilometre upon kilometre of the same chaos of green, with nothing to distinguish one part from any other – the random monotony of the jungle that Manne knew so well. Occasionally a colourful swarm of parrots would rise up from the trees and swoop down on the boat, like the reconnaissance aeroplanes Manne remembered from the war.

Most of the passengers were bunched up at the front of the boat, enjoying the cooling wind. In search of some solitude, Manne made his way to a small lower deck at the stern, abandoned because some of the engine smoke blew onto it. He managed to find a protected corner, though, and sat down on a bench by the rails. He was going to read his book, and opened one of his bags to get it out, but then changed his mind. He found himself rifling through a folder of papers slipped down one side of the case. His passport and birth certificate, a few envelopes, some other documents with his name on them.

One by one, he dropped the papers over the side of the boat, shocked and thrilled by his own action. The papers turned in the wind and swirled about in the wake like darting birds. He'd boarded the French boat as Manne, which was dangerous enough, but he couldn't risk entering French territory under his own identity. At some expense he'd acquired another passport from a trafficker in Caracas, just a few weeks before. It bore his photograph, and the name of Paul Hartfeld, born in Brussels. Had such a person ever existed? He did now, in any case. There'd been a few weeks when Hartfeld and Manne had shared the same body, but Manne was gone now. He felt a pang of regret or emptiness, but it passed quickly enough. He was Paul Hartfeld. Almost identical to Manne, and yet in some as yet indefinable way quite different.

Dusk. The boat turned a final bend to reveal a floodlit industrial plant, with AMERICAN ALUMINUM CO., MOENGO painted in colossal letters along its side. A startling sight, deep in the heart of the jungle. Manne let the other passengers disembark first, then made his way down the gangplank and wandered the length of the single street. A company town – not much here but the monstrous plant, some worker accommodation, a general store, a bar. No hotel, but after asking around Manne was offered a government room above the police station for a few florins. Just enough space for a bed and mosquito net, with a faded picture of the Dutch queen on the wall.

At the bar he found a Chinaman heading for Albina first thing next morning. A plate of stew and a couple of beers later, Manne began to feel his head spinning: sheer exhaustion probably, combined with the vile chemical fumes the plant belched out. He managed to make it back to his room and collapsed on his bed. Sleep came instantly, once more troubled by dreams of Edouard, none of which he could remember in the morning.

A loud banging woke him up: five o'clock, still dark, the

Chinese trader at his door ready to leave. Minutes later, he found himself crashing along in a battered old Ford with no suspension. The road itself was nothing more than a dirt trail in the jungle, so narrow at points that branches swept in through the open sides of the car. The back heaved with bags of rice and flour, and it seemed the only way to keep the car going was to rattle on at top speed and rely on momentum.

Even if the Chinaman had been a talkative type, the engine noise precluded all conversation. But halfway along they stopped for bread and water, and Manne felt compelled to fill the silence: 'You live in Albina?'

The Chinaman shook his head. 'Delivery.' He jabbed his thumb in the direction of the sacks in the back.

'What's it like, Albina? Nice place?'

He shook his head again. 'Nothing to do there. So quiet, people must go to Saint-Laurent for fun!' He broke out in raucous laughter as if he'd just cracked the most hilarious joke.

On along the trail at breakneck speed, stopping one more time to fill the hissing radiator with water. A couple of hours later the road suddenly widened, and Albina and the river came into view. The car pulled up alongside a general store; Manne collected his bags from the back. Albina seemed not much more than a row of tidy whitewashed houses in the colonial style. The river, on the other hand, was a vast expanse, a good couple of kilometres across. It was a relief and also a little overwhelming to be able to see so far, after the claustrophobia of the jungle. The sunlight bounced off the water's rippling surface, dazzling him.

'Where you go? You want a room?' asked the Chinaman.

Manne shook his head, pointed out across the river. He'd been going to spend the night in Albina, but what was the point?

'Saint-Laurent?'

'Yes.'

'Go to the water. Boni man will take you across. You give one florin. One florin only!'

II

Customs House: a corpulent official with a florid moustache asked for his papers, and Manne handed over the fake passport. Hartfeld, he reminded himself. You're Paul Hartfeld now.

'How long are you staying?'

'I'm not sure.'

'You have permission to stay?'

'Here's the visa.'

The official looked it over, shook his head. 'This is for Cayenne. Not for the penal territories. You need permission from the governor's office to stay more than twenty-four hours.'

'I did forward a letter of introduction to the governor from Caracas. There's a copy of it here.'

He proffered the letter he'd had forged, with its fancy letterhead for a non-existent institute of tropical botany in Belgium.

'I'll check with the governor's office,' said the official. 'You'll have to report back tomorrow. Where are you staying?'

'I don't know yet.'

'Well, there's only one place to stay here.'

Manne stumbled back out into the bleached streetscape. He

found himself panting a little – the heat was quite different from on the coast, where a constant breeze made it tolerable. Here, the air was so heavy that it felt at times like a solid mass weighing down on you.

Opposite the Customs House, Manne noticed the statue of a man staring out over the river, with two black men cowering at his feet. He walked up to the statue to read the little plaque: 'Victor Schoelcher, liberator of slaves'. Then he wandered further up the main boulevard, past a string of well-kept administrative buildings and an attractive-looking hospital with wide verandas. For a tropical town, everything seemed well scrubbed and impeccably clean.

Here and there, men with wide straw hats and striped uniforms were gently pushing a broom, or leaning down to prise a weed from a crack in the pavement. In the intensity of the noonday heat, they moved with an exacting slowness, as if time itself had wound down to a painful crawl. They seemed totally unsupervised. A long wall, then a gigantic arched gateway came into view, marked CAMP DE LA TRANSPORTATION. The gates were open. Convicts wandered in and out, with no apparent purpose.

A Creole woman walked past Manne, a loaf of bread under her arm. He was in a tiny commercial district now, a block long. There was a *boulangerie* to his left, a bank and a post office too – the letter box the same shape and colour as in France. Beyond the shops, a neatly laid-out residential quarter stretched out, with its squat bungalows, tidy gardens, ugly little church. It was different enough from anywhere else he'd been in South America. None of the overripe, baroque fantasy favoured by the Spanish and Portuguese colonists. No, this was more like the drab suburb of a provincial town in some nondescript corner of Picardy.

Soon after, the boulevard crumbled into a dirt path, the bungalows giving way to little lean-tos and shelters made from corrugated iron. Just like any shanty town, on the outskirts of any city. A few white men in rags were slumped in front of their makeshift dwellings, playing cards or simply staring into space. *Libérés*, no doubt – men who'd finished their sentence but weren't permitted to return to France. Then beyond the shanty town, nothing. The dirt path petered out into a little trail that pierced the darkness of the forest. Saint-Laurent was small, smaller than Manne had imagined it. You could see it all in twenty minutes.

In the dead of the afternoon, a bell was tolling, its single note ringing on and on. Manne wandered back along the boulevard in search of the town's only hotel. The temptation to stop and stare at the *bagnards* as he passed was too strong to resist. Their slow, silent movements lent them a certain gravity, as if they were the apostles of a new religion. Marked, wrinkled faces stared blankly back at him like a distorting mirror. Manne towered above most of them. Impossible to imagine Edouard among these broken remnants of an underclass. Not for the first time, he wondered whether Edouard's letter wasn't some kind of hollow, eccentric joke. It was hot, so hot he had to stop from time to time to get his breath. The breeze itself felt as if it were on fire.

Au Petit Coin de Paris: he found it on the rue Voltaire, just behind the commercial block, in front of a sort of wasteland. A small café-bar, with a few rooms to rent at the back. A mulatto woman stood behind the bar, some kids played outside in the dirt. Manne sat down and ordered a coffee, then called over one of the kids and gave him a few coins to collect his bags from the Customs House. He tasted the coffee and inwardly grimaced: in a continent where they grew so much of the stuff, how could it be so awful? On the bar top lay a few yellowing magazines. He flicked through a months-old copy of *La Vie Parisienne*. Theatre reviews, society women, photos of a ball at the Hôtel de Crillon . . . He had a memory of dining there with a lover once, before the war. Such a long time ago. Paris seemed unreal. It was this café, this simulacrum of a town, that was the real truth of life.

He got out his journal and started to write:

The same streets, the same hotel rooms. You travel a thousand kilometres, only to find the same face in the mirror. I don't feel hopeful about what I have come to do. I'm not depressed. But I feel no drive, no urge to swing into action. Perhaps it's the heat.

He closed the journal again. That was all that would come these days, a phrase here, a phrase there. Before, he was capable of writing pages and pages at a sitting. That too, in any case, had been pared down to the bare minimum.

'Your room's ready now.'

The mulatto woman was standing in the doorway at the back of the café, holding a key.

'Thank you. Do you have a safe, somewhere I could leave valuables?'

The woman looked at him as if she hadn't understood the word. 'Don't worry. It is safe here. Very safe. Many police, many soldiers. They come and drink here. There is no trouble here.'

As he took the key from her, she said: 'I am free, all afternoon. If you want, I am in the bar. I will arrange anything.'

It was hard to follow her Creole French, and he wasn't sure if she was offering herself, or some other woman. Her face was pleasant and pretty enough; her rounded figure wavered somewhere between voluptuous and plump. Manne imagined kissing her, undressing her, taking her to bed. The sex would be brisk, matter-of-fact, enjoyable. It was a fantasy that lasted no more than a split second, and yet it was enough to sate him.

'Thank you, I'll be fine.'

A washbasin and mirror, a table and chair, a bed with a mosquito net – much the same as last night's room in Moengo. Manne flopped down on the bed, still thinking of the mulatto woman, of sex. The last time he'd slept with a woman was in Caracas. He'd briefly kept a mistress there. She'd actually been a prostitute – it had been several years since he'd slept with any other kind of woman. But she'd played along with enough humour and grace, and he remembered with affection her face, her conversation, the look and feel of her body. He'd take her out to lunch or dinner a few nights a week, would delight in buying her clothes and jewellery, paid rent on a room for her in a nice part of town. The liaison had lasted around a month. It was a pattern that had played out in many of the ports and cities he'd stayed in for any length of time. And it was always at that point, about a month in, when the purity of the commerce would start to feel corrupted, and one or the other would put an end to it.

Now he threw off his clothes, washed himself as well as he could at the basin. Always greasy with sweat in this climate, impossible to feel crisp and dry and clean. He stared at himself in the mirror, examined his face carefully for the first time in days or weeks. The handsome boyishness was still there. The sculpted bone structure, the thick lick of hair – bleached blond in the tropical sun – made him look at least a decade younger than his forty-two years. It was only when he looked very closely that he could make out the minuscule lines running through his face, under his eyes, like a thousand hairline cracks in a Chinese vase.

A few books spilled out of his suitcase. He'd ordered them from the Librairie Française in Caracas – the memoirs of a convict, a guard, a doctor who'd served their time in the Colony. Their stories took on an air of fiction now that he was actually in Saint-Laurent. The novel he'd started on the boat seemed more real. He lay down on the bed to continue reading it, but quickly drifted off into an uneasy sleep. Dreams came to him again: some grotesque, some sexual, some about the novel, some about Edouard.

The rain woke him up – a pummelling tropical shower that made the ceiling shudder. By the time he'd got dressed, the rain had stopped, abruptly, as though someone had turned it off with a switch. Outside, a humid, fetid odour rose from the streets swept clean by the savagery of the downpour. The water hadn't really refreshed the atmosphere, hadn't brought relief from the heat, either.

On his noonday walk, Manne had already located the botanical gardens – 'the most beautiful in South America,' a woman on the boat had insisted. Past the large iron gate was a sweeping expanse of gravel, with rows of what looked like horse chestnuts on each side. At a cursory glance, it could have been a large municipal park anywhere in France, and it made Manne realise why he felt so strange in Saint-Laurent. It wasn't the tropical setting, or the convicts in the street, or the Creole families, or the *camp de la transportation*. No, it was the fact that, despite all that, he was back in France, for the first time since the war. The same unease he'd felt on the boat, with its little microcosm of Gallic life revolving around the captain's table. It was France that felt exotic to him now – its boredom, its rituals, dangers – rather than the gargantuan river and forest that surrounded him here.

He tried to see himself in the faces of the convicts who

tended the gardens. Had Manne been caught and arrested after the war, he might well have ended up among them. Theoretically, he still could. Or had there been an amnesty in the intervening years? The only thing he knew for certain was that he'd been declared missing in action, presumed dead, back in 1917: months afterwards, in Geneva, he'd seen his name on a list in a French newspaper.

Someone was clipping at a bush, his back turned to Manne. He was tall for a convict, and for an electric moment, Manne thought it was Edouard. But when the man turned around, he could see it wasn't. The convict stared, as if it were Manne who was the bizarre creature, then lifted his straw hat slowly and bowed with exaggerated courtesy.

'I'm looking for someone who works here, in the gardens. By the name of Edouard. Do you know where I can find him?'

The man shook his head solemnly. 'No Edouard working here, sir. But I've only been in the gardens a few months. Best ask old Xavier. Been here for years.'

The convict indicated where to find him, in a corner by a shed, beyond the gravel and rows of trees. Here, a different kind of vegetation was bursting out of myriad little pots – a riot of purples, reds and yellows, with the familiar wiry stems and drooping petals of orchids. Manne recognised most of them, but there were some he'd never seen before, and instinctively he found himself mentally noting dimensions, colours, symmetries.

The man was sitting on a stool, contemplating the orchids, even talking to them, since his mouth was silently moving. Shrivelled and toothless, he looked impossibly old.

'I knew Edouard,' he said after a long pause. 'Liked him well enough. He was here a year or two. Think he was waiting for someone. Maybe you? But he's not here any more.'

'Where is he?'

'He got moved.'

'Where to?'

'Camp down the river. An old scam. They move a man down the river. Then his lover, he has to bribe the bookkeeper to get moved up there too.'

'I've no idea what you're talking about . . . I just want to know where I can find Edouard.'

'I saw him not so long ago. Maybe . . . two months ago. Sneaked back in here one day. Just like that. On the run, I'd say. Took some of these roots here. Took his drawings, too. He'd left them in the nursery office.'

'Where did he go?'

The man waved vaguely towards the river. 'Took off with Bonifacio's gang, so they say. Didn't get far, by all accounts. They got Bonifacio. Skulking around, up near Renée.'

'What's Renée?'

'Camp up north.'

'What about Edouard?'

The man shrugged his shoulders. 'Who knows? Probably hiding out up that way, too.'

'This other man. Bonifacio. Where can I find him?'

'Ah! Too late for that now. The bell. Didn't you hear the bell?'

In the twilight, the town felt different, somehow more sinister. Convicts made their way back to barracks; Creole women scurried through the streets as though they too were under curfew. Manne wandered slowly back through the gardens and along the boulevard in a daze of thought.

The mulatto woman looked up as he walked into the café. 'Letter for you.' Manne ripped it open – an invitation to a cocktail reception at the governor's residence, tomorrow evening.

A tedious, dangerous night of colonial small talk, no doubt. Was there any way to get out of it? No, he could hardly refuse. He ordered a beer, drank it down quickly, ordered another. A small crowd of men stood at the bar. Next to Manne, two uniformed men were drinking rum, shot after shot, bottle on the bar top. Manne could tell that one of them was watching him warily out of the corner of his eye. Maybe strangers – of Manne's sort, anyway – weren't so common in this town.

'What a business,' the other one was saying, 'what a business!'

'Only wish I could've been there.'

'I'll give him this. He didn't start blubbing, like most of 'em do.'

'Know what someone told me? He'd had "CUT HERE" tattooed around his neck.'

'I couldn't see well enough for that. It was over in a minute. Frogmarched him straight to the block. Practically carried him there. Didn't want to give him a chance to try anything on.'

'No last words, then?'

'He did shout something. Just as they were about to strap him under. I couldn't make it out. Antoine thought it was "*Je suis le bagne.*" That's what he heard it as.'

'Doesn't make any sense.'

'They don't tend to make much sense, by then.'

The man who'd been eyeing Manne now turned to him. 'Well, sir. You and I both seem to have missed the big show today.'

Only now did Manne recognise him: the fat, surly officer who'd questioned him at the Customs House. The drink seemed to have loosened him up.

'What was that?'

'You didn't hear the bell?'

'I heard a bell . . . I thought it was the Angelus.'

The man laughed. 'They ring the bell when there's an execution. Famous killer, this time around. Name of Bonifacio. Expect you've heard of him.'

'No.'

'Surely you've heard of the Bonifacio gang? The heists in the Place Vendôme? Caused quite a hullabaloo at the time.'

'I don't recall.'

'Well . . . anyway, he killed a guard, not so long ago. The guard killers . . . we always get them in the end. Don't we, François?'

'Like to think we do,' said the other man uncertainly. He was in colonial whites, a large pistol holstered at his hip. There was a silence for a minute or two as the men drank.

'I'm curious,' said Manne eventually. 'How often are these executions?'

'Oh, not too often,' replied the customs officer. 'Depends. Some years, there's only a couple. Others, a dozen or more. Bonifacio's the fourth this year, I think.'

The man with the pistol downed the rest of his drink, made to go. 'Can't sit here getting drunk all night. Tomorrow's the big day.'

'Why, what's happening?'

The man raised an eyebrow. 'You don't know? New convoy's coming in. You should go down to the pier and take a look. It's quite the carnival. The only type you'll get in Saint-Laurent, at any rate.'

After a dinner of rice and meat, Manne went back to his room and took off his clothes. He threw himself onto the bed, confused and exhausted by the events of the day. The news about Edouard was still sinking in, making him feel giddy. The toothless convict in the gardens had been a touch senile ... or had he been toying with Manne? One thing seemed certain enough. Edouard really had been here, in Saint-Laurent. The old man could hardly have been making it all up, not with that detail about Edouard's drawings.

Had Manne acted as soon as he'd received Edouard's letter, everything would have been so straightforward. He'd have come to Saint-Laurent and found Edouard still at the Botanical Gardens. Instead, he'd spent a few months dithering, moving from town to town in Colombia, through the jungle. Then on to Venezuela, where finally he'd decided. He'd been a couple of weeks in Caracas, ample time for the city to no longer feel new or different. And still he'd had to wait out another month there while he assembled the forged documents, the visas, the permits, the bank transfers, before he could finally get out, move on.

The roof leaked, he couldn't see from where, but the walls were damp, as if they too were sweating. Under his mosquito net, Manne felt like a caged animal. He remembered the words he'd written in his journal only a few hours before: *I'm not depressed.* They worked on him like a reverse spell. A vision of the convicts he'd passed in the street came back to him, with their tatty, striped uniforms. The blankness of the gaze, which spoke of lives worn smooth through repetition. It made some sort of sense that Edouard had ended up here after all.

As usual, the heat woke him early. Manne sat in the bar for an hour or so drinking bad coffee, wondering what to do with the hours that stretched out before him. Years ago, a day without duties had been a thing to be savoured; now it felt like a constraint. He wandered along the main avenue for a while, his mind eternally drifting back to Edouard. No longer in Saint-Laurent, but somewhere north of here, hiding out. In which case, there was a good enough chance of finding him – if he wanted to be found. No doubt he could survive for weeks or even months in the jungle. After all, most orchid hunters ended up getting lost at some stage, forced to live off the jungle until they found their way back to civilisation.

Manne wandered back to the botanical gardens. There was no one around except a few convict gardeners, desultorily clipping or digging. He recognised the tall man he'd almost mistaken for Edouard, and walked up to him. 'I'm looking for the old man I talked to yesterday. Where can I find him?'

'He's not here today. Took ill in the night. I think he's at the hospital.'

Manne wandered back out again, somehow unsurprised at the old convict's absence. Saint-Laurent's few streets were filling up with people. They were all heading in the same direction, towards the pier. Without anything better to do, Manne followed them down to the river.

A whistle blast pierced the air. As Manne got closer, a huge grey ship came into view, almost the size of an ocean liner. It had just docked at the pier. Even given the width of the Maroni, it was disconcerting to see anything this big so far up a river, by the jetty of such a small town. Quite a crowd had formed by the foreshore: Creole men in suits and hats with their women in multicoloured dresses and headscarves; half-naked native boatmen; dozens of guards, too, pistols glistening at their hips. Faces bobbed at the thick glass plate of the ship's portholes.

Sailors lowered the gangplanks; slowly, the convicts began to disembark. Again, Manne was struck by how short most of them seemed, how young, too. He watched as two prisoners clumsily carried a third down one of the gangplanks. Once they'd set the man down on the pier, it was clear that he'd lost the use of his legs, that he was a paralytic.

'*Mais c'est un cadavre!*' exclaimed a bemused official who was overseeing the disembarkation. 'What's the use of sending me men like this?'

The official was one of several who were standing about, in their spotless whites and pith helmets, chatting to the guards on the pier. A number of their wives were there, too, shading themselves under parasols as they stared at the disembarking convicts. The younger ones were bare armed and in elegant summer frocks; they looked wildly out of place – more like flapper girls from the chic quarters of Paris. One of them turned to Manne. 'Which one's Boppe?'

'Who?'

'Boppe!'

'Sorry, but I don't know who that is.'

'Oh, you must have heard of him! That millionaire who killed his wife.'

'Afraid not.'

She looked at him oddly, then turned back to the convicts, peering at them through opera glasses as they lined up on the pier, ready to be marched to the *camp de la transportation.* Manne turned the other way, pushing back through the crowds. The sight of hundreds of convicts standing to attention under the sun made him feel light-headed. He'd read in a book that a third of them – or was it half? – usually died within the year.

Back past Customs House, the statue, the pretty *hôtel de ville*... but when he got to the hospital he stopped. Even here, doctors and orderlies loitered outside its impressive façade, waiting to see the new convoy marched along the boulevard.

Manne climbed the stairs to the entrance, and then through to a high-ceilinged atrium. Beyond, he could see a large hall with men lying on long rows of beds, panting in the heat. There didn't seem to be any guards about.

'Yes?'

A bored-looking man in a white smock was sitting behind a desk.

'I want to see a patient. Not sure of his last name, his first name's Xavier. An old man. He works in the botanical gardens. He was taken in during the night.'

'Couldn't have been during the night, could it?'

'Why not?'

The man looked up in surprise. 'They lock the barracks. Then they don't open them till morning.'

He was consulting some sort of *cahier*, flicking back through the pages. He hadn't bothered to ask Manne who he was or why he wanted to see the convict patient. The man's arms were covered in tattoos – so he, too, was a convict.

'Bonnefoi, Xavier, age sixty-three, brought here at six this morning.'

'Must be him. Could I see him?'

'If you go to the bamboos.'

'What do you mean?'

'You don't know the bamboos? Where they bury the convicts.'

'Oh . . . you mean he died.'

The man nodded. 'Probably dead when they brought him here.'

Manne made his excuses, then ducked down an alley back to the café, back to his room. Already tired from the heat, he was thinking about the conversation he'd had with the customs officer the night before. About executions. About the guillotining of the gangster, Bonifacio. The man Edouard had escaped with, if the old convict was to be believed. Now the convict was dead, too, only hours after their conversation. Everything was tenuous – the faint traces of Edouard's existence in the Colony already fading under the sun and rain. He felt angry at the old man for dying like that, for not waiting to explain himself more clearly. Absurd, of course. It's what old men do, after all. They die.

Once again, Manne couldn't escape the feeling that Edouard was playing a trick on him, an elaborate game of seduction. He remembered an expedition up near the Panamanian border, several years ago. He'd stopped at an Indian encampment for supplies and water, only to be told that another team had passed that way just three days before. Led by a tall European, dark hair, strange eyes. Almost immediately, Manne had set out once again, taking with him a couple of local Indians. He'd abandoned his planned itinerary and set the Indians to track Edouard. One morning a couple of days later, they saw plumes of smoke rising on the horizon. It wasn't until the late afternoon that they'd got to the area: a whole swathe of forest had been burnt out. Edouard had discovered something there – something valuable. Not only that, he'd also known that Manne was in the vicinity, and had burnt out the area to destroy any other specimens. For weeks, Manne had continued to track Edouard. On one occasion he'd even come across a campsite with still-warm ashes from the night fire. It had been around then that Manne's health had started to fail. His feet had swollen up and a malarial fever had laid him low for a week or two. Still he'd pressed on. During the endless drudgery of the journey, he'd often wondered just what he'd do should he find Edouard out here in the jungle. Rob him, or threaten him, or murder him, or offer to team up with him? Maybe he'd got it the wrong way round, it had once occurred to him. Maybe it was Edouard who was following *him*.

Manne's condition had got progressively worse, until finally he'd had to limp back into Panama City, mentally and physically at the end of his tether. The weeks in the jungle had nearly killed him, had got him nowhere. He'd found nothing of real interest, had merely accumulated enough new specimens to cover expenses.

A tasteless meal, a sleepless siesta, then a visit to a Chinese tailor to hire evening wear. By now the sun was low in the sky, about to sink into the jungle. His room behind the café had begun to feel like a prison cell, but it was still too early to go to the governor's residence. Instead he wandered aimlessly south of the pier until he came to a muddy beach, sitting down on a rock that jutted out of the grey sand. For a long time Manne simply gazed into the river, with its melancholy ripples of sunset orange and yellow. Then he stared over to Albina, the tiny, whitewashed settlement on the other bank. His mind spun away into that occult place halfway between thought and dream.

Something had changed in him since he'd crossed over the river. He couldn't pinpoint what exactly. It had to do with the vertigo he often felt, in dreams mainly but sometimes in waking moments too. A sensation of falling, forever falling, that he'd been falling for years. Since the war at least, or maybe all his life. Without ever reaching the bottom, or even knowing if there was one. Well, he'd reached it now. Before, up had been the same as down, forward the same as backward. No longer.

The river, sky, jungle were melting away into the blackness – night fell so quickly here. Manne was perfectly used to it, though. What seemed alien to him now was the thought of those languorous European twilights, with their eternal shadows and filtered light. Manne got up from the rock he'd been sitting on and headed back to the café. There he changed his clothes and walked slowly back up the boulevard.

He'd passed the governor's residence before: a rather splendid affair on a wide street shaded with mahogany trees. An immaculately turned-out butler let him into a sumptuous garden, bursting with exotic vegetation. Manne followed the man down a path, through the huge front door, then on to some sort of reception room, where he was announced. A couple of dozen people were being served cocktails by an army of servants. The men were mostly in smart military uniform, the women in summer frocks, adorned with jewellery that in Paris might have been judged too showy. Manne could feel eyes wandering over him with a small-town intensity. The tedium of garrison society hung heavily over the room.

For a few minutes Manne stood by himself, sipping his cocktail, until a pudgy, balding man approached him and bowed curtly. 'Monsieur Hartfeld?'

'That's right.'

'Please allow me to introduce myself – Captain Leblanc. I'm the governor's secretary. I'm afraid he couldn't be here this evening, but he asked me to . . . ' The captain stopped mid-flow, peered at Manne. 'But this is most odd . . . haven't we met before?'

'I don't think so.'

'You didn't serve in Belgium, did you?'

'I wasn't in Belgium. I don't think we've met.'

'I'm sorry . . . could have sworn . . . to tell you the truth, you look awfully like someone I served with. Now I think about it, poor chap died in action. Silly mistake of mine.'

'That's all right.'

Leblanc continued to look at him oddly for a moment, then snapped out of it with a smile. 'In any case, why don't you tell me about your mission here? The governor is most anxious to help in any way he can.'

'Well, we're hoping to receive funding for a botanical survey of the lower Maroni area. We think this could be of immense scientific and commercial interest to the Colony and the French government. The institute has sent me out to do a preliminary feasibility report...' Manne hadn't thought it through, but what came out sounded plausible enough. The captain asked him a few questions, and Manne found himself effortlessly extemporising – as always, the bigger the lie, the easier to tell.

'Your first stop here should probably be the botanical gardens. The old convict in charge, he's been there for years, if not decades. Probably knows more about the local flora than anyone else. He's something of an expert on local orchid species, so they tell me.'

'Thank you, I'll bear that in mind.'

'Of course, outside Saint-Laurent, things will be more difficult. This is penal territory, so you'll understand there'll be restrictions on your movements. The inland and coastal camp areas are out of bounds, for a start.'

'That shouldn't be a problem. It's the river system that's the focus of the study.'

'Well, there's relatively easy access to the river between here and about fifteen kilometres south. Beyond that is the *camp de la relégation*, which is under different jurisdiction, so you might have to apply to Cayenne for permission to enter.'

'What about to the north?'

'To the north it's all penal territory. There are labour camps. A couple on the river: Saigon, then further up there's Renée. There are paths along the river, right up to the coast. Although, as I said, the coastal camp areas are out of bounds.'

'And the river camps? If I wanted to stay at one of them, would that be possible?'

'Oh, you'd *have* to stay at one of them. Outside Saint-Laurent, you must report to the authorities every evening. And I'm afraid I'd also have to ask you to sign a promise not to publish anything about the camps or take photos of them. You've probably read some of the sensationalist tripe journalists have written about the *bagne*. It's been most damaging.'

'I've no interest in writing about the camps, I can assure you. It's the flora I'm here for.'

'Good. Well, yes, as I said, to the north there's Saigon, which is pretty basic. Beyond that there's Renée. The camp commandant's built a rather grand house there. If you do want to go north, he'd probably put you up.'

A bored-looking girl of about fourteen or fifteen had been hovering about, listening in on the conversation, eyeing Manne. Suddenly she broke in: 'Oh, do go to Renée and tell us what's happening up there!'

'Oh ... hello, dear,' the captain said. 'Monsieur Hartfeld, let me introduce you to my daughter, Elodie.'

'How do you do.'

'Elodie, this is Monsieur Hartfeld. He's a botanist.'

'How d'you do ... Oh yes, do go up to Renée! Has Papa told you about the commandant's wife?'

'Really, Elodie. Monsieur Hartfeld is not in the least interested in local gossip.'

'Oh, rot! Everyone likes gossip!'

'Well, now,' said Manne. 'You've certainly piqued my curiosity.'

'See, Papa?'

'Elodie, why don't you run along and see how your mother is. Monsieur Hartfeld and I have things to discuss.'

The daughter sloped off, a look of profound *ennui* on her face. If she'd been two or three years older, Manne mused, she'd have flirted shamelessly, tried to seduce him even, out of sheer frustration with the claustrophobia of colonial life . . .

'Ha ha, you must excuse my daughter! She's going through a rather blunt stage.'

'Nothing to excuse. She seems delightful.'

'Thank you.'

'And I must say I'm rather intrigued now about this commandant and his wife.'

'Well, if you do want to go up to Renée . . . I suppose you might as well know that the commandant's regarded here as rather a rum chap. He . . . well, his family's very rich, and he's built his house up there with his own money, most unusual. He's also invested in some building and agricultural schemes that have not, um, met with universal approval . . . but as long as it's not the Administration's money, I suppose it's his own affair.'

'And his wife?'

'Strange business.' The captain lowered his voice. 'She simply appeared here in Saint-Laurent one day, a few weeks ago. In a most awful state. Bedraggled, hysterical. Walked all the way from Renée through the forest by herself to get here. Not a *sou* on her, no papers, nothing. She was asking about for help to get to. . . I think it was Buenos Aires. Somewhere absurdly far away, in any case. None of us had even met her before – the commandant had whisked her straight up to Renée the moment her boat had got in. So we couldn't even be sure she was who she said she was . . . until her husband turned up the next day. In the meantime, we'd put her up in a room here. Fed her, gave her some clothes. By the next day she'd calmed down. My wife tried to get her to talk, but she wouldn't. When the commandant appeared . . . well, we were expecting a frightful row. But she went back with him. If not happily, at least not unwillingly. All most bizarre. As you can imagine, the whole business set tongues wagging.'

A few more minutes of conversation, before the captain excused himself to greet a newcomer. Leblanc – such a common name. Not one that would stick in the mind. Even if he'd once known him, Manne might not recognise him now. A decade ago, Leblanc had probably been slim, with a full head of hair. Men who'd fought in the war often aged more quickly than others. Manne's own still-boyish looks were a perverse exception.

III

Black clouds scudded low across the sky. In the forest, everything was still, and in the stillness Manne could hear the thud of rain, a couple of kilometres away. It would be upon them in minutes, and Manne scouted about to find some cover for himself and the boy convict who was accompanying him on the trip up to Renée. Eventually they ducked under the branches of a mahogany tree. Moments later, the rain came down in what seemed like a solid mass. As if an enormous lake had stood suspended just above the forest canopy.

Manne had hardly exchanged more than a handful of words with the convict boy so far. He hadn't wanted a servant. It was Leblanc who'd imposed one on him, and Manne still felt angry about it. The meeting in Leblanc's office had been wholly different in tone from their initial chatty encounter at the cocktail reception, two days before. This time, there'd been no gossipy stories about colleagues and their wives. Leblanc had been rather cold, and if not obstructive, then not terribly helpful either. At one point, Manne had caught Leblanc staring at him oddly again. And when Manne had insisted he needed no servant, Leblanc had insisted otherwise. But it was Leblanc who was signing the permits, so there was nothing Manne could do about it.

As the meeting had wound up, Leblanc had said to him: 'Hartfeld ... Jewish name, is it?' Manne had replied no. Although now that he thought about it, he had no idea whether it was or not. After all, he was only gradually getting a feel for who Hartfeld was, and in what ways he differed from Manne. It was true that in certain military circles 'Jewish' was code for subversive, unreliable, unpatriotic, *dreyfusard*.

Manne had been tempted to ask who it was that Leblanc had initially mistaken him for at the cocktail party. But it might have looked suspect – and he'd already made himself more conspicuous than necessary. As he'd marched through the forest in silence, Manne fell to wondering why he had to be accompanied, when in any case he reported to an official every day. The best he could come up with was that he was being spied on.

Now immobile beneath the mahogany, Manne looked around for almost the first time since plunging into the jungle. A palm tree was practically bent double from the force of the rain. In the lower reaches of the canopy, he could make out small clumps of orchids, their petals twisting into each other in a sensuous grip. One of the commoner varieties of *Cattleya* – nothing worth shinning up a tree for. A few months ago, he'd have climbed up anyway, just to be sure.

Next to him under the tree, the convict boy was hunched up and shivering under the rain. After a while, Manne noticed that the boy wasn't only shivering, he was also snuffling and crying, but trying to hide it as well. Manne felt suddenly ashamed of his suspicion that the young convict was a spy. This simple lad, lost in a new country, terrified by the solitude of the jungle ...

'What's your name?'

The boy uttered something long and unpronounceable. Arabic. It was the first time Manne had even noticed that the boy was Arab and not French. 'The others call me Guépard. You can call me that.' He had dark splotches running all the way down the left arm and leg, probably some sort of birthmark.

'How long have you been in the Colony?'

'Came in on the last convoy, *m'sieur*.'

'Just a few days, then?'

The boy nodded. He must have been sixteen or seventeen, although he looked more like fourteen.

'What did you do to find yourself here?'

A thick North African accent made the story almost incomprehensible, but from what Manne could gather, the boy had been sentenced for the murder of a café proprietor in Algiers, during a botched robbery. The boy hadn't even been present, he insisted, but he'd been rounded up along with the guilty ones, since they all lived on the same street and ran around together. His French was poor and he hadn't been able to defend himself properly at the trial.

As he told his story, the snuffles gradually dissolved into outright sobbing, the boy's body shaking as if in spasm. He gripped Manne's arm. Through his tears, he implored: 'Please help me, *m'sieur*! You can help me! You can talk to the governor, please! You can write to France! I'm an honest boy, I did nothing wrong. Please help me!'

'I'll see what I can do. Don't worry. I'll put in a good word for you. I'll do what I can.'

His reassurances seemed pitifully insufficient. He thought: at the very least I'll write a note to Leblanc commending him. The feelings of compassion the boy had aroused in him made Manne feel good about himself, then, seconds later, bad about himself. Bad that he needed the misfortunes of another to feel good. The rain dropped to a drizzle, continued for another ten minutes, then cut out altogether. Steam rose up from the ground. It was as if something were trapped underneath, trying to push its way out. A rolling sea of mist was spreading noiselessly across the river. They moved on through the silence.

Manne watched the young convict as he walked a few paces ahead, clearing the path of stray branches. He wondered whether it was fatherly concern that he felt for him. Not exactly. If the boy were his own son, then he'd do anything for him, make whatever sacrifice necessary. And what a relief it must be to feel that way, he now thought. To be wholly absorbed in someone's problems and pleasures, and yet without having to *be* that person. A means of finally escaping yourself.

Orchids dotted the canopy. It was refreshing in this heat to contemplate their frozen grace. Edouard was right – the Maroni would offer rich pickings for the orchid hunter. No doubt only a handful of hunters had ever passed this way, owing to entry restrictions for the penal territory. Who knew how many new species might be sheltering up there? In the greenhouses of Europe, they withered and died without constant attention. Here, it was the opposite. The orchids flourished, twisting their way towards the same sun that flayed the European exiles.

Several hours later, the path ended abruptly. Without any forewarning, Manne found himself at the base of a wide avenue. Administrative buildings and barracks lined the avenue, and at the top, work was in progress on a new structure, shrouded in wooden scaffolding. Some sort of arch. With the exception of the arch, the camp resembled one of those military garrisons he'd come across in the Colombian jungles.

Not many people were to be seen. A guard pointed him in the direction of an administrative building which apparently housed the camp commandant's offices. The building seemed relatively deserted as well. At a desk by the main entrance sat a man in a soiled white uniform, playing solitaire. He showed no sign of putting the cards away as Manne approached.

'I'd like to see the commandant.'

'He's not here.'

Manne waited for an explanation, but the man said nothing further.

'Could you tell me where he is?'

'He's never here in the afternoons, is he? He's at his house.'

'Could you show me where it is, then?'

The man eyed him suspiciously. 'This is penal territory. You can't just wander in here. You need a permit. What's your business here?'

Annoyed, Manne pulled out Leblanc's letter from one of his bags. 'I have a letter of introduction from the governor's office.'

'Let me see that.'

The man tore open the envelope carelessly and skimmed over the letter. Manne felt a sudden fury: the letter was addressed to the commandant, not this slovenly official. He was about to say something but then checked himself. No point in making a scene. He remembered that he'd even contemplated opening it himself after Leblanc had given it to him, but had finally resisted the temptation.

The official handed the letter to Manne's servant boy. 'Take this down to the commandant's house, along with *monsieur*'s luggage. You can ask one of the men outside for directions.' He turned to Manne. 'And you, sir, if I might detain you a moment while I register your details.'

No offer of water or any other refreshment, after a long day's walk through the jungle. The official wandered off in search of the correct forms, leaving Manne to leaf through a weeks-old copy of *La Dépêche Guyanaise*. It was as bland as any provincial newspaper might be – no doubt it was under military censorship. As he turned the pages, his eye was caught by a *fait divers*. It was about the murder of a Cayenne street artist – probably a *libéré*, although the article didn't say. The murderer's wife had owned a portrait of a man, which she'd cherished and gazed into every evening. She wouldn't tell her husband who the man was, but she did tell him who'd painted it. So the husband had gone out and killed the artist. That was all there was in the article. It didn't explain the logic behind the murder, and seemed to take motive for granted.

Manne turned the story around in his head for a few minutes. A very old memory came to him, of a painting in his mother's bedroom in the family home. After she'd died, he'd had the habit of stealing in there most days, and staring at the picture for minutes at a time. It was such a long time since he'd last thought of this; the memory swept through him with an extraordinary force of emotion. The painting was a landscape, he remembered, probably a copy of a Poussin or a Le Lorrain. A vast green panorama, utterly dominating the tiny figures in the foreground. Off in the distant hills, a walled town, with its turrets and steeples. It was infinitely intriguing, and the young Manne had had the fantasy that he might one day penetrate its artifice, go through its oils.

The official came back with the forms, and spent another quarter of an hour questioning Manne and filling them out.

'When's the rest of your luggage due?'

'I don't have any more luggage.'

The official looked at him quizzically. 'You're a botanist?'

'That's right.'

'You don't have any equipment with you?'

'No.'

For once, Manne was too tired to make anything up. The

official waved his hand dismissively. 'You'd better get down to the commandant's house now. It'll be dark soon.'

A convict showed him the path to the commandant's residence, back through the jungle. The sun was already setting over the trees, but he'd been told it was only a ten-minute walk. Back into the darkness of the forest. For a while, as he walked, he couldn't shake the image of his mother's painting from his mind.

Now a break in the jungle. A large house – like a country residence in the French provinces – came into view. It had extensive grounds; some effort at landscaping them had been attempted and, it seemed, abandoned. A vast lawn had been laid out with turf, only the turf had gone a reddish brown, the colour of dried blood. Something about it all reminded Manne of his great-uncle's house in Chiswick, where he'd been sent to stay soon after his mother had died. The size and layout were much the same, except that where his great-uncle had had his greenhouse, here there was a peculiar-looking construction, with a brick base and wooden slats holding up a palm roof. Beyond that, Manne could see the immense expanse of river, even wider than at Saint-Laurent.

As he got closer to the house he could hear music. A man singing, accompanied by a piano – Schubert Lieder, by the sound of it. The effect, out in the jungle, was distinctly unsettling. Especially since there was something off-kilter about it, as if the piano were out of tune, or the man not in time. Only when he was at the door did he realise it was a gramophone record.

A butler showed him into a large office. Most of it was taken up by an architect's model of what looked like a town, spread out across two tables. It was very detailed, with little carved blocks and plaster casts representing buildings and tiny model trees making up the limits of the forest. There were even models of people, like toy soldiers, strolling up and down the thoroughfares. Manne remembered Leblanc's words about the commandant's 'unusual' building schemes.

To one side of the model, a man was bent over the gramophone. He was taking the needle off the record, replacing the record in a dust cover. 'Sound's not terribly good, I'm afraid. The records have all got warped in the heat. But I'm used to it. I like to listen to music while I work.' He extended his arm. 'You must be Monsieur Hartfeld.'

'That's right.'

They shook hands. The commandant was tall, an imposing figure. A wiry body; thinning hair cropped close to the skull – there was something of the monk about him. A long face, as if it had been stretched like a rubber mask. And marked with some kind of suffering, Manne fancied. He didn't look like a war veteran, though, despite his military rank. Manne had a knack for picking out veterans – something about the way they talked or moved their body; he couldn't be more precise than that. Leblanc had had it; this man didn't.

'I see you're looking at my model.'

'Indeed.'

'I'm rather proud of that. Took a couple of convicts a good month's work to come up with it. Come and get a closer look.'

He beckoned Manne over. On the edge of the model rested a tumbler, half full, probably of rum. The commandant was drunk, he realised. Not very drunk, but Manne could nonetheless see it in the glassiness of his eyes.

'It's a plan of the camp, or the settlement, I prefer to call it. It's how Renée will look once the first phase of construction is finished. You see here? This is the avenue you would have arrived at. There'll be trees planted along it eventually. It's where all the administrative buildings will be – I'm relocating the convict barracks further north, in their own quarter. Between the avenue and here, I mean the river, there'll be a residential quarter, with three main roads . . .'

The commandant carried on in this vein for another few minutes. Not a word enquiring about Manne's mission. At one point, Manne broke in: 'And this, up here?'

He was pointing to the carefully carved model of an arch, at the top of the avenue.

'This? It's a monument. To the war dead. My Arc de Triomphe, ha ha . . . But you must think me awfully rude; can I offer you a drink or something? I usually have an *apéritif* about now, rum I'm afraid, I've rather gone native. But I have some whisky. And plenty of red wine. Not much point in drinking white, there's no way to keep it cold.'

'Not just yet, thanks, perhaps later.'

'Of course. I'll ask Charles to show you to your room. No doubt you're tired after the trip. Charles!'

Manne followed the butler through a corridor and up a wide sweep of stairs. It was getting dark now, and the house evidently had no electricity. Everywhere, it gave the impression of being not quite completed. Skirting boards only partly laid, a wall unplastered, a section of balustrade missing. Simple things, but things that looked as if they'd remained undone for months. On the other hand, there were paintings on the wall – good ones – that would almost certainly end up eaten away by damp and mould.

On one side of the landing were a couple of rooms; Manne could see a narrow bar of light escaping from under one of the doors. The butler led him over to the other side of the landing. Manne's bedroom was large, and yet the heat somehow made it feel claustrophobic. The thick stone exterior walls were unsuitable for this climate – wooden walls allowed the night coolness to penetrate, while stone stored up the heat during the day and discharged it during the night. Surely the architect should have known this.

The butler lit the several lamps in the room, then left. Manne's bags were on his bed, opened. His clothes already put away in the wardrobe – by Guépard, he guessed. He went through his affairs, to check that nothing had been taken. No, everything was where it should be.

For no good reason, he took out the two drawings of the Vera Cruz orchid that Edouard had sent him, and stared at them for some time. In his daze of exhaustion, he found the drawings mesmerising. There was the *trompe-l'oeil* of the brown cross within the petals, with the twisted strands that well enough represented a man hanging from it. But Manne had seen too much bizarre orchidry to be impressed by that alone. It was something about Edouard's meticulous, unsentimental draughtsmanship. There was none of the fantasy or sensuality that tended to creep into even the most scientific of orchid drawings. These were clean-lined, technical perfection, like an architectural plan of something yet to be built, that perhaps never would be. Almost as if the thing depicted were not alive at all.

Apparently, Edouard's artistic efforts hadn't always been like this. Once, in Rio de Janeiro, Manne had got chatting to a middle-aged Frenchman who was teaching at the Escola de Belas Artes. The man had invited him for a drink, and the two had ended up having dinner together. By chance, Edouard's name had come up in conversation. It transpired that the art teacher had briefly known him in Paris, about twenty years before. Edouard had been a young painter then, and known as a rather flamboyant character. He'd gained a certain notoriety for his obscene paintings, which he'd sell to *maisons closes*. Not much appreciated at the time, the works had since become collectables among a certain clientele. They were painted in a strikingly modern manner, the teacher had told Manne.

It was hard to imagine the terse, ascetic Edouard ever being 'flamboyant', but this secret, romantic past of his had amused Manne. A year later, he'd run into Edouard at the Hotel Grande in Havana. They'd spent the evening talking about the trade, in the circumspect way that plant collectors do when they get together, careful not to give too much away. At one point Manne had remembered the conversation he'd had with the teacher in Rio. 'Seems you've got something of an artistic reputation back in Paris,' he'd said, recounting the story. Edouard had stiffened, transparently wondering for a moment whether he could deny the whole thing. And despite Manne's questionings, he would barely talk about his past as an artist. The paintings he'd done were 'garbage'; he'd only done them for money; he had nothing but contempt for the 'charlatans' of the art world. This outburst had put a dampener on the evening, and the two had gone their separate ways soon after. Had that been their last encounter? Maybe it had. Later, there'd been that ill-fated expedition south of Panama. And that was the last Manne had heard of Edouard, until he'd received the letter.

Manne turned away from the drawings, opened his journal.

I wonder what E. looks like now. I have a fear that I won't recognise him, although I don't see why I shouldn't. The last time I saw him could only have been five or six years ago. He was probably forty then, mid-forties now. Men don't change a great deal in their middle years. By then, they have already become who they are. And yet I have the impression that this rule doesn't apply to me.

He closed the journal, aware that once again he'd written himself into a corner. Manne dozed fitfully for a while, until the butler woke him. 'Dinner will be served in twenty minutes, sir.' He got up, went to the basin and washed his face. As he dressed, he could hear someone climbing the stairs, a door slamming, fierce whispering.

IV

There were place settings for three people. The commandant hovered by the table, waiting for Manne to sit down.

'What do you care to drink? I've decanted a bottle of Burgundy. A Nuits-Saint-Georges. But Charles can easily...'

'Some Burgundy would be a pleasure. I'm surprised you can find it out here.'

'I had it shipped out especially. Of course, as soon as I got here, I realised it was impossible to lay down, due to the climate. We might as well drink it all up now before it goes bad.'

Manne noticed that the commandant himself was still on his rum, refilling his glass at regular intervals.

'Charles has managed some duck for this evening. How the devil he got hold of it is a mystery to me.'

'Sounds splendid.'

More small talk ensued. The commandant's mood seemed to have changed since their initial meeting. Before, he'd been garrulous and relatively at ease; now he looked nervy and spoke in staccato phrases. The empty place setting was opposite Manne, and he waited for the commandant to mention his wife, even if just to say that she would be down in a minute. But he didn't. Then halfway through a remark, the commandant stopped and looked up. Manne had his back to the staircase and turned around in his chair. She was coming down the stairs, but very carefully and slowly, as if on a swaying ship. The commandant jumped to his feet, waited until she got to the bottom of the stairs, then wrapped a solicitous arm around her. Manne got up, too.

'*Chérie*, this is Monsieur Hartfeld. He'll be staying with us for a few days. Monsieur Hartfeld, I'd like you to meet my wife Renée.'

'*Enchanté, madame.*'

The butler materialised with bowls of soup. After the introductions the conversation quickly dried up, and they started on dinner in an embarrassed silence. As he sipped at his soup, Manne glanced across the table at the commandant's wife. Her face was amazingly pale for this climate. In the tropics, even the most sun-conscious woman ended up with a little colour on her face, her arms.

'Monsieur Hartfeld is a botanist, dear,' the commandant finally managed. 'He's up here for a survey of riverside flora.' He waited for his wife to reply – she had her spoon to her mouth, but when she put it down again, she said nothing. 'Well, in any case it'll be pleasant to have a scientific man in the house,' continued the commandant. 'Someone interesting to talk to, at any rate.' The remark hung awkwardly in the air as they continued with their soup.

She looked to be in her early thirties, although a glazed look about her eyes might have added a few years. The lines of her *décolleté* hung crookedly between her breasts, as if she'd just woken and hurriedly thrown on some clothes. Poorly combed hair framed a striking face, sensuous, and yet with a strong, well-defined bone structure. It contrasted with the curves of her figure, which were feminine to an old-fashioned degree – the opposite of the straight-waisted flapper look.

'And how have you spent the day, my dear?'

Again she didn't reply, and again a strained silence filled the room.

'My dear, I asked you a question. I asked you how you'd spent your day.'

'You know perfectly well how I spent my day.'

The butler cleared the soup bowls. The woman stared down at her place mat, which depicted an old hunting scene. Manne noticed that the commandant hadn't touched his wine, but had continued to serve himself rum throughout the first course. He found himself wondering whether the couple had any children. It was perfectly possible that they had, staying with relatives, or being schooled in France. But Manne thought not.

'Monsieur Hartfeld, did you know that another botanist has recently arrived in the Colony? Not a professional, but a very good amateur one, I believe.'

Surprised by the woman's sudden remark, Manne took a moment to realise that it was addressed to him.

'No, I didn't know that. Who is he?'

'A fellow named Pierre Boppe. Strange chap. I used to know him. We moved in similar circles. A long time ago.'

'I think I heard that name in Saint-Laurent. But isn't he one of the . . . one of the *transportés*?'

'He is. You probably read about his trial. Caused quite a stir, back in France.'

'Renée dear, where on earth did you hear all this?'

Manne glanced over at the commandant, who toyed nervously with his glass as he spoke. His wife stared past Manne, past the staircase and through the window to the river.

'Charles told me. I knew Pierre. He was part of that Riviera set. Even then, I remember botany being his hobby. He used to disappear into the hills of Provence on the hunt for plants. I hear he's shipped over crates of botanical equipment. The authorities are creating a post especially for him. Apparently, he wants to write a book about tropical flora. I thought it might interest Monsieur Hartfeld.'

'Indeed, that's certainly interesting,' said Manne. 'If you don't mind my asking, what exactly did he do to find himself here?'

'He murdered his wife,' the woman replied in a matter-of-fact voice. 'I knew her, too. I'm surprised you didn't read about it. He's the heir to the Fernand fortune. He . . .'

'Renée,' interrupted the commandant, 'I think that's enough.'

'Enough?' she replied coolly. 'Enough what?'

'I really don't think this is a suitable subject for conversation.'

'Why ever not? I was answering Monsieur Hartfeld's question.'

'I said that's enough. Quite enough. It's rather morbid.'

His wife shrugged her shoulders in irritation. 'Honestly. Where do you think we are? What are we supposed to talk about?'

'I said it's *enough!*' the commandant snapped, his face suddenly flushed. He put his hands to the table, as if he were about to lever himself up. 'When I say it's enough, I mean you to listen to me! Look at you! I asked you to dress properly for dinner! *Look* at you! You're a mess!'

An artery in his neck stood out horribly, as if inflamed; he waved an arm wildly in his wife's direction. Her face bore an expression of astonishment rather than fear.

Manne's words cut through a bizarre pause: 'With respect, sir, it's true that I did ask her that question. I'm sorry if I caused any trouble. I think it's best if we all calm down.'

The commandant turned to him, still apparently in the grip of his rage. 'This has nothing to do with you, Monsieur Hartfeld. Nothing to do with you!'

'In that case, I must ask you to excuse me.' Manne placed his napkin beside his plate and got up from his chair. 'Although first I wish to say that I don't much care for the way you treat your wife in front of a guest.'

'I find that most impertinent, Monsieur Hartfeld. Most impertinent. You have no idea of the situation. May I remind you that you are staying in my house.'

'I'll leave in the morning.'

The commandant's wife broke in: 'Monsieur Hartfeld, there's no need to leave.'

Another agonising pause. The commandant slumped back in his chair. 'Yes, please sit down, Monsieur Hartfeld. I'm afraid I lost my temper. I owe you an apology.' His voice was flat now, like that of a corrected schoolboy. 'In fact, I offer my apologies both to you and to Renée. Please accept them.'

The duck arrived. It was dry and chewy, but edible enough. For minutes at a time, an excruciating silence reigned. Small talk was a virtual impossibility now, although near the end of dinner, Manne and the commandant's wife managed some sort of discussion, mainly about Manne's travels in South America. The commandant sat there limply like a child's cloth animal, occasionally sipping at his rum, taking no part in the conversation. Finally, the butler cleared the plates away.

The commandant rose from the table. 'Can I offer you a *digestif*, Monsieur Hartfeld? A cigar, perhaps?'

'Thank you, but no. I'm very tired after the journey up. I think I'll retire, if you don't mind.'

'Very well.'

Manne bade them good night and made his way up to his

room. He flung himself onto the bed, physically exhausted from the trip, mentally exhausted from the dinner. Too tired even to sleep. He wondered whether the commandant was physically violent with his wife. His guess was no, despite the dinner scene, despite Leblanc's story of her flight. He didn't know exactly why he thought that, only that the look of surprise on the woman's face at dinner had seemed genuine enough. He found himself visualising her face, her body, wondering what she would look like naked.

In the hope of some air, he got up to open the windows. In this climate, a man sweated day and night; sweated so much liquid away while sleeping that he'd wake up thirsty. Manne lay back down under the mosquito net and drifted off into a state somewhere between dozing and heat delirium. At some point, he could hear the sounds of a Bach cello suite wafting into his room like a cool breeze. He couldn't tell whether it was real or he was dreaming it.

Morning: the sun streamed into the room. He stood at the window looking out at the river and the shards of light that bounced off its ripples. As he washed at the basin in the corner of the bedroom, Manne found his thoughts turning to Edouard again. No obligation, no obligation, Edouard had written in his letter. Manne could walk out of the commandant's house, pay a Boni to take him across the river, out of France, out of the penal colony for ever. It was a temptation. The question was where he'd go next. Because the years of criss-crossing the continent were over, Manne realised. If those years had taught him anything, it was that when pushed to its extreme, travel turned into a type of immobility.

Downstairs, the commandant sprang up to greet Manne at the breakfast table, showing no outward signs of his heavy drinking of the evening before. 'Morning. I trust you slept well?'

'Yes, thank you.'

'I'll have Charles bring you some coffee and *tartine*. Unless you'd prefer tea?'

'Coffee will be fine.'

'Good, good ... I ... Let me apologise once again for my behaviour last night. Really quite inexcusable.'

'Please, let's speak no more of it.'

'Very gracious of you ... I put your servant in Charles's room. He's in the kitchen now, I think, helping Charles out, but any time you need him, just ask Charles to fetch him.'

As Manne ate his breakfast, the commandant continued talking at him: 'I do hope you'll find time to come and see some of the building works at the settlement. I'd be most obliged to have your opinion ... My wife, to be honest, my wife hasn't been well and that's why I try to avoid morbid subjects with her. I know it's difficult for her out here, but she needs to cultivate an interest ... Do you know how to use a pistol? If you're going north from here, I'd advise you take one of mine, there are *évadés* up that way, or so they tell me, in any case ...'

Later, Manne found Guépard weeding the small vegetable garden outside the kitchen. 'Leave that for a moment. Come up to my room. I want to talk to you.'

Guépard trailed behind him as he climbed the stairs. Opening the door to his room, Manne noticed that an unmarked envelope had been pushed under it. Inside was a single sheet of paper covered with an uneven scrawl. He shoved it into his pocket.

'Sit down, sit down.' Manne tidied some clothes off a chair and guided the boy to it. 'Now listen. I'm going to do what I can to help you here. I can't work miracles, do you hear? I can't get you a release. But I can write to Algiers and get a lawyer to look over your case again. See if there are grounds for appeal. And I can write to the governor commending your service to me. Recommend you for domestic duty. Do you understand me?'

The boy wrung his hands nervously, refused to look Manne in the eyes. '*Oui, m'sieur, merci, m'sieur*, you are a good man, *m'sieur*, very good man.'

'In return, you can do something for me. I understand there are convicts who come down here to work. Or I might send you on an errand up to the main camp. What I want you to do is ask around for some information on an *évadé*. I'm told he's hiding out near the camp. His name is Edouard Holmes.' He pronounced the surname OL-MESS, the way he'd heard Edouard himself say it. 'A tall man with dark hair. And a glass eye. Or perhaps an eyepatch. He used to work at the botanical gardens. You say he's your friend. You tell the other convicts that you're looking for a friend, a man named Edouard. Do you understand me?'

'*Oui, m'sieur.*'

Manne repeated the essentials in his rudimentary Arabic: 'Tall man, dark hair, called Edouard. You say he's your friend.'

Guépard looked at him, wide-eyed in astonishment. 'Yes. I understand,' he replied in Arabic, and then rattled off something else that Manne didn't catch. He nodded, nonetheless – best let the boy think his Arabic is better than it is. He'd picked some up in the Lebanon years ago, but Guépard was from Algeria: different dialect, different accent. Guépard continued to stare at him in frightened surprise, as though by speaking some Arabic, Manne could see right through him.

After he'd dispatched Guépard, Manne sat musing for some time. He was aware of something scraping against his thigh. He put his hand in his pocket and brought out the stiff fold of paper he'd stuffed into it. He'd forgotten about the note that had been slipped under his door. Now he unfolded and read it:

> *I should like to talk to you in private. Please follow the path at the far side of the garden, through the trees. You'll find a hut at the end of the path. If you can, meet me there this morning at eleven.*

It was signed with an illegible squiggle, in a female hand. Perplexed, Manne crumpled it up and tossed it into the bin by the desk. Then he thought better of it, fishing the note out and putting it back into his pocket. Someone snooping about might find it; he'd get rid of it later on. Across the landing was the woman's bedroom. He thought to go and knock on the door, then decided against it. Instead he gazed out of the window, across the garden that stretched along the river. He couldn't make out any path at the end, but no doubt it was there.

Manne sat back down by the desk, opened his journal and flipped his way through from start to finish. Read this way, it was clear how the smooth chronology of the first few pages slowly gave way to the disjointed abstractions of the latter part. He could feel his mind nonetheless trying to glue the fragments into some kind of narrative thread, only they refused to cohere. He picked up his pen, deliberately continuing with a theme he'd already touched on:

> *I look at E.'s drawings, again I try to work out what fascinates me about them. It strikes me now that the precision of their style signals not a beginning that could ever lead anywhere. They're a culmination, an end.*

* * *

That was all that would come for the moment. He lay down on his bed, closed his eyes and conjured up the face of the commandant's wife, with her black-blue eyes. Leblanc had implied that the woman was mentally unbalanced. So had her husband, in a more roundabout way. And yet Manne hadn't particularly gained that impression. She'd seemed to him simply unhappy, very unhappy. Of course, madness might be a transformed version of unhappiness. If so, it was a transformation that had always eluded Manne.

Later, he thought to see the commandant, to discuss plans for an expedition down the river as part of his 'mission'. The office door was ajar. Manne knocked, but there was no answer and he went in. There again was the vast, intricate model spread out over the two tables. At the end of the avenue, where the arch was positioned, was a gigantic *rond-point* that spiralled out into further avenues, not yet built into the model but lightly pencilled in. The effect was like a map of the western *arrondissements* of Paris. Everywhere, the commandant had scribbled in various specifications, remarks. And yet the architects Manne had known had worked from plans, detailed blueprints, and not models, which were used simply to give the client a general idea of the finished project.

Books lined one of the walls – Manne skimmed over the titles. Manuals on hydroelectricity, construction, medicine, botany, agriculture, cattle farming – a promiscuous selection of 'how to' books. The library of an autodidact. A man who thinks he can do everything. There was a whole row of dictionaries and grammars, of English, Dutch, Spanish, Portuguese, half a dozen other languages. Manne pulled out a manual for Taki, the lingua franca spoken by the Bonis and Indians up and down the Maroni. He flicked through it; written by a missionary, it dated from the mid-nineteenth century and included swathes of translated gospel. Manne put it aside. He'd take it up to his room to study; it might turn out to be useful. Manne picked up languages easily. In Latin America, he was often mistaken for a native Spanish or Portuguese speaker. By contrast, the French and English often assumed he'd been brought up elsewhere – some distant colony perhaps.

Underneath one of the bookshelves was a cupboard, with a key in the door. He was just bending down to investigate when he heard a discreet rustling behind him.

'Can I help you, sir?'

Manne straightened up. 'I was looking for the commandant.'

'He's gone up to the main camp, sir.'

'When will he be back?'

'He'll be back for lunch, sir. At half past twelve.'

'I see,' said Manne, leaving with the book he'd pulled out. As he climbed back upstairs he could hear the butler closing the door to the commandant's office. The man rubbed him up the wrong way.

He spent an hour skimming through the book on Taki, then read a few pages of *Arthur Gordon Pym*. Sweaty and itchy, he squirmed about in his chair – it was hard to get comfortable in the heat and humidity, to relax enough to concentrate. And yet the tropical climate was something he'd never had a problem with before. In fact, he'd always prided himself on coping better than most Europeans. It was age – he simply couldn't take it as easily now that he'd hit his forties. And all the time, as he tried to read, at the back of his mind he was wondering whether he'd make the rendezvous with the woman or not. Then at ten-thirty, without really having decided, he found himself getting up from his chair and putting his shoes back on in readiness to leave. He was going to meet her after all.

Downstairs all was quiet. He went down a dark corridor,

then through a side door that led out into the garden. By the river he could see a couple of white men, convicts probably, stripped to the waist, lounging about, seemingly not doing anything. He wandered across the lawn, slowly, as if out for a stroll. The vast, dead turf, burnt brown by the sun, looked alien. Up away from the river he could see long flower beds too, filled with weeds and dead plants. Huge expense must have gone into the landscaping of the garden. It was as if, just at the moment of its completion, it had been abruptly abandoned.

The sun was pounding at the back of his neck and, under the intensity of the light, his vision seemed to have gone dark. Feeling dizzy and weak, Manne made his way to one side of the garden where a mangy hedge gave some shade. He passed a hand through his hair; it was soaking with perspiration, as if he had a fever. Poor timing, if that were the case. At the very least, he should get himself a hat.

As he sat there recovering from the dizzy spell, an idea struck Manne. He was a plant collector, and had necessarily learnt a great deal about botany, about horticulture, above all about tropical plants and climates. For instance, the type of turf that had been laid down here was quite wrong for the location; whoever had been responsible had been poorly advised. Manne could have a word with the commandant. He could draw up some specifications, and instruct Guépard on what to do. If he could get Guépard a position here, as a gardener, he'd feel that, whatever else, he might have at least achieved one thing. He got up again, still feeling vague and dizzy.

The entrance to the path was obscured by ferns, perhaps deliberately, because behind them the route, though narrow, was well cleared. Manne walked on, relieved to be shaded from the punishing sun. In a few minutes he found himself in a circular clearing. In the middle stood a small, equally circular stone hut with a palm roof. It seemed newly constructed.

There was a door, closed. He knocked and it immediately opened. She looked smaller and more vulnerable than before. Her dark hair was tightly pulled back; she wore no make-up. Tiny lines circled the corners of her mouth.

'Thank you for coming.' They stood staring at each other wordlessly. 'We don't have long. My husband is up at the camp. Charles is buying meat at the native village. They'll both be back shortly.'

Manne took in her face, hips, the shape of her breasts. She didn't look away, but at one point stepped back slightly, as if to protect herself from the ferocity of his gaze.

'You're probably wondering why I asked you here.'

'Indeed I am.'

'I want to ask for your help.'

'What kind of help?'

She took a breath. 'I have to get away from here. I need someone's help to do it.'

Behind her, on the wooden floor, lay a lamp, a blanket, a few personal effects. Through the slats of the shuttered window, Manne could see tall palms rustling in the trade wind.

'Here? What do you mean by here?'

'The camp, the Colony...' She made a sweeping gesture with her hands that seemed to encompass the entirety of things.

'Why would you need my help for that?'

'I don't have any money, for a start. I don't have any means of leaving.'

'Why don't you ask your husband?'

She shook her head. 'I can't do that.'

'You want to leave him, is that it?'

'Yes.'

'In that case, can't your family send you money?'

She shook her head again. 'My father's not about to help me leave my husband, I can assure you. Besides, he has no money. He lost it all in the war.'

'Why do you want to leave your husband?'

'That's my business, don't you think?'

'If you're asking me to help you, perhaps it is my business. I'm here as your husband's guest, after all.'

She didn't reply. After a pause, Manne continued: 'Is he violent? Is that it? In which case, why don't you report it to the authorities?'

'My husband *is* the authority. But I don't wish to discuss my marriage with you. As I said before, it's none of your business.'

Her tone was dismissive. They continued staring at each other, neither flinching.

'What exactly do you want me to do?'

'There are various possibilities. One is to organise a boat across the river. Then accompany me up to Paramaribo. And lend me enough money for a passage out. When I get work, I'll be able to pay you back.'

'That's a pretty tall order. Do you have any idea of what you're asking?'

'I fully understand what I'm asking.'

'Even if I did help you get to Paramaribo, where would you go then?'

'I have a good friend in Buenos Aires. If I can make it to Argentina, she'll put me up. Help me get a job. I'm an excellent seamstress; I've always made my own clothes.'

'Do you know how far Buenos Aires is from here? Thousands of kilometres. You're living in a dreamworld.'

'I know exactly what my choices are. I know what I'm doing. You'll just have to accept my word for it.'

'Why don't you write to your friend in Buenos Aires? Why ask me? I don't know you. It will put me in a difficult . . . in an impossible situation.'

'I can't receive letters without my husband finding out.' She gazed past him. 'I'm not particularly expecting your help. But there's no one else to ask. You're the first civilian to stay at the house. So I'm asking you. It's as simple as that.'

'What's to stop me reporting all this to your husband?'

'Nothing at all.'

She seemed too contained, too coldly in control of herself. Fleetingly, Manne had a vision of something else – a scene where she would break down crying. Beg him, flatter him. *I'm asking you to do it out of the goodness of your heart, because I can sense that you're a kind man . . .*

'You won't help me?'

He shook his head.

'There's nothing I can do to persuade you?'

Through the shutter, a shaft of sunlight caught Manne in the eye, momentarily blinding him, confusing him. He wanted to put his arm up to protect his eyes from it, but he couldn't seem to move. The dizziness again, overpowering him.

'Take off your dress.'

Her blank expression remained. A long pause, an almost imperceptible shrug. Pushing her dress down, she wriggled a little until it fell to the ground. Memories of other women, performing exactly the same action, mostly prostitutes, shimmying then stepping out of their clothes. Her arms rested now at her side, exactly mirroring his, rigid, every muscle taut.

'Take off your brassiere.'

Twisting her arms up behind her back, at one point she turned away from him, presenting her shoulders to him as if she wanted his help in undoing a strap. He didn't respond. He stood blocking the doorway, making it impossible for her to leave. She didn't cross her arms over her breasts to hide her nakedness. Her vulnerability was like a weapon against him. The sweat from Manne's sodden hair trickled into his eyes.

'What are you going to do now?' she said flatly. The words sounded shockingly loud. 'Are you going to force yourself on me?'

'Of course not.'

He'd been holding his breath; he hadn't even noticed. The tension had broken, and the woman was bending down now, picking up her brassiere. Abruptly he turned around, walked out the door. He found himself striding back along the path, as fast as he could without actually breaking into a run. He stumbled over a root and almost lost his balance. He stopped for a few seconds, tried to calm his shaking with deep breaths. A knot in a tree trunk caught his attention: it looked like an eye, staring out at him, following him as he moved on again. Along the path, the bleached tropical light punctured the canopy randomly, but then broke over him as he came out into the garden. Once again, he found himself walking across the expanse of dead turf.

He'd got halfway across the garden when he noticed Guépard at the back door of the house. Manne slowed down, resisted the temptation to look behind to see if the commandant's wife was following him. Guépard was wearing an apron, and was sitting on the doorstep. As Manne got closer, he saw that the boy was polishing shoes. He continued to take deep breaths in an effort to control himself. At the door, he got out his packet of cigarettes: the tobacco might calm him. He offered the packet to Guépard. 'Cigarette?'

The boy looked up nervously. '*Non, m'sieur, merci, m'sieur.*'

Why must the boy be so damned tense around him? Manne lit his cigarette, drew in the smoke; he could feel the nicotine wash through his body like a barbiturate.

'Any luck yet?'

The boy looked at him in surprise. 'I don't understand, *m'sieur*.'

'You do remember what I asked you to do?'

'*Oui, m'sieur*. I will do it, *m'sieur*. I will do it. You trust me, *m'sieur*.'

'I trust you.'

But of course the boy hadn't had the time to make enquiries yet. That interview with him in his bedroom had only been an hour or two ago. It felt like days. The sense of time was escaping him: things that happened a decade before could be so clear, things of only minutes ago a distant memory.

'How are you settling in here, Guépard?'

Again the boy looked up in astonishment. 'E-e-everything very good, *m'sieur*. Thank you, *m'sieur*.'

Yes, the boy had a slight stutter – he hadn't noticed that before. Manne stood there smoking his cigarette as the boy continued polishing shoes, horribly self-consciously, no doubt wishing Manne would go away.

'How would you like to stay here for a while?'

'I d-don't understand, *m'sieur*.'

'I noticed you tending the kitchen garden this morning. Do you like gardening?'

'Y-y-yes, *m'sieur*. I used to look after my mother's vegetable patch, *m'sieur*.'

'What if I could get you a post here? A domestic post? How would you feel about that, Guépard? I could ask the commandant on your behalf.'

The boy looked bewildered. '*Oui, m'sieur.* Whatever you think, *m'sieur.*'

'All right then, Guépard. I'll see what I can manage.'

Upstairs in his room, Manne took his clothes off, filled the basin and put his head in the water. Afterwards, he lay down on his bed, but quickly got up again. Finally, he pushed his desk chair over to the window. For an hour, he sat staring out at the lawn – a rusty brown expanse, pregnant with loss. He'd tell the commandant to get a tougher, better-adapted turf variety shipped from Belém. He kept staring out, watching to see if the woman would come back from the hut, but she didn't. If she returned, if he heard her on the stairs, he'd go and see her, tell her that he'd help her leave, apologise for his behaviour, blame it on the confusion of fever. Yes, he could certainly feel himself on the cusp of fever – the shaking, the sweating, the hallucinatory memories. But he was at that stage where you could still beat it, where if you really concentrated, you could stop it coming on through force of will alone.

A gold chain and crucifix had dangled between the woman's breasts. Had he actually seen that, or was it his imagination? It was as if he'd dozed off by the window, dreamt that he'd got up and walked to the hut, and then woken up here again in his chair. If she decided to tell her husband what had happened, then it'd be better if Manne were to leave immediately. Melt away into the forest. If only he had the confidence that he could still do it, the way the climate got to him now. Under the sun, after the endless kilometres, he could feel the fragmentation, the pieces chipping off as if from an old statue. His journal hadn't lied; it told the story well enough. It sat there accusingly, where he'd left it on the desk. What if he destroyed it now, burnt it? The cities he'd visited, the languages he'd spoken, the people he'd met, the plant collectors, the art teacher in Rio, the mistress in Caracas ... his journal was the sole, unifying record. The rest was nothing but the falsehoods of memory.

He was no one: a ragbag of tics and tricks, echoes and clichés. A vague homesickness invaded him – but for somewhere he'd never been. Missing people he'd never known, and longing for lovers never touched.

V

'Drink, Hartfeld?'

'I'm afraid lunchtime drinking doesn't agree with me in this climate.'

The commandant had poured himself a large rum. Once again, there were place settings for three at the table, although Manne hadn't seen the woman return from the hut. He'd almost begged off lunch himself, but the thought of the commandant and his wife alone at table changed his mind. He wanted to say something to her before she spoke to her husband.

'Thought you might like to come along with me this afternoon, take a look at one of the construction sites. Might interest you. I'd appreciate your thoughts as well.'

'Kind of you to offer – yes, I'd like that very much.'

Why did one tend to automatically accept unexpected invitations? Manne took a forkful of the grey stew he'd been served, which turned out to be edible enough. The butler hadn't waited for the woman to arrive, and as the commandant prattled on, Manne mused on this. Perhaps she sometimes came down to lunch, and sometimes didn't, and the butler could never be sure which.

A pause in the monologue: the commandant seemed to expect Manne to say something now, show interest.

'So how many convicts do you have here at the camp in all?'

'Oh, I think it's about three hundred.'

'And what are they here for, mostly? I hope you don't mind my asking.'

'No no. Of course not.' Nonetheless, the commandant looked uncomfortable. 'Murder, I'd say. Half of them at least. Maybe more.'

'Really? That many?' It did actually interest Manne. The butler cleared the plates off the table, then disappeared into the kitchen. 'Your man, for example. What brought him here?'

'Charles?' The commandant lowered his voice. 'That was murder. Killed his wife, I believe.'

'I see. And you're not worried about his being around your own wife?'

'No, I'm not, but...' he frowned. 'It's difficult to explain, but let me try. There are career criminals... and there are the violent types... but they get sent to the Islands, or they stay in the camp barracks. For domestic service, we use a different type. Often convicts who've committed just the one murder, in the heat of the moment. A violent row with an unfaithful wife. That sort of thing. They're not going to do it again. These criminals have one crime in them, that defines them. I'm not explaining myself very well...'

'No, I think I understand what you mean.'

'Good, good.' The commandant looked embarrassed, as if he'd let slip something private. 'Now, if you've finished, why don't we have some coffee in my study and I can show you where we're heading this afternoon.'

* * *

245

The two of them set out through the forest, up the path towards the camp. Neither spoke much. There was something about the forest and its random noises that suppressed general conversation, Manne had found during his years of wandering. At one point, out of habit, Manne stopped and looked up to the canopy.

'What is it?'

Manne pointed. 'See up there? That clump of purple flowers? An unusual orchid species. Not exactly rare, but not common either.'

The commandant squinted up. 'Ah yes, I see it.' He stood stroking his chin. 'Are there a lot of orchids about in the forest?'

'I should think there are, around here.'

'Could they be collected or cultivated? Would it be easy?'

'They could be collected. The commoner varieties can be cultivated, yes. You have to know what you're doing, though.'

'Interesting . . . I actually had some orchids shipped in from Florida. For an orchid house I had built in the garden. But they all died.'

'Most of them would, normally. You'd be better off harvesting them from the forest. Take a look in the botanical gardens next time you're in Saint-Laurent. There's some sort of fertilising project there.'

They moved on. Manne was thinking about orchids again. He was remembering his great-uncle's house in Chiswick, with its greenhouse that took up most of the garden, and the reflections of the orchids that would bounce off the glass walls. The morgue-like stillness of everything inside was what had most impressed. Row upon row of little pots, each carefully numbered and labelled. He could see his great-uncle toiling away with his orchids, potting them, repotting them, feeding them, enveloping them in a fine water mist, lavishing his love on them, day in, day out, always the same, year after year. He'd been an enigma to Manne as a child. But now Manne thought he understood his great-uncle well enough. It was an existence that had been smoothed, polished and finished until it was like a perfectly round, shiny pebble, with no irregularities, a life that admitted no way in and no way out.

Manne's great-uncle had rarely left his own house and grounds, had probably never been abroad. But his library had been full of the exploits of botanists, explorers, the famous orchid hunters of the nineteenth century. It had been a very different game in those days, when prized orchids could fetch extraordinary sums of money, and hunters took to the forest with great armies of coolies. Back then, there'd been a certain romanticism, or so it had seemed to Manne as a boy. Few of the territories had been properly explored, and the hunters had to wander far off the map for months or years at a time. Well before the turn of the century, though, things had changed. Many of the mysteries of orchid fertilisation had been unlocked; nurseries had begun to breed them by the thousands in Europe and America. Orchid mania had subsided with their easier availability. Hunters now operated alone or with just a few hired hands, and if their earnings were sufficient, they were generally modest. Orchid hunting was past its prime. It was no longer the business of gentleman explorers and their aristocratic patrons. Rather, it was a marginal world of the exiled, the eternally restless – the men from nowhere and everywhere.

They were back at the main camp. It felt disconcerting to see people again – convicts and guards wandering about aimlessly up and down the dirt thoroughfare. At the commandant's office, they stopped for a few minutes.

'You were talking about orchids,' the commandant said as

he shuffled through some papers. 'That shipment I got from Florida. Cost me quite a bit. I wonder if there's a business opportunity there. We could build nurseries here and export the orchids.'

Manne shook his head. 'You're too far from the main markets. And you'd need proper experts to set up and run the nurseries.'

'I'm sure you're right. Just thinking aloud. My wife, you know, she's rather fond of orchids. That's why I had them shipped out in the first place. I was going to build an orchid house for the garden.'

'I was thinking about your garden. Seems there's no one to look after it at the moment. Pity to see it go to ruin like that.'

The commandant sighed. 'I had a gardener. A real professional. He did the landscaping. Really knew what he was doing. Sadly, there are so few like him. I would have done a lot for him. But what is one to do?'

'What happened to him?'

'Vanished!' The commandant spat out the word with surprising bitterness. 'Made off with Bonifacio's gang, so they tell me. Robbed me of a few hundred francs to boot. After all I'd done for him. I'd even given him money. No, you can't trust them. Not even the good ones.'

'I'm sorry to hear that. As for your garden, I don't believe it's beyond repair. The landscaping has mostly been finished. It's a question of planting and upkeep. Replacing the turf is the main problem. I could set my man to the job. He has some experience with gardens, he tells me. I'm sure he could make headway fairly quickly.'

'Very kind of you,' the commandant replied distractedly. 'Why don't you see Charles about it?' He was poring over his maps and plans. 'I've lost faith in it myself, but if you think you can do something with it, by all means ...'

Shortly after, they set off again down another track, the commandant ahead, striding on determinedly. If the governor's secretary, Leblanc, represented one type of colonial administrator, with his squat figure, red face and expanding waistline, the commandant represented the opposite. Tall and thin, painfully thin, as if desiccated by life's frustrations.

Manne was thinking about the commandant's wife, about the fact that she hadn't returned to the house, hadn't turned up to lunch. An incident from his early childhood came back to him. There was a teenage girl who'd lived in a nearby village, whom Manne had known vaguely. Apparently, she'd been the victim of 'improper advances' from a local farmhand. Afterwards, she'd thrown herself into the river.

They'd arrived at an enormous clearing, surrounded by forest. The ground was a bog of baked mud, tree trunks and roots. The commandant gestured towards the vast empty space. 'This is where we're building the new penitentiary.'

Convicts were levelling the ground. Most were stripped to the waist, burnt nut brown under the sun. Many of them had tattoos; Manne noticed one of an entwined naked couple that moved suggestively when the convict's back muscles were flexed.

The commandant had spread out plans on a sawn tree stump. 'It'll be very different from what you find at Saint-Laurent or in the other camps. I'm working from an American model. Large circular exterior walls; barred cells around the inside walls and a sentry station in the middle. That way enables better control, you see, better surveillance. At every moment, the guards will be able to see exactly what any prisoner is doing. The present system is chaos. We lock the prisoners into their barracks at night and leave them be till morning. You can imagine what goes on. Revenge killings. Gambling, theft. And all manner of perversity.'

As he spoke, the commandant continued to stare intently at his plans, making occasional annotations with a pencil, almost as though they were the important things, and the building site there simply to justify them.

'Looks like a huge project,' said Manne. 'Where are you getting the stone from?'

Giant slabs were piled up on one side of the site, already sinking slowly into the mud.

'Quarries upstream. On the other side of the river. Nothing here, of course, so we have to buy from the Dutch. And they bleed me dry for it.'

'What's the purpose of relocating the prisoners here?'

'I want to free up the main avenue. So we can start rebuilding there. Start developing a proper commercial centre. The idea is to attract the traders, investors. Settlers. Open up the surrounding land, farm it, exploit it . . .'

'I see. I didn't realise how ambitious your plan was. You want to build a whole new settlement.'

'That's right. That's exactly right. A fresh start.'

The sun was setting by the time they got back to the house. Manne climbed the stairs up to the landing. There was no light from under the woman's door. He thought to go and knock anyway, but then heard the commandant coming up the stairs behind him.

Back to his bedroom. He didn't bother to light the lamps for the moment. Day and night in the tropics were such absolutes that the brief twilight – with its shadows, ambivalences – felt like a respite. He was still thinking of the woman; he'd been thinking of her the entire day. On the way back to the house, he'd formulated a credible apology in his head, and he strained to remember what it was now, but it was no good, he'd already forgotten it. He considered the possible escape route the commandant's wife had sketched out to him – across the river to Albina, overland to Paramaribo, then a boat out. Not only was it the reverse of the route by which Manne had arrived in the Colony, but it was also more or less what he'd been planning on himself, when the time came to get Edouard out, should he ever find him. Then he thought for a while about the commandant's project. The clearing with its gigantic circular building. A little like the hut where Manne had met his host's wife, but blown up to a preposterous scale.

After that, he must have dozed off for a while, because a tap on the door woke him. Dinner would be served in fifteen minutes. Befuddled by sleep, he splashed some lukewarm water on his face, dressed and went down.

The woman was already there, seated. He'd expected her to be absent, or at least to make a late appearance. He certainly hadn't imagined that she might transform herself in the way she had. Gone was the sloppy dressing, uncombed hair and unmade-up face. Sleekly groomed now, she was wearing a smart, low-cut top and skirt with discreet earrings and a small necklace of dark stones. The effect was insolently seductive – and quite different from the cocktail women of Saint-Laurent, with their showy outfits that overcompensated for the drabness of colonial life.

The commandant was beaming, in visibly good form. 'Ah, there you are, Hartfeld. I was just telling Renée about our afternoon.'

Manne turned towards her. 'Yes, your husband was good enough to show me around one of his construction sites.'

'Oh good. What do you make of his grand plans? I'm persuaded he thinks he's a latter-day pharaoh.'

The commandant gave a nervous 'Ha ha!' – whether out of embarrassment or pleasure it was hard to tell. His wife, on the other hand, looked supremely self-possessed, smiling, staring at Manne straight in the eyes.

'Very impressive. Seems like an ambitious, courageous project.'

'Thank you, thank you!' said the commandant.

'I'm glad you had an interesting afternoon,' continued his wife. 'I trust you had an equally interesting morning?'

'Why... not quite as interesting. I was taking notes in my bedroom. Then I went for a walk in the garden.'

'Garden's rather gone to seed, I'm afraid. But there are some nice walks down along the river. You didn't pass by the folly, did you?'

'I don't think so...'

'A stone hut, down a path, at the other end of the garden. My husband had it built for me, didn't you, dear? It's rather delightful!'

'I'll certainly take a look tomorrow.'

'Yes, do. I like to imagine it to be the place of romantic trysts. The runaway convict and his guard's wife, perhaps.'

'You do have a vivid imagination, my dear.'

The butler interrupted the flow of conversation as he served the entrée. Then as they started eating, the woman continued with her interrogation: 'Now tell me, Monsieur Hartfeld – and please forgive me if I seem to be prying, it's just that we have so few guests here – I was wondering whether you were married.'

'I'm afraid not.'

'Not married? Well, I must say I'm surprised. Handsome fellow like you.'

'Now, Renée, really!' the commandant said. 'I'm sure you don't want to embarrass our guest.'

'It's perfectly all right,' Manne said. 'No, I suppose I've always travelled a lot, and been very involved in my work, so the married life wouldn't really suit me.'

'Well, Monsieur Hartfeld. I wouldn't have put you down as a confirmed bachelor. Not much use for women, then?'

'On the contrary. I'm always charmed by their company.'

'I'm sure the sentiment is reciprocated.'

'Renée! Really!' Manne could feel the commandant searching for a good-natured tone for his remonstrance, anxious to avoid a repeat of the night before.

'Oh, he doesn't mind my idle prying, do you, Monsieur Hartfeld?'

'Of course not.'

'Yes, I can well imagine how you went down with those society ladies of Saint-Laurent.'

There was a natural silence for a minute or two as they ate. It wasn't so difficult to keep up the urbane exterior, but Manne could feel his heart thumping against his ribcage. He wondered how far she'd go with the barbed flirting, and whether she was leading up to a denunciation. He looked for a hint of hysteria in her, or hostility, or even complicity. But there was nothing.

'Tell us something about the project you're working on here, Mr Hartfeld,' the woman said.

'It's not at the project stage yet. We're considering a botanical survey of this stretch of the Maroni. I'm here to make an initial feasibility report.'

'What's of special interest on this particular stretch of the river?'

'It's an area that's never been properly surveyed.'

'I mean, wouldn't it be a lot easier to survey the Dutch side, and avoid the problem of working in the penal territories?'

'Well, we're hoping to sell the report to the French government.'

'Surely one side of the river isn't going to be much different from the other?'

'Well . . . these reports . . .'

The commandant came to his rescue. 'I'm sure all parties concerned have their reasons. Isn't that right, Monsieur Hartfeld?'

'Indeed.'

His feeble response hung in the air as they continued eating. With people like the commandant or Leblanc, Manne knew he could hold his own, under any circumstances. But he struggled to think of something to say now, a way of shepherding the conversation to safer ground. Before he could formulate anything, the commandant's wife had cut in again.

'Perhaps you could have my friend seconded to you.'

'Your friend?'

'You remember the man I was telling you about. Yesterday at dinner. Pierre Boppe.'

'Ah yes. The convict.'

'He may well be the only other botanist in the Colony. He could be of some help to you.'

'That's certainly an idea. Although I don't expect to be here very long.'

'Worth a thought, in any case.'

'Yes. I'll think it over.'

'You know, his is a strange story indeed.'

'I can only imagine it is.'

'He claimed his wife had been unfaithful to him. With a house guest.'

Manne glanced at the commandant. His *bonhomie* had

evaporated, and he was now looking rattled. But it was clear that he wasn't going to try to stop his wife saying whatever she wanted.

'So, do you know what he did?' she continued. 'He shot her while she slept. Only she didn't die straight away. She even managed to sit up and look at herself in the mirror.'

Her eyes flickered away from Manne to her husband, to gauge how far she might go.

'Apparently, she said something like: "Pierre, did you do this?" And he replied yes. Then she said: "But what will you tell the children?" And he said: "I'll tell them you killed yourself." Then finally she said: "I'd like to see a priest before I die." And he replied: "What do you need a priest for? You went to Confession only yesterday." That's how he told it to the police, in any case.'

The commandant was looking down at his plate. A disconcerting silence had invaded the room. To break it, Manne said: 'What a very bizarre story.'

'Isn't it? Especially when it's about someone you know.'

She was staring directly into his eyes. Suddenly she broke out into a smile.

'But as my husband always says, mustn't linger on the morbid. Now I wonder what Charles has managed for dessert?'

The rest of the dinner dissipated in harmless small talk, although the story of the Boppe murder left a peculiar aftertaste. Just before coffee was served, the woman rose and said: 'If you'll excuse me, Monsieur Hartfeld, I think I'll retire for the evening. I'm feeling quite tired tonight, for some reason.'

'Not at all. I might well follow you shortly.'

'Oh, come now, Hartfeld,' said the commandant. 'Stay at least for a *digestif*, I beg of you!'

There was something pitiable about the commandant's

pleading. Manne had seen it often enough in the colonies – educated men drowning in a backwater, desperate for talk, for any sort of conversation with a peer.

'All right, then. Do you have cognac?'

'Of course.'

As they waited for coffee and drinks, the commandant said: 'You must forgive my wife. She can be rather direct about everything. She's not so used to being in society, and I...'

'There's nothing to forgive. I find her perfectly charming.'

'Oh, she can be charming, all right.' Manne caught a look in the commandant's eye that he didn't know how to interpret. 'I don't know what nonsense she was talking about that convict, Boppe. It's extremely unlikely he'll end up in this camp. They'll find something easy for him to do in Saint-Laurent. Until his pardon comes through. As it no doubt will.'

'Why do you think he'll be pardoned?'

'People of his sort rarely get transported. When they do, they generally only serve a year. Then they're quietly pardoned, once all the press interest has died down.'

'I see.'

'People with education, with real skills, with leadership abilities, with ingenuity, with any quality at all, we don't get them here. Not in the convict population, not in the Administration, either. The ones needed to build a new country are precisely those who are weeded out. It's hopeless.'

'Well, you at least seem to be making headway with your building projects.'

'To be frank with you, Hartfeld, I've pumped a lot of my own money into this enterprise. It'd have been fruitless to ask the Administration for funds; they wouldn't have been interested.'

'Why not?'

The commandant sighed. 'There's no will to make anything

of the Colony. Almost all the officials are corrupt. The convicts are no help, either. I was naive when I first got out here. I looked at what the British managed in Australia last century. I thought, why not here? Give convicts land to cultivate, and an opportunity to make something of their lives.'

'Makes sense, I suppose.'

The cognac had arrived. The commandant drank his down quickly and poured himself another.

'I thought so, at first. But the convicts come from the lowest rungs of society. They can certainly escape, and many of them do. But they can't escape their mentality. They've no imagination. They can't understand what's best for them. They're doomed. Even when they don't start out that way, the convict culture dooms them.'

'How do you mean?'

'Well . . . take that gardener fellow I was telling you about earlier. I thought, now here's a young man who has a skill, who has some wits about him. Here's someone who could help build a new sort of Colony. And whom the Colony in turn could help. But no, it turns out he preferred petty thieving and escape fantasies, just like all the others.'

'What was his original crime, this gardener?'

'Was he the chap who strangled his fiancée? I can't remember.' The commandant dismissed the gardener with a theatrical wave of his hand. 'Anyway, after he ran off, I changed my mind about things. It's pointless trying to make citizens out of convicts. No, what interests me now is a community of free settlers. It's the only way to exploit the possibilities here. After all, who's getting the most out of the Colony right now? Not France, not the Creole population. No, it's foreign traders, the Chinese, the Brazilians. We need to attract a free French population interested in commercial enterprise.'

'Where do the convicts fit in?'

'For a while I thought we'd be better off without them. Close down the penal colony. What the do-gooders back in France want to do. Now I'm not so sure. If you look more closely at what the British did in Australia, they had migrants. Free settlers. Who rented the convicts from the government, as cheap labour. Almost like slaves. That's how they built the country. Not by government decree. But by free enterprise and forced labour.'

The commandant leant forward, his eyes gleaming with alcohol.

'Now, the difficult part is to morally justify such a system. But that's the beauty of the convicts. Because they're actually here to be punished. That's their purpose in the scheme of things. Let them be punished, then!'

'So it doesn't matter what happens to them?'

'I aim to treat the convicts as humanely as possible. But beyond that... these men are already dead. There's no hope for them. Even if they finish their sentence, they're still not allowed to return to France. The very idea of redemption is a legal nonsense.'

The commandant had been talking excitedly, but went quiet as the butler came in to serve more drinks. Manne had noticed the phenomenon before – as if the free men were under surveillance from the convicts. Then as soon as the butler left, the commandant started up again. But Manne wasn't listening to the commandant's peculiar theories any more. The cognac was going to his head, after the heat and exertions of the afternoon. He felt detached from the situation. The impression was that he was watching himself sitting there, as though it were someone else entirely. In a sense, it was. Hartfeld, not Manne, was talking and listening to the commandant. Hartfeld, who hadn't existed a short while ago, but whose character was becoming ever more sharply defined with each passing day. And it was Hartfeld, too, who had met the commandant's wife in her 'folly', and had ordered her to undress.

The commandant was talking about his construction plans, about the giant penitentiary he was building. In his mind's eye, Manne saw the clearing again, bathed in its powerful, unsubtle tropical light. It reminded him, he now realised, of the night patrols in Belgium, out in no-man's-land. At some point, he or someone in his scouting party would send up a flare to illuminate the scene. For a split second, everything would explode into light, a grey light, and the endless devastation would be apparent: the blasted-out foxholes, the bodies, the barbed wire, the sculptural wreckage of a shot-down reconnaissance plane. That was what the clearing had looked like, with its chaos of mud, tree stumps and gnarled roots, its hundreds of semi-naked men, and the stone slabs piled up like sandbags.

VI

He'd heard rustling; had wondered whether there was a mouse or rat in the room; had wondered also whether he'd dreamt it; and had then dozed off again, despite the dawn light streaming in through the window. When he'd got up an hour later, a cream envelope, with its slip of folded paper inside, was by the door. It simply read: 'Meet me at eleven.' Immediately, he'd thrown on some clothes, gone across the landing and tapped on the woman's door. No answer.

By the time he'd got down to breakfast, the commandant had already left the table. Just as well, since Manne was in no mood for yet more stilted conversation. An unsettled night, troubled by dreams, had exhausted him before the day had even started. In one of them, he recalled now, he'd been with his mistress in Caracas. They'd been in bed, her back towards him – they'd just had sex. But when she'd turned around, she'd transformed into the commandant's wife. The fog of that dream had yet to clear. He could see her now, across the table, in the low-cut top she'd worn at dinner. The well-defined bone structure of her face struck him again. Like the androgyny of a classical statue. The staring eyes were those of Coptic portraits he'd once seen at the British Museum. The dark hair, with its photographic play of shadows across the face . . . he wasn't really reminded of a woman, but of a dozen representations of them.

Music came from the commandant's office. It jolted Manne out of his daydreaming – or pushed him deeper into it. It was one of Schubert's Lieder, something Manne himself used to play as a boy. His mother had sung, while he'd accompanied. He hadn't heard those songs since then, but he'd completely internalised them. He could still recite the Heine poems they'd been set to. The memory of this music had an extraordinary force, maybe even more powerful than the trench hallucinations that struck him when feverish.

Mechanically, he rose from the breakfast table and went back upstairs. He should be out pretending to survey the area. But he hadn't the head for it now. All he could think about was the meeting with the woman. Nor could he even plan for that in any meaningful way, because he had no idea what she would say to him. He was pacing the room, working himself up into a feverish state again.

Eventually he managed to sit down at the desk. He opened his journal and forced himself to write something, anything:

The music from the commandant's office. A memory that hasn't been distorted or polished over time, lying there undisturbed, like an object in a pharaoh's tomb. And yet the next time I hear that music, it will have lost its power over me.

The idea refused to go any further. He put his pen down for a moment, before continuing with a different theme:

Vera Cruz orchid. This is what I know about the Vera Cruz orchid. Found across the Amazon region. First so named by Jesuit missionaries, I think. Flowers every few years; no foliage. When not flowering is simply a mass of roots, indistinguishable from certain tree roots. Figured in various 16th & 17th c. treatises on the teleological argument. Considered lucky; dried flowers used as talismans. Extensively harvested in 19th c., now rare. Pollination requirements unknown.

He'd learnt all that one afternoon at the Biblioteca Nacional in Caracas, the day after he'd received Edouard's letter. There were other details he remembered now, such as the theory that the orchid ultimately killed its host tree by strangling its roots. He'd note that down another time. The concentration involved in writing had calmed him.

For a while he sat studying the manual on the riverside lingua franca that he'd borrowed from the commandant. At one point the sound of a door slamming echoed through the house. Manne looked through the window to see the commandant making his way up to the path that led to the camp. He glanced at his watch: a quarter to eleven. He flicked through his notebook – the vocabulary list he'd been working on stretched back four or five pages. Somehow, the hours had passed.

Outside, the sunlight struck his face with a violence. Manne walked slowly towards the folly, past the abandoned construction that he took to be the orchid house the commandant had mentioned. Once again it reminded Manne of his great-uncle, and of that other orchid house that had grown and grown until it had swallowed up most of the garden. He remembered now that at one stage his great-uncle had even set up a bed and table in a corner of it, and had had his housekeeper serve his meals there. It was the kind of behaviour that had set relatives talking, that had led to Manne being reclaimed by his father and returned to France. Looking back now, though, Manne thought he understood his great-uncle's actions perfectly. Moving the bed to the greenhouse had been a kind of journey, an internal emigration.

Manne stood by the door of the folly for a minute or two, staring at it, trying to compose himself. Noiselessly it swung open. She was in a simple summer frock and sandals, as though just off for a walk in the park. Everything inside was the same as before. A blanket, a lamp, one or two other objects on the floor. Nothing to sit on.

'Well?'

'Well what?'

'Are you going to help me? Are you going to help me?

Her bluntness had thrown him off balance again. He'd been rehearsing different apologies in his mind; now he realised that it didn't matter any more. She was already ahead of him.

'I don't know.'

'Don't know what? Don't know if you're going to help me?'

'I'm thinking it through.'

'You're thinking it through?' She folded her arms. 'What do you need to think about? What else do you want from me?'

To be engaged so directly – without any of the usual filters of convention – felt savage, too intimate. Manne could see his own tiny image reflected in her eyes, warped and distorted as in a fairground mirror. She kicked off her sandals and started unbuttoning the front of her dress. It had happened so fast – in a moment – leaving Manne struggling to respond.

He let his eyes roam over her body. There was something brutal about her nudity. She had a little belly, heavy breasts, some weight around the thighs – not a perfect body. Perfection was a lifeless thing, though. It was the opposite of erotic.

'Do you just want to stand and watch me? Is that it?'

'No.'

She put a hand to his cheek; he flinched. Her arms were around his neck, as if they were old lovers. Hips and breasts, lips and neck, perspiration, the smell of hair – adrenaline and desire charged the atmosphere. He thought he could sense something through her skin, a relief at being touched. Or maybe she just wanted to get it over with. He pressed her closer, in a movement that was more violent than intended. They were pulling and grabbing at each other like children fighting. Briefly they disentangled while Manne struggled with his clothes and the woman threw a blanket over the wooden floorboards. She was on her knees, tugging him to the ground. Everything had become inward, had folded in on itself, like the smooth, edgeless walls of the folly.

Slowly, the blanket, lamp, strewn clothes came into focus again. Noises from the river and jungle filtered back in through the shutters. The familiar feeling of loneliness after sex, only this time more intense than usual. The woman was resting on her side now, turned away from him, propping herself up on an elbow, staring at the wall. He noticed a beauty spot under her shoulder blade, like a minuscule tattoo. She trembled slightly, and Manne had the feeling she was silently crying.

'You'll have to leave now. He'll be back soon.'

She hadn't turned around to address him; her voice had a flat quality to it. He got to his feet, fished his clothes out of the pile and began dressing. The woman remained there, immobile, as Manne buttoned up his shirt, then tied his shoelaces. He wavered at the doorway, looking down at her back and buttocks, still marked with the impression of the blanket weave. He wanted to put a hand on her shoulder. That was impossible. If he stayed a moment longer, he had the feeling she'd do something, she'd scream *Get out!* The folly, with its womb-like intensity, had suddenly become unbearable. He headed out into the heat.

Back in the house, Manne made his way to the kitchen. Guépard was at the stove, stirring what looked like a large pot of stew. The butler was sitting by a table, smoking a cigarette.

'*Oui, monsieur?*'

'I'm feeling a little under the weather. I won't be down for lunch. Send me up some bread and cold meat. Please inform the commandant and convey my apologies.'

'*Très bien, monsieur.*'

The butler had neither got up nor put down his cigarette as he'd addressed Manne, which irritated him hugely. For a moment he thought he'd say something to the commandant about it, before realising that he was overreacting.

In his room, listless and restless, he seemed unable to do anything, unable to think. He stood by the window, watching the commandant march in across the garden at his military pace. But no sign of the woman. He guessed she'd stay in the folly all afternoon. Surrounded by jungle, the sense of confinement was so great that you automatically sought it out. He himself found his room claustrophobic and yet here he was retreating to it again.

After his lunch he flipped through some old copies of *Le Petit Parisien* he'd found in the drawing room downstairs. There was an article about the new Musée des Colonies that had recently opened in Paris, and photographs of the murals that had been painted for it – Edens of exotic plants, animals, savages. Manne gazed out through the window across the river to the other bank. The Dutch side. Exactly the same as here, yet completely different. Like a photograph negative. The same plants and animals, the same climate, same mix of natives and

Europeans. He remembered the commandant's wife asking him why he didn't survey the other riverbank instead, since it at least was not part of any penal colony.

It was hard to think of anything else but her, to visualise anything but her body. The shock of the encounter – he recalled what had happened in the folly in a series of erotic fragments. A wretched, hollow feeling invaded him.

He forced his mind to other things. To Edouard's escape, for example. In Saint-Laurent, Manne had made discreet enquiries, but no one had been able to tell him much. It was known that the *évadés* had bought a boat, and that one had been spotted at dawn at the headlands one morning, sailing straight out into the ocean. How it was that Bonifacio had ended up back at Renée remained an enigma, though, since he'd refused to say anything after his recapture. All that was left were his last words: '*Je suis le bagne!*' Manne thought of the commandant's gardener, who'd also escaped with Bonifacio's gang. And therefore must have known Edouard. Given their professions, it was possible they'd known each other previously. It might be an avenue to pursue. He wanted to try out his thoughts on paper. But it was unwise to write down anything too specific about Edouard in his journal, in case anyone should read it. Ideas continued to circle and shadow each other in his mind.

The spectacle of the sunset over the jungle. The afternoon lost in a maze of thought. He focused on the shattered colours of the river, the deep reds and yellows. The sun was dramatically puffed up and grandiose, as though it were the last sunset ever at the end of the world.

On his way downstairs, Manne heard voices from the commandant's office. At first he assumed it was the commandant and his butler, but when he stopped to listen, it seemed one was his own servant. The commandant raised his voice, as though he were remonstrating with Guépard. All Manne could make out was the occasional *oui, m'sieur* and *non, m'sieur* from Guépard. He waited by the door until Guépard finally emerged looking flustered. On seeing Manne, his expression had turned to shock. But he'd scuttled off before Manne had time to stop and interrogate him. No matter. He'd catch him after dinner, or in the morning.

She was already at the table. Again, she'd dressed smartly and in black, with a hint of provocation in the tightness of her blouse against her breasts. She hardly looked up from the book she was reading as he sat down.

'What's the book?'

Without a word, or even interrupting her reading, she flashed him the cover of a battered copy of *La chasse spirituelle*. For a moment Manne was on the verge of making some comment about it, but stopped himself. Polite conversation would be an absurdity. It was as if they'd gone directly from the stilted formalities of strangers to the silent indifference of a long-married couple.

'Hello, dear. Evening, Hartfeld. Sorry to have kept you both waiting – had some work that needed finishing.'

The commandant had brought his glass of rum with him and sat down uncertainly. His wife put her book aside as the butler served the *entrée*. A light drumming on the roof signalled the beginning of the evening rains. Here, no one ever commented on the weather, since it rarely varied. The clockwork of dinner chat had to be triggered in other ways.

This time, though, they ate in silence. Tonight's dinner had a subdued, post-coital feel to it after the high tensions of the last two. Even the commandant seemed to be in a reflective mood and avoided his usual, awkward attempts at conversation. As

Manne ate, he found himself indulging in a fantasy – that they'd all been living in this house for years; that the commandant was fully aware of his wife's affair with Manne, which had also been going on for years; that he and Manne were old friends and, despite or because of the circumstances, had somehow remained so . . .

No one wanted coffee, and the commandant's wife again quickly excused herself after the meal. The butler had brought out the drinks tray and Manne accepted a glass of cognac; he had no wish to sit and talk to the commandant, but felt the desire to get a little drunk.

After a few banal pleasantries, the commandant started in on his construction plans again, with Manne interjecting the occasional reply. This time he was talking about building an airfield, to link his settlement to Cayenne and the French West Indies. The commandant's words were tumbling over each other – for once, drink seemed to be affecting his control. At one point he leant forward, touching Manne on the knee. 'You know, it's a relief to be able to talk these things through with somebody like you. Trouble is, I'm so isolated. No one I can speak to. My wife is the only person I feel is my intellectual equal out here. And she's simply not interested in all this.'

Difficult to know how to answer that. Eventually Manne said, 'What sort of things *is* she interested in?'

'She . . . well, she reads a lot. But . . .' He poured himself more cognac. 'As I've already told you, she hasn't been well lately. I can't help feeling your presence has pepped her up, though. Oh, I'll tell you one thing she's interested in: your orchids. I knew her as a child, you see. Our families were close. Occasionally I used to take her on trips to the mountains, in the Savoie. She used to collect wild orchids.'

'Really? I wonder why she hasn't mentioned that.'

'She doesn't like talking about the past.'

'Why not?'

The commandant quickly downed what remained in his glass and cast an unsteady look up the stairs, as though his wife might be listening in.

'Probably shouldn't be telling you this. Can see you're the discreet type, though. Truth is this. There was a family tragedy. You see, my wife was originally engaged to her cousin, Paul. Friend of mine, boyhood friend. We went to military school together. Then just before he was due to be mobilised, he drowned in a river that ran through the family estate. They found the body kilometres downstream. She took it badly.'

Abruptly, he stopped talking. The staccato phrases had been fired out as if the pressure to expel them had been building for months. Now he was staring into the middle distance, lost in thought. In the silence, Manne could hear the squawk of monkeys fighting in the canopy, somewhere not far from here. Once, when trekking through the jungle, he'd seen a young male push another out of a tree, killing him.

'Took it badly,' the commandant repeated, seemingly minutes later. 'She was resting, in Switzerland. Things went from bad to worse. Her father had made some unwise investments. For a while I took it upon myself to cover her expenses. Some might have considered that improper. But I did it because I was a friend of the family. And also because I was a good friend to her fiancé. I felt the responsibility. When she finally accepted me, she made me the happiest man in France.'

That final cliché struck a sombre note. One of the table candles sputtered to its end in a pool of wax. The commandant stirred himself, then stared at Manne, as though he'd forgotten that Manne was there or even who he was.

VII

He could hear birds calling to each other along the river as he lay in bed, caught in the disorientating moment between sleep and waking. Finally he opened his eyes, swung himself out of bed and went straight to the door. Nothing. No note pushed under it. He sat back down on the bed, filled with a sense of overwhelming disappointment.

Manne went to the basin and washed the sleep from his eyes, then got dressed and went downstairs. Again, too late for the commandant, and he found himself breakfasting alone. As the butler served him coffee and toast, Manne said: 'Please go and find my servant and tell him I'd like to see him.'

Minutes later Guépard arrived, anxious and breathless.

'I want to speak to you after breakfast. Go and wait for me in my bedroom. Sort out my laundry while you're there.'

'*Oui, m'sieur.*'

A copy of *Le Figaro* lay on the table; the commandant must have left it out for him. It was only a few weeks old and had probably come in yesterday with the evening post. Manne scanned the front page, but he didn't recognise the people mentioned and couldn't follow the stories – he'd have been more at home with a newspaper from Caracas. Only the place names reminded him of the deeper connection: the rue de Rivoli, the Comédie-Française, the avenue Montaigne, the boulevard Montparnasse – they were like a grid, placed over another life.

Upstairs, Guépard stood quivering by the bedroom door. He'd got himself into a state of complete nervousness, to the point where he was finding it hard to speak. Manne put his hand on the boy's shoulder. 'What are you worked up for? There's nothing to worry about. Sit down, I just want to ask you a few things.'

'*Oui, m'sieur.*'

'I was wondering what you were doing in the commandant's office yesterday.'

'*M'sieur?*'

'Just before dinner. I saw you come out of the commandant's office. What did he want to see you about?'

'I . . . I don't know what you mean, *m'sieur.*'

'I heard you talking. I saw you come out. And you saw me too. What was it all about?'

Guépard shook his head. 'I don't know anything, *m'sieur*. I swear it.'

'Guépard, I'm not accusing you of any wrongdoing. I just want to know what the commandant said to you.'

'No, *m'sieur*. I never spoke to him, *m'sieur.*'

'I don't know what you take me for. I *saw* you. You *saw* me.' At that, the boy started to whimper. 'Well, if you won't tell me, I won't force you. I shall ask the commandant. Now, another thing. You remember what I asked you to do the day before?'

'*Oui, m'sieur. Le bagnard, m'sieur.*'

'Go up to camp today, ask around, find out anything you can. Get me some writing paper from one of the administrative offices while you're up there – that can be your pretext for the trip.'

'I can't do it today, *m'sieur*. The butler's told me to . . .'

Manne interrupted him with an irritated wave of the hand. 'Tomorrow then, for God's sake. Now be off with you.'

Guépard bolted like a frightened cat. Gramophone music wafted up from the ground floor. Manne was on the verge of going down and having it out with the commandant, but then thought better of it. He stared out of the window, thinking of the woman, her dark hair. A horrible frustration filled him, both sexual and intellectual.

He remembered the day he'd arrived in Saint-Laurent. Sitting by the river and watching the sun set, struck with the feeling that everything had changed. Later that same evening, he'd been at the cocktail party at the governor's residence, and Leblanc had told him about the commandant's wife, and her flight from the camp. Just from the tone of his voice, Manne had understood that she was beautiful. Could it be that he'd already wanted her, even then? Could that have been the *moment*? He wrote in his journal:

Those moments. The tiny instants when, almost imperceptibly, one's world tilts, then tips over into something else entirely. One day, you might be holed up in your trench section, under sporadic enemy fire, your socks and boots wet through with the winter mud. A day not unlike a hundred others you've already endured in the same place, under the same conditions, in the same war. The only difference is that today you're enjoying the fine cigar you just received from your father, by some miracle neither lost, damaged nor pinched in transit. The nicotine sweeps through your body like a narcotic, the cigar fumes envelop you in a cloud of solipsistic well-being. It occurs to you that the passageway leading to the service trench is just opposite where you're sitting at the moment, as you enjoy your cigar. From there on, there are other passages to other trenches even further behind the front positions. In fact, you can probably walk a good kilometre back along various trench routes. As an officer, there's even a decent chance no one'll stop you, especially since there's a major assault planned for three o'clock the next morning and everything is in a chaos of preparation. Without even much thinking about it, you find yourself winding your way back from the front line, past troops huddled against the spitting rain, smoking and clutching their tin mugs of hot drink. Somewhere, a soldier is singing an old music-hall melody you remember from your childhood. You stop to draw on your cigar, and it fills you with a marvellous sense of calm. The further back you get, the fewer actual troops you encounter; the trenches widen out and are divided into little offices for army administration. Even further back are temporary wards for the wounded. It's like the outer suburbs of a city. In fact, there's no firm point where the trenches stop and the fields and farms begin. Presently you find yourself walking along a country road. You pass by convoys of troops and trucks making their way up to the front. People look at you strangely but no one stops you or even asks you where you're going. If they had, you'd have said you were on a half-day leave and cadged a lift back. You're near the village now, which would normally be teeming with officers, and where most likely you'd bump into someone you know. You decide to take a detour, avoiding the village and cutting through the fields instead. Again, there seems to be no firm point where a few hours of excusable AWOL might turn into desertion. But somewhere you must have finished your cigar and thrown the end away without even thinking about it. More fields. You come across one that's intersected by a stream. You take off your boots and trousers to wade across. It's deeper than you suppose and you end up having to swim a few strokes, holding your clothes above your head. You get out trembling and feeling numb and ill. What a stupid thing to have done in the middle of a northern European winter. You rub your legs and body to get the circulation going and put your clothes back on. You walk on briskly. The exercise warms you up and you start to feel better. For a moment even, a certain exhilaration fills you. Lighting the cigar was one of those moments, crossing the stream another. You rejoin the road. You pass by a roadside café and stop for a late lunch. Nothing more than sausage, cheese and wine, but it'll do. You're a lone officer, on foot, not far from the front line – you wonder if the proprietor suspects something, but if so, he doesn't do anything about it. And you walk on. Soon it's dark, but you know if you stick to the road you'll end up at a town and a railway station. Your mind wanders as you walk, although never focusing on anything, simply alighting here and there on a memory or a thought, like a butterfly among garden flowers. You have no idea what time it is when you reach the outskirts of the town. But when you get to the station there's a big clock that says twenty past ten. You look at the train timetable; the last Paris train is due to leave in five minutes. Even if you had enough money on you, and you don't, there wouldn't be time to get a ticket, and you wouldn't have the necessary military permit anyway. So you rush to the platform and jump on. Most of the passengers have settled in and are dozing. You can't do that, though, because you know the ticket inspector will be along at some stage. What will happen then? Suddenly it all hits you. At the next big station you'll be handed over to the transport police, who'll hand you over to the military. From there, it'll be arrest, back to barracks, and a quick court martial. You're an officer with privileged knowledge of a major assault; the court will be pitiless. There might be a long prison sentence, or with luck an insanity verdict. But most probably, the firing squad. You sit there, rigid in your seat. The inspector seems to be taking an eternity. And the dreamy sense of well-being that has lingered since you first lit the cigar has curdled into paranoia. Finally you hear a carriage door slam. Vos billets, s'il vous plaît! *You get up, make your way to the WC. An old trick that's most unlikely to work. Still, you never know. In a moment of inspiration, you leave the WC door ajar, banging gently with the rhythm of the train, and then you squeeze behind it. That way, the inspector might think it's unoccupied and not bother to look too closely. A horrible anxiety grips you, actually not too dissimilar to the feeling you get the night before going over the top. You hear the inspector clumping along the corridor. Closer, closer. Then you see a uniformed arm reach out, grab the handle of the swinging door, pull it shut. More clumping and then he's gone, on to the next carriage. But you're so frozen with fear you can't even move. How long you stay like that in the WC you don't know. When the door opens again, you're confronted with the surprised face of a lady in a fur coat. Just a minute, you say. You pull yourself together and go back to your seat. Somehow, time passes. And somehow you find yourself at the Gare de l'Est. You look about for military police, but you don't see any. You make your way quickly to the exit. What a relief to disappear into the anonymity of the Paris night! By now, it must be about two in the morning. Your small apartment's across town, on the rue la Boétie. You've been walking all day, you've another hour to go, but you don't feel tired. You don't feel anything. All you can think is thank God it's late at night, I'll avoid the concierge and with any luck I won't bump into anyone on the stairs. The streets pass by in a dream. And the carriage entrance of your building looms out of nowhere. You cross over the cobbled court-yard and make your way upstairs in the dark. Slowly, quietly, you creep into your apartment. For a minute or two more you're bursting with nervous energy. You don't know what to do with yourself.*

You pour yourself something alcoholic. You check the small safe in your bedroom and find that you have ten thousand francs in cash. Well, thank Christ for that. Then from one second to the next you're so tired you can barely stand up. You collapse on your bed. You've already decided you'll have to be up early, well before light, to leave Paris and make for the Swiss border. You wonder whether you'll wake up in time. Or whether you'll sleep until the military police come banging on the door. To be honest, you don't care any more. As it happens, you don't sleep at all, you're too tired even for that. You fall into that delirious state where the world recedes and proper thoughts are hard to distinguish from random fears and fantasies. The reality of your situation hasn't sunk in yet. You see it, but you don't really understand that there's no turning back, and no way home. It hasn't hit you that you'll never see this apartment again, this city again, this country again, your family again, your lover again. It'll be months before you read that French newspaper in Geneva and find your name in minuscule print on a pages-long list of those missing in action, presumed dead. And months again before you board the ship in Liverpool, bound for Brazil. No, all you can think of as you lie there on your bed for the last time is that it's the cigar, it's because of the cigar, and if you'd never received that cigar today, or even if you'd saved it for another day, then none of this would have happened.

Manne put down his pen. The words had come out in a single flow – it was the most he'd written in months, and the effort had exhausted him.

Later, he watched from the window as the commandant finally disappeared in the distance. Even before looking at his watch, he knew it was a quarter to eleven – the commandant's habits had the dead inevitability of prison life. Downstairs, everything was quiet. Right after the commandant's departure, the butler always disappeared somewhere as well. Perhaps he had a mistress in the native village.

Across the lawn, then down the little path to the folly – he threw the door open without knocking. She was sitting cross-legged on the ground, and seemed to be knitting or darning something. Whatever it was, she put it aside and got to her feet.

'What're you doing here?'

'I wanted to see you.'

They stood facing each other confrontationally. The woman had her arms crossed beneath her breasts.

'Well, you're seeing me. What do you want?'

He took a breath. 'I can't stop thinking about you. I can't concentrate on anything else, I can't think of anything else.'

The clichés withered on his lips. He moved forward, put his arms around her waist and started to kiss her. She pushed him away.

'No, no, stop it, *stop it*!' The woman was wiping her mouth with the back of her hand. 'For Christ's sake!' Another moment's silence, then she shook her head. 'Listen to me. I didn't ask for your attentions. I don't hope for your regard. I just wanted you to help me get away from here. If you won't do that, then please God leave the camp immediately. If you won't leave, I'll feel constrained to tell my husband about the situation.'

'You'll tell him what happened yesterday?'

'What happened yesterday was a mistake. It won't be repeated.'

'I can't leave the camp. At least, not until I've done my work here.'

'Your work here?' She made a dismissive gesture with her hand. 'I don't know who you are or why you came here. I don't believe a word of your story. You may be able to fool my husband, but I'm not taken in.'

'What do you mean?'

'I mean I don't believe you're a botanist. I don't believe in your tropical institute or your project. I haven't a clue what you're doing here and I don't care to know, either. That's what I mean.'

It was as if someone had just kicked him in the stomach and winded him. 'You don't know what you're talking about.'

'Don't I?' She snorted derisively. 'I've known botanists. You don't look the part. You don't act the part. You don't even sound as if you've been to Europe since the war – you're all wrong. Your accent, your behaviour, everything. I could probably guess some of your history if you like.'

He shook his head. 'You're a fantasist.' That was all he could manage for a moment – then he felt a sudden fury at her frontal attack, and a desire to respond in kind. 'You live here in isolation. You're lost in your own world. I heard the story about your turning up in Saint-Laurent without a *sou* to your name. You're like a naive girl running away from her finishing school. And you want me to help you!'

He stopped; the fury had passed as soon as it had come. He was thinking now about how she'd seen through him so accurately. Yes, he probably did look wrong to someone fresh out of France. The years of exile do something to a person. Back home, language, customs and everything else continue to evolve. Not so for the expatriate. He's frozen in the moment of departure. To cover up, he adopts a neutrality in appearance, behaviour, accent. As though he came from nowhere. Manne had seen this in countless colonials. And yet it hadn't occurred to him that others might see it in him.

'Think what you like,' said the woman coldly. 'I really don't care. I'll find a way of leaving here.'

'You think you can run away? What will you do in the end?

Go back to France? Go back to your family?'

'No. France is finished.'

'Where, then?'

'I told you. I'll go to Buenos Aires.'

'And what then?'

'Work. I don't know. Start a business.'

'And what then?'

'What then, what then!' she snapped. 'Isn't it enough for you? Why do you care?'

He couldn't explain why; he watched her in silence. Although her hair was heavy and sometimes swept over her face when she was excited, he noticed that she never bothered to pat it back into place.

'Perhaps it's not enough,' she continued tonelessly. 'Who knows. It must be better than this.'

For a moment he thought she might break down, but she didn't. She merely stared blankly at the wall behind Manne. She shrugged her shoulders. 'Anyway. You got what you wanted.'

'How do you know what I want?'

'You know what I mean by that.'

'Spell it out for me.'

She turned to him. 'Do I really have to? All right, then. You treated me like a prostitute.'

'What absolute rubbish.'

'You played your game. Now leave me in peace.'

Manne said nothing. He didn't move. All he could feel was the hollowness again.

'You heard me. Leave me in peace. Get out. Get out, *get out*!'

She was screaming, loud enough for anyone to have heard it back at the house. Still Manne stood there, watching as she bent down, picked up the lamp from the ground and hurled it at him. He made no effort to get out of the way, and its metal edge caught him just above the eye, swinging him back against the wall. The pain was searing. A beautiful spectacle of glass shards filled the air, glistening with oil and the sunlight filtering in through the shutters.

His last image of the folly was of her standing there, open-handed, in shock at what she'd just done. Manne walked back along the path feeling light-headed. He put his hand to his forehead; there was blood, quite a lot of it. His clothes were splashed with oil.

In his bedroom, he took off all his clothes and examined himself in the small mirror above the washbasin. The light-headedness had given way to a dull headache. The cut hurt like hell. He washed the wound clean and tied a towel around his head to stop the bleeding.

There were no other shirts to wear; Guépard had taken them to be laundered. Instead, he put on his dressing gown and lay down on the bed, trying for a moment of lucidity. On the bedside table were Edouard's drawings of the Vera Cruz orchid. Manne picked one up and stared into it. He remembered his sole encounter with that particular orchid. He'd never seen one in the wild, but his great-uncle had once bought a pair of them, probably at enormous expense. Manne had been fascinated by the fragile filaments that stretched from petal to petal, as though they'd been delicately glued on – fascinated by the way nature could be so unnatural. Like Edouard, Manne's great-uncle had most likely been experimenting with pollination techniques. Unlike Edouard, he'd no doubt failed.

Manne got up, went to his trousers, which were lying on the floor, and fished out one of the woman's notes from a pocket. He held it up to the light, along with the orchid drawing. The same watermark. No, he hadn't been imagining things

– they were written on the same expensive, cream writing paper. He turned this coincidence around in his head. Where would a convict have got hold of such paper? He had the impression of pieces that would perfectly slot into place if only he knew the trick to the puzzle. Absurd – in a place as small as Saint-Laurent, there was no doubt only one supplier of quality writing paper. There was no need to read any more into it than that.

He heard someone on the stairs, and went to the door. The butler was loitering on the landing.

'Charles. Come here a moment.' The butler walked over, none too quickly. 'Could you please ask my servant to come up to my room.'

'I'm afraid I don't know where he is, *monsieur*.'

'He told me you'd given him some task today . . .'

'*Non, monsieur*.'

'Well, no matter. I need a change of clothes, but my shirts are being laundered. Could you find something for me to wear, please.'

'You mean . . . you'd like to borrow one of the commandant's shirts?'

'If need be, yes. There's another thing. As you can see, I've cut my head. I slipped on something, down by the river. I need a bandage to dress the wound, and some disinfectant.'

'We don't have anything like that here, *monsieur*. You'd have to go up to the camp hospital.'

'I see. Well, go and see about the shirt.'

'*Oui, monsieur*.'

Manne shut his bedroom door. Once again he felt angry at the butler, who should have at least offered to fetch the bandages and disinfectant himself. On second thoughts, Manne wasn't feeling physically too bad, and the walk up might do him some good.

The butler returned with a clean white shirt, London-made, obviously the commandant's.

'Wait, Charles. I've been talking to the commandant about the state of the garden. My servant has some experience with gardens. I've offered his services. Instead of his kitchen duties, I want you to put him to work weeding the plots on the north side of the house. I'll be drawing up some specifications for the garden when I have time.'

The butler raised an eyebrow. 'The commandant hasn't said anything to me about this, *monsieur*.'

'Nevertheless, that's the situation.'

'I'll see the commandant about it, *monsieur*.'

'As you like.'

Manne wandered along the main avenue of the camp. Today it had a dilapidated, semi-deserted feel to it that reminded Manne of gold rush-era towns he'd passed through in the Brazilian interior. No one showed any interest in him or asked what he was doing, and eventually he had to ask a *bagnard* to direct him to the 'hospital'. The man pointed to what appeared to be a converted barracks. A number of convicts were queuing up outside it.

Just inside the entrance, a doctor in a white coat sat on a stool, cursorily examining the men who stood in line, occasionally giving them a pill or bandaging a wound. Beyond him, in the dark, half-naked men lay on grubby mattresses on the dirt floor, immobile, staring up at the ceiling. Only one of them was sitting up: a man counting endlessly on his fingers: '27, 28, 29 – 27, 28, 29 – 27, 28, 29 ...' An air of terminal apathy pervaded the room. No one seemed to be paying any attention to the men.

Manne approached the doctor. 'I'm staying with the commandant. I've cut my head. I need it properly bandaged.'

'Let me see.' The doctor squinted up. 'Doesn't look too serious. Wait for me in the mess hall. I'll see to it when I'm through with these men.'

'When will that be?'

'About an hour.'

Manne walked back out, not unduly bothered that the doctor hadn't given him precedence over the convicts. He continued slowly up the main avenue, towards the large arch that was under construction. A toy Arc de Triomphe, crowning a toy Champs-Elysées. A breeze blew down from the river; for once it felt cool and refreshing. Manne sat on one of the park benches bizarrely placed on the side of avenue.

The camp was disorientating, the 'hospital' depressing, and yet it was a relief to escape from the commandant's house and the folly. As Manne sat watching the convicts wandering up the avenue, he could feel his mind clearing. He kept thinking about the woman. He wasn't angry with her. He didn't know what would happen now, whether she would tell her husband, whether he would leave tomorrow. He felt only a disinterested curiosity about it all.

The hour passed; he made his way to the mess hall. The doctor, a small man with a neat moustache, examined his head. 'How did you do it?'

'Fell onto some rocks.'

'Feel any dizziness?'

'No. Yes. A little.'

'Pain? Headache?'

'It comes and goes.'

The doctor got a roll of bandages from his bag. 'I've used up all the disinfectant I brought with me. Rum'll do just as well.'

He poured some over the cotton wool and dabbed it on Manne's forehead, then wound the bandage loosely round his head.

'Keep it disinfected. Rum or any spirit'll do. Put some on a few times a day. It'll probably throb tonight. D'you want something to help you sleep?'

'Thank you, yes. What do I owe you?'

'Have a drink with me. That's all the payment I need.'

'With pleasure.'

The same desperation to talk to a peer that Manne had seen in the commandant. The doctor poured him a glass. 'What brings you this way?'

'I'm doing preliminaries for a botanical expedition here.' Manne quickly changed the subject. 'So how long have you been at the camp?'

'Oh, I'm not based here. I'm at Saint-Laurent. I do a round of the river camps, once every ten days. You're lucky to catch me.'

'There's no doctor here? Who looks after those convicts I saw, at the hospital?'

'Hospital?' The doctor laughed sourly. 'It's not a hospital. It's a *mouroir*. There are convict orderlies. They do the job as well as any doctor could, in the circumstances.'

'Circumstances?'

'You saw the place. I've no drugs. We're in fever country, the stores have no quinine. I'm forced to buy it on the black market, at my own expense. Take my advice, don't get ill up here. The only half-decent treatment you're likely to get is in Saint-Laurent. And that's a day's walk away.'

'Have you brought all this up with the Administration?'

'You haven't had many dealings with the Administration, have you?'

'Not really. I met the governor's secretary in Saint-Laurent. Captain Leblanc. And I'm staying with the commandant here.'

'Leblanc's a fool. Though no greater or lesser one than any of the others. As for the commandant . . .'

'What about him?'

'Strange man.' The doctor poured them both another glass of rum. 'When I was first here, I used to go and talk to him in his office. Thought we saw eye to eye. He agreed to refurbish the hospital, create a medicine stock. Then he lost interest. Almost from one day to the next. We had a huge row about it. So I have to avoid him now. All the time we were talking about the hospital, it was right there, not five hundred metres from his office, but he's never visited it. It's all abstract for him.'

'He's building a new penitentiary. Kilometre east of here. He took me to see it. I imagine he'll be transferring the hospital over there. That's probably why he lost interest.'

'I know. How long will that take? A year? Two years? What's he going to do about the hospital in the meantime? How many'll die? It's a charnel house. That's what I said to him. Know what he replied? "Sometimes you have to cure the patient at all costs, even if you have to kill him to do it." What the bloody hell is that supposed to mean?'

'Certainly an odd thing to say.'

The doctor shook his head. 'Everything about him's a bit odd. From what I heard, he has no permission from the Administration for the new building work. Never asked for it, never got it. The Administration didn't know what to do. But he's using his own money, so in the end they did nothing.'

'Perhaps he's doing the right thing. Scrapping the whole

set-up and starting from scratch may be the only thing to do.'

The doctor shook his head. 'You can't improve something that's fundamentally rotten. That's what I'll be writing in my report. I've got friends in government, and when I get back to France I'll be working as hard as I can to get this disgrace of a penal colony shut down. I said all that to the commandant as well.'

'How did he react?'

'He laughed!'

Manne wished the doctor well with his crusade against the penal colony; he meant it too. And yet, it occurred to him as he wandered back towards the river, in a way he could see the commandant's point of view as well. The idea of building a new colony – who wouldn't be seduced by it? Not for the first time, Manne found that he could consider two opposing notions and then accept both, without fundamentally believing in either.

The images of Edouard were fading, the mystery of his letter diminishing in importance. It was a process that had started the instant the commandant's wife had touched his cheek with her hand. He visualised her again, with her sweep of black hair. He thought of the story the drunken commandant had told him: the fiancé dead in an accident; the father who'd lost his fortune in the war. Then marriage with the commandant. That had been the first escape, presumably. From family and poverty; from the misfortune of a death. Strange fate, then, to end up in a penal colony. And now, rather than suffocate in a lifeless marriage, she was trying to leave, again, under adverse circumstances. That was courageous, wasn't it? That was a kind of bravery.

By the time he got back to the house, his head had started throbbing again. He told the butler he wouldn't be at table for dinner, then went straight to his room. At some point the butler brought up a dinner tray, but the throbbing had intensified and all he could manage was some soup. With his head, with the various other aches and pains he'd accumulated in the past few days, with his increasing discomfort in the heat, he felt not so much ill as old. The feeling was new; it had only hit him since being in the Colony. But it didn't surprise him much. Age hadn't crept up unforeseen; he'd been patiently waiting for it.

A barely audible knock. Manne raised himself from his bed. '*Entrez.*'

She opened and closed the door noiselessly. 'Charles told me you'd been up to the hospital. Whatever our differences, it wasn't my intention to injure you. Please accept my apologies for my behaviour.'

'No need to apologise.' She was staring at his bandaged head. 'It's not as bad as it probably looks. Just a cut on the forehead. And a blazing headache.'

'That's a relief. All day I've been convinced I hit you in the eye.'

'No. Just above the eye. I'll be fine tomorrow.'

'Good.' The conversation had been flat, neutral in tone. She stood there uncertainly, as if unsure whether she wanted to say something further. 'Well . . . good evening, then. If there's anything I can get Charles to bring you . . .'

'No, wait a second.'

Her hand was on the doorknob; now she turned back to face him.

'I've thought about it. I'm prepared to do what I can to help you. Of course, I understand if you simply want me to leave. In which case I'll go just as soon as I feel well enough to . . .'

She raised her hand to silence him, and put her head to the door. Manne could hear the faint sound of footsteps. Someone downstairs, or perhaps on the landing, trying not to make much noise. In the concentrated silence, Manne thought he could hear a clock ticking, although he didn't have one in the room.

The woman snapped out of position, as if coming out of a trance. She turned to him again. 'I don't know what to think any more. I don't trust you. We can't talk here, though. Come and see me tomorrow, if you feel up to it.'

She opened the door slightly, stared through the crack for a moment, then disappeared. Manne lay there listening to the night noises from the forest and the river. He got up and found the sleeping powder the doctor had given him, dissolved it in some lukewarm water and swallowed it down.

VIII

'Put it down on the bottom of the bed, thank you.'

The butler was standing over him, a breakfast tray balanced on one arm, '*Oui, monsieur*. Also, the commandant wishes to see you, at your convenience, in his office.'

'Tell him I'll be down just as soon as I'm dressed.'

'*Très bien, monsieur.*'

The headache had mostly gone. Although refreshed from a proper night's rest, he felt slightly groggy from the sleeping draught. He climbed out of bed and walked over to the mirror. Blood had glued the bandage to the wound, and he removed it with difficulty. Above his eye, his forehead was now swollen and purple-blue. It looked awful, worse than it felt. He washed, dressed, had his breakfast.

Strains of music wafted out from the commandant's office. Manne knocked hard on the door: 'Ah, Hartfeld. Come in, come in.'

The commandant was on his feet, making some annotation on the model that took up most of the room.

'You wanted to see me about something?'

'Yes I did.' The commandant was staring at Hartfeld with

detached curiosity. 'Charles told me of your . . . misadventure. I trust you're feeling better now?'

'It's nothing serious. Just a cut and a bruise. Rather foolish of me, I'm afraid.'

'Good. Not that I want to rush you if you're not feeling well. But I was wondering how much longer you need to stay here.'

'Not much longer. Another two or three days.'

'I see. It's, what, Thursday today. So that means leaving on Sunday at the latest.'

'I suppose so. I hadn't thought it out.'

'Well, let's say Sunday. Sunday morning.'

'If that's what suits you.'

'It's not a question of what suits me. I just like to know what's going on in my own house.'

The tone of aggression in the commandant's voice was hard to miss. Now the gramophone record had come to an end, its scratchy inner groove looping over again and again.

'As you wish. I'll leave by Sunday morning.'

'Fine. That's all I wanted to see you about.'

The commandant had already turned back to his plans.

'Oh,' said Manne. 'There's something I wanted to ask.'

'Yes?'

'You know the boy who came with me. Guépard. I've asked Charles to put him to work in the garden. I don't know if Charles mentioned it to you.'

'No. He didn't.'

'Well, he's a very reliable boy. But I don't need a servant, not here or in Saint-Laurent. He told me he has some experience with gardens. If I run up some specifications and explain to the boy what he needs to do, he could probably have your garden looking reasonable within a month or so.'

'Do you owe this boy something?'

Manne shook his head. 'He's very young. And it'd surely be best for him to have a job away from the other convicts. At the same time, it's a pity to see your garden go to ruin through lack of elementary care.'

'Well . . .' The commandant stared at him coldly. 'I'll see to the boy. Don't you worry about him.'

Back in his room, Manne's thoughts sped ahead of him. The commandant's unfriendly tone was perplexing. Then again, it mightn't signify anything. Alcoholics were prone to mood swings, after all. Manne had seen it himself in the commandant's fury, that first dinner here.

In any case, whatever the woman said to him today, it was clear now he'd be leaving by Sunday. He thought of his two months in Caracas, of the mistress he'd left there. He remembered a game they used to play. It involved his pretend-asking her to marry him, and her laughing, then pretend-accepting. Perhaps that's what he should do. Go back to Caracas and find her, then ask her to marry him, only this time for real. The idea briefly flared up in his mind as a way out, a possible escape route. Even as he entertained it, he knew it was another fantasy. Besides, when he tried to visualise his mistress now, what he actually saw was another body. A fuller figure. The *grain de beauté* on her shoulder blade, a curtain of hair over her face. That was what he wanted, wasn't it? It was just as impossible.

'I saw your husband this morning. He wants me to leave, by Sunday. His behaviour was odd. I wonder if he knows something.'

The woman stared past him, through the slats of the folly's small window.

'About what?'

'About . . . us.'

It felt ridiculous to verbalise it in that way. As if they really were lovers.

'You'd better hope not.'

'Why? What would he do?'

'He's under a lot of pressure. Strange things happen here.'

'I think I can look after myself.'

A brief pause, then the woman said: 'Anyway, we'd better act fast. If he wants you out by Sunday.'

For a second or two, Manne didn't know what she was talking about. She'd already moved on, made her decision, leaving Manne stumbling a few paces behind.

'You want me to help you – is that it?'

'You're still willing?'

'Of course.'

'We'd better start organising, then.' She sat down cross-legged on the floor, signalling for him to do likewise. 'First, we have to decide when. If my husband's expecting you to go on Sunday . . . what, early in the morning?'

'I suppose so.'

'Then we'll have to leave on Saturday. Which gives us two clear days to prepare. It should be enough. There's a native village about a kilometre south down the river. I suggest you go down this afternoon and negotiate a boat to Albina with one of the Boni traders. Can you do that?'

'Yes . . . I can do that.'

'Don't mention me. Just say you want a boat over for yourself – we don't want any gossip. Also, pay for a return journey, coming back the next day; that'll be less suspicious. As for the timing . . .'

She rushed on ahead. Even as he focused on her words, Manne could feel the tug of someone else, haunting the periphery of his mind. Edouard. A diminished presence, certainly. And yet still there.

'There's one big problem,' she was saying now. 'My husband has my passport, all my papers. I don't know where he keeps them. Can we manage without? Could I get new papers in Paramaribo? What do you think?'

'Makes things very difficult. If you enter Dutch Guiana illegally, your husband might get you detained and deported. You'd be on the run from the word go. Maybe the French consul in Paramaribo would give you a *laissez-passer*. But you'd be at his mercy. The governor at Saint-Laurent could very well order him to turn you over to the Dutch.'

'What if I just boarded a ship directly in Paramaribo?'

'Without papers? Not many boats would take you.'

'What about false papers?'

'Possible. I don't know anyone in Paramaribo, though. Do you?'

'No.'

'Well . . . I could probably arrange it. But it'd take a while. In the meantime, you couldn't stay at any normal hotel, because they'd ask for your papers. And then remember that afterwards you're under a false name. Wherever you end up, you're there illegally. Is that what you want? That kind of strain?'

The woman sat there pensively, gently pulling at her hair. Manne continued: 'If you've no papers, you should forget the idea of escape. You should go to Saint-Laurent and tell the governor that you wish to separate from your husband.'

She shook her head. 'I can't do that. He'd never let me leave the Colony. He'd write to my father. He'd . . . no, I can't do that. We'll just have to find my papers.'

'Any idea where they are?'

'If they're in his office up at the camp, then I'm stuck. But they're probably down here, in the house. Either in his bedroom or in his study.'

'We'd better look there, then.'

'Yes.' She glanced at her watch, got to her feet. 'We've about half an hour, probably. You can do the study, I'll do the bedroom.'

'What, right now?'

'If you've a better idea, tell me.'

There was a second's pause while they stood facing each other. Fragments of sunlight from the shutter speckled her face. Behind that façade of self-assurance, Manne caught a glimpse of profound uncertainty.

'You're right. Let's do it.'

She nodded. She was still staring at him: 'How's your head? It looks . . .'

She'd lifted her hand as if she were going to put it to his forehead, but stopped herself mid-motion.

'Not as bad as it looks.'

'Good.' She turned away. 'We'd better hurry. You go first. I'll follow a little later.'

A quick tour of the house – no one about, as far as he could make out. He'd sent Guépard up to the camp, to ask after Edouard. He tried the door to the commandant's study. Locked. Manne knelt down to examine the lock. Shoddy piece of work – not difficult to dismantle, but he'd have to do it quickly. He worked on it with his penknife. If anyone looked at all carefully, it'd be clear enough that it had been tampered with.

Five minutes later he had the door open. Another few moments to screw the lock back on left him hardly any time to look around. The window blinds were down. The gigantic model of the commandant's settlement loomed out of the semi-darkness. It reminded Manne of those table-sized battle maps he'd seen the generals use during the war.

There was the cupboard. Not open, no key in the lock, and no time to take the lock off. Manne bent down, eased the small door open with the point of his knife – without doing too much damage to the wooden frame, he thought. Inside, a few neat piles of papers. One of them seemed to be of official documents. He rifled through them. A marriage certificate, some title deeds, various financial papers. Almost too easily he found the woman's passport. He flicked through it to check that it was the right one, then pocketed it.

Next to the official-looking documents was another pile, of letters in their envelopes. These, too, Manne cursorily flicked through, looking for something about or from the commandant's wife. Disappointingly, there was nothing of that sort. But all the while, he was thinking of her. Trying to make sense of how their relationship had changed, under the shadow of their sexual encounter, even though he could barely remember it now – just his eyes roaming her body, moments beforehand.

The handwriting on the envelope on the top of the pile looked familiar enough, but he couldn't place it immediately – for a second he felt a *frisson* at the thought that the commandant might know someone he knew. Then it came to him: it was the governor's secretary, Leblanc. The same schoolboy-ish loops as on the letter of introduction Leblanc had written him. Manne pulled the letter from the envelope. At once his eye homed in on the scrawl of his name, Hartfeld. He quickly scanned the relevant paragraph: 'In response to your enquiry about Mr Hartfeld, we are still pursuing our investigations. Keep him under surveillance, and under no circumstances permit him to leave Renée.'

The words burned into his head. As he took in their implications, Manne could feel a presence in front of him. He looked up. The butler was staring, almost as if he were studying him. The cupboard door was wide open.

'Hello, Charles.'

The butler didn't say anything. He simply stood there by the door, his face unreadable.

'Listen, Charles,' Manne found himself saying, 'I've been meaning to have a word with you. I'll be leaving soon. I wanted to ... give you something to thank you for your services while I've been staying here.'

The words had tumbled from him without his really knowing what he was going to say, as if it were someone else, Hartfeld, who took control in times of emergency. Manne reached into his pocket, pulled out his wallet. The woman's passport almost spilt out as he did so. He opened his wallet, took out a sheaf of notes. A hundred francs at least, but he didn't bother to count.

'Here you are.'

The butler took the money without hesitation, without a thank you, and slipped it into the pocket of his waistcoat.

'Will you be here for lunch, *monsieur*?'

'No, I won't. I have some work to do.'

'Very well, *monsieur*.'

Hartfeld walked out of the commandant's office as calmly as he could. On his way upstairs he tapped on the woman's door. No answer. He tapped again, whispered: 'It's me.' Nothing. Filled with childish impatience, he was desperate to tell her that he'd found her passport. He crossed over the landing to his room, where he paced about for a few minutes, unable to compose himself. He forced himself to stop, and to draw regular breaths until his heartbeat had dropped to near normal.

Through the window, Manne could see the commandant emerging from the forest, ant-like against the immensity of the trees. He was still thinking of Leblanc's letter to the commandant. But he couldn't recall the exact succession of events after he'd looked up from reading it to find the butler staring at him. He felt in his pockets, but the letter wasn't there. In the shock of the moment, he must have left it on the sideboard or dropped it. And the commandant would find it. Then again, if the letter had shown anything, it was that Manne's position had already been severely compromised. Keep him under surveillance, it had said, under no conditions allow him to leave camp – something like that. In which case, why had the commandant made a point of asking him to leave by Sunday? Manne felt lost in the maze of other people's motives. But he had the woman's passport. He felt alive, electrically alive, for the first time since he'd received Edouard's letter.

IX

Naked children played in the dirt. Semi-naked women sat cross-legged on the ground, breast-feeding babies, or working at something intricate, although Manne couldn't quite make out what. Most of the women didn't even bother to look up from their work as Manne passed through the village. One seemed slightly startled, but then stared up into the distance beyond him, as if she'd heard a noise but Manne himself was somehow invisible.

'*Monsieur! Monsieur!*'

Manne turned around. It was a male villager who'd appeared out of nowhere.

'Boat, yes? Boat?'

Manne nodded, surprised that the man should have immediately known what he was after. With a mixture of gesticulation, broken Dutch and French, he made the man understand that he wanted to be taken across the river, the mid-morning of the day after the next. The boatman nodded, punctuating his disjointed speech with a staccato laugh. Once Manne was sure that the boatman had understood, he pulled out some money from his wallet and handed it over. At that, the man wandered off back down to the river. Manne watched as he climbed into a canoe and paddled over to the Dutch side – shrinking until he was nothing but a black spot against the brutal green of the trees on the far bank.

Like finding the woman's passport, it had all seemed too easy. He walked slowly back along the path towards the house, unsure of what to do with himself. Several hours to kill before dinner. His mind flitted from one subject to another, without settling on any one in particular. Thursday afternoon, and they wouldn't be leaving until Saturday morning – now he had the woman's passport, he couldn't see the point of the delay. Especially after finding Leblanc's letter. In general, once a decision had been taken, Manne liked to act upon it immediately, and felt frustration when he couldn't. Perhaps it was in compensation for a larger, overarching procrastination. He stared across to the Dutch side of the river.

Back in the house, he went to the door of the woman's room and knocked; no response. Nothing to do now but return to his own room, where he lay down, overwhelmed with tiredness. As he dozed in the afternoon heat, he dreamt of an endless column of men marching through a jungle. Some of them were dropping to the ground along the way, out of sheer exhaustion. Manne ran forward, hoping to get past them. Moments later, he found himself at the front of the column. A man in military uniform was leading it. The face was familiar, but it was younger, thinner than the last time Manne had seen it. He woke up, opened his eyes with the image of that same face still there in front of him. He was certain now that he had known Captain Leblanc at the front in Belgium. No wonder Leblanc had been so shocked at the sight of him. It must literally have been like seeing a ghost.

A timid tap on the door. That was what had awoken him.

'Guépard. What do you want?'

'I come back from the camp, *m'sieur*.'

'Yes?'

'You ask me to go to the camp, *m'sieur*. To look for your friend.'

Manne struggled out of his dream. Yes, he could remember asking Guépard to go up to the camp. It felt like weeks ago.

'I ask a lot of people. And I find someone who knows, *m'sieur*.'

'Knows what?'

'Where your friend is hiding.'

'Where?'

'He doesn't tell me. He says not very far away.'

'What does he want? Money?'

'He says he wants to see you. He wants to speak only to you.'

'Why? Why did you mention me? I told you to say it was *your* friend, for God's sake.'

Guépard cringed as though he were about to be struck. 'Very sorry, *m'sieur*. I said nothing, *m'sieur*. You must believe me. He knows who you are. He knows you are looking for your friend. I do not know how.'

'Where does he want to see me? How do you know he's telling the truth? How do you know he's not trying to leech me?'

'I describe your friend, *m'sieur*. Tall, one glass eye, called Edouard. The man, he says he knows where your friend is. Not far away, he says.'

'What does this man want me to do?'

'He meets you tomorrow morning, *m'sieur*.'

'Where do I have to go?'

'He comes down here, *m'sieur*. He comes to see *you*.'

'What's his name?'

'I do not know his real name, *m'sieur*. They call him Masque.'

'What's he going to do? Come and knock on my door?'
'He says there is an old ruin here. By the edge of the trees.'
'Yes, I know where he means.'
'He will meet you there, at eight o'clock in the morning.'

After Guépard had gone, Manne paced up and down his room in a state of total consternation. This talk of Edouard would probably come to nothing. Guépard had no doubt been taken in by a convict on the lookout for a few francs. Nonetheless, Manne could feel the adrenaline pumping through him as he fumbled for cigarettes and matches. Already he'd dismissed Edouard. Already he'd set this other escape in motion, and already, in his mind, he was visualising it, taking the woman across the river, leading her through the jungle to Moengo, then up to Paramaribo. The woman was *there*, flesh and blood, and Edouard wasn't, had merely been an idea, a memory. He couldn't ignore that. And yet, all of a sudden, here he was again, resurrected.

Manne sat down by his desk, opened his journal and began to write:

I remember E. once telling me of a trip he made to New Guinea in search of tiger orchids. In the remote mountain area he was exploring, he had come across a group of native men, hunting in the forest. He had tried to communicate with them using signs and the smattering of the regional lingua franca he had picked up. They had seemed terribly excited at having found him, and were evidently asking him to do something for them, but he couldn't understand what. They had led him on a trek through the forest, to an enormous, rectangular clearing. At one end of it, E. had been astonished to see a biplane. He now understood that the clearing was supposed to be a runway, and what they wanted him to do was pilot the plane. As he got closer, he realised that it wasn't a plane at all, only an extremely good replica, its body made out of forest wood, its wings palm leaves sewn to a wooden frame, all dyed a vivid red. Its tail sported a German cross and, along the side of the body, what had appeared at a distance to be a few letters in Gothic script. On closer inspection, they turned out to be mere approximations, generic squiggles. The natives had bade him climb into the cockpit. There, too, were skewed approximations of engine controls, as if seen from afar.

Frustratingly, Manne couldn't recall how Edouard had said he'd extricated himself from the situation. He couldn't even remember where and when Edouard had told him about it. The story floated free in his brain, without connection to anything else. Manne flicked forward through the empty pages of his journal. They'd never be filled now. Because with Edouard's story, his journal had somehow come to its end, however unsatisfactorily. There was nothing more to write.

X

All afternoon, Manne had kept an eye out for the commandant's wife, watching the garden from his window, listening for her footsteps on the stairs, several times crossing the landing to knock on her door. And yet when he finally came downstairs, there she was, elegantly dressed for dinner and already seated. He risked a glance in her direction, and caught an expression that was penetrating, questioning. Quickly, he glanced away again.

'You know, Hartfeld,' the commandant said as he poured the wine, 'there was no need to send your servant up to camp.'

'I beg your pardon?'

'Your servant. You sent him up to Renée for some writing paper, didn't you? No need for that. I've plenty of writing paper in my office. You only had to look in my office.'

The butler served the meal, and they ate in silence. Manne considered the commandant's sally, examined it for its implications. Writing paper, the office . . . an oblique reference to Manne's being caught reading the commandant's correspondence? In any case, the comment irritated him: surely it was up to Manne to do what he liked with his servant.

The commandant now turned to his wife. 'My dear, I heard

some news up at the camp that might interest you.' The woman said nothing, and the commandant continued: 'About your friend. The convict botanist. Damned if I can remember his name. What was it, my dear? What was his name?'

'Boppe. Pierre Boppe.'

'Ah yes, that's right. I'd forgotten. Pierre Boppe.'

He rolled the name around in his mouth. He hadn't forgotten, obviously. The commandant was drunk, more so than usual, or so Manne first thought. But it might have been something else. Tonight he seemed in an excitable, febrile mood.

'Well, it seems he had an accident. Apparently he drowned. Swimming in the river.'

'Oh . . .' The woman put her hand to her mouth, clearly taken aback at the news.

The commandant now turned to Manne. 'Astonishingly common here, actually. The current's much stronger than it looks. And quite a few convicts drown every year. Of course, some can't swim. They go to the river to cool off and then get swept off their feet by the current. But often enough it's swimmers who are trying to escape. They take it into their heads that they can make it over to the other side.'

The commandant shrugged his shoulders, went on with his meal, noisily clunking his knife and fork against the plate. Manne looked over to the woman, who had stopped eating and was visibly subdued. Another interminable stretch of silence, this time continuing throughout the rest of the meal. Manne's impression was that the commandant's comments had meant to be gentle assertions of authority; instead they'd killed the dinner completely. In the silence, Manne lost himself once more in thought. All sorts of details and problems about the escape had occurred to him. He wondered how long it would be before the commandant discovered that they'd gone. And what might happen if they couldn't get a ride immediately out of Albina. The commandant might get the Dutch police to stop them, after all. They'd be so much safer in a large town, rather than Albina or Moengo.

As they finished dessert, Manne looked over to the commandant's wife, for the first time since the beginning of dinner. She mouthed 'my room' to him, before getting up from her chair. 'Think I'll turn in. I'm very tired tonight.'

'As you wish, my dear. You'll stay for a cognac, though, won't you, Hartfeld?'

'Well...' Manne caught an almost imperceptible nod from the commandant's wife.

The butler poured the two men drinks. For a good few minutes, dinner's silence continued. Finally, the commandant said: 'You're not a religious man, by any chance, Hartfeld?'

'Why do you ask?'

'It's just that a priest comes up to the camp once a month, to say Mass. It so happens that tomorrow he'll be here. Just thought I'd let you know, in case you were the churchgoing sort.'

'I'm not, I'm afraid.'

'Didn't think you would be. Scientific man like you.'

'You're a churchgoer yourself?'

'Not in the least. Dreadful superstition. Mind you, the Gospels make for a marvellous story. Oh, I quite believe in the crucified Christ. It's the resurrected one that makes no sense.'

'Why not?'

'It's a strange end to a tragic tale, is it not? It's... well, as if Hamlet had survived and were crowned king, if you follow my example. Everything that had come before would have lost its sense.'

Manne could think of no reply to that. For a moment he

thought the commandant was going to say a lot more, as though the story of Christ were the subject of an eccentric pet thesis. But he fell silent, moodily gazing into his drink. Manne sat with him for a few more minutes before draining his own glass. He stood up to bid goodnight to the commandant, who barely looked up, waving his hand as he might to dismiss a servant.

As he approached the woman's door it opened silently, and he slipped into her room. Inside, everything was grey and dim, with just a single lamp casting long shadows. Facing him, a full-length mirror that almost looked like another door. It was a shock to catch his reflection in it unexpectedly. In the gloom, he looked insubstantial, hardly there at all. A tiny cascade of thoughts ran through his mind. Usually, he realised, when he looked at himself in the mirror, he framed himself in a certain way, in fact to look just like he did in his mind's eye. But it was not how others saw him. That other person, the object and not the subject, was someone different, a stranger. All this struck him in a split second. Now he turned to the woman. She'd changed out of her elegant robe, into a plain white nightdress.

'I found it,' he whispered. 'I found your passport.'

'I know that.' She didn't elaborate. 'You went down to the village? Did you get a boat?'

'Yes. For the time we agreed. Eleven o'clock the day after tomorrow.'

'Good. Good.'

Behind her was a bed, the sheets in a state of rumpled disorder. Next to it was a small table, on which stood a framed photo of the house itself, with the vast river in the background.

Manne was about to say something when the woman cut him off with a 'shhh!' In the void, he could hear her breathing and her husband's heavy, drunken step on the stairway. With a single fluid movement, the woman went back to the door and quietly turned the key in the lock. The steps were closer; the commandant was on the landing now. An eternity later, Manne could hear him slowly turning the door handle, trying not to make any noise. When it wouldn't open, he turned it with more insistence, then finally rattled it violently. Finally a banging at the door that tore through the fragile silence. 'Renée! Open this door!'

Manne stood stock-still, every muscle taut, frozen as he gazed into the woman's eyes. She stared back. The contact felt so powerful that he forced himself to look beyond her, at the photo of the house on the bedside table.

'Open this door. Open up!' Again she didn't reply. After another brief silence, the commandant raised his voice to a shout: 'Renée! I order you to open this door immediately!'

'No. Go to bed. You're drunk.'

Another rattling of the door, another silence, this time longer. Manne pictured the commandant on the landing, wondering what to do next. Eventually, he heard the uncertain footsteps again, then the opening and closing of another door.

'Wait a few minutes,' the woman whispered to him.

The two of them stood there like statues, centimetres away from each other but not touching. Under her nightdress he could make out the contours of her body, whose absolute foreignness both seduced and frightened him. He could feel her eyes scrutinising his face, just as he scrutinised hers, every tiny feature magnified a thousand times.

'I think he's gone,' the woman whispered finally. 'He may be waiting on the landing. I'll have a look.' She silently unlocked the door, put her head around it. 'You go now. We can talk tomorrow.'

Manne crept back to his room. For a long time he prowled

about, smoking cigarette after cigarette, unable to sleep until the tension inside him had wound down. He went through the details of the escape with the woman, wondering what the best strategy would be to ensure the Dutch police wouldn't stop them. It somehow pleased Manne that there was still plenty to think about, because he had the impression that once he'd imagined every detail, actually carrying out the escape would be almost superfluous.

XI

He woke just before dawn, jolted from an indistinct dream that seemed filled with desire. Downstairs, Manne found the breakfast table already set. He wandered over to the kitchen.

'Charles, I wonder if you could tell the commandant when he rises that I would like to see him.'

The butler turned his attention away from the stove, fractionally too slowly for Manne's liking. 'I'm afraid he's gone up to the camp, *monsieur*.'

'What? At this hour? It can't be much later than six.'

'I'm afraid he's already left.'

'When will he be back?'

'It is not for me to say, *monsieur*. Normally he returns for lunch.'

'I see. Well, could you please serve me some breakfast.'

'*Oui, monsieur*.'

He'd have liked to ask Charles whether it was very common for the commandant to be up and gone by six. He'd have liked to ask him whether he'd found Leblanc's letter and put it back in the cupboard. Or whether he'd said anything to the commandant about finding Manne in the study.

After breakfast, he went back to his room and on several

occasions tried to see the woman. Each time he opened his door, there was the butler, apparently cleaning something on the landing, or in the dining room at the foot of the stairs. As he sat fretting in his bedroom, an idea came to him. His servant, Guépard, was still on his mind. It occurred to him to call for him now and ask him if he wanted to join himself and the woman on their escape. He would provide the boy with funds, lodge him secretly in Paramaribo, get some papers made up for him there and buy him a passage out of the town. The boy might even accompany the woman to Buenos Aires as her servant. As soon as the idea came to him, he realised it was ludicrous, merely idle fantasy. As if Manne were not enough of a liability to the woman, without her having to contend with an escaped convict.

Later, Manne crossed the lawn to the ruin by the edge of the forest. Despite his scepticism, he'd decided to keep the appointment with the convict Guépard had met, who'd claimed to know where Edouard was. The ruin was not much more than a crumbling wall; Manne wondered what it had once been. He imagined some other commandant, years ago, who'd decided to build his house there, and had been defeated by it.

Manne cast about in the undergrowth with his feet, for want of anything better to do. As he looked down he noticed what seemed to be a large hole, disguised with branches. He got down on his hands and knees to examine it more closely. The branches looked freshly cut; he pushed them aside, put his hand down into the hole and touched something smooth. He peered into the hole. Three lidded barrels were secreted there, plus another larger, lidless one. He prised the lid off one of the barrels. Inside was a series of parcels, carefully wrapped in greased paper. Manne opened one of them and found some dried, salted meat. His guess was that the butler was smuggling foodstuffs out of the house to sell later on the black market. He rewrapped the meat, put it back in the barrel.

Half an hour, an hour . . . the convict wasn't going to turn up. The whole thing had been a sting that the convict had considered and then thought better of. It meant that Edouard was gone for good. Manne visualised his long face and dark hair, his glass eye staring at him, his own reflection staring back in miniature.

Now it was time to prepare for the escape. To jettison everything that wasn't needed. Always a sense of anguish with every departure, however desired. And always an urge to strip himself of everything but the essential, as if to counter some inner deadweight. There wasn't much left to him now that was extraneous. He stuffed some banknotes into his back pocket, and put the rest of his money and bank orders into a canvas bag. He'd give it all to the woman. She needed it more than he did; he could always find a way to make money. But he also had a sense of foreboding. A feeling that something would go wrong. That they wouldn't be escaping after all. Not together, in any case. He picked up his journal, and put that into the bag, too.

Crossing the garden, Manne stopped at one point and turned back towards the house. The butler was standing by the door, arms folded against his chest, staring at him, or beyond him. He made no movement to acknowledge Manne's presence. Manne inwardly shrugged. What did it matter now?

Before, various bits and pieces had been scattered over the floor of the folly – a rug, the lamp, a couple of books, maybe some clothes. There was nothing there now. It had been cleaned out. The room looked bare and forlorn. He thought he could make out a mark where the lamp the woman had thrown at him had dented the wall.

Manne wandered about the small clearing in which the folly was set, waiting for the woman to show up. There was some scrubby bush by the folly wall and, out of the corner of his eye, Manne caught a glint of colour. He bent down. A tiny orchid had attached itself to the wall. Manne knelt down and gently removed its roots from the wall with his penknife. A spider orchid, but not an especially rare one. And yet to the best of Manne's knowledge, it was native to Florida only. How could that be? He stared at it.

'Is that for me?'

He hadn't heard her come, it was as if she'd simply appeared. Manne got to his feet.

'If you like. Have it.'

She shook her head. 'I've never much liked orchids.'

'Why not?'

'I don't know. Something unpleasant about them. Unnatural.'

'Not this one. It was growing here in the wild. That's natural enough.'

'Unnatural is the wrong word. They look unreal. Artificial.'

'And yet your husband told me that you loved orchids.'

'Did he? What would he know? Actually, I don't think I care much for flowers in general.'

'What *do* you like?'

But the absurdity of their conversation struck them both simultaneously, and the light mood now evaporated. Manne picked up the canvas bag he'd left on the ground beside him as he'd been collecting the orchid.

'I brought this for you. There's some money in cash here. Some of it in francs, some of it American dollars. Also some

American bank orders you should be able to cash in Buenos Aires.'

She opened the bag, pulled out some of the banknotes. 'I don't need all of this. It's very kind of you, but I'm not asking you for so much. Just to help me get to Paramaribo and pay for my passage out.'

'Take it anyway. I don't need it.'

'I'd rather make my own way as far as possible.'

'I'm offering it to you. Take it.' He desperately wanted the woman to accept the money. But she didn't reply. 'Well, I'll hide the bag here. I don't feel it's safe in my room. I don't trust the butler. I'll decide what to do with it later.'

'As you wish.'

She followed him into the folly. Its bareness struck Manne again – everything smooth, circular, like a little chapel. There was a slightly loose floorboard he'd noticed once before, and he thought there'd probably be room underneath to hide his canvas bag. He dropped to his knees, got his penknife out. The board came up surprisingly easily. He felt about under it for somewhere to put the bag, and his hand came up against something hard and cool. An old jar, with a screwtop lid. With some difficulty, he got the top off. The contents spilled out over the floor.

'Photos, by the looks of it.'

Manne flipped through them. Mostly old holiday snaps, some of them half-eaten away by fungus.

'Show them to me.'

She peered at the top photograph intently, as though examining a specimen through a microscope. Finally she put it down and moved on to the next one, to which she gave the same treatment. Then the next one, and the next. All in all, there were around a dozen. She sat there wordlessly, as if deep in thought – subdued, as at dinner, when her husband had told her about the death of her convict acquaintance. She shook her head several times.

'What is it?'

'They're of me,' she said without looking up. 'They're all of me.'

She pushed them back into the space on the floor between them. Through the mould stains, Manne could make out the same girl in each of the photos. Here she was, fresh-faced at a debutantes' ball. Men in uniforms, must have been during the war. Here she was again, at the beach, in a swimming costume, smiling gaily, innocently, at the camera. Thinner, younger. But not much. Probably only a few years ago. And yet, at the same time, impossibly long ago.

'How did they get here? You didn't put them there?'

'No.'

'Who did, then?'

'I don't know.'

Photographs. The more inept, the more blurred or poorly framed, the more they haunted. And the people in them, whether still living or dead, were ghosts just the same . . . The woman's head was bowed over them now as she spread them out on the ground. The expression on her face was transparent, filled with remembering. Looking at the photos, Manne, too, was struck with a sense of nostalgia, although the pictures were a private shrine. Nostalgia for things never known. Manne remembered his French grandfather and the glimpses of Second Empire life he'd gleaned from him, odd memories of the war with the Prussians or drinking in Latin Quarter cafés. Details that could suddenly breathe life and longing into a long-dead, never-experienced era.

The woman's voice cut through his thoughts: 'The first time

I came here, there was someone camping out in the folly. He must have just come out of the jungle. He asked me to get him food. And so I did.'

'An *évadé*?'

'I supposed so.'

'You weren't afraid of him?'

'I was, yes. But . . . not so much. He was in a pitiful state. Half-dead. He wasn't about to do me any harm. He was only here for a couple of days. Twice I brought him food. Then he disappeared. It was only after he vanished that I started coming here.'

'You didn't tell anyone about him?'

'No. I'm opposed to transportation.'

'Do you know who the *évadé* was?'

'No. Although not long afterwards, I heard that a famous jewel thief had been caught near here. Perhaps it was him. But I'm told there are quite a number of *évadés* up and down the river.'

'Whoever he was, you think he had something to do with these photos.'

'No. Yes. I don't know what to think.'

She went silent again. The photographs, the spider orchid, the convict hiding out at the folly . . . it seemed to Manne that they were all elements of the same thing, which he couldn't quite seize in its entirety. As if a blanket had been thrown over an unknown object, revealing only the bumps and angles of its exterior shape.

'This one of me dancing. That man there in the background, in the left-hand corner. How very odd. I had no idea he was there that night. It was before we met.'

She was almost talking to herself, lost in her discovery. The man in the photo was just a black sliver, a blur in a bow tie.

'Who is he?'

'He was my lover.'

'Your cousin?'

She looked up at him bizarrely. 'Of course not. What on earth do you mean?'

'You were going to marry your cousin, weren't you?'

'My husband told you that, too?'

'Yes.'

'Well, let him believe it if he likes.'

'He told me you were engaged.'

She shook her head. 'We grew up together. That's all. One day he thought he was in love with me. I wasn't in the least bit interested. Not in that way.' Her mood darkened. 'What does it matter now?'

She was looking at the ballroom photograph again, still lost in it, far away. 'The dancing. It's what I miss. Possibly most of all. I used to go to a lot of dances. My husband brought his gramophone all this way. And yet he didn't bring a single record you might dance to.'

'I know where that photograph was taken,' Manne said. 'It's at the Crillon, isn't it?'

'Yes. That's where it was.'

'I went to a ball there once as well. A long time ago. Before the war.'

The woman was now staring at the folly's blank white cornerless wall, softly humming a melody to herself. Manne recognised that, too. A Tchaikovsky waltz. One of those infectious, physical melodies that he too had once danced to, years ago, a lifetime ago.

A bewitching mood had settled over the folly, which now filled with sound, with music, pushing back its walls. Manne found himself on his feet. The woman was in his arms. The technique came back to him; he swept her around the tiny room. It was the Crillon, he was with his lover, the one he'd never seen again after his desertion. The woman, too, was at the Crillon, he was sure enough of it. Their respective fantasies intertwined and fused as they danced together, memory and sensation blending seamlessly. The music filled him until he could feel nothing else but its sounds and rhythms, and the woman held lightly against him.

How long had it lasted? Two minutes? Twenty minutes? After the dancing, they disentangled from each other and sat down on the floor again. For a while he still felt overpowered by the sense of music in the air. The mood had spun away into something else again by now: an easy, comfortable *tristesse*, as if the two had just made love. Something had changed in him; for a moment he felt that it didn't matter what happened now. Slowly, they broke into conversation, which came in fragments, as if each were confident that the other could mentally supply what was left unspoken.

She was talking about her husband. 'He comes and stares at me sometimes, at night. He comes into my room. I pretend I'm asleep. After a while, he goes away again.'

Then later: 'I could have done it so easily before. I could have got away. We had a huge row and I just took off one morning, in a rage. Not really knowing what I was doing. I walked to Saint-Laurent. When he came to collect me, that was that. He took my papers away. Put me under surveillance. Somehow, I wasn't surprised to end up here, like this.'

They sat opposite each other, knees almost touching. At one point Manne uttered her name, and she replied: 'Don't call me Renée. Only my husband calls me Renée.'

'What does everyone else call you?'

'Mathilde.'

A long silence, and then: 'What are you hiding? Why did you come here?'

'You said I don't look like a botanist. But I'm a sort of botanist. I collect plant specimens.'

'That's not why you're here, though.'

'No. I came looking for someone.'

'A friend?'

'Not really.'

'A *bagnard*?'

'Of course . . .'

'You haven't found him.'

He shook his head.

'If he wasn't a friend, why were you looking for him?'

'He has some valuable information. He offered to share it with me. He offered me a deal.'

'You're still wondering whether you shouldn't stay here.'

'No. I have to leave now. Tomorrow isn't soon enough. Your husband suspects me.'

'Suspects you of what?' She stared at him with curiosity. 'You've committed some sort of crime. That's it, isn't it?'

He didn't immediately answer. For a long time he just stared back at her, taking in all the details of her face, as he'd done in her bedroom the night before. She met his gaze unflinchingly. Outside he could hear the mid-morning rain thrum down on the trees, intensifying the atmosphere of intimacy and confinement within the folly.

'Listen,' he said now. 'Come with me. We can go anywhere. I'll support you. The money I have could last us a couple of years. I'll do whatever you want me to do. We could go to New York. Or Buenos Aires. I could help you start a business, if that's what you want. I know Buenos Aires well enough. I know people there who could help us.'

Even as he said that, he realised he knew the city only in the same way as he knew any other city – hotel rooms, restaurants, bars, brothels, merely skimming the surface. The woman shook her head, and there was nothing further for him to say. The rest was just form.

'You frighten me. You're handsome. But you're a dry root. I can't give you what you need. Even if I could, I don't want to. I have my own life to lead.'

'I understand.'

The rain had quickly died down to an uncharacteristic drizzle, to a whisper down the walls. Bars of grey light, filtered through the shutters, criss-crossed Mathilde's face.

'You might have seduced me. You didn't have to spoil it all the way you did.'

'No.' He felt cleansed of feeling. 'I didn't have to do that.'

'You'd better go now. My husband will be back soon. I won't be at lunch today, but you'd better be there. I'll see you at dinner – certainly not afterwards, not after last night. Tomorrow we'll meet as arranged.'

XII

The thought of his room in the commandant's house filled Manne with a sort of horror. Instead of returning there, he went to sit by the river, until it was time for lunch. For an hour he watched the tiny waves lick at the riverbank; in the distance, glints of light dazzled across the water's surface. Further downstream, disappearing into the haze, Manne could make out Boni canoes darting through the current, a paperchase of gulls trailing them.

The sense of being cleansed of feeling hadn't gone away. Never had Manne felt more empty. Something had happened during those snatched moments of dancing in the folly – but in the end he'd failed to draw Mathilde into a world of complicity, of sensuality. His mind worked its way back to other failures he'd suffered in his life. The carefully laid plans that had gone awry; the wrong paths taken. The lover who had killed herself. Friends who had long since fallen silent.

Once he'd helped Mathilde onto a boat in Paramaribo, Manne had no other plans, good or bad. No ideas. Clearly, he wouldn't stay in Paramaribo. Clearly, he'd move on. The world was a vast prison: it was immaterial which particular corner he ended up in. Perhaps Edouard had reached the same point of no return. If Edouard too was a deserter, as Manne suspected, then he might have come to the Colony quite deliberately. The fear of exposure was not so far from the hope of it. And the men who spent a life in hiding were often enough the ones who wanted to be found.

Meanwhile, back in the here and now, there was lunch to get through. It struck him forcefully that the commandant had been holding out on him, had not told him about the letter he'd received from Leblanc, had not told him that Manne was under investigation. Even so, the commandant had no moral duty to tell him. In any case, Manne had received the commandant's hospitality under false pretences. He had made advances to his wife, had even cuckolded him. Mathilde, in turn, had her own secrets. The eternal roundabout of deception and betrayal.

Judging from the sun, directly above, it was close to midday. Manne had barely got through the back door when the butler appeared in the corridor. 'The commandant would like to see you, *monsieur.*'

'Where is he?'

'Waiting for you in his study.'

'I'm just going to wash first. I'll be down shortly.'

'I will inform the commandant, *monsieur.*'

Back to his room, finally. There was his bag on his bed. It contained not much more than a change of clothes. A few books lay beside it. The language manual he'd borrowed from the commandant. The novel he'd started to read on the boat, and would now never finish. He didn't like the sound of the commandant asking for him. He looked out of the window. His bedroom was on the river side; it wouldn't be too difficult to snake down the wall, get to the river unseen. There was the problem of Mathilde. If he could be sure she was still in the folly, then that's what he'd do. Manne opened his door: he wanted to check she wasn't in her bedroom. The butler was on the landing, just standing there, not even pretending to be there for any other reason than to keep watch. Manne made as if he'd forgotten something, and retreated into his room. He only had a minute to act, before being locked into whatever the commandant had in mind for him.

The moment he'd found Leblanc's letter, the very moment he'd paid off the butler... that was when he should have left, without further ado. He'd felt it at the time, but hadn't acted upon the intuition. Even afterwards, even this morning in the folly, he'd been going to suggest to Mathilde that they leave at once, when instead he'd given her his pleading speech. A wave of fatalism washed through him. Manne opened the door again, and made his way past the butler towards the commandant's study.

'Hartfeld. Good of you to come. Please sit down.'

The commandant held up his hand as if inviting in an old friend. The *faux bonhomie* was the flimsiest of façades. He had a wild stare and his face was haggard and grey. Clearly, the commandant was only just holding everything together, the alcoholic shake barely under control.

'Charles...' The butler was there. He must have silently followed Manne down the stairs. 'Please go and fetch Mr Hartfeld's servant.'

'*Oui, mon commandant.*'

The commandant now sat down heavily at his desk, next to the model of the camp.

'What has my servant got to do with anything?'

The commandant seemed incapable of saying anything for the moment, and merely grinned maniacally. Moments later, Guépard arrived, the butler hovering behind. Manne tried and failed to catch his servant's eye.

'Ah, there you are. Now, I'd like you to repeat what you told me just now.'

'*Oui, monsieur.*' He was still avoiding Manne's eye. 'This morning, I see Mr Hartfeld. He walks across the garden. He goes to a small house in the jungle. I see him go there before. I follow him, just like you tell me. I see him at the small house. Then I see *madame*. Now she talks to him. I don't hear what they say. They go into the small house. I go closer. I try to see them through the window. I try to see what they do. I see them kissing. Then I think they see me. So I go back.'

'*Merci.*'

The commandant could hardly get the word out, such was the state he was in. Guépard stood there uncertainly, unsure whether he'd been dismissed or not. There was a bottle on the commandant's desk. The commandant poured himself a glass of rum and drank it down. It seemed to calm him, but only for a moment.

'Well then, Hartfeld. Have you anything to say?'

'Whatever I might have to say, I'd prefer to say it in private. Guépard, could you go upstairs to my room and wait for me, please?'

Guépard didn't move at first. Manne caught a nod from the commandant to Guépard, who then took off at a run.

'Charles, I want you to go up to the camp. Find the captain-at-arms. Tell him to accompany you back here with two properly armed guards.'

'*Oui, mon commandant.*'

Now the butler disappeared. The commandant opened a drawer in his desk and took out a service revolver. Such was the mad look in his eye that at first Manne thought the commandant was going to blow his brains out in front of Manne. Instead, he put the revolver in his lap.

'Have you anything to say about what your servant just recounted?'

'I don't think so. Not about the uncorroborated testimony of a convict. I certainly don't intend to say anything while threatened with a gun.'

'It's a precaution. I have no intention of doing you any harm. Please stay seated until the guards arrive.'

'Are you putting me under arrest?'

The commandant fiddled with the revolver. 'What were you doing with my wife?'

'I can assure you there was nothing criminal involved. Nothing that might require my arrest. Under the circumstances, I think it would be appropriate if I got my bags now and left this house at once.'

'Don't you leave this room!'

The commandant was brandishing the gun and his grey face had flushed a dark purple. There was a long, heavy silence as they stared at each other. A mass of tiny tics and twitches had invaded the commandant's body. Slowly he put the gun down again, back in his lap. Manne felt calm. He mentally calculated: it was a ten-minute walk up to camp. Ten minutes there, ten back, then probably a further ten minutes for the butler to find the captain-at-arms. It would be another half an hour before the guards arrived.

'This is penal territory. I need no further authority to detain you. Even if I did, I already have it, since you're here illegally.'

'That's not true. I have the permits from the governor's office.'

'You have papers for one Paul Hartfeld. That's not your name, is it? It's Jean Capgras. You served as an officer in the 101st regiment, B Company. You were reported as missing in action in 1917.'

Manne started. He wasn't surprised that the commandant knew about him. The probable sequence of events flickered across his consciousness: Leblanc had remembered who he was, had made some telegram enquiries, and had quickly discovered Manne's story. In retrospect, it seemed so inevitable that he wondered how he'd ever thought he might safely return to French territory. No, what had shocked him was to hear the name Capgras. To be sure, it was what was on his birth certificate. But he'd never used it, not even when small. He'd always taken his mother's family name instead. And Capgras felt no more or less real than Hartfeld.

'I had confirmation of that yesterday. And today I received the order to detain you. But do you know what? I actually had no intention of having you arrested. I was going to tell you about the warrant, and ask you to leave immediately.'

'You can still do that. I'll cross the river. You'll never hear from me again.'

The commandant shook his head. 'What did you do to my wife? Why? Why?'

He was waving the revolver again. Manne didn't reply. Despite the revolver, despite the commandant's building hysteria, Manne wasn't yet worried for his life. He thought it unlikely that the commandant could hit him in the state he was in. He'd sent the butler away. At the house, there was only the commandant, his wife, Manne, perhaps the maid from the village. It even crossed his mind that the commandant wanted him to get away, and that this was some kind of elaborate suicide theatre. All that remained was to decide what to do, and to do it within the next fifteen minutes.

'What do you intend to do with your wife?'

'That's my business!' the commandant snapped.

He gulped down more rum. The sweat glistened on his

hands, which could hardly hold the glass still enough for him to drink. He started raving again: 'You think I'm a fool, don't you? What did she tell you? What did she do for you? Was it the first time? Or were there times before? Is that it? Is that it?'

He let out a high-pitched laugh. Again, the silence, the staring. Something in what the commandant had said – or the way he'd said it – made Manne wonder whether the marriage had ever been consummated.

'What will you do with me now?'

The commandant shrugged with drunken exaggeration: 'The guards will take you back to camp. You'll be escorted to Saint-Laurent tomorrow morning.'

'And then?'

'You're a deserter, aren't you? You'll be sent to France. Or perhaps you'll go before a military tribunal here. I don't know.'

Manne tried one more time. 'Let me leave now. I'll disappear into the forest. I'll be gone for good. But if I get sent back to Saint-Laurent, I'll tell the authorities what's happening up here. I'll tell them you're keeping your wife here against her will.'

'Are you trying to blackmail me?'

'Take it as you wish.'

'You won't get far with that.' The commandant seemed to sober up. 'What sort of nonsense has she been feeding you? Did she tell you that she spent eighteen months in a psychiatric ward? That she was released into my care? That the provisions were that she remain under my roof? You think I'm a fool. But it's you she's taken in with her delusions.'

'Why did you take her passport from her?'

'She tried to tear it up once when she was . . . but it doesn't matter now. She's not here against her will. In fact, it was she who insisted I take this post.' The commandant waved uncertainly towards the cupboard. 'I've told her that her papers are there when she wants them.'

As he gestured towards the cupboard, the commandant took his eye off his prisoner for a second. Manne saw his opportunity in an unthinking instant, leaping from his seat to launch himself blindly at the commandant. There was a blur of confused violence as Manne felt his hands grasping desperately at the commandant's neck, then a brief image of the commandant's astonished face before the chair overturned, followed by an ear-splitting noise. Something hit Manne in the head, an almighty knock that left him helpless and befuddled for a few seconds. He'd somersaulted over the commandant and now lay on the ground, face up. From above, tiny objects seemed to be raining down on him, slowly, pricking at him as they fell. It felt as though this continued for minutes on end, although afterwards he realised it obviously couldn't have. The vision had a hallucinatory intensity to it and it took Manne a moment or two to understand what had happened. The two men had fallen onto the huge model of the camp, which had collapsed under their weight. The tiny objects were the scale buildings and figurines – the miniature convicts and guards – that had peopled the model camp, flung up as the trestle tables flipped over.

Gradually, the rest of the room came into focus. There was a little blood on his shirt, more on the floor. He found he could move his arms, and put his hand to his head, expecting it to be sticky. It wasn't. The commandant was lying next to him, among the debris of the model, moving like a sick animal and groaning. Manne struggled to his feet, his head a little clearer. Now he realised that the blood on the floor was not his but the commandant's, from a gently pulsating bullet wound to his wrist. Properly bound, it was unlikely to be fatal. For a second,

Manne even considered staying to bandage the commandant's wrist. But the commandant was probably conscious enough to know what to do; in any case, the guards would be here shortly.

Pity for the commandant flashed through him. Even though on the face of it Manne was in an infinitely worse position, he couldn't repress the feeling that at least he had a chance. But the commandant? He had no chance. Manne cast a final glance over the room. With the model broken down the middle, the little buildings and figurines scattered over everything, it looked like a comic apocalypse. The commandant was feebly shaking his uninjured hand in Manne's direction, and whispering something inaudible.

Upstairs, Manne thumped on Mathilde's door. No answer. He tried the handle but the door was locked. He cried out her name a couple of times, banged at the door again. He was considering breaking it down, but then heard noises downstairs. The commandant getting up. Or perhaps the guards arriving. He crossed over the landing and opened the door to his own room.

'Guépard!'

The boy was cowering in a corner, shaking violently.

'Get out. Just get out!'

As he shouted, Manne was still blocking the doorway. A fury had stormed up in him at the sight of Guépard. If he'd had a knife in his hand at that very moment, he'd have used it, brought it across Guépard's throat. But the fury passed through him as quickly as it had come. He stood away from the door.

'Go to the commandant's office. Go and see if he needs help.'

The boy darted out. Manne went to the window and opened it. Across the river, the far bank was quite lost in the midday heat haze. It left him with the impression of being at the edge of a vast ocean. He thought of the ocean crossings he'd made in his life. The countless ports he'd passed through. Always haunting the edge. That was what a port was, wasn't it? An edge. The point at which civilisation dissolved into water, into nothing. He climbed out of the window, started scaling down the wall. He'd forgotten his bag, left sitting on the bed. It hardly mattered, though.

There was a short dash from the house to the river, the only moment of exposure. A low stretch of greenery separated the riverbank from the house and garden, allowing Manne to crawl slowly along the scrubby beach without being seen. But then about halfway along, his vision blurred. He was seeing double, and he had to sit down. It passed in a few seconds. The bang on the head, which at first he'd thought was a bullet. What actually must have happened was that he'd hit the edge of the model as he'd crashed into it. The second blow to his head in almost as many days. He got up and continued along the river-bank until he arrived at the little path that he knew led up to the folly.

The door was ajar; he pushed at it. No one inside. Only a few hours ago he'd been sitting there on the floor, Mathilde in front of him. Standing, dancing, the music still in his ears. And there was the jar that he'd found under the floorboards, that had contained the photographs. It was lying on its side, empty. Mathilde must have taken the photographs back with her. Manne dropped to his knees, pulled up the loose board and felt around. Nothing. No canvas bag. It wasn't a shock: somehow he'd expected it. He'd offered it to Mathilde, after all. She was gone, and it was gone. All that was left to him now were the clothes he was wearing, and a few hundred francs in his back pocket. A confusion of emotions passed through him.

Anger, relief. Desperation, resignation. Fear for his life. And at the same time, he'd never felt more alive.

He sat there for a while, in a daze. He noticed a damp patch on the floor. A trickle of water had stained the wall: a hole in the roof, no doubt. In this climate, the folly's demise would be quick enough. Within a year, the roof would be gone; within two, the folly would be a ruin, reclaimed by the forest. Just the stone walls remaining, for someone to discover and wonder at years from now...Eventually Manne heard voices, distant enough but coming from the path that linked the folly with the garden. For an instant he thought he might stay put. But it was as if someone else took him over in these moments of indecision: he found himself creeping out of the door and running across the small clearing, into the nearby forest. He dropped down behind the huge trunk of a dead, fallen tree.

Presently, Manne saw two figures emerging from the path. He had the impression that the smaller one was Guépard, but didn't dare raise his head any further to check. He saw the two going into the folly, then coming out a minute or two later. All this time they were talking, but Manne couldn't hear what they were saying. He could just catch the intonation and occasionally the expressive hand movements, which seemed to translate mild uncertainty. After about five minutes of toing and froing, the men left again. Manne listened to them clumping back down the path, focusing on the sound until it finally dissolved into the forest.

For what seemed a long time, Manne simply sat behind the tree trunk. He felt incredibly tired and faint. He tried to stand up, but at first found it impossible. He wondered what Mathilde would do with his journal when she discovered it in the canvas bag. And if she read it, what she'd make of it. He thought of everything that had happened that day, then the day before and the day before, a spiral of consequence that could all be traced further and further back, to some vanishing point.

High up above where he was sitting, Manne could hear a tiny rustling sound. It was a bird or some other small animal scrabbling about in the branches. Although barely audible, the noise invaded the stillness of the forest. When the rustling abruptly stopped a minute later, Manne finally managed to get to his feet. The profound silence now surrounded him once again. It was as though it emanated not from the forest at all, but from somewhere inside.

XIII

Through the jungle, down a criss-cross of animal runs. It was slow going, but he knew he didn't have far to go. As he weaved through the undergrowth, it struck him that he too was now an *évadé*, like Edouard. A convict story he'd heard in Saint-Laurent came back to him. A guard's wife had bought a live chicken at the market, and had given it to her convict chef to cook. When he refused to kill it, she'd retorted: 'What? You'll happily murder your next-door neighbour, but you won't wring a chicken's neck?' To which the cook had coolly replied: 'Wringing a chicken's neck would upset me so much more.' The story reminded Manne of the mutilated horses on the battle-field in Belgium, and how common it was for men to be more upset about them than their wounded comrades.

Now he was at the edge of the camp, watching the occasional guard or convict pass by from a vantage point just inside the forest. As usual, there seemed to be few people about; no doubt the bulk of the camp was up at the commandant's new construction site. If he were going to do anything at all, he'd have to be brazen about it and do it now, before word got out about what had happened down at the commandant's house. He cut around the side of the camp until he reached the path that led to Saint-Laurent, so he could make it look as if that was where he'd come from.

Manne emerged at the bottom of the grand avenue the commandant had built, with its arch at the top. Close by were what he took to be convict barracks, half a dozen of them. He passed by a couple that seemed deserted. Near the entrance of the third one, an old black man sat on a stool under the shade of a tree. On his knee sat a kitten. One end of a dirty piece of string was tied to the kitten's paw, the other to the man's wrist – like a manacle locking the two together. The man was idly tapping the kitten on the nose, sometimes quite hard. The kitten would flinch, then retaliate, batting at the man's out-stretched hand, which he'd pull away at the last moment like a bullfighter. There were no guards about.

'I'm looking for someone. I don't know his real name. I'm told people call him Masque.'

The man continued tormenting the kitten for a moment, then looked up and stared blankly in the way that convicts sometimes did. He said nothing, but made a gesture with his head towards the thick iron doors of the barracks.

'He's in there?'

The convict nodded. Manne walked past him and through the doors. Inside, it took a moment for Manne's eyes to adjust. There were no windows. Just the light behind him, flooding in from the entrance, making it feel as if he was walking into a cave. A complicated matrix of shadows deepened towards the back wall. Two long bed benches ran the length of the barracks. At first it seemed completely empty, but in the far corner Manne made out a body on the bench. He walked towards the figure. Under a tattered image of a showgirl that had been pinned to the wall, a bulky lump of a man came into focus.

He stirred, looked up. 'You're the one who sent your friend looking for me.'

Surprised, Manne took a moment to reply. 'I waited for you this morning. Where I was told you'd be. You didn't show up.'

'I had other things to do. I knew you'd find me if you wanted to.'

He lay languidly on the bunk, eyeing Manne up, his hands resting behind the back of his head. A sinister carnival of tattoos covered his face. He was bald on top but had tattooed in his hair; around his eyes, there were tattooed glasses. On one cheek, an ace of spades; on the other, an ace of clubs. A freak, in any other circumstances.

'So you're looking for Edouard.'

'You know where he is?'

'Sure, I know where he is,' the man drawled. 'The question is what you're prepared to sacrifice.'

'I've got money, if that's what you mean. I'm prepared to pay.' His voice echoed in the emptiness of the barracks. 'How can I be sure you really know Edouard?'

'Want me to describe him to you? Tall, thin. Mid-forties. Black hair. Doesn't say much.'

'Anything else?'

'His eye. He has a glass eye.'

Manne shook his head. 'You'll have to do better than that. You've just rehashed everything my servant told you.'

The man shrugged. 'As you wish. It's neither here nor there to me.'

Manne focused hard on the convict's face in the half-light, until it seemed to dissolve into a seething mess of tattooed images, contrasted by the pure blue of his reptilian eyes ... A knife appeared out of nowhere. Masque started casually polishing it with an oily rag.

'Tell me something else about Edouard. Any little detail.'

The man put down his knife for a moment. 'Well, I remember something. He has a tattoo. A small one, of a flower. On his back.'

Manne pulled out the last of his money and handed it to Masque. It disappeared instantaneously in some sort of sleight-of-hand.

'All right, then. He's over the other side of the river. Should be easy enough to find. You cross the river directly from here. Get a Boni to drop you off at a point where a path leads up to a ridge. Once you get up to the ridge, you turn right. About a kilometre along, there's a path to your left. You follow that up. There's an old ruin up there, where Edouard lives with a native woman.'

'How do you know all this?'

'He cleared some land up there. Planted a garden. He grows vegetables. Some he sells, some he trades with the natives. Sometimes he crosses back over the river. He sells stuff to the barracks keepers. I'm a barracks keeper.'

Manne walked out into the white light of the afternoon, with the impression of having been transported to somewhere else. He looked around for the black man and his kitten, but they'd vanished, although Manne could only have been in the barracks for five or ten minutes. Nonetheless, there were a few more people about than there had been when he'd arrived at the camp. Convicts and guards were slowly, placidly, trickling back from the construction site. Surely the news about the commandant must have spread. But there was nothing, no urgency at the camp to suggest that.

Now he was back in the forest, retracing his way to the river through the animal runs. Already, his return to the camp and the encounter with Masque had started to seem fantastic, otherworldly. It wasn't just Masque. Everything that had happened since his altercation with the commandant had an air of unreality about it. He went back over what Masque had told him about Edouard. That detail about the tattoo on his back. In fact, Manne had no idea whether Edouard had such a tattoo. It had just struck him as an unlikely thing for Masque to have made up on the spot. And the image of Edouard clearing some forest to create a garden seemed a likely one. Edouard, the jungle Crusoe. It made sense to Manne, and he found himself believing what Masque had told him.

Then there was Masque's sibylline remark about what Manne might be prepared to 'sacrifice'. Manne toyed with possible meanings, but only for a moment. He had no desire to analyse things further, he was too tired, too incurious, only able to think one step ahead. His mind marched on to other, more practical matters – how to get across the river, whether he should try to contact Mathilde, if so, how, and so forth.

At one point, he felt faint and weak again, his legs giving way under him. He lay on the ground for several minutes, panting, trying to gather his strength. This dizziness, this unreality – it probably had something to do with the knock on the head he'd received. In which case, things would soon either get better or get worse. It occurred to him that he was very hungry, too, and that it was now late afternoon, and he hadn't eaten anything today except some bread and coffee at six o'clock in the morning. Eventually, he got to his feet and continued on.

Another few minutes and the forest started thinning out. Ahead, he could make out the silhouette of the house against a colossal sun, low in the sky. He dropped to his knees, crawling along until he reached the edge of the forest. In front of him some scrub, then the carpet of dead grass. It was difficult to make out what was happening at the house, but he could hear voices and there seemed to be a fair few people about, coming and going, or loitering about outside.

Manne crawled around the garden's border until he was at the crumbling wall just inside the forest, the place where he was supposed to have been meeting Masque that morning. He had a half-formulated plan in his head. He'd stay the night there, behind the wall. There were the barrels of dried foodstuffs he'd found there. He'd be able to assuage his hunger at least. The food and the rest would give him the strength to go on. Then at first light, he'd find a way to get across the river.

Almost immediately, though, the plan fell apart. He searched around for the hole where the barrels of food had been hidden under branches. There it was – and yet the barrels were gone. Manne sat there dumbfounded for a moment. He even wondered if he'd imagined the barrels, dreamt them into existence. His hunger pangs had dissipated somewhat, although all that meant was that he'd wake up in an even weaker state tomorrow. A day without food would be nothing, nothing, if it weren't for this dizziness, these faint spells that kept assailing him at intervals.

It was still light, but nightfall wasn't so far off. He sat down by the wall. An infinite drowsiness had overwhelmed him. He had the impression that if he didn't get up now, he'd never be able to get up. Closing his eyes, he imagined scaling the wall of the house, to the window of Mathilde's room. That was what he'd been thinking of doing, until he'd got to the house and seen the activity there, the guards at the doors. Nonetheless, the image was fixed in his mind, he was inside that erotic moment, and it felt real, as if he were actually at her window, waiting for her to open it, staring at her, then past her to the photograph on the bedside table.

He shook himself out of it, shook himself awake. The guards would probably do a search of the environs in the morning. In all likelihood, they'd find him here. What he needed was somewhere much safer than this, to lie low for a couple of days. He needed to get out of French territory altogether, over the river, over the border. Another idea struck him. He had no money left; he'd given the last of it to Masque. But he'd already paid for his trip over to the other side from the Boni boatman. He'd get down to the village and find that man. For another few moments he remained seated by the wall, confusion still washing over him. That feeling again, of being in a maze. The puzzles of the past few days being the intersections of this maze – the points at which different paths could have been taken. The maze itself had no meaning. There was simply the question of whether he'd traverse it, or find himself terminally lost in it.

With enormous effort he managed to get himself up on his feet. A green-grey twilight was descending over the forest. Dim, flickering candlelight from the house. Noises, too: laughter, the clinking of bottle and glass. The guards had found the commandant's supply of rum. Gambling that they'd all be inside drinking, Manne edged his way across the garden. Then down the little path that led to the riverbank.

The Maroni stretched out before him in all its immensity. Its preternaturally smooth surface was like a screen thrown over the water. Manne stood on the bank and gazed out. His mind wandered through a jumble of incidents and conversation fragments, all coming together in dream-like juxtapositions. He recalled a tale he'd heard at the café-bar in Saint-Laurent. Of a man in Paris who'd been accused of murdering his wife, when in fact she'd poisoned herself. Imprisoned while awaiting trial, he'd been tortured by a sadistic prison warden. After weeks of this, he'd lashed out and killed his tormentor. At his trial, he'd been acquitted of his wife's murder, but then sentenced to transportation for killing the warden.

A man's voice tore through the background of forest and river noises. It felt right close by, but it was impossible to judge distances in the jungle. The words had a French cadence to them, although Manne couldn't catch what they were. Instinctively, he dropped to the ground. For ten or twenty seconds, nothing. Then a sloshing about in the water. A light, slapping noise repeated itself at jerky intervals. Manne was on his stomach now, peering out through the scrub. A full moon was directly overhead. It cast a metallic sheen over the river.

A canoe was darting across the water, upstream from where Manne was hiding. A man was paddling, and Manne could tell it was a Boni, because of the characteristic way Bonis crouched down to paddle. By contrast, his passenger was European. In the canoe she sat up regally, dangerously, in a way that no Boni would. The boat skimmed along, hugging the bank, heading directly to where Manne was hidden in the scrub. It swooshed past him in a moment. Manne turned his head. The moon shed its pale light over her face, draining it of colour and giving it a shadowy, black-and-white feel. She'd been facing the rear, and so now she was looking in his direction, staring past him, to the house or beyond, to a future accelerating away from her as she began her long journey back.

The boat progressed further downstream before veering into the current, shooting its way over to the other side of the river. Only then did it occur to Manne that he should have stood up and shouted out Mathilde's name. Only when it was too late, when he could no longer make out the canoe's shape in the silvery darkness. He thought of Mathilde's bluntness. Her rush to get to the point and then beyond it, and how that in some ways reminded him of Edouard. He thought of their final meeting, her almost final words to him: *You might have seduced me.* His hopeless fantasy of escaping into each other. He wondered why he could never have said something very simple, like telling her that she was beautiful, for instance.

Manne found himself getting up, tugging at his shirt and pulling it off. Then his shoes, trousers, underclothes. The slight breeze on his skin, coming from downstream, from the sea, felt good. His clothes lay there limply under the moonlight. They were like a person he'd just climbed out of, the crumpled shell of someone that he already no longer knew.

The water was intoxicatingly cool. Immersing himself in it set off a mini-chain of childhood memories. Of swimming on hot July afternoons at the family holiday house in Normandy before his mother had died, of the sensuousness of salt and sun prickling at the skin. And the swimming was easy for the first few minutes; he even thought he might make it over to the other side relatively quickly. But at one point the current picked up and he could feel himself being pulled downstream. He knew not to try to swim against the current, but across it. As long as he continued to make some progress towards the other bank, he thought, it didn't matter how far down he was swept.

The Maroni was a couple of kilometres across – an hour's swim, he calculated. And for the first twenty minutes or so he continued to feel confident. But then gradually he found his strokes getting slower and slower, and it was harder and harder to lift his arms. After a while, without noticing when it had happened, he realised he was just going through the motions. He wasn't really swimming any more, wasn't making any progress towards the other side. He was just bobbing up and down, pulled along by the current, pulled into the centre of the river.

Now he was flailing around, lunging at the water, fighting the rising panic. It was the thought of being swept out to sea, the horror of drowning. The panic didn't stop the cascade of images. On the contrary, Manne had a vision of himself naked at the river's edge again, jumping into the water. Always seeing himself in the third person. A sense of hopelessness invaded him. Decisions could always be changed, overturned, reversed in some way. Every decision, that is, except the one he'd just taken. A world of boundless possibility had been revealed to him, a world hidden until now, the very moment when it would be denied him. Of course I'm going to drown, he thought, I knew it before I even jumped in. He was still struggling, throwing his arms against the current, but the more he struggled, the more disorientated and tired he became. Then slowly, miraculously, the panic began to subside.

Sometimes his head was above water. Here, noises seemed harsh to him, his movements jerky, the objects within his visual field angular and sharply defined; he was in pain, he choked and wheezed, gasping and gulping down the air. And sometimes his head went below the water's surface. This world was so different. Here, all movements were slow and graceful; perspective rounded and soft; sound dulled; colours dimmed. Here, breathing was impossible, but the desire to do it had also dimmed, had begun to flicker out.

For a while he alternated between the two worlds. The last time he had his head above water, he thought he could even glimpse the other shore. But by now it was a matter of indifference as to whether he got there or not. His head went down again, back into the amniotic darkness, and a deep sense of peace filled him, of himself flowing out into the water, just as the water flowed into him. He marvelled at the way people hung on so tenaciously, in the most terrible circumstances, when in reality it was easy to let go. Whose life was anything but a temporary fix, an eternal plugging of holes? He was aware of living within a tiny fragment of time, stretched out to all infinity...

Point on a matrix. A million discrete moments that didn't add up to a life. 'Release me. You're a better man than that.' He drifted weightlessly, effortlessly, in a world with no ups or downs. Hartfeld was a sham, waterlogged and falling apart. Manne had never been born. Somewhere behind it all was Capgras. The block of marble he'd chipped away at, until there was nothing left.

The years of roaming. Of departing before he even arrived. Everything since the war now falling away, dissolving into the water.

In the end, what was clearest in his mind – the one image that stayed with him – was his great-uncle's greenhouse. The orchids, all flawlessly aligned in rows. Their reflection in the frosty glass, one winter morning. And their still, perfect beauty.

COLONY THREE

The sun is in his face. It's ferocious; he's shielding his eyes from it. That's the moment he realises that he's *there*, conscious. For a while he's been feeling something, the wet ground beneath him, but in a primitive way, as a reptile might feel it. Now he peeks from between his fingers – a dazzle of yellow, and a blue so pure it's hard to look at. He experimentally moves his head, then raises himself up on his elbows. The fact that he can actually do it surprises him. He's lying half in the water, half out. He's naked. His skin is all grey and red and puckered and swollen – from the water, or from the sun. In any case, he doesn't feel as bad as his skin looks. In fact, there's a sort of lightness about him. It's no effort at all to spring to his feet.

Who is he? Where is he? At first the confusion feels disturbing; then later, liberating. He looks across the river, determines which way the current is flowing. He's on the Dutch side. Impossible to tell how long he's lain there, whether hours or days. He looks around, takes in the surroundings. Nobody about, no sign of human life on the bank, nor on the river. At the water's edge, magnificent coconut palms stretch up endlessly into the sky, as if trying to take flight, to escape the world.

It's a steep climb up away from the river. Soon enough he's

plunged into the forest. On the one hand, it's a relief, the trees protecting his nakedness from the sun. On the other hand, some sort of rapier fern is cutting at his feet, and it's not long before everything below his knees is covered in blood. As he gets further up, the ferns thin out, the ground dries up and levels out.

He's on a rocky ridge. He's climbed up maybe a kilometre. He should be exhausted, he should be in pain, but he's not. There's a store of raw energy in him, still there, still ready to give. Even where the ferns have torn at his feet and legs, he feels nothing. There's only his ravenous hunger: that's the only thing that might slow him, stop him.

In a nearby tree, wild bananas are growing in the higher branches. He shins up the trunk, then climbs from branch to branch. His agility astonishes him. In seconds, it seems, he's reached the bananas. He breaks one off, peels it, smells it, tastes a little. Despite his hunger, something tells him not to eat it. He tosses it to the ground, but pauses a moment before climbing down again. This high up, a vista has opened up to him. He looks down at the river, blinking in the sun. A silver sinew, pushing its way towards the absolute of the sea. Still no sign of activity on it. No settlements to be seen on the other side, either. It feels as if he's a thousand kilometres from anyone, in total solitude, with nothing and no one to measure his impressions against.

Back down on the ground, he starts walking along the ridge. His terrible hunger is the only thing bothering him. It has become a physical pain inside him. At one point he comes across a dead *urubu*, a scavenging bird, and he contemplates building a fire to cook it. But the bird's legs come apart from the body as he tries to pick it up. It gives off an unholy stink of rotting flesh, and he sees that it's been eaten away by maggots.

He continues on. He's not thirsty, although he forgot to drink any water before climbing up to the ridge. No, it's the gnawing desperation to put something solid in his stomach.

A little way along, he comes to what looks like a path. Or it could be an animal run. But he thinks not, judging from the way the ground is impacted and stripped of undergrowth. If he's right, it's the first sign of human presence he's seen since waking up. The path branches away from the river. It's on a gentle incline, and he follows it up. As he walks, he's mostly glancing about to the left and right, on the lookout for anything to eat. But at one point he stares upwards. The sky has turned from deep blue to a crystal grey.

Somewhere off to the left, there's a large gap in the trees. Through it he glimpses a stone construction. There's no path directly there, and he clambers off through the undergrowth to reach it. What he finds is a section of wall – the remains of a farmhouse, probably – with a lean-to built against it. Beyond that, further fragments of wall that seem to enclose a garden. It's been cleared, and there are rows of different plants, but the garden looks as though it's recently been abandoned. Some of the plants are flourishing, some are half-eaten by insects or animals, others are already dead. In the borders, the forest has begun to invade, to reclaim ownership.

He crouches down to enter the lean-to. It's oppressive and dark inside. Such a contrast to the harsh light outside, that at first he can't see anything at all. Gradually things come into focus. A scene of chaos: plates, clothes, gardening tools, cooking utensils, all jumbled up together, lying haphazardly on the dirt floor. There's an acrid, fetid smell of sweat and bodily waste. In one corner, what looks like a mess of bedclothes. Only when he looks closer does he realise that there's someone there.

'You've come back. Have you? You've come back.'

It's a woman's voice, croaking, whispering, in pain. He peers through the gloom. She's lying there amidst the blankets, dark-skinned, naked, breathing laboriously. He kneels down beside her. She's glistening, shaking, her eyes closed.

'Yes. I've come back.'

'Thirsty. Very thirsty.'

'I'll get you water. I'll go down to the river.'

She nods, closes her eyes. She's weak, in a fever. She could be almost dead, or she could be only an hour away from recovery. Impossible to tell with these fevers.

As he's about to leave, she whispers: 'Come closer.'

He's beside her, he can't see how he can get any closer, but he moves his head above hers, so she can see his face, if she opens her eyes.

'Closer, closer.'

He notices her swollen belly. He lowers his head further. Their lips are almost touching. Her eyes are still closed. She reaches out and touches him on the cheek. 'You're there, aren't you? You've come back?'

'I've come back.'

Her hand flops down, as if it was an enormous effort to move it.

'I see things. I can't tell what's real, what's not.'

'I'll be back shortly. I'll get water for you.'

'No, don't go. Don't leave me again.'

'I'll be back very soon. Don't worry.'

'Edouard . . .'

Outside, he takes great gulps of fresh air to shake the dizziness brought on by the close, humid atmosphere of the lean-to. In moments, he feels himself again, light on his feet, coiled with energy. He looks around. Remnants of a previous life are scattered over the clearing. A rusted wheel. A hoe. An old water pail. He picks it up. It'll do, he'll take it down to the river with him. He calculates that it'll take him forty minutes to get down there, an hour to get back up. He looks up at the sun. It's mid-afternoon. There should be time enough.

On his way down, he catches sight of a large iguana sunning itself a couple of metres up a tree. He freezes, then slowly reaches down and finds a heavy stone. In a short, brutal movement he hurls it at the tree. The iguana drops to the ground with a thud. He runs up to where it fell, another stone in hand, in case he has to beat it to death. No need: he crushed the skull with his first throw. Dark red blood wells up, glints in the sunshine. He slings the dead iguana across his shoulder, continues down the river. He'll cook it once he gets back up to the ruins where the woman is lying. He'll fill his belly, and try to get her to eat a little of it as well.

Now he's back at the river's edge. He has the impression that it's the same place where he woke up, but of course it can't be. That would be a couple of kilometres downstream. For the first time that day he feels tired, febrile with the hunger. He sits down by the water for a moment to regain his strength for the steep climb back up, now laden with the pail of water and the iguana.

Still nobody to be seen. Not a single boat or canoe. Mesmerised by the water shimmering in the heat, he lets his mind wander. And now the riverscape fills out. A vision of bridges crossing from one bank to the other, some straight, some arched, others descending at oblique angles. A few of these bridges are covered in hovels. Cords cross each other and disappear, ropes rise from the shore. The dome of St Paul hides somewhere behind that of the Beaux Arts. Further back, the minarets of Al-Finar.

He looks away from the river. Within the cocoon of his

body, he can already feel the transformation – two lives compressed with such extreme violence that they breach each other and fuse. He prepares to make his way back to where the woman lies in the lean-to, by the falling-down wall. In his mind he rights the wall, fills in its gaps, builds around and on top of it, until once again he can see it whole. A dark farmhouse, silhouetted against the twilight. His imagination is torn to pieces, scattered to the winds. Inside him lies a vast, empty landscape. It has always been there. Trackless plains stretch out endlessly towards the horizon. And then beyond, to unknown lands, waiting to be colonised.

ACKNOWLEDGEMENTS

I have adapted episodes and/or the occasional sentence from a number of works, principally *Dry Guillotine* by René Belbenoit (Berkley, 1975); *Au bagne*, by Albert Londres (Serpent à plumes, 2001); *Bagnards: la terre de la grande punition* by Michel Pierre (Autrement, 2000); *Damned And Damned Again* by William Willis (Dell, 1974); *Devil's Island* by J.J. Maloney (www.crimemagazine.com); and *Journey Without Maps* by Graham Greene (Vintage, 2002). I have also used some lyric fragments from *Tilt* by Scott Walker (Mercury, 1995). For specific references, please contact me at hugowilcken@hotmail.com.

Thanks to my family, particularly Patrick Wilcken for his critical reading of the text. Thanks also to Lisa Darnell; to Catherine Heaney at Fourth Estate; to Ian Peisch for providing me with work space in Paris; to Helen and Paul Godard for their hospitality in Nîmes; and to everyone else who helped in the writing of the work.

And a very special thank you to Julie, for her all-round support and valuable editorial input.